CW01431141

The Indian Bangle

Fergus Hume

The Indian Bangle

Copyright © 2024 Indo-European Publishing

The present edition is a reproduction of previous publication of this classic work. Minor typographical errors may have been corrected without note; however, for an authentic reading experience the spelling, punctuation, and capitalization have been retained from the original text.

ISBN: 979-8-88942-489-5

CONTENTS

The Fourth Scene: In Florence

The Fifth Scene: In London

The Sixth Scene: At Casterwell

PROLOGUE

PART I

A letter from Mrs. Purcell, of Bombay, to Miss Slarge, of Casterwell, England:—

"29th of May, 189—

"My Dear Sister,

"By this time you will have received my previous epistle, in which I announced the apoplectic seizure and subsequent demise of my beloved husband, Joshua Ezekiel Purcell, lately a faithful and distinguished servant in the Indian Civil Service of her Most Gracious Majesty the Queen and Empress. As over a month has elapsed since my lifelong companion joined the angelic choir, I am now becoming more resigned to my widowed condition, and I begin to contemplate with equanimity the prospect of a solitary future, enlivened, I trust, by the acceptable companionship of sympathizing friends. In thus submitting myself to the inevitable, I have obeyed the inspired advice of the great lexicographer, as expressed in his masterly ethic poem 'The Vanity of Human Wishes':—

'Pour forth thy fervours for a healthful mind,
Obedient passions, and a will resigned.'

Thus in some measure I may emulate, as a Christian gentlewoman should, the philosophic composure of the sage Doctor Johnson.

"Passing to more mundane considerations, I may mention that the late partner of my joys and sorrows has left me fairly well endowed with worldly wealth. Notwithstanding his elegant hospitality, and the regrettable depreciation of the rupee, he contrived to save and invest considerable sums of money, the interest on which has been assured for life to his mourning widow by a generous and provident testament.

"On entering into the necessary details with my worldly adviser—Mr. Deson, the lawyer—I find that my income will slightly exceed the yearly sum of two thousand pounds sterling, an amount which will amply suffice to maintain me in the dignified and easy position to which I have hitherto been accustomed. On my decease these moneys will be divided amongst the relatives of my late husband. Thus I shall be unable to devise any personal property by will other than that which I save or become possessed of during my widowhood.

"This consideration troubles me but in a minor degree, for, as you—my sole surviving relative—are in no need of pecuniary aid, it is only just that, after I have done with earthly vanities, my late husband's riches should benefit those of his blood who deserve well of his generosity.

"My position being thus assured, I have decided to leave the 'gorgeous pd home of my youth, to lay in due time my bones with those of my kindred in the family vault at Casterwell. But, prior to my departure from this torrid clime, it is my dutiful intention to erect over the remains of the most beloved and generous of men a monument of stainless marble, inscribed with an appropriate tribute to his excellent qualities, and an explanatory inscription of his widow's grief.

"And now—to touch on lighter topics, and thus relieve my mournful mind—let me inquire, my dearest sister, about your health, and concerning your interesting attempt to prove that the Romish Church is the inheritrix of the Babylonian superstitions so frequently condemned by the Hebrew prophets. Also, I must not omit to request special information regarding your charge, Olive, the daughter of my dear, but, alas! departed friend, Mr. Bellairs. I trust that the girl, who was singularly controllable, if I remember rightly, is growing in beauty and wisdom, and that she is beginning to reflect on the responsibilities of wealth and position which the near approach of her twenty-first birthday will shortly render it incumbent upon her to assume. With such a companion as you, my dear Rubina, and with so admirable and conscientious a guardian as the rector of Casterwell, I feel satisfied that our beloved Olive has become possessed of those elegant and necessary accomplishments which should embellish the character of a young gentlewoman.

"The moral Mr. Brock, in his double capacity of clergyman and adviser, must also have succeeded in impressing on her plastic mind the sacred precepts of the Established Church, and the needful principles for the guidance of her conduct towards virtue and discretion.

"When I meet her again—if an over-ruling Providence should

permit the occurrence of so much-desired an event—I shall expect to find Miss Olive Bellairs the model and paragon of our sex. Do not let us forget, my dear Rubina, that as a twig is bent so does the tree grow, and that early moral training in a refined and Christian circle is invariably productive of a happy result in those fortunate enough to have been placed by their Maker is so enviable a position.

"The mention of Olive leads me by an obvious sequence of thought to speak of Mr. Angus Carson, to whom—by a family arrangement—she has been engaged since her early childhood. I have lately had the gratification of a somewhat lengthy interview with that young gentleman, and I made use of my opportunity to observe and question him closely, so that I might transmit to you an accurate estimate of his character. He informed me that his respected father lately departed this life, and that he—young Mr. Carson—was passing through Bombay on his way to England by the Peninsular and Oriental steamship Pharaoh. It is his declared intention to complete the family arrangement, spoken of above, entered into so many years ago between Mr. Bellairs and Dr. Carson, both now deceased.

"As it is not improbable that in your arduous studies you may have forgotten the precise details of this matrimonial scheme which concerns so nearly your charge, and thereby yourself, I think it advisable to recapitulate the same, that it may be freshly impressed upon your mind. This long and explicit letter is mainly written with this object in view, and I beg that, for your own sake, and for the sake of Olive, you will give your whole attention to the details which I am about to recount concerning the physical and mental attributes of Angus Carson. We are informed by a very excellent proverb that 'forewarned is forearmed,' therefore my communication—if read with due care—will place you in the position of knowing Mr. Carson, so to speak, before you make his personal acquaintance.

"The benefit of such knowledge—having regard to the fact that neither one of this engaged pair has seen the other—will be of incalculable value to you, their well-wisher and supervisor. This being the case, I shall proceed to relate, firstly, the details of the domestic contract entered into between the parents of our young friends; and, secondly, the impressions I derived after conversing for two hours—not unprofitably—with young Mr. Carson.

"It is a matter of general knowledge that between the years '57 and '59 of this century, our supremacy in Hindostan was endangered by the revolt of the native troops. During that disturbed period, Mr. Mark Bellairs and Dr. Alfred Carson, then young and ambitious soldiers, were united in the bonds of ardent friendship; and afterwards they gave their affection to Mr. Julian Brock, then a missionary labouring amongst the benighted heathen. These three friends were together during the time of the disturbance, and side by side they witnessed the horrors of Cawnpore and Lucknow, as you have often heard the ingenious Mr. Bellairs relate, when, to quote Dr. Goldsmith, 'he fought his battles o'er again,' in the retirement of his luxurious and stately home. In the year '60 these comrades on many a field were parted by the exigencies of existence; and, while Mr. Bellairs and the Rev. Mr. Brock returned to settle on their native shores, Dr. Carson, having an unconquerable passion for Orientalism, preferred to remain in India. However, no doubt wearied of warfare, he beat his sword into a ploughshare, and, withdrawing himself from public life, secluded himself in the near neighbourhood of the gigantic range of mountains which are known to geography as the Himalayas. I understand that he dwelt there as a solitary for ten years, at the end of which time, feeling that it was not good for man to live alone, he contracted a marriage with a young Eurasian lady. It is sad to state that his marital happiness was not destined to continue more than twelve months, for, in the year '71, his wife died in child-bed, leaving behind her a son—the Angus I speak of—to solace his distracted surviving parent.

"In the meantime Mr. Bellairs, by the death of his father, had become possessed of the ancestral acres at Casterwell, and had taken up his abode in the family mansion to superintend his heritage and enact the agreeable part of an English squire. As a mark of his constant friendship for Mr. Brock, and in token of his appreciation of a blameless and moral character, he presented him with the living of Casterwell, a position which our reverend friend has held these many years to the satisfaction of all who are acquainted with his manifold good qualities. Mr. Bellairs, as you know, also remained single for a considerable period, but, bethinking himself that for the dignity of his name and the welfare of his tenants it was incumbent upon him to beget heirs of his body, he followed the example of his medical friend, and married the accomplished Miss Sophia Seymour in the year '74. By a strange coincidence—which you, my dear sister, will have no difficulty in recalling—the lady of Mr. Bellairs also died within a year of her nuptials, leaving, as a pledge of love to her sorrowing husband, our dear Olive. On hearing of his friend's loss and gain, Dr. Carson wrote a kind and judicious letter, in which he proposed that, further to cement their early friendship, his son Angus should be contracted in marriage with Mr. Bellairs's daughter Olive. To this proposition Mr. Bellairs readily agreed, with the proviso that the ceremony should not take place until his child attained the age of twenty-one years. On this basis the matter was arranged, and for the last twenty years Olive and Angus have been betrothed, although—the first dwelling in England, and the second restrained by filial duty in India—they have never met to enjoy in one another's company the pre-nuptial pleasures of Cupid's votaries. But these chaste delights will no longer be deferred, for, now that the lamented father of young Mr. Carson has journeyed to that bourne whence no traveller returns,' the impatient lover is hastening to greet his lovely, but, alas! fatherless, mistress. What joy it will be to you, my dear Rubina, to witness the coming together of these young hearts, to contemplate their amiable qualities, and discreetly to superintend their joyous meeting.

"Mr. Carson is a gentle and well-bred youth of twenty-five, not without parts, although of too retiring a nature to display them in company. He is tall, slender, elegant in shape, and from his mother inherits a somewhat swart complexion. Indeed, so apparent are the traces of his foreign blood, that in England, doubtless, he will be taken for a native of Italy. His hair and eyes, and the thick moustache which adorns his upper lip, are black in the extreme, resembling in their hue that 'raven down which clothes the night's vast wings;' and although I own to a predilection for the golden fairness of our Saxon race, yet I cannot deny that this young gentleman is prepossessing in no ordinary degree. I regret to say, however, that, like many half-castes, he is delicate in health, and owns that his heart is weak, so much so, indeed, that when excited in any violent degree, he is liable to be so overcome by emotion as to lapse into a state of insensibility. Therefore, my dear sister, when he greets your charge, be careful that you restrain his transports of joy, else it's more than probable that you will see him extended at your feet—a calamity which may cast a shadow over the united pair. I must admit that Mr. Carson is somewhat effeminate in his dress and looks. He even goes so far as to wear a bracelet of gold on his right wrist. In India we term this a bangle, and frequently such an ornament is worn by native princes who yet retain barbaric tastes; but I ventured to remark to Mr. Carson, that in England the wearing of a bangle by one of the male sex would not be looked upon with favour. I am bound to say that he took my expostulation in the most good-humoured manner, and he explained that the bangle was a sacred ornament taken from a Hindoo idol. It had been presented to his late lamented father by a certain notability, or Rajah, whose son he had skilfully cured of a deadly disease, upon the symptoms of which young Mr. Carson did not dilate. He also informed me that the bracelet had originally been placed on his arm above the elbow by his ayah, or Indian nurse, when he was a boy. As gradually he attained to the full size of manhood, the bangle was slipped down by degrees to the wrist, whence it cannot now be removed without filing through the broad band of gold of which it is composed—no very easy operation, as you may guess. Moreover quite recently Mr. Carson hurt his hand while out shooting in the hills, whereby some of the small bones have become diseased, and the breadth of the member much extended; indeed, the whole hand is largely swollen. I advised him to undergo an operation in England, and at the same time have the bracelet removed; in fact, I imagine this would be necessary. He promised me the suggestion should receive his most careful consideration. He was then pleased to exhibit the bracelet for my inspection, and I examined it with much interest and curiosity.

"It is a broad band of ductile gold, wrought with the idol figures of the Hindoo trinity—Bramah, Siva, and Vishnu—interwoven with the sacred lotus-flower and other heathen symbols. I confess that I was weak enough to covet this work of art, for it is not only extremely beautiful as an exhibition of how exquisitely a goldsmith can manipulate the precious metal, but it is also an ornament of great antiquity, and, being sacred, no doubt there is attached to it a strange and eventful history. Mr. Carson has had golden wrist-buttons made to match this unique bracelet, wrought after the same style, but of vastly inferior workmanship.

"On the whole, my dear Rubina, I am prepossessed in favour of my visitor, as he appears to be modest and intelligent and high-principled. Notwithstanding his delicate health and effeminate looks, I am confident that he has a strong will and a somewhat stubborn nature, both of which may be productive in the future of either good or evil. If Olive be soft and yielding, her married life with young Mr. Carson will no doubt be happy and easy, as he requires, I suspect, to be deferred to in every way, having full confidence in his own judgment. If, on the contrary, she be wilful, and refuse to acknowledge her husband as the head of the house, I fear that their union will not be so perfect a one as we could wish. To use a trite image, Mr. Carson resembles the iron hand in a velvet glove, so of this you will do well to warn Olive. 'Verbum sat sapienti,'

x

as the Latin poet has it; the same may be stretched, my dear, to include our own sex, although in the estimation of the male, we are not considered to be gifted greatly with wisdom. Of course, I dissent from this view, and—but you know full well my opinion on the subject; therefore, I will not add to this already lengthy epistle by enlarging upon it.

"Mr. Carson is accompanied to England by a certain Major Horace Semberry, who is, I understand, an officer in one of our native regiments. He has obtained leave of absence in order to act as a kind of social tutor to our young friend. I was informed that the Major met Dr. Carson whilst shooting in the Himalaya Mountains, and so won his goodwill by an attractive exterior and fascinating manners, that the doctor asked him to conduct Angus to Europe, and arranged, most generously, that he should be paid a handsome stipend for his services.

"Thus it comes about that young Mr. Carson and Major Semberry are travelling in company; but I must confess that the late Dr. Carson might easily have shown more wisdom in the selection of a companion for his son. Major Semberry is a fair, handsome man, an excellent sportsman, a well-bred gentleman, and he is possessed of a charm of manner which would impose upon many people. However, it did not impose upon me, my dear, for I judge this Horace Semberry to be one of those plausible scamps who roam the world like social Satans, seeking whom they may devour.

"This is a strong sentiment, I admit, but no stronger than is necessary, for you know that I am an excellent judge of character, and that it is not my habit to quote Holy Writ unless the occasion demand: it. The occasion, my dear Rubina, demands it now, and my earnest advice to you is to discourage the visits of Major Semberry to the Manor, and to break off; if possible, the intimacy which now exists—to my great regret—between him and Olive's future husband. I speak for his sake as I speak for hers, and you may take my word for it that the less they see of this military Belial, the better it will be for both of them.

"And now, my dear sister, I must conclude my long but, I hope, not uninteresting letter, by inquiring after our mutual friends and acquaintances. I trust that young Lord Aldean is in good health, and that he is benefiting to the utmost extent of his mental powers—not that I think much of them—by the instruction of his tutor, the amiable Mr. Mallow, whom I esteem greatly for his many admirable qualities. If Lord Aldean only emulates the moral and social and scholastic example of his friend and tutor, I am convinced that he will prove a useful and ornamental member of our House of Peers, in which, doubtless, he will shortly take his seat.

"Let me also inquire after Miss Ostergaard, the young lady of Danish extraction, from New Zealand; you will remember how highly I approved of her on the occasion of my last visit to Casterwell. It is to be desired that Olive should make an intimate friend of this charming young gentlewoman, in order that she may have constantly before her eyes a character of such sterling merit. Miss Ostergaard is a particular pet of mine, and I could wish our dear Olive no better fortune than that she should become just such another delightful girl.

"I presume that Dr. Drabble is still in our parish, practising his profession during his intervals from political excitement and Radical speeches. It is to be regretted that such a firebrand should endanger the peace and rustic charm of our quiet corner of England, and, as I always said, it would be much more to Dr. Drabble's credit if, instead of promulgating dangerous dogma, he gave more attention to his hard-working wife and her too-numerous family. The man is a red Anarchist, a subverter of law and order, and I fully expect that he will end by throwing a bomb into Casterwell Church—a circumstance which is the more likely to occur from the fact that he is an atheist and an ardent follower of Monsieur Voltaire, to say nothing of the infidel Thomas Payne, and that abominable American, Colonel Ingersoll.

"Concerning myself, my dear sister, I am in moderately good health, considering the recent loss of my beloved husband, for my friends here are all that can be desired in the way of sympathy and kindness. Also I have the company of Pontius Pilate, who, though only a dog is so intelligent as to afford me the greatest comfort in my terrible and overwhelming affliction. The dumb animal seems to be aware of my bereavement and in his own way tries to solace me with caresses and canine attentions generally. Therefore, you will see that the solitariness of my position is in some degree mitigated.

"And here I must conclude this long letter with the hope that we shall shortly meet again in England, when I can find in you, my dearest sister, a relative upon whose bosom I can recline, and pour out my sorrow for the loss of the best and most excellent of men.

"God bless you, my dear, and may His shield be extended in protection of our dear Olive. Such, my dear Rubina, is the heartfelt prayer of

"Your affectionate and resigned sister,
"Priscilla Purcell.

"P.S.—On my arrival in England, I wish you to accompany me to Paris, in order to assist me in the choice of my widow's garb of woe, for I am but ill-pleased with such garments as I have been able to procure here."

PART II

"Peninsular and Oriental Steam Navigation Co., Ltd.,

"Head Office: Leadenhall Street, London, E.C.

"June 24, 189—

"NOTICE

"R.M.S. Pharaoh arrived this morning at Gravesend. She is expected to dock by the afternoon tide in the Royal Albert Docks."

PART III

Extract from The Morning Planet, dated June 29, 189—:—

"A startling discovery was made yesterday at No. 64A, Athelstane Place, Bloomsbury. Thomas Gale, a baker, of Tottenham-court Road, complained at the local police station that for two consecutive days he had been unable to see the occupant of the house. As the window blinds were drawn, and the doors locked, he believed something to be wrong. Inspector Jain, and a constable proceeded at once to Athelstane Place, and, after vainly ringing and knocking, forced the area door. The house proved to be empty, but in the drawing-room the dead body of a young man was found, mutilated in a shocking manner. On an examination being made by Dr. Rayner, of Bloomsbury Square, it was discovered that a steel knitting-needle had been thrust into his heart, and that the right hand had been cut off at the wrist. The missing hand was afterwards found in the grate. Dr. Rayner is of opinion that the deceased was murdered about two days prior to the discovery of the body. The police have taken possession of the house and corpse, and are actively searching for evidence which shall throw light upon this atrocious crime. The result of their inquiries will be made known at the inquest, which is to be held to-morrow in the Bloomsbury Coroner's Court."

PART IV

Extract from The Morning Planet, June 30, 189—:—

"Mr. Mappin held an inquiry yesterday afternoon in the Bloomsbury Coroner's Court into the circumstances attending the death of the unknown man who was found dead in the drawing-room of No. 64A, Athelstane Place. Mr. Julian Pyke, owner of the house in question, deposed that it was rented from him on June 19th last by a tall, fair-haired man with a beard, who wore smoke-coloured spectacles, and gave his name as Francis Hain. He informed witness that he was a scientist, and that he required a quiet retreat in London in order to carry out certain experiments, the nature of which he did not disclose. Mr. Hain took the house furnished for six months and paid a quarter's rent in advance, an arrangement which was considered entirely satisfactory by the landlord. Witness saw the man but once, as the agreement (on a printed form) was approved and executed at one interview. He knew nothing of the man's antecedents, and his business with him was confined solely to the business as between landlord and tenant.

"Thomas Gale, of Tottenham-court Road, baker, deposed that on June 20th a woman called at his shop. She stated that she was the housekeeper of Mr. Hain, 64A, Athelstane Place, and requested him to supply the house with bread. She did not give her own name. Her appearance was refined and ladylike. She spoke excellent English, though she had a foreign accent. Witness concluded that she was either Italian or French. She was of medium height with a particularly pale face, large black eyes, and smooth black hair untouched with grey. She was not a young woman—about forty, witness thought. Her hair was worn in bands, and she was dressed entirely in black. Witness presumed she was a widow—at all events, she looked like one. She herself took in the bread each day, and paid for it on the spot. He saw no one else in the house, although he called there up to June 29th. Witness never saw deceased.

"Richard Brass, of Tottenham-court Road, butcher, gave much the same evidence. The same woman called on him, and gave a similar account of herself. He was to call each morning for orders at 64A, Athelstane Place. He did so up to June 29th, and was paid cash on delivery of the meat up to the 26th. The woman appeared to be the only person in the house, and he saw her last on June 26th. But on the 27th and 28th no meat was taken in, and the house appeared to be deserted. He thereupon informed the police. Witness never saw either Mr. Hain or the deceased.

"Amelia Rankin said that she was employed as a domestic servant at the house opposite to No. 64A. She saw a tall, fair-bearded man enter it on several occasions; also a pale, dark-haired woman, but she did not pay much attention to either. Once she noticed a young gentleman with a dark moustache looking out of the first-floor front window. He was laughing and talking with some one inside whom she did not see. He appeared to be quite happy. She believed, after viewing the corpse, that the young gentleman she saw was the deceased. She heard no noise, and saw nothing likely to arouse suspicion in any way. As a rule she was in the kitchen with her mistress (who kept a boarding-house), and it was seldom either of them was in the front of the house during the day. It was possible many people might have gone in and out without her being aware of it.

"Several witnesses resident in Athelstane Place gave much the same evidence. Some saw Mr. Hain, some the housekeeper, but none save Amelia Rankin caught a glimpse of the deceased. Nearly all the houses on either side of and opposite to No. 64A are boarding-houses, from which the lodgers are absent all day, and as the landladies and their servants are mostly occupied in the back premises, No. 64A was not observed in any special degree. Indeed, there was nothing about the house to arouse remark in any way.

"Dr. Rayner, of Bloomsbury Square, stated as the result of a post-mortem examination that in his opinion death was caused by a wound in the heart, apparently inflicted by some such instrument as a steel knitting-needle. The clothes over the breast: that is to say, the waistcoat, shirt, and undervest, were unbuttoned, tending to show that the deceased was unconscious when the wound was inflicted. With an instrument of the kind supposed, it would

xv

probably be necessary to open the clothes. The right hand had been cut off, and, judging from the neatness of the operation, a surgical instrument would seem to have been used for this purpose. The hand itself, distorted and swollen, was found in the grate. The bones of the hand were diseased, but not sufficiently so to warrant amputation. Witness was of opinion that the hand had been cut off by a surgeon. He did not believe that an untrained person could have performed the operation with the requisite skill. Deceased had been murdered—judging from the condition of the body—two days before the discovery of the remains on June 28th; that is to say, on June 26th. In answer to a question put by one of the jury, witness stated that there was no smell of chloroform perceptible about the clothes of the deceased or in the room.

"Inspector Jain, who discovered the body, said that it was lying on a sofa placed behind the drawing-room door. The clothing over the chest and region of the heart had been disturbed, and the collar and necktie removed. The shirt-studs, sleeve-links, and watch of the deceased were missing, and the pockets were empty. The marks on the linen had been cut out. There were no rings on the fingers of the left hand. The deceased was tall and dark-complexioned, with smooth dark hair and a small black moustache.

"From the condition of the body—the nails, for instance, were extremely well-cared for—deceased had evidently been a man accustomed to the refinements of life. His underlinen was of the finest quality, and the suit of grey tweed was evidently the work of a high-class tailor. The boots were of Russia leather, and were particularly well-shaped. Witness thought deceased must have been a gentleman in easy circumstances. On searching the house neither trunk, clothes, linen, nor papers of any kind were to be found; in fact, nothing which would be likely to reveal deceased's name or position. The only strange thing he had noticed was the fact that the clothes smelled strongly of sandal-wood. The furniture and appointments of the house were the property of the landlord, but neither Mr. Hain nor the housekeeper had left anything behind them by which they could be traced. Up to the present, in spite of all efforts, no clue to the whereabouts of either the tenant or his housekeeper had been found.

"After a brief deliberation the jury returned a verdict of 'wilful murder' against some person or persons unknown."

PART V

Extract from The Morning Planet, July 1, 1891—:—

"Despite the triteness of the proverb, We are constrained to remark with regard to the Athelstane Place murder that once again truth is stranger than fiction. Had one of our writers of detective stories imagined so extraordinary a crime as having taken place in the heart of a busy neighbourhood, within hearing, almost within sight of hundreds of people, he would have been scoffed at for exceeding the bounds of probability. It would, we assert, have been termed exaggeration of the wildest order. But it has been proved possible in fact, and No. 64A, Athelstane Place, Bloomsbury, now enjoys the distinction, albeit no enviable one, of having provided London with a mystery so unfathomable that it is extremely doubtful whether it will ever be plumbed by the keenest of detectives. For the unravelling of so complex a riddle we need the Sergeant Cuff of Wilkie Collins, or the Monsieur Dupin of Edgar Allen Poe—in a word, a fabulous detective such as we have not at the present time amongst us.

"Plainly stated, the facts are these:—A house is taken by a man who calls himself by the, to us, obviously false name of Francis Hain. Beyond the fact that he wore a pair of smoked-glass spectacles, there appears to have been little about him to cause remark. The payment of a quarter's rent in advance appears to have answered satisfactorily those questions which the landlord would otherwise surely have felt it incumbent upon him to ask; at all events, the usual formalities with respect to references were in this case entirely dispensed with. Ostensibly, the house was rented with the object of carrying out certain experiments of a scientific nature. A nameless woman, calling herself the housekeeper, is the active agent between Mr. Hain, so called, and the local tradesmen. Observe, the butcher and the baker see no one but this woman; they neither of them see the tenant of 64A or the deceased. By chance a domestic servant sees both, but naturally enough takes small notice of either. Up to June 26th the housekeeper herself receives the food from the tradesmen, and pays them for it in cash. This, of itself, might or might not be indicative of a preconceived intention to leave the house suddenly. After the 26th the housekeeper is seen no more, and on the 28th the house is broken into, and the dead man's body is discovered. The medical evidence goes to prove that he was done to death on the 26th, and it is from that day also that we lose sight of Mr. Hain. Both tenant and housekeeper vanish as completely as if the earth had swallowed them up. Thus we are deprived of the only two persons who at this time seem to have had any connection with the dead man. Their disappearance, coincident as it is, of itself arouses suspicion. Moreover, by the careful removal of all marks from the linen of the deceased, we are left without what otherwise might have lent an important clue to his identity.

"Here, then, is the problem with which our detective force is confronted. For ourselves, in a case like this, where the elementary facts are so completely concealed, we can at most theorise and surmise. For some reason, impossible to guess, the victim would seem to have been inveigled into the Athelstane Place house. As his right hand was diseased, it is not impossible that he went there, or, as we think, is more likely, was taken there by some accomplice ostensibly to have an operation performed. That a surgical instrument was used we may safely conclude from the evidence of Dr. Rayner. Mr. Hain called himself a scientist, and he may have been that, and that only; but at all events he, if he it was, was evidently skilled in surgery so far as to be able to accomplish an amputation at the wrist neatly. Let us then assume that Mr. Hain was to operate upon the hand of the deceased. The first thing he would do would be to administer an anæsthetic. This in all probability would be chloroform, for as the body was not discovered until two days after death, and as the air was warm during the interval, it is likely that the chloroform would evaporate. We take it, therefore, that the deceased was choloroformed by Mr. Hain with his own consent, since he was about to undergo a painful operation.

"Up to this point our assumption is comparatively clear; but, when we are asked to say why this Mr. Hain should have preferred a knitting-needle to either of the two means which were at his disposal for the accomplishment of his end (we refer, of course, to the instruments which he must have had at hand, and to the chloroform), and further, why the diseased hand, when amputated, should have been thrown into the grate, we confess ourselves absolutely in the dark.

"In short, our assumption, such as it is, becomes hopelessly worthless when separated from evidence wholly circumstantial; and circumstantial evidence is, as we know, frequently misleading. Before we can hope to obtain data more reliable it is necessary first that the deceased be identified, and further, that one, if not both of the persons who were known to be occupants of the house, be traced. We presume that in the ordinary course a full and sufficiently minute description of the deceased man will be disseminated by the police. He is apparently a gentleman, and may be said, therefore, to have occupied a certain social position. It is fair to assume that he has friends and acquaintances who will recognize some, if not all, of the characteristics put forth in the description. Further, he probably has a home if not relatives somewhere in the kingdom, and if he does not return within a reasonable time, inquiries will doubtless be made. It is probably by some such means as this that the deceased will be identified. Once that is done, there may be some chance of capturing his murderer.

"It is remarkable that the deceased's clothes smelled of sandal-wood. This is essentially an Eastern perfume, and a man, especially a gentleman living in England, would hardly be in the habit of using it. We are not aware, indeed, if it is used even in the East as a scent, though many nations of the Far East, such as the Indians and the Chinese—particularly the latter—make chests of sandal-wood. If, then, this unknown man had at any time lived in the East, it is possible he might have been in the habit of keeping his clothes in such a chest, which would account for the odour detected by Inspector Jain.

"This clue is slight; still it is tangible, and it is moreover possible to assume from it that the unknown man came from the East, and further, that his arrival in England must have been comparatively recent, since, had he been here for any length of time he would surely have exchanged this cumbersome box for the portmanteau of Western civilization. We suggest, therefore, to the police that, supposing, of course, nothing be forthcoming from the deceased's relatives or friends, a thorough search be made through the shipping offices and the neighbourhood of the docks for the existence of any passenger answering to the description of the deceased, who might recently have disembarked from one of our great liners.

"Again, we say, the clue is a slight one; but in such a case as this no fact, however insignificant, is unimportant, and the most slender circumstance may, if rigorously followed up, ultimately lead to results wholly unlooked for and disproportionate to it.

"Here, then, is a splendid opportunity for our detectives to cover themselves with glory, and, by the capture of the perpetrator, to prevent this—one of the most terrible crimes of recent days— from being relegated to the already too well-filled limbo of unfathomable mysteries."

THE FIRST SCENE
AT CASTERWELL

CHAPTER I

DAVID AND JONATHAN

Towards the first week in July two young men were seated in a smoking-carriage on the midday express from Paddington to Reading. They were alone in the compartment, and at the moment there existed between them that peculiar silence of sympathy which can be only the outcome of a perfect friendship. The Jonathan of the pair was slim, tall, and dark, with a military uprightness of bearing, and a somewhat haughty expression on his clean-shaven face. His David was younger in years, but considerably greater in size, and like his namesake of Judah, was ruddy and of a fair countenance. The one was an eager, anxious, highly-strung Celt, with his Irish impulse and impetuosity trained into well-nigh complete obedience by years of experience; the other a phlegmatic Saxon, of small brain and much muscle. Jonathan's nineteenth-century name was Laurence Mallow. David answered to the title of Lord Aldean. They had been tutor and pupil respectively, and they were still fast friends. The elder possessing the stronger and more imperious will, continued to control the younger.

Mallow was not popular, nor did he wish to be so. He chose to be feared rather than loved. He was brilliantly clever, and, therefore, had many admirers; on the other hand, his intolerance of stupidity lost him many friends, so that to his expressed satisfaction he moved more or less isolated amid a crowd of fair-spoken, back-biting acquaintances. And yet perhaps it was a knowledge of the guarded manner in which he was received that made him cling the more to the solitary friend he possessed. People thought and people said that there was but little about good-natured, thick-headed Aldean to attract the brilliant young Irishman. There were those

1

who went so far as to hint that the boy's title and wealth explained all that, albeit Mallow was well-nigh aggressively independent.

Left an orphan with comparatively little money at an early age, he had won prizes and taken scholarships at a great public school, and had maintained himself at Oxford by these early efforts. He left the University with a full brain and empty pockets, and he had undertaken the tutorship of Aldean to gain breathing-time while he cast around him for choice of a career. When Aldean came of age, Mallow left him, a fair enough scholar and an admirable athlete, and went himself to London. He became a journalist and a power with his pen. He attached himself to a weekly publication of high aim and small circulation, conducted by a genius who had failed to profit by his pen because he could not write obviously enough for the taste of the general public.

Mallow became one of the props of this journal. When it failed, by reason of its too lofty aims, he went to India to write letters about the incomprehensible East, for a newspaper. A while after he returned, and published a novel which was much condemned and widely circulated. At the present time, having netted a few hundreds out of the book, he was going down to Casterwell to stay with Aldean, and to renew his friendship with Olive Bellairs, whom he loved ardently, though—knowing full well that she was engaged to a certain Mr. Carson—hopelessly, in his own peculiar, wrong-headed way.

Aldean, who was now twenty-four, and as good-naturedly stupid as ever, was in truth more akin to Goliath than to David. He was a gigantic son of Anak, considerably over six feet in height, and as wide as a church door. He was sparing of his words, and he usually assented to whatever was said to him as the safest way out of an argument. But in spite of his lack of conversation, and the rareness with which he gave expression to such ideas as he possessed, he had a fund of shrewd common sense, which, in his position, was worth far more to him than genius would have been. It was with all his heart and soul that he admired Mallow, and the very naiveté with which he would express his admiration endeared him to the young Irishman. Habitually Mallow's tongue was razor-like in its acerbity, but Aldean—though he took full advantage of the friendship between them, and spoke pretty plainly when he judged his lordship deserved correction—he invariably spared where he would have spared none else. They had indeed established their friendship on a very durable basis, by the extremely simple process of shutting their eyes to one another's faults and opening them very

2

wide to one another's virtues. The young Irishman had his brilliant flashes of silence. It was on these occasions that he found Aldean so agreeable a companion—in fact, the boy was as a pet dog to Mallow; agreeable company, and not given to criticism.

"Aldean!"

"Eh yes, what?" asked his lordship, looking up from Ally Sloper.

"Have you read the account of this Athelstane Place murder?"

"Yes—fellow killed with a knitting-needle, isn't it?"

"Yes, thrust into the heart—devilish queer case. The Morning Planet seems to think the unfortunate beggar came from India."

"Who told the 'M.P.' so?"

"No one, apparently; it is a theory based on the fact that the man's clothes smelled of sandal-wood."

"Bosh! there's plenty of sandal-wood in England."

"No doubt; but Englishmen are not by way of scenting their clothes with it. I shouldn't be surprised to find that the Planet was right. At all events it's some sort of clue."

Aldean shook his head. "I thought you said it was a theory?"

"So it is; but a theory may develop into a clue," retorted Mallow, lighting another cigarette. "If only I had the time, there is nothing I would like better than to follow up a case like this."

"Well, surely you have the time?"

"I have not; I am giving you what spare moments I have."

"You are—now. But at Casterwell Miss Bellairs, I guess, will see a good deal more of you than I shall. The moth and the candle, eh?"

"Not at all, Aldean; your simile is quite inapt. I am not a moth, neither can Miss Bellairs be compared to a candle. She is not the kind of girl to scorch any poor butterfly that flutters round her."

"All right, old chap, you needn't take one quite so seriously. But as you do, I may as well be serious too. Do you know I am thinking of getting married?"

"No; that's news to me. And whom do you intend to honour so far, may I ask?"

"Miss Ostergaard, if she concurs." Aldean heaved a huge sigh. "By George! she's a ripping girl."

"Certainly, you might do worse," replied Laurence, musingly. "She's a very good girl, and clever too. Does she reciprocate?"

"I don't know; she laughs at me."

"That may be just her method of showing her affection. She will be hard to please if she is not satisfied with a titled Hercules like you."

"Oh, I don't think she bothers in the least about the title," said his lordship, dolefully, "she is quite a radical, a—a—what do you call it—Anarchist, you know. Dr. Drabble has been converting her. He's a proselytising beast, that Drabble."

"Oh, that's all rubbish. 'In the spring a young girl's fancy lightly turns to thoughts of love'—not anarchy."

"But it isn't spring," said the literal Aldean, "and Miss Ostergaard isn't the girl to marry for rank."

"Then make love to her properly, and she'll marry you for love."

"I wish I could; but I'm not a clever chap like you, Mallow."

"My dear boy, I'm not clever; on the contrary, I'm a fool—a perfect fool, for do I not love Miss Bellairs like an idiot, when all the while I know well she is going to marry this Carson man from India?"

"So she is; that's queer," said Aldean, reflectively.

"Queer! how do you mean?"

"Oh, nothing, old man. I am thinking of this murder case; and the fact of both men coming from India struck me, that's all. You see Carson's just on his way home now."

"Is he? I didn't know that," said Mallow, alertly.

"Yes; Miss Slarge—you know, the Babylonian, mark-of-the-beast woman—told me that her sister in Bombay had written Carson was on his way home by the P. and O. liner Pharaoh."

"The Pharaoh arrived some time back," said Mallow, gloomily. "He must be at Casterwell by this time."

"He was not there two days ago when I ran up to town."

"Well, it must be quite two weeks since the Pharaoh arrived. What an ardent lover the chap must be. I wish I stood in his shoes, that's all. I wouldn't let the grass grow under them on the way to my 'own true love'—not that Miss Bellairs can strictly be said to stand in that relation to a man she has never set eyes upon. The very fact that she has to marry him should be sufficient to make her hate him."

"By Jove! What a rum go it would be if Carson turned out to be the man murdered in Athelstane Place!"

Mallow stared. "What on earth put such a wild idea into your head?" he said.

"I don't know; nor do I know why you should be so ready to call it wild. The man who was killed came from India—as you say——"

"I don't say so. It is the theory of the Morning Planet."

"It is just possible that it might be Carson, seeing that he hasn't

4

turned up at Casterwell," continued Aldean, not heeding Mallow's interruption.

"Really, Jim, I didn't credit you with such a vivid imagination."

"Oh, of course it's merely an idea, Mallow. But what strikes me is that if Carson arrived two weeks ago, he certainly ought to have put in an appearance at Casterwell before this, if only out of curiosity to see his future wife."

"My dear fellow, Carson may need a kit before he calls on Miss Bellairs. He surely would wish to create a good impression, and I don't suppose he would present himself in sandal-wood scented clothes."

"I never said he would. But even so, that wouldn't take him a fortnight."

Mallow leaned back and pinched his chin reflectively. He had no great faith in his friend's prognostications, still he could not help being struck by the suggestion coupling Carson with the victim of Athelstane Place. It was certainly queer that this man from India should be two weeks in England without fulfilling the very object for which his journey had been made. He had arrived in the Pharaoh on the 24th of June the murder had been committed on the 26th, yet so far he had not presented himself at Casterwell. The prime facts certainly coincided. It was very odd; Mallow could not deny that.

"But the idea is incredible," he said aloud. "Hundreds of men arrive from India every week; besides, Carson never was in England in his life—Miss Bellairs told me so. Why should he be murdered immediately on his arrival—where was the motive? You have found a mare's nest, Jim."

"I dare say," replied Aldean, stolidly: "it's a bare idea."

"A very wild and a very absurd one, my boy. There is nothing to connect the sandal-wood man (as you call him) with Carson."

"Perhaps not, Mallow. But if Carson does not turn up soon I shall begin to think that my idea is not so ridiculous as you say."

"If he does not turn up," repeated Mallow with emphasis, "that's just it, but he will turn up if it is only to take from me the only girl I ever really cared about—a trite saying no doubt, but a true one in this case."

"Every fellow says the same thing," said Aldean, as the train slowed down into Reading Station. "Here we are."

Casterwell lies—as every one knows or should know, seeing that it is one of the prettiest villages in the home counties—amongst the Berkshire hills, some ten miles from Reading. Lord Aldean's cart was waiting for himself and his friend. Mallow walked leisurely out

5

of the station into the sunshine, and watched the porter transfer his portmanteau to Aldean's groom. Whilst he was standing on the edge of the pavement a plump little man, rosy in face and neat in dress, stopped short before him. He carried a black bag, but dropped this to hold out a friendly hand to Mallow.

"Well, well," he chirped, just like an amiable robin; "and who would have thought of seeing you here, Mr. Mallow? You're here on business, I presume?"

"I have come down to stay with Lord Aldean at Casterwell, Mr. Dimbal," replied Mallow, graciously.

"Miss Bellairs' busi—— Ah, here is his lordship. How d'ye do, my lord? On the road to Casterwell, eh? I'm going there myself."

"To see Miss Bellairs, did you say?" asked Mallow, impatiently. "There's nothing wrong, I hope?"

"Good gracious, no. Why should there be anything wrong?"

"Why, indeed," said Aldean, laughing. "Lawyers and wrong never go together."

"Ha, ha! very good, my lord; but we are a much-maligned profession. No, Mr. Mallow, nothing is wrong with Miss Bellairs. On the contrary, everything is very right. I bring her the good news that Mr. Carson has arrived."

"Oh," said Mallow, with a glance at Aldean, "have you seen him?"

"Yes, he called yesterday at my office, and to-morrow he comes to Casterwell to see his future wife. Well, well; good-day, good-day, I see my fly, I must be off. Good-day, Mr. Mallow; my lord, good-day," and the little lawyer bustled off.

"So Carson isn't the sandal-wood man, after all," observed Aldean.

"No, God forgive me! I wish he were," replied Mallow, and frowned.

CHAPTER II

THE SEALED LETTER

Casterwell is an aggressively antique village, the delight of landscape painters and enthusiasts of the hand camera. It has been painted and photographed times without number, and its two crooked streets, its market cross, its mediæval church and ruined castle are all of them familiar enough to the frequenters of London art galleries. Bicycles converge to it from the four quarters of England, transatlantic tourists twang the melodious American tongue under the gabled roof of its principal inn, the omnivorous kodaker clicks his shutter at donjon, battlement, and ivy-covered tower, and unscrupulous authors thieve its local legends for the harrowing of the public in Christmas numbers and magazines. The name is obviously of Latin origin, and from the Castraville of the middle ages we have the Casterwell of to-day. On the brow of an adjoining hill the circumvallations of the ubiquitous Romans show that the village originally received its name from a military post of the days of Caractacus and Boadicea. But the Imperial legions have marched into the outer darkness, the baron of the castle is a handful of dust, the founders of the church lie mouldering in their ornate tombs, and Casterwell survives them all: a quaint, pretty, peaceful spot, beautiful even in its decay.

The village lies in a dip of the ground—hardly to be called a valley—between two wooded hills swelling gently from the surrounding plain. On one of these rises a square palace of white free-stone ornate, and conspicuous by force of its many windows and lofty tower—this latter well-nigh offensively incongruous with the general architectural design. This grandiose barrack is "Kingsholme," the country seat of Lord Aldean. In it he lives like a mouse in a haystack. It is many times too large for a single young orphan, and it takes much more of the orphan's income to keep up than he likes.

Thither Aldean and his friend spun as fast as a quick-trotting mare could take them. As they turned into the park Mallow cast a wistful look towards the other hill, where, surrounded by its ancient woods, lay embosomed the dwelling of Miss Olive Bellairs—the lady of Casterwell Manor. The soul of this hapless lover was full of regret in that he was not the occupant of Mr. Dimbal's fly, and he sighed as he mastered his feelings, in subservience to the exigencies of social intercourse—a necessity for the moment, but one by no means to his taste.

Meanwhile the fly—the tortoise to the Aldean hare—crawled doggedly along the dusty road. Mr. Dimbal, with a complacent smile on his rosy face, and his black bag established safely on his knees, glanced absently out of the window. Through incessant clouds of dust he caught glimpses of the flowering hedges, and now and again behind them of the corn waving in the hot wind. Then a cottage or so with its thatched roof and tiny garden marked the proximity to the village, and soon he was rumbling through Casterwell High Street. At last the avenue leading to the Manor House came in sight, and, as his eye rested on the mansion, Mr. Dimbal heaved a sigh of relief to think that he was at his journey's end. Three hours of continuous travelling on a hot midsummer day are not exactly the height of bliss to a comfortable elderly gentleman.

The house was typical of its kind. Here were diamond-paned casements, tall oriel windows, lofty-tiled roofs surmounted by stacks of twisting chimneys, terraces of grey stone with urns and statues—in fact, all and everything which we are accustomed to associate with the conventional old English manor-house.

The whole place was radiant with roses. The walls of the house were draped with them; they clambered over the balustrades of the terraces; they flamed in the wide-mouthed urns; they clothed the antique statues, and rioted round the lawn in prodigal profusion, dazzling the eye with their glorious tints, and filling the air with their perfume. "A dwelling fit for Flora, truly"—it was an unusual flight of fancy for Dimbal, but he gave way to it even as he stepped from out his dusty old fly. He raised his eyes, and lo! the "lady of flowers" was waiting to greet him. In truth she was comely enough, this young woman, for the most beautiful of goddesses. Not an ideal Venus perhaps, or an imperial Juno, but an eminently healthy and withal dainty goddess of spring was Olive Bellairs—a trifle reminiscent maybe of Hebe, the girlish and ever young.

Neither divinely tall nor unduly slender, her figure was neatness exemplified. Her hair was brown, so were her eyes; while, did you seek to compare her complexion, you must perforce fall back upon the well-worn simile of the rose-leaf.

She was dressed in pure white. "And how are you, Mr. Dimbal?" she said. "For a whole hour have I been watching for you."

"If, like the Lord Chancellor in 'Iolanthe,' I were possessed of wings, my dear, you would not have had to wait at all."

"Well, now you are here, I'm sure you're very hungry. Lunch is quite ready; come along!"

"Yes, my dear, and I am quite ready, too; but I should not eat my luncheon in peace did I not first discharge, at least, the more important part of my mission."

"Oh dear," pouted Olive, "won't the horrid thing keep for an hour?"

"My dear," said Dimbal, taking the girl's hand in his own, "let me make myself quite clear. I am here to impress upon you the terms of your father's will, which, as you know, has been in my possession since you were a baby, and to hand to you a sealed letter which he left for you. Until this is done, I cannot eat my meal in comfort."

"A sealed letter?" queried Olive, leading the way into the drawing-room; "why was it not given to me before?"

"Because your father's instructions were that you were not to have possession of this letter until after the arrival of Mr. Carson in England. Well, Mr. Carson has arrived. He was in my office yesterday; so, you see, I have lost no time."

Olive sat down and took off her sun-bonnet. She looked put out. "I know that Mr. Carson is in England," she said; "I got a letter from him three or four days ago, in which he says he is coming down here at the end of the week."

"Oh, well, I hope you are pleased," said Dimbal, looking dubiously at her. The kind-hearted little lawyer feared, from her expression that she was not.

"No, Mr. Dimbal," replied the girl, decidedly. "I cannot pretend that I am. You must remember I have never seen the man. Indeed, I do not want to see him, and I am very sure I do not want to marry him."

"But you must marry him, Olive."

"I don't see that I must marry anybody I don't like. I am sure I shall hate him!"

"My dear, you really must not talk like that. Remember you lose a large sum of money if you do not fulfil the conditions of the will."

"I would rather lose anything than marry him," said Olive, recklessly. "I don't love the man; why, I have never seen him; how can you—how could papa expect me to marry him? He may be horrid—indeed, I am sure he is horrid."

"Mr. Carson is a very charming and handsome young man," was Dimbal's reply, as he opened his bag. "You will find that he is everything your heart can desire."

9

"My heart does not desire him at all. I object to being married without being consulted."

"But Olive—dear child, remember, you loved your father!"

"Yes"—the girl's face grew very tender, "my father was the dearest and best of men. I loved him very dearly—better than any one else in the world. You know I love his memory still."

"Then you will surely obey his last expressed wish?" said Dimbal, persuasively. "In that way alone can you show your love and affection for him."

"Mr. Bellairs's heart was set upon your marrying the son of his oldest and best friend."

"Where is this letter, Mr. Dimbal?" asked Olive, irrelevantly.

"All in good time, my dear. Let me first explain the will to you."

"Do you wish Miss Slarge to be present?" said Olive, as the lawyer spread out the formidable parchment.

"Oh, that is not necessary. I suppose she is busy?"

Olive shrugged her pretty shoulders. "She is hunting, I believe, through Layard's Nineveh in search of Nimrod," she answered. "Lucky Aunt Rubina, she hasn't got to marry a man she doesn't care two pins about."

"I don't suppose Miss Slarge would marry any one, my dear. She has always been the consistent advocate of celibacy."

"I only wish my father had been the same."

"Would that really please you?" said Dimbal; he knew a good deal more about Miss Olive's likes, if not about her dislikes, than she had any idea of. "I met Mr. Mallow at Reading Station," the artful lawyer continued, significantly.

"Oh!" said Olive, the colour mounting to her face.

"Yes; he has come down to stop for a week or two with Lord Aldean."

"I—I—well, I really don't care. Why do you look at me like that, Mr. Dimbal? Don't, please! Mr. Mallow is really nothing to me."

"Or you to Hecuba. Well, if you don't know, Olive, I'm sure I don't. Let us get to business. By this, my dear," he said, smoothing out the parchment, "you inherit all the real estate of your father, consisting of the house, lands, farms, tenements, etc., etc.—all of which combine to bring you in an income of some three thousand pounds per annum. Into possession of this you will enter upon your twenty-first birthday."

"That is next month," said Olive, nodding.

"Quite so. On August 24th you attain your majority. You will

10

then receive your rents, and become absolute mistress of the estate."

"Without conditions?"

"Certainly—without conditions. Those of which I am about to speak apply only to the personal estate. This consists of some fifty thousand pounds, excellently well invested in railway stock and shares for the most part, though some small portion of it is in the Government funds. If within a month of your majority you become the wife of Angus Carson this money passes to your husband, and he is to use it for the benefit of you both."

"Oh, indeed and I have no say in the matter, I suppose?"

"Well, not legally speaking. Although Mr. Carson can only obtain this money by marrying you; that done, he has full legal possession of it; and, although there is no absolute charge upon the capital providing for it, there is a strong wish expressed by your father—so strong as to amount to an absolute obligation in the mind of any right-thinking man—that the sum of a thousand pounds per annum shall be set apart from out of the interest of this money by your husband for your own separate use. But of the principal, you understand, he has absolute control."

"But suppose Mr. Carson is a scamp and a spendthrift?"

"We will not suppose any such thing, my dear. I admit," added Dimbal, looking at the document—"I admit that the powers given to Mr. Carson are very great, and should perhaps have been controlled, if not restricted, in some measure—indeed, I suggested something of the sort to your father; but he contended you were amply provided for by the real estate, and he had every hope that young Mr. Carson would prove to be as good and as honourable a man as his father had been before him."

"What is your opinion of him?" asked Olive, abruptly.

"My dear, I saw Mr. Carson but for half an hour, so I can scarcely be expected to answer that question. He appeared to me to be an amiable and pleasant young gentleman, and I have no doubt he will make you an excellent husband."

"Oh, I dare say; that is, of course, provided I consent to marry him," said Miss Bellairs, tartly. "Well, Mr. Dimbal, thank you. I quite understand all you have told me. When I marry Mr. Carson, he gets fifty thousand pounds to do exactly as he likes with."

"Well, certainly that is one way of looking at it; but you must not forget that he is to pay you quarterly the sum of two hundred and fifty pounds," said Mr. Dimbal, hastily.

11

"Quite so. I get one thousand to his forty-nine!"

"No, no, my dear—not at all."

"Oh, well, in any case he has the best of it," said Olive, wilfully. "If he chooses to make ducks and drakes of the capital there will be but a small chance of my getting any income."

"That would be to argue Mr. Carson a thorough scamp, my dear. I do not think he is that."

"How do you know—you say yourself you only saw him for thirty minutes—you can't read a man's character in that time."

"Perhaps not; but Mr. Carson appears to me to be an exceptionally well-conducted young gentleman; and, after all, Olive, supposing he does waste this money, you have always three thousand a year of your own which he cannot touch."

"And a husband I don't want," she replied bitterly. "Well, Mr. Dimbal, suppose I refuse this arrangement?"

"Well, in that case, my dear, the whole of the money goes to the Reverend Manners Brock, Rector of Casterwell."

"Yes, so I remember you told me before. Why, may I ask, does it go to him?"

"Really, my dear, I can hardly say. Mr. Brock was the most intimate friend of your father and Dr. Carson. Failing the fulfilment of his primary wish, it is evident your father decided to pass on the money to his best friend. That is how the will stands, though, as I have said, it is not easy to approve of it in all respects."

"It is a hard and cruel will," said Olive, despondently. "I am sure I don't wish to rob Mr. Carson or any one else of the money, but, on the other hand, I have no wish to become the wife of a man who is a complete stranger to me. My affections are not a regiment of soldiers, to be ordered about in this way."

"Well," said Mr. Dimbal, fishing up a blue envelope with a red seal from the depths of his black bag—"well, Olive, here is your father's letter. It may perhaps explain his reason for making what, I allow, is a most extraordinary disposition of his personalty."

Olive took the letter in silence, and, rising from her chair, opened it at the window with her back to the lawyer. It contained a single sheet of paper, on which were written eight lines in her father's well-known hand. They were shaky and faint, as though they had been penned—as indeed they were—by a dying man.

"My Darling Olive,

"When you read these lines you will know that it is my last wish and command that you should marry Angus Carson, to whom you have been engaged since your birth. Marry him, I implore you—not so much for the money, as, because if you do not become his wife, evil, terrible evil, will come of your refusal. If you ever loved me, if my memory is dear to you, fulfil my dying wish, and marry Angus Carson within a month of your twenty-first birthday. If you refuse, God help you!

"Your loving father,
"Mark Bellairs."

As white as ashes Olive let the paper flutter to the floor.

"What does it mean?" she murmured faintly. "My God, what can it mean?"

CHAPTER III

AT THE MANOR HOUSE

"What about to-day, Mallow?" asked Aldean, as with his friend and mentor he enjoyed a morning pipe, pacing the terrace of Kingsholme.

"The day is right enough," replied Laurence, morosely; and he looked with a jaundiced eye on the green country stretching beyond a fringe of trees towards the blue and distant hills.

"I don't think you are," retorted his lordship; "you have not spoken two words the whole of breakfast."

"I'm never fit for rational conversation till noon, Aldean. I should be tied up this morning."

"Liver!" grunted Aldean, with a fond look at his pipe. "Let's get out the 'gees,' and shake ourselves into good humour."

Mallow placed his hands on the young man's shoulders and swayed him to and fro. "That is all the shaking you need, Jim," said he, in a more amiable tone. "If I were as good-humoured as you I should be content—all the same, I wish you would confine yourself to the Queen's English."

"Your speech is like a hornet, the sting's in the tail. Have you read the papers this morning?"

"No," replied Mallow, listlessly. "What's in them?"

"The usual nothing. France is abusing us, Germany is envying us, Russia is warning us, and the U.S.A. are beginning to see that blood is thicker than foreign ditch-water."

"And what are we doing?"

"Holding our tongues and picking up unconsidered geographical trifles. Silence is ever golden annexation with us."

"Upon my word, Jim," said Mallow, with good-humoured astonishment, "you are getting beyond words of one syllable. You can actually construct a sentence with a visible idea in it."

"I am growing up, Mallow; age is coming upon me."

"Well, Jim, suppose we take a walk."

Aldean laughed, and pointed with the stem of his pipe towards the red roofs of the distant manor house, "Over there, I suppose?"

"Jim, you have no tact. If our steps do tend in that direction, wandering in devious ways, I—I—well, I have not forgotten that Miss Ostergaard is paying a visit to—to—Miss Slarge."

"True enough," replied Jim, winking. "Let us pay a visit to—to—Miss Slarge."

"We might do worse," said Mallow; and sighed.

"I expect we'll do better," was Aldean's response.

Mallow groaned. "Oh, Jim, Jim, I am a fool. I know that she is going to marry this Carson; and yet—and yet I cannot help making myself miserable by calling to see her."

"Buck up, old man, she isn't spliced yet!"

"James, you are incurably vulgar."

"If you pay me any more compliments, Mallow, I shall forget the respect to my former tutor, and chuck you out of this gangway. Come for a walk."

So Mallow allowed himself to be persuaded, and in due time, as he knew they inevitably would do, they found themselves in the grounds of the Manor House.

Striding up and down the lawn was an elderly lady with a lack-lustre eye and the gait of a grenadier.

"How do you do, Miss Slarge," said the visitors, almost simultaneously. And they waited for the priestess of Minerva to wake up and return their salutation.

Miss Rubina Slarge was a maiden of forty-five years. She was sufficiently well-looking to have married a score of times. However, early in life she had become convinced that it was her mission to

14

expose the errors of the Romish Church, and she felt that for this purpose she should dispense with a husband. Her knowledge was extensive, but apt to be inaccurate. It was her firm impression that the idol worship of Babylon still existed in the Papal Church, and she was writing a voluminous book to prove this. Nimrod and his wife Semiramis were still worshipped, she declared, and the festivals and ritual of modern Rome were identical with those of ancient Babylon. She thought of little else, and lived in a world of Biblical prophecy and mythological lore. Therefore, although she was supposed ostensibly to look after Olive, that clear-headed young lady looked after her, and the house to boot. Olive called her Aunt Ruby, but she was really only a distant cousin, connected by blood with the late Mrs. Bellairs. Absent-minded and dogmatic, Aunt Ruby was nevertheless amiable and kindly, and Olive was really fond of her. But it was rare for her to leave Rome or Babylon to speak on commonplace subjects. She was difficult to manage, and required no little humouring.

On seeing two young men standing bareheaded before her, she stopped and looked bewildered. Then she recognized them both and smiled. Finally she pointed a lean finger at Lord Aldean.

"Septem alta jugis toti quæ presidet orbi,'" said Miss Slarge, solemnly. "What does that mean, Lord Aldean?"

"Great Scott!" gasped Jim, cramming his hat on his head, "I don't know."

"Yet you call yourself a scholar, sir?"

"No, I don't, Miss Slarge. I call Mr. Mallow a scholar. What is it, Mallow?"

"The lofty city with seven hills which governs the whole world," translated Mallow.

"I know that," snapped Miss Slarge; "it is a simple sentence from Virgil. But what city?"

"Rome, of course; what other city has seven hills?"

"I was certain of it," cried Miss Slarge, triumphantly; "the chief seat of idolatry under the New Testament. Mystery, Babylon the great—that is Rome!"

"Is it indeed," said Aldean, for her eyes were fastened upon him. "What a rum idea!"

"Jim, Jim," reproved Mallow, smiling.

"It is a very wonderful idea," said Miss Slarge, reproachfully. "Do you know, Mr. Mallow, I made a most remarkable discovery last week? The two-horned mitre of the Romish bishops is nothing but the mitre worn by Dagon, the fish-god of the Babylonians."

15

"I do not quite understand, Miss Slarge."

"It is not difficult," replied the lady. "Dagon was depicted as half man, half fish."

"I know," cried Aldean; "he had a fish's tail, like a mermaid."

"True enough," assented Mallow; "but that does not explain the mitre."

Miss Slarge became excited. "The head of the fish, with open jaws, was worn on the god's head!" she cried, "and the scales and tail formed a cloak. The bishops of the papal church don't wear the tail, but they place the open-jawed head on their brows, and call it a mitre. Now do you see?"

"Oh yes. It is truly wonderful, Miss Slarge."

"Osiris also wore such a mitre, Mr. Mallow. How then can you doubt that the Pope of Rome is not the modern representative of the Philistine, of the Babylonian deity. Why, if——"

By this time Miss Slarge was taking a breather on her hobby horse, and might be expected to gallop that tiresome animal for a considerable time; so, leaving Mallow to endure the martyrdom, Lord Aldean edged away from the pair by degrees. The cunning rascal had caught a glimpse of Miss Ostergaard out of the tail of his eye, and, preferring flirtation to instruction, managed to place himself by her side whilst she was filling a small basket with roses. All this apparently without her knowledge.

The young lady from New Zealand was one of the most charming of young ladies; and Aldean went so far as to make no reservation in favour of any one. She had been sent to England to be educated, and, having gone to the same school as Olive, a close friendship had sprung up between them as rapidly as had grown Jonah's gourd. Happily the friendship was more enduring than the plant, and for three or four years these two had been like Helena and Hermia, two cherries on one stem. Miss Ostergaard, whose Christian, or rather Maori name, was Tui, loved Olive as her other self, and frequently came to stay at the Manor House. She was now twenty years of age, and so pretty that she won every heart left uncaptured by Olive. With dark hair, dark complexion, and two wonderful dark eyes like wells of liquid light, she made such havoc amongst young and susceptible males that she should have been shut up as a too delightful damsel dangerous to the youth of the community. Her last victim was the hapless Aldean. Having impaled him on a pin, she was watching him wriggle. Not that Jim objected to the process—indeed, he rather liked it—for if he wriggled on the pin no one else could, for the time being; and thus he secured all the sweet torment unto himself: a most gratifying monopoly.

Of course Tui knew that Olive was in love with Mallow, and equally, of course, Olive was aware of Aldean's passion for Tui; and of course both of them discussed their lovers to their hearts' content. Tui was distinctly in favour of Mallow as a suitor for her darling Olive, and was enraged at the mere thought of her friend being handed over, with fifty thousand pounds, to an unknown suitor from the back of beyond. Therefore she was glad to see him, and she hoped that he would rescue Olive from the Indian dragon as a true knight should; for Olive was very wretched and very tearful, and had been so ever since the departure of Mr. Dimbal.

"Poor dear!" sighed Miss Ostergaard, thinking of her friend.

"That is me, isn't it?" asked the artful Aldean.

"You?" said the lady, snipping vigorously—"as if I was thinking of you, Lord Aldean. Oh, you men, you men!—and they say that women are vain!"

"You have something to be vain about," said Aldean, seeing his way to a compliment.

"I have, indeed—with you. No, I was thinking of Olive. You know that she is going to be married?"

Aldean cast a commiserating look at his friend, who was still being assailed with Babylonic information by Miss Slarge, and nodded.

"But she may not marry the chap after all, you know?"

"Oh yes, she will. Mr. Carson is coming down here in three days, and Olive has fully made up her mind to accept him. I am so enraged," cried Tui, "that I could (snip) cut his (snip) head off (snip, snip)."

"She has never seen Carson, has she?"

"No; that's the worst of it. Fancy marrying a veiled prophet—a Mokanna!"

"Never heard of the Johnny, Miss Ostergaard. Who is he?"

"He is a fable, Lord Aldean."

"Pity this Carson man isn't," said his lordship, with a grin.

"I wish he were," sighed Tui, walking towards the house. "I am sure he is a beast—a beast with a big, big B!"

"Who deserves a big, big D!" cried Aldean, emphatically. "Oh, what a beast!"

"Are you talking of the beast from the Persian Gulf," cried Miss Slarge, who, having pulverized Mallow, had glided behind them; "the beast who taught the Babylonians arts and sciences?"

17

"This beast comes from India," said Aldean, smiling at Tui, and with a side glance at Mallow; "he is called Car——"

"Oh, there is Olive," interrupted Miss Ostergaard, waving her hand; "Olive, here are two visitors!" and Olive, pale and listless, descending the steps, turned yet paler at the sight of the man she loved and who loved her.

CHAPTER IV

A QUEER COINCIDENCE

When Olive saw who was standing on the lawn, she felt very much inclined to fly from so dear yet dangerous a foe. But maidenly pride came to her aid, and, doing violence to her feelings, the better to conceal them, she saluted Mr. Mallow with so much frigidity as rather to disconcert that young gentleman.

"Mr. Dimbal told me that you were here," she said. "He saw you at Reading Station yesterday."

"Mr. Dimbal is very kind to save me the trouble of announcing myself," said Mallow' dryly. "So unimportant a person as I am should feel much flattered."

"No friend is unimportant, Mr. Mallow," reproved Miss Bellairs, gently.

"I believe that—when there is something substantial to be gained from the friendship."

"What a cruel remark!" cried Tui, shaking her head. "I hope you do not practise what you preach, Mr. Mallow."

"Mallow's bark is worse than his bite," chimed in Aldean.

"And the horse is the noblest of all animals," said Mallow' ironically. "Go on, Aldean; I love these dry chips from the tree of knowledge."

"The Hebrew tree of knowledge was stolen by them from the Chaldeans," said Miss Slarge, loudly. "The serpent legend, so intimately connected with it, came from the same source. Well, young people, I must really return to my studies. Lord Aldean—Mr. Mallow; I hope you will both stay to luncheon?"

Aldean consulted Mallow by a side look, but seeing no encouragement in his moody face refused the invitation on behalf of them both; whereat Miss Slarge shook hands in the nineteenth-century fashion, and returned to her studies and the primæval days when Nimrod began to be a mighty one on the earth. The four young people were left standing, and a short silence prevailed, which was broken by Mallow.

"'Hence, loathed melancholy!'" he spouted theatrically; "we have had enough of that dismal goddess. Miss Bellairs, smile; Aldean, make a joke; Miss Ostergaard, laugh for goodness' sake."

"I can't," replied the last-named lady, "until Lord Aldean makes his joke. One can't make bricks without straw or mirth without jests."

"I always have to think out my jokes," said Aldean, innocently; which remark brought forth the required mirth.

"You are like the man whose impromptus took him years to invent," said Olive, beginning to be merry. "Mr. Mallow, what is the latest news from town?"

"Men are in love; thieves are in gaol, and women still use looking-glasses."

"Also Queen Anne is dead," laughed Tui, swinging her basket. "Oysters and news should both be fresh, yet you talk truisms."

"Have you heard of that awful murder?" put in Aldean. "Murder! Oh, the horrid word, you make me shudder!"

"Aldean is like the fat boy in Pickwick," said Mallow, and quoted, "I wants to make your flesh creep.'"

"Is that the Athelstane Place crime, Lord Aldean?" asked Olive.

"Yes. Fellow was killed with a knitting-needle. I wonder who did it?"

"A woman, you may be sure."

"What makes you think so, Miss Bellairs?" demanded Mallow, quickly.

"Because men don't use knitting-needles, and women do," replied the girl. "I dare say it was a case of jealousy."

"Perhaps; but even a jealous woman would hesitate to cut off the right hand of a dead lover."

"Unless she came from the East," said Aldean, suddenly.

"Why should she come from the East?"

"Well, the Morning Planet says that the man came from India."

"From India!" cried Olive and Tui in one breath; and their thoughts centred at once on Angus Carson.

19

"Oh, that is only a theory of the newspaper!" said Mallow, hastily. "Can't you find a pleasanter subject to talk about, Aldean?"

"Yes," replied Aldean, looking meaningly at Tui. "Only——"

"Only I am wasting my time, and you are helping me to do so," cried that young lady, briskly. "I must tie up my roses."

"Let me help you."

"I am afraid your help would be a hindrance," said Miss Ostergaard, as she moved towards the house, followed by her huge admirer. "However, if you are very, very good, you may hold the ball of string."

Left alone with Mallow, Olive felt in so dangerous a position that she assumed a demeanour even more reserved.

"So Mr. Carson has arrived in England," remarked the young man, gloomily.

"Yes; who told you so?"

"Mr. Dimbal, the lawyer. Of course, it is an open secret that you are to marry him."

"I see no reason why it should be a secret at all," retorted Olive, with a flush. "If my father wished for the marriage, no one can say a word against it."

"I am not saying a word against it. If I did, I should probably say too much."

"Then don't let us discuss the subject," said Olive, hurriedly; "you only make my position the harder."

"Do you consider it hard?"

"You have no right to ask me that question, Mr. Mallow."

"I beg your pardon," said the young man, reddening. "I admit that I have no right—unless you give me one."

"Mr. Mallow, I really do not understand you."

"I don't understand myself, Miss Bellairs; usually I am not timid when I should be bold."

"'Be bold—be bold, but be not over bold,'" quoted Olive, trying to turn off his speech with a laugh—an attempt which Mallow resolutely refused to countenance.

"I suppose you will marry Mr. Carson?" he inquired anxiously.

"I suppose I shall," replied Miss Bellairs, with a coolness she was far from feeling.

"Is it absolutely certain?"

Olive felt a quiver pass through her frame, and it was with difficulty she prevented her emotion from overcoming her. She thought of the man who was coming to claim her, the man she had never even seen; of the undeclared lover who was by her side dreading the answer which she should give. Finally the memory of the sealed letter, with its menace of coming evil passed through her mind, and dictated the reply—

"It is absolutely certain—absolutely."

"In that case there is nothing for me to do but to offer you the customary congratulations on your—your good fortune."

"My good fortune!" she burst out. "My good—oh yes, of course. Thank you, Mr. Mallow. I congratulate you, in my turn, on your penetration." And before he could recover from his amazement at this attack, she flitted across the lawn, swept past the astonished couple on the steps, and vanished into the house.

This incident brought the visit to a close, for as Olive did not reappear to explain her sudden anger, Mallow said good-bye to Miss Ostergaard, and departed with the reluctant Aldean. The young lord, guessing that his friend and Olive had come to words, more than expected to have a peevish companion for his homeward walk, instead of which Mallow was quite uproariously merry. By this time he had fathomed the cause of Olive's wrath, and he cursed himself for a fool not to have seen and known that she was not the woman to wear her heart upon her sleeve. Her sudden retreat after her foolish speech had been the result of fear at having betrayed her real feelings. These were not for Carson, he was sure of that now, but for himself—Olive loved him; and whether the pre-arranged marriage took place or not, nothing could alter that fact. As the thought became conviction, Mallow found it impossible to suppress the joy he felt, and he forthwith indulged in antics which would have shamed a schoolboy.

"What is it?" asked Aldean, amazed at this conduct in so grave a man.

"What do you think it is, Jim?"

"Lunacy, I should say, on the face of it."

"No, my boy; but a word much the same in meaning, which begins with the same letter."

"Larking?" guessed the obtuse Jim, with a grin.

"I can't say much for your penetration, Lord Aldean," said Mallow, with a laugh. "Love is the word I mean—love is the feeling which thrills me, for 'to-day the birthday of my life is come.'"

"One would think you had been celebrating the occasion with strong drink," retorted Jim, soberly. "Have you spoken to Miss Bellairs?"

"No, sir; I have done nothing so foolish."

"Then has she perhaps given you to understand——"

21

"Of course not; do you think for one moment she is the woman to do such a thing?"

"I don't know; once or twice girls have pretty near proposed to me. I've had some trouble with them, I can tell you. Then how do you know it is all right?"

"Because I do know."

"That isn't an answer; it's a statement."

"Then you will have to take the statement for your answer, my dear old thickhead. Olive loves me, the angel that she is."

"She ran away from you."

"I know she did, but she loves me."

"She was in a pelting rage; I saw her face."

"I know she was, but she loves me."

"Oh, come home," growled Aldean, putting his arm within that of his enigmatic friend. "You're a human cuckoo."

Mallow laughed, and went back to Kingsholme with an excellent appetite, which went to prove that he was no lover out of a sickly romance. For the next two or three days he made no attempt to see Olive, but lived on the memory of her self-betrayal. In spite of Jim's insidious hints that the pleasantest walks tended towards the Manor House, Laurence kept away. With his host he rode and drove and played golf. He spun over the country on his Humber, and fought Jim valiantly in singles on the tennis-lawn.

Then the news came that Angus Carson and his friend Major Semberry had arrived, and were in possession of the garden of flowers, and presumably of the nymphs who haunted it. Mallow's spirits suddenly went down to zero, and, in a moping mood, he worried Aldean for two whole days. On the third he resolved to meet his rival face to face; so, taking advantage of Aldean's absence at Reading, he walked over to the Manor House, and was duly shown into the drawing-room.

Remembering their last meeting, Olive blushed as she gave Mallow her hand. Then, to cover her confusion, she presented Mallow to a tall, slender young man in a grey tweed suit, with his right hand in a black silk sling.

"Mr. Mallow, this is Mr. Carson."

Laurence bowed, and as he did so he became aware of a faint drowsy odour.

It was the perfume of sandal-wood.

22

CHAPTER V

THE SUSPICIONS OF LAURENCE MALLOW

O all things odours are the most powerful to stimulate a dormant memory; to bring back in a flash an especial scene, a peculiar face, a particular conversation. Nothing was further from Mallow's mind than the mysterious murder of Athelstane Place, yet the moment that whiff of sandal-wood titillated his nostrils, he recalled at once the theory of the newspapers and the wild suggestion of Lord Aldean.

For the moment he was so bewildered that he stood tongue-tied before Mr. Carson. That young gentleman, on his part, appeared to be amused, if a trifle astonished.

"You have seen me before," he asked in a pleasant voice, with a slight and agreeable accent. "No? Is there anything strange about me then that you——"

"I—I—I really beg your pardon," stammered Mallow, scrambling out of his unpleasant position as best he could; "but I—that is—I fancied I did know your face."

"You have been in India, then?"

"Yes, Mr. Carson; I was in India some months ago."

"Then it is quite possible that we met there, Mr. Mallow, although I cannot recall having seen you. This is the first time I have visited England. Forgive me if I am somewhat lax in the observance of your social customs—one always shakes hands here, I believe, when presented; you must let me then give you my left hand."

"Is your right disabled?" asked Mallow, shaking the hand this affable young man extended.

"I am sorry to say it is, Mr. Mallow. I hurt it some months back, shooting in India; the bones are diseased, and, since my arrival, I have been having it attended to by one of your clever London surgeons. I am relieved to say that he did not consider amputation to be necessary."

Here, again, was another circumstance which immediately struck Mallow as peculiar. The right hand of the dead man in Athelstane Place had been cutoff; the right hand of Mr. Carson was diseased, and had narrowly escaped amputation. This was a strange coincidence.

"I am charmed with your country, Mr. Mallow," continued Carson, who seemed bent upon making himself agreeable. "After the arid plains of India, these green fields are very refreshing to the eye."

"Yet I have seen marvellous verdure in the Himalayas," replied Mallow.

Carson shrugged his shoulders. "Oh yes; every land has its season of greenness, you know, but India is undeniably dry."

"How do you do, Mr. Mallow," said a voice at the young man's elbow, and he turned to see the lean form of Miss Slarge. "We have quite a large gathering to-day, have we not?—Major Semberry, Dr. Drabble, and Mr. Carson."

"Last and least," smiled that gentleman.

Mallow laughed also, seemingly out of politeness, and glanced round the drawing-room at the people referred to by Miss Slarge. Major Semberry, a fair, handsome, soldierly man, was paying great attention to Miss Ostergaard, who had apparently forgotten Aldean in the ardour of her present flirtation; and Dr. Drabble, tall and thin as a telegraph-pole, and with about as much figure, was talking loudly with Olive Bellairs. When Laurence withdrew his eyes, Miss Slarge, who was quite modern at the present moment, was chatting with Carson in her high-pitched voice.

"My sister, Mrs. Purcell, describes you as being like an Italian," she was saying; "and I quite agree with her—don't you, Mr. Mallow?"

"Certainly, Mr. Carson has the appearance of a Tuscan."

"My mother was Eurasian," explained the young man; "I am supposed to take after her. There is a great similarity between dark people, don't you think so? Yes?"

"Well, putting negroes out of the question, I suppose there is, more or less," assented Mallow. He thought Carson much more like the pure Italian than the Englishman of mixed blood. Certainly there was no hint of the Anglo-Saxon about him.

"So Mrs. Purcell has been giving you my character," said Carson, smiling blandly on Miss Slarge.

"Oh dear me, yes. She wrote me quite a long account of you—all about your looks, and conversation, and I don't know what else."

"Really? I feel flattered by the notice she has taken of me. I confess I should very much like to see that letter."

"If you like I will read you those parts of it which refer to you," said Miss Slarge, amiably. "You will see then how keen an observer my sister is. Excuse me, I will fetch the letter."

24

As Miss Slarge slipped out of the room on her errand, Mallow detected a sigh from Carson—a sigh that sounded like one of relief. At the same time he appeared—so Mallow thought—to be uneasy, and while continuing his conversation he frequently glanced at the Major. Semberry instinctively became aware of this, and once or twice turned his head. Finally he left Miss Ostergaard, and came slowly across the room, as though drawn in spite of himself to the side of his friend. Again Mallow heard from Carson a sigh of relief, after which his uneasiness gave place to a more confident manner, and he presented Major Semberry to Laurence with perfect ease.

"We need no introduction," said Mallow, smiling. "Major Semberry and I met at Simla some few months back.

"Ah, yes," replied Semberry, in his crisp, abrupt way; "Mallow the sportsman. I remember."

"Say, rather, Mallow the scribe—in India, Major. It was my mission to scribble out there."

"By George, yes. Read some of your letters in paper. You dropped on us hot, Mallow—deuced hot. What are you doing in these parts?"

"Idling, Major, at the expense of Lord Aldean."

"Met him in London," said Semberry, staccato; "nice boy, make good Army man. No brains, plenty muscle."

"Oh, Aldean has a good deal more mental power than people give him credit for."

"Dark horse, eh?"

"Well, he may yet prove to be so. As to your no brains for the Army,' Major, I fancy you depreciate your profession. They don't make the fool of the family a soldier now—they certainly did not in your case."

The Major acknowledged the compliment with a bow, but did not reply.

"Do you know, Semberry, that I am about to hear my character?" said Carson, blandly.

"Eh, what? From our friend here?"

"No," explained Mallow; "it seems that Mrs. Purcell has written an account of Mr. Carson to Miss Slarge, and your friend is to hear it verbatim."

From long exposure to the sun, the natural hue of Semberry's complexion was brick-dust, yet at this it became still more red, and he put up a hand and tugged uneasily at his moustache. His manner reflected the recent anxiety of Carson, and Mallow was at once on the alert to discover the cause of their joint discomfort. There was a

25

hint of mystery about the swift glances they exchanged which piqued his curiosity, and from that moment he was silently observant of their every look and word. What he expected to learn he hardly knew, but that there was something to be learned he felt convinced. But then Mallow was distinctly prejudiced against Carson as his rival.

When the Major's hand came down from his moustache, he observed that "Mrs. Purcell was a charming woman, and that she wrote an amusing letter." He then turned to face Olive, who was approaching with Dr. Drabble.

"It is not kind of you three gentlemen to exclude us from your conversation," she said brightly. "What are you talking about?"

"Mrs. Purcell's letter," said Carson, with a glance of proprietorship. "Miss Slarge has promised to read aloud the character which her sister is so good as to give me."

"It is a better one than you deserve," replied Olive.

"Ha, ha!" roared Drabble, who was a noisy creature at best, "isn't his character to your liking, Miss Bellairs?"

"If it is not," said Carson, before the girl had time to answer, "Olive shall make it to her liking in two months."

Miss Ostergaard, who had joined the group, laughed. "Can an old dog learn new tricks?" she said mischeviously.

"A young puppy might," muttered Mallow, whose hot Irish temper was rapidly rising, both at Carson and at Olive.

He was enraged at the mere fact of the man calling the girl by her Christian name, and he was annoyed at the complacent way in which she seemed to listen to him and his babble. Luckily for the peace of the moment, his remark passed unheard by all save Tui, and she nodded approbation.

"What ridiculous things you say, Tui," said Olive, with pretended severity.

"Extraordinary name, 'Tui,'" called out Drabble, elegantly. "What does it mean, Miss Ostergaard?"

"It means me, in the first place, Dr. Drabble," she replied smartly; "and in the second it is the native name for the New Zealand parson bird."

"By George, parson bird!"

"Why rookery, Miss Ostergaard? or, to be more precise, why parson bird?"

"Because it is all black, Mr. Mallow—a beautiful glossy black, with two white feathers in its throat like a parson's cravat. We have christened it the parson bird; the Maoris call it the Tui."

"It is inappropriate to you, Miss Ostergaard," said Carson, smiling. "You never preach, I am sure."

"Oh yes, I do; but I keep my sermons for Olive."

"Ho, ho! I should like to be a member of that congregation."

"As an Anarchist, Dr. Drabble, you are not fit to be a member of any. You don't like preaching—other people's preaching, I mean."

"That depends upon the preacher, Miss Ostergaard."

"Madame Death-in-Life, for instance."

With a snarl Drabble turned on Mallow, who had made this remark.

"What do you know of Madame Death-in-Life?" he snapped.

"Only that she is the most noted Anarchist in Europe," retorted Mallow, coolly. "Why not? I know her, you know her, the police know her; and a few stray kings will know her some day to their cost, if she isn't guillotined—as she ought to be.'

"I wonder you know such a horrible woman, Mr. Mallow," said Olive.

"Oh, my acquaintance with her is not personal, Miss Bellairs."

"Neither is mine," said Drabble, who had recovered his good humour. "I don't approve of Madame Death-in-Life's methods. It is not my plan to terrorize the world by bombs and murders. The pen, sir, the pen is mightier than the explosive; so is the tongue. Pamphlets and lectures—that is my system for bringing about the much-needed social millennium. The woman you speak of does harm to the cause; she should be suppressed."

"Just what I said—and by the guillotine."

"No, sir!" thundered Drabble. "No legal crime, if you please."

"Anarchists prefer illegal murder," said Semberry, smiling grimly.

"And no punishment to follow," remarked Carson, arranging his sling.

"Except that of their own conscience," chimed in Olive.

"No Anarchist possesses one," said Tui; at which all present burst out laughing at the expression on Dr. Drabble's face.

In the midst of this merriment Miss Slarge returned with the letter and an apology.

"It took me some time to find," she explained to Carson. "Listen; this is how my sister describes you. Perhaps it is better not to give it to you in my sister's own words, for her style is founded upon Dr. Johnson's, and is apt to be prolix."

"Paraphrase the description Miss Slarge," said Mallow.

"Mr. Carson," said Miss Slarge, glancing at the letter, "is

27

twenty-five years of age, gentle, well-bred, not without parts, and modest."

The gentleman in question clicked his heels together in quite a foreign fashion, and bowed low. Mallow noticed the continental air of the whole action, and remembered it.

"He is tall, slender, elegant in shape, of a swart complexion, inherited from his mother, and his eyes and moustache are of the deepest black. He looks like an Italian."

"By George, Carson! Mrs. Purcell describes you exactly," said the Major; and in his heart Mallow, who had followed the description closely, was obliged to confess that this was true.

"He is delicate in health, and has a weak heart."

"I know that to my cost," sighed Carson, "and a swollen hand. Does Mrs. Purcell mention that fact, yes?"

"She does, Mr. Carson, and she also says that you are effeminate."

"Ha, ha!" bellowed Drabble—"effeminate, eh?"

Carson reddened. "And why, Miss Slarge?"

"Because you wear a bracelet."

"That is true enough," assented the young man; "but I can't get it off, and it has been on my wrist all my life—in fact, ever since it was placed there by my ayah."

"Oh, do show us the bracelet!" cried Tui. She had a thorough woman's love for jewellery.

"Bracelet, hum! bangle, India!" muttered the Major, and tugged his moustache.

"Show me the bangle, Angus," said Olive, persuasively; and Mallow winced.

Mr. Carson with great care, and evidently with some pain, took his arm from the sling and drew up his shirt cuff. Loosely encircling his wrist appeared a broad band of pale gold, elaborately wrought with the hideous forms of three Hindoo gods.

As he displayed it, Miss Slarge read aloud the description of the ornament from her sister's letter:—

"It is a broad band of ductile gold, curiously wrought with the idol figures of the Hindoo trinity: Bramah, Siva, and Vishnu, interwoven with the sacred lotus-flower, and other heathen symbols."

"Most extraordinary," said Mallow, looking at it; "good trade-mark, eh, Mr. Carson? None genuine without this device."

"What do you mean, sir?" cried Carson, pulling down his sleeve with an angry jerk.

28

"Mean! why, what should I mean?" replied the Irishman, and smiled innocently.

CHAPTER VI

THE REVEREND MANNERS BROCK

The young men were seated on the terrace in the warm summer twilight. The plains of corn beyond the dark trees were filled with floating shadows, and the pale radiance of the long-set sun still lingered in the western skies. Overhead a few stars shone with mellow lustre in the warm, purple arch; but the moon had not yet rolled her wheel over the distant hills, and the dusk was faintly luminous, so that the landscape was indistinctly visible, as through a filmy veil. There was no breath of wind, and the trees seemed to extend their opaque shadows, even to the verge of the glimmering white terrace. At intervals a nightingale filled the dusk with silvery strains, and occasionally the hoot of a distant owl sounded like depreciative criticism of the bird music. So still, so dreamy, so peacefully beautiful, it was a magic night for love and lovers, for dancing elves and poet's singing. Yet this unromantic pair were talking the crudest commonplaces—harsh music for such an hour, for such a scene. But there are times when man sympathizes with Nature as little as does she with him.

"Well, Jim," said Mallow, after a pause and a sip of warming liqueur, "it is now a week since those marplots came on the scene. What is your candid opinion?"

With a flick of his finger, Aldean sent the stump of his cigarette flying over the balustrade.

"That is what I should like to do," he said, in his deep voice; "chuck them both into space."

"I did not ask you what you would like to do to them, but what you think of them."

"They are two bounders—at least, Semberry is one."

"You are prejudiced, my James," said Mallow, coolly; "Semberry is a well-bred man, but Carson—ahem!—Carson is not a gentleman."

"In other words, Carson is not Carson."

"Upon my soul, Jim, I don't believe he is." Mallow jumped up, and balanced himself on the railing of the terrace immediately before his friend. "I don't believe he is," he repeated. "He is supposed to have come from India. Well, he knows precious little about India, although I have questioned him repeatedly. He talks with a distinct foreign accent; his every action is suggestive of continental society, and he looks like an Italian. See here, Jim"—he slipped down, clicked his heels together, and made a stiff bow from the waist—"is that English?" He mimicked Carson's speech: "You think so, yes? Is that English, Jim? I ask you plainly, is there anything English about the man?"

"Well, he isn't English, you know," was Jim's reply.

"His father was a Saxon, and, from all accounts, a public school boy, a University man, gently born and well-bred. Why isn't his son—if this man be his son—more like him?"

"The poor chap hasn't had his father's advantages, Mallow. His mother was a half-caste, and, I suppose, no pattern of breeding. He has been brought up in exile amongst niggers, and has received a scratch education. I don't see what you can expect. Carson's pretty good, considering his disadvantages."

"Confound you, Jim; don't desert to the enemy!" cried Mallow, in a huff.

"I'm not deserting, but I see both sides of the question, and you don't. You believe that the real Carson is dead, and that this man is an impostor."

"And if I do," said Mallow, defiantly, "it was you who put the idea into my head."

Aldean laughed.

"You don't usually take my suggestions so seriously," he said, smiling. "Besides, I had no proof for my assertion, and you—however much you wish to—can't find one. On the other hand, there is ample evidence to show that Carson is the man he declares himself to be. Mrs. Purcell's letter describes him exactly: he has a weak heart and an injured hand; also, he wears the golden bangle, which, as he showed Mrs. Carson in Bombay, cannot be removed. Finally, Carson has been in Semberry's company ever since he left his father's death-bed."

"Semberry is a plausible scamp," growled Mallow, biting his fingers. "I heard no good of him in India."

"Perhaps not; but a man can be a scamp without being a blackguard."

30

"Pooh, pooh! you split straws. That is a distinction without a difference."

"Well," rejoined Aldean, with equanimity; "let us say that a fellow can be a spendthrift and a Don Juan without being dishonest. I hardly think, Mallow, that Semberry would risk his commission and his position in the world by supporting an impostor such as you believe Carson to be."

"You have certainly found your tongue, Jim," said the Irishman, recovering his good humour, "and your arguments are moderately convincing. But you seem to forget that some fifty thousand pounds are involved in this marriage contract."

"Who told you so?"

"Miss Slarge. She is a dreamy, up-in-the-clouds old lady, as you know, but she can open her eyes and descend to the contemplation of ordinary things occasionally. Olive is the apple of her eye, and her wish is to see the girl happy; therefore, she does not approve of this marriage.'

"Isn't she pleased with Carson?"

"No, she dislikes him thoroughly, and she believes that he is marrying Olive solely for the sake of the money. Now Major Semberry is a chronic bankrupt, and half—even a quarter—of fifty thousand pounds would be a great temptation to him."

Aldean looked earnestly at his friend.

"I see what you mean," he said slowly. "Your idea is that Carson was murdered at Athelstane-Place, and that Semberry has substituted this impostor so that the marriage may take place, and they may share the proceeds. My dear Mallow, if you argue thus, you argue a rope round the Major's neck."

"Bosh! Did I say that Semberry was a murderer?"

"I am only bringing your argument to a logical conclusion, Mallow. If the real Carson has been murdered, Semberry must know of it, else he could have no reason to substitute the false one. Admitting as much, he must either have killed Carson himself, or he must know who did. In either case he is a criminal. Q.E.D."

Mallow shook his head.

"Even assuming that I am right, Semberry could not have murdered Carson, as it would be sheer folly for him to support an impostor when the real Simon Pure was his friend. However, I don't say that the real Carson has been murdered, nor do I identify him with the Athelstane Place victim; although," added Mallow seriously, "it is a strange thing that the clothes, both of the living and the dead, should smell of sandal-wood."

"It is strange," admitted Aldean, "and not to be easily explained. But we have argued the subject threadbare. What is your final opinion?"

"My original opinion—Carson is not Carson."

"Mallow, you are developing a monomania. Come and unbend your great mind over billiards."

The Irishman laughed and agreed. For the next hour or so they were taken up with cannons and breaks, and they left further discussion of Carson's identity to a more fitting occasion. The argument was not renewed that evening, and Mallow retired to bed with his mind less taken up with the subject than usual, and had a good night's rest. However, he woke early the next morning, and his thoughts at once reverted to Olive and her doubtful lover.

Beyond the fact of the sandal-wood perfume, he had no reason for connecting the man who had put in an appearance at Casterwell with the victim of Athelstane-Place, and his good sense told him that this was but a slender foundation upon which to build the superstructure of an imposture. And yet there remained with him an instinctive feeling that all was not right. Do what he would, argue as he might, he could not get rid of the idea that Semberry and his friend were brother rogues, bent upon obtaining the dowry of Olive.

"I cannot believe in Carson until I find some one who can identify him," thought Mallow, as he dressed himself. "If Mrs. Purcell were only in England, she would settle the question at once. But, according to Miss Slarge, she will not be back for three months, and this man is to marry Olive in two. On the 24th of August she comes of age. By the terms of the will, she must become Mrs. Carson before the 24th of September. After that date, be the man genuine or an impostor, I am powerless."

The matter agitated him so greatly as to render him irritable and restless. Unwilling to inflict his state of mind on Aldean, as it was yet early, he slipped out of the house and walked down to the village. He found the rural population astir and busy in the freshness of the morning air. During his tutorship of Aldean he had become friendly with many of these villagers, and those who met him now were glad to renew acquaintance with him. After strolling through the quaint High Street, admiring once again the old-fashioned houses, with their black beams diapered on the whitewashed walls, he turned into the churchyard, and strolled round the sombre grey building, which was the oldest of all the old things in Casterwell. The blackened tombstones, their queer inscriptions half obliterated by brown moss and yellow lichen, toppled askew amongst the uncut dewy grass, and from out the general untidiness rose the ecclesiastical fabric, its obtuse roof hidden by the open stonework and crocketted pinnacles. The massive square tower, draped with fresh green ivy, loomed out at the western end, and round it the swallows were wheeling and glancing like flying arrows. Thrush and blackbird and starling piped in the adjacent thicket, white pigeons whirled overhead, and wreaths of smoke curled from the village chimneys. Mallow enjoyed to the full the freshness of it all—the mellow sounds of waking life, the atmosphere surrounding him. The peace and beauty of it soothed his mind, and he fell to musing. He started when a voice at his elbow greeted him.

"Ah, good morning, Mr. Mallow, this is an unexpected pleasure!"

"Mr. Brock!" cried the Irishman, turning suddenly. "I thought you were away."

"So I was," rejoined the Rector, holding out his hand. "I have been recruiting by the sea. I only returned last night. I see you are like myself, Mr. Mallow; you love the freshness of the early morning."

"I felt restless within doors, Mr. Brock, and came out to be soothed."

The Rector nodded approvingly.

"'You fly to Nature's breast for Nature's balm,'" he quoted in a deep, rolling voice. "It is to be regretted that all young men are not so sensible. Well, Mr. Mallow, and how are you?"

"I am in capital health and spirits," replied Laurence, lightly. "And you? You are not looking quite so fit as usual."

"Age, sir, age. Years are beginning to tell on me. After sixty the human frame begins to fail. I lose tone. My recent visit to the seaside was to restore it."

Mallow thought to himself that the result had not been wholly successful, for Mr. Brock looked sallow and wrinkled and hollow-eyed. He was a handsome, burly man, and he carried himself with an air of importance which many a bishop might have envied. His face was clean-shaven, and his features were clean-cut. His skin was of the particular hue one associates with old ivory, and a halo of silvery white hair lent an air of benignity to his expression. The Reverend Manners Brock had been vicar of Casterwell for over twenty years, and was as well-established as the church over which he presided. He was an industrious worker, an excellent orator, and a general social favourite with rich and poor alike. There was not in

33

England a rector more popular or more admired. He might certainly have been a bishop, and—granting that the welfare of the community was the aim of those in power—he perhaps stood a good chance of becoming one. That he would adorn the position, as he adorned the rectorship of Casterwell, there could be no doubt. But, so far, there had been no hint of any such elevation for Mr. Brock.

As he strolled up and down chatting with Mallow, the click of the church-gate was heard. Simultaneously they turned to see a dark young man, with his arm in a sling, advancing along the grassy path. Mr. Brock started when he saw the face of the newcomer, and clutched the arm of his companion.

"Who—who is that?" he asked, his face grey and drawn, and his frame literally trembling with nervous agitation. "That is Mr. Carson," said Mallow, wondering.

"Carson! Oh, my God! Carson? Do—do the dead return?"

Mallow feared the old man was about to faint.

CHAPTER VII

MARGERY

Carson, with his usual amiable smile, came jauntily along the path, looking directly at Mallow and the Rector. He appeared to be amazed at the white and perturbed face of the latter, but, ignoring it, he held out his left hand in greeting to Laurence.

"Good morning," he said pleasantly. "I see you are an early bird like myself. I have been accustomed to rise at dawn in India, and to drop old habits is difficult, is it not? Yes?"

"India?" gasped the Rector, before Mallow could reply. "Do you come from India?"

"Yes. I arrived in England only a few weeks ago."

"Your name is Carson?"

"Angus Carson, at your service;" and the young man clicked his heels and bowed.

"The son of my old friend, Alfred Carson?" pursued the Rector, who was recovering his self-control somewhat.

34

"Yes. Are you Mr. Brock? Are you my father's friend? Yes?"

"I am," said the other, in a voice of emotion. "Ah! no wonder I felt queer when I saw your face. It was as if the dead were come to life."

"I am supposed to be very like my father," returned Carson, easily. "I don't wonder you were startled. My dear father often spoke to me of your devotion to him."

"Yes, yes; poor Alfred!" The Rector seated himself on a flat tombstone and fought down his natural feelings. "I wish I had known you were here, Angus; your great resemblance to your father has given me a shock. I feel ill—I—I feel very ill."

"Shall I go to the rectory and fetch you some brandy?" said Mallow, who was sorry for the old man.

"If—if you would be so kind," muttered Mr. Brock, burying his face in his handkerchief. "Poor Alfred!"—and his emotion again overcame him. Carson stood by and looked sympathetically on at this proof of a long-remembered friendship; but he made no remark, until Laurence returned from his errand.

"Thank you, Mr. Mallow; you are most kind," said Brock, gratefully, as he swallowed the brandy.

"Believe me, I am sorry my sudden appearance should have so alarmed you," said Carson, politely. "Did you know that I was coming to this place? No?"

"Certainly, I was aware of it," answered the Rector, in a stronger voice, "for Miss Slarge read me a letter from Mrs. Purcell. I also saw the communication you addressed to Olive from Bombay, advising her of your coming. But I have been absent, and I returned only last night; and the sight of your face—your extraordinary resemblance to your father—startled me not a little."

"Such emotion is natural," said Mallow; "the more so as you were so attached to Mr. Carson."

Mr. Brock rose and sighed. "He was my dearest friend," he said sadly; "and even thirty years have not banished his memory from my heart. I feel like a father to you, Angus—you must permit me to call you Angus?"

"I beg of you to do so," answered the young man, gracefully, giving his left hand to the Rector. "Who should do so, if not you, the oldest friend of my father, and the guardian of my dearest Olive."

Mallow bit his lip, and turned away to conceal his anger, for after all, being engaged to her, the man had every right to speak of Olive in affectionate terms. Angus, who had long since discovered that the Irishman was his rival, smiled blandly at this exhibition—

35

for it did not escape him—of jealousy. But he had sufficient discretion to make no remark. With an inclusive nod to both men, Laurence walked away, and his feelings on climbing the hill on his way home were anything but enviable. He felt that fate was dealing hardly by him.

"Have you hurt your hand?" asked Brock, when the unnecessary third person had vanished through the gate.

"Yes, many months ago while shooting," replied Carson. "Indeed, it was this hand that detained me from paying my respects to Olive and yourself earlier. I arrived on the twenty-fourth of last month, and intended coming here at once; but my hand was so painful that I waited in London to see a surgeon about it."

"Where did you stay?" asked the Rector.

"With my friend, Major Semberry, in St. James's Street. Semberry took rooms there, and I made it my home. Indeed, my luggage is there at the present moment."

"St. James's Street!"

"Yes; that is, a little street off it—Duke Street, I believe it is called, No. 80B."

"No. 80B, Duke Street, St. James's," repeated Brock, slowly. "The first address you gave me was somewhat misleading."

"My ignorance of social customs in your large city," replied Mr. Carson, with a charming smile. "I am quite a barbarian, am I not? Yes?"

"Indeed, no; if Olive is not pleased with you she will be hard to satisfy."

"I think she likes me, Mr. Brock, but she does not love me."

"Oh, love is a matter of custom with young girls. You will gain it sooner or later—if not before marriage, then afterwards."

"I fear Olive has no love to give me," said Carson, shaking his head. "It is my impression that she has already given her heart to that gentleman who has just left us."

"To Mallow? Nonsense. She looks upon him as a friend."

"As a very dear friend, don't you think? Yes?"

"That may be," rejoined Mr. Brock, gravely. "She has known him for many years, for Mallow lived here a considerable time as tutor to Lord Aldean. But I am sure Olive is not the girl to disregard her father's dying wish. She will become your wife, Angus; be sure of that."

"I shall endeavour to deserve my good fortune, Mr. Brock."

"By the way, Angus, did your father send no message to me?"

36

"He spoke of you kindly and tenderly on his death-bed," replied Angus, gently; "but he sent no message."

"He gave you no letter for me?"

"None. Had he done so, I would have sent it on to you."

"I suppose he told you about our early friendship?"

"Well, no; he spoke always of you with affection, yet he gave me no details of your association with him."

"Yet Bellairs and I were his nearest and dearest," sighed the Rector; "but I should not complain. A man might forget many things in thirty years. Poor Alfred!—he was one of the best men I ever knew. I hope you will try to emulate his virtues, Angus."

"I shall do my best, Mr. Brock," said Carson, glancing at his watch. "It is getting near breakfast-time. I must return to the Manor House."

"No," said the Rector, taking the young man by the arm. "I cannot so readily part with the son of my old friend, who brings back all my youth to me. You must breakfast with me."

This invitation did not appear to please Carson over much, and he would fain have declined it, but the Rector was peremptory; so, in the end, he accepted. Mr. Brock was pleased, and showed his pleasure.

"I am a bachelor," he said, showing his young friend the way through the quick-set hedge; "but I have an excellent housekeeper and an admirable cook. You shall have a good breakfast, Angus."

"Well, sir, I bring a good appetite," answered Carson; and, arm-in-arm with his father's old associate, he passed into the rectory grounds, making himself as agreeable as he knew how.

Mr. Brock became rejuvenated in the presence of his old friend's son, and questioned the young man closely concerning the dead-and-gone companion of his youth. It was a merry breakfast enough in one way; yet in another it was sad. In the hereafter it afforded Mr. Brock much food for reflection. But, if a man will be so rash as to raise the ghost of a dead past, he cannot expect to be other than melancholy.

Honest enough to avow that his suspicions concerning Carson had proved baseless, Mallow was not patient or amiable enough to discuss the matter with Aldean. After a short explanation Laurence passed on to more agreeable subjects, and his friend was in no way unwilling to leave unprofitable argument for pleasant conversation. The Irishman concealed his disappointment, and, deciding that there was little sense in crying over spilt milk, made himself as entertaining as possible. He enjoyed his meal with Aldean, after which—in completion of his cure, as Mallow put it—they rode together. Returning late in the afternoon, they came upon the residence of Dr. Drabble. A slatternly-looking dwelling it was, on the outskirts of the village. Here Laurence announced his intention of paying a visit to the doctor's wife. Aldean expressed himself agreeable. He liked the doctor's children infinitely better than he liked the doctor. Beckoning two small boys to hold their horses, they went up to the door.

"As untidy as ever, I see," remarked Laurence, as they walked up an overgrown brick path, through a wilderness of neglected flower-shrubs.

Aldean shrugged his shoulders. "What can you expect?" he said. "The doctor is one of your world-reformers, who sweeps every doorstep but his own. Reformation never begins at home with these fanatics—more's the pity."

Had Mrs. Drabble heard this last statement she would probably have endorsed it. She was a weary-looking, white-faced woman, worn out with family cares and domestic worries. Seven children, one servant, and a neglectful and exacting husband, were enough to account for her aspect. The room into which the visitors were shown was as untidy as the garden, and Mrs. Drabble was as untidy as the room. She gave her hand to Lord Aldean with a wan smile, and greeted Mallow with an apologetic air.

"For, indeed, I am quite ashamed that you should find us in such a state," she complained languidly; "but I have so much to do that I can do nothing."

The epigram was, if unintentional, none the less true. The poor, weak head of this domestic martyr was literally dazed by the constant abuse of her neglectful husband and the burden of her clamorous children.

That Mrs. Drabble was a byeword in Casterwell for untidiness was not altogether her fault. In truth, she possessed neither the strength nor the capability necessary to reduce her domestic chaos to something like order. A more helpless, hopeless creature never lived. She had been a pretty girl enough when she had married Drabble, and that would-be reformer was largely, if not entirely, the cause of her degeneration.

"And how is my young friend Margery?" asked Aldean, who had known Mrs. Drabble and her household ever since he was a small boy in petticoats.

"Oh, Margery is well enough," sighed Mrs. Drabble (she naturally took a despondent view of life). "Her brain is too big for

38

her body, and lately she has taken to writing poetry. As if that would help one? Then there is Cade, and Brutus, and Danton—all of them growing boys, who eat enormously and spoil their clothes dreadfully. I'm sure I often wish their father was more of a parent and less of a Radical," finished the poor lady. "I can't do everything; it's not to be expected—nobody can deny that."

A crowd of children—all named after notorious Republicans—at that moment surged past the sitting-room door, which would not shut. Giggling and whispering, they appeared and disappeared like rabbits in and out of their burrows. Shortly Margaret, the eldest, tripped into the room, and shook hands with precocious composure. She was a pretty little girl of some twelve years, with a nobly-formed head, a profusion of curly reddish hair, a complexion of cream, and dreamy grey eyes. Altogether a noticeable child. She already displayed considerable brain power, and, indeed, she was the only one of his children in whom Dr. Drabble took the smallest interest. The display of his affection took the form of inculcating her with pernicious Anarchistic doctrines, the meaning of which the poor child, intelligent as she was, was quite at a loss to understand. As Hamilcar made his son take an oath of eternal hatred for Rome, so did Dr. Drabble instil into his small daughter a detestation of the world and the world's social system. Poor little Margery innocently piped diatribes which would have done credit to the hags of the Revolution.

"Well, Margery Daw," said Mallow kindly, "have you forgotten who I am?"

"Oh no," answered the child in her pleasantly low voice, "you are the gentleman Olive is so fond of."

Lord Aldean laughed, Mallow coloured, and Mrs. Drabble, much shocked, apologized for her daughter's candour.

"But indeed she is such a sharp little thing that there is no keeping anything from her," wailed Mrs. Drabble; "and the doctor, I am sorry to say, tells her many things that a child should not hear."

"I am a Red Anarchist, like father," announced Margery, proudly. "We intend to make everybody equal."

"Do you, indeed?" laughed Aldean, drawing the child to his knee. "And what is to be done with me?"

"You are to be called Mr. Aldean, and made to work."

"You will indeed be clever if you can make Mr. Aldean work, Margery," said Mallow, smiling. "I have never been successful so far."

"Please excuse her, Lord Aldean," said the shocked Mrs.

39

Drabble. "It is her father who puts these ideas into her head. Margery, how can you?"

"Oh, we all know that the doctor is working for the social millennium, Mrs. Drabble; the time when there will be neither rich nor poor, and we shall all practise communism."

"I'm sure I wish the doctor would practise his profession, Lord Aldean. But Mr. Dyke, that new man, gets all his best cases, whilst he is constantly in London working for the cause. As if preaching in Trafalgar Square is of any use to me. I never know the day when he may be in gaol; and then what shall I do with these seven children?"

"I'll support us all with my poetry, mother," said Margery, grandly.

"Poetry!" said Mallow, laughing. "And pray what kind of poetry do you write, young lady?"

"The poetry of Revolt; that is what father calls it;" and Margery, stretching out a lean arm, proceeded to recite these terrible lines:—

"Tyrants tremble in your beds,
We shall cut off all your heads,
Take your money and your land,
And as freemen take our stand;
This is not a foolish gabble,
But the word of Margery Drabble."

The young men roared, both at the poetry and the fierce attitude of the child.

"You are quite a Revolutionist, Margery," said Aldean, "and a poetess to boot. E. B. Browning; Sappho in a Phrygian cap, eh?"

The little girl shook her red curls. "I aspire to be like Louise Michel," she said solemnly, "the noblest of all women."

"Wouldn't you rather grow up like Miss Bellairs," said Mallow, persuasively.

"Ah!" groaned Mrs. Drabble, dismally, "where are the education and money to come from?"

"I love Olive. I am very fond of Olive," said Margery judiciously, "but I do not approve of her choice of a husband."

"Don't you indeed," laughed Mallow.

"No. I have advised her to marry either you or Lord Aldean."

"Margery, Margery, do not be so pert."

"I am not pert, mother, I am a Thinker."

"With a large T," said Aldean, rising. "Well, Margery, you must come and see me soon, and we will ravage the orchards."

"Apples, strawberries, peaches—oh my!" cried Margery, a child for the nonce, "I should like to have as many as I could eat."

"Well, I dare say we can satisfy even your appetite. Come soon, and bring us some more poetry with you. Mr. Mallow and I must be going now. There, dear, you won't refuse that, will you?" and he slipped a half-sovereign into the child's hand.

"No," replied Margery the Communist. "'What's yours is mine'—father says so—but thank you very much, Mr. Aldean."

"Lord Aldean, Margery," corrected her mother.

"Father says there are no lords, mother; this is plain Mr. Aldean."

"There is a reflection on your lordship's good looks," said Mallow. "Well, Margery, when you begin cutting off heads, I hope you will spare us, eh?"

"Fear not," said Margery, dramatically; "I'll stand by you in the day of trial."

CHAPTER VIII

JEPHTHAH'S DAUGHTER

Save her honeymoon, probably the happiest time in a woman's life is the period of her engagement—the time when she is being adored by her lover, congratulated by her friends, and is delightfully employed in expecting and receiving the customary offerings of her friends and acquaintances, and in making those varied and numerous purchases which seem to be considered de rigueur on such occasions.

For the time being she is, at all events, the supreme centre of interest amid her own immediate circle; her life teems with pleasure and expectation generally; a beautiful halo is around the most commonplace of things; the present is enjoyable, the future entrancing, and she—the luckiest of women, surely?—dances along over her rose-strewn path, under her cloudless sky, happy in the conviction that smiles and eternal sunshine are to be her lot.

What if, after marriage, the sky is ofttimes clouded and the path of life grows stormy, and the smiles disappear in frowns—and we know that such a change does sometimes come over the spirit of the most beautiful of matrimonial dreams—what if some of the early illusions are mercilessly murdered?—there is always that pre-nuptial period to be looked back upon with fondness, if also with regret. She has snatched from fate at least one hour of supreme and unalloyed delight—there is true satisfaction in the thought. And happy is the mortal who enjoys even that much happiness in this troublous world. The years of the Moorish Caliph were sixty and more; his hours of perfect bliss—five!

Olive, had she been engaged to Mallow, would have enjoyed her supreme hour with all the zest of a naturally happy disposition. As it was, she was wretched in the extreme. She detested her affianced husband, and she knew how deep was her love for the man she would have had in his place. Tossed about like a shuttlecock by these extremes of feeling, she anticipated her wedding-day with dread—almost with terror. The loss of the money would have been of no account with her; it was the dying wish of her father that she felt she could not disregard, to say nothing of the hint of unknown evil which the sealed letter contained. Why her father should have expressed himself so strongly, and yet so vaguely, she could not conceive. She could only conclude that he had committed some error in his life for which she was to pay the penalty. Jephthah vowed rashly, and circumstances brought about the sacrifice of his daughter that he might not be forsworn. Likewise she was to suffer for her father's sake by contracting this loveless marriage. There were times when she was resolved to throw all to the winds, to let Fate do her worst, rather than suffer what was before her; but in the end her affection for her dead father prevailed, and she bent her will to the force of circumstance.

On the subject of such unqualified obedience, her friend Tui did not hesitate to express herself strongly, for she was an independent young lady with ideas the reverse of favourable to what she termed family slavery. That any parent should command or expect to receive blind and unquestioning obedience was not her way of thinking. She was, therefore, exceedingly wrathful at her friend's decision.

"When a human being arrives at years of sense, he has every right to shape his own life," said she, ex cathedra. "Our religion teaches us that every one has to answer for his own sins, therefore certainly he should choose his own wickednesses."

42

"You speak in the masculine sense, dear," rejoined Olive; "besides, I do not intend to commit any sin, that I am aware of."

"I speak for woman as well as for man, Olive; and if you marry a creature you don't care two straws about, you will be committing a sin, and a very great one."

"Oh, Tui, darling!"

"It's no use saying, 'Oh, Tui, darling,'" replied Miss Ostergaard, vehemently; "you know in your own heart that I am right. Do you or do you not love Laurence Mallow?"

"I do, with all my soul."

"Then why don't you marry him?"

"He hasn't asked me yet," replied Olive, with attempted carelessness. "I do not even know if he loves me."

"My dear, you know well enough that he does. Why, he would give his ears to make you his wife; and it is only his scruples about this wretched engagement that makes him hold his tongue. Believe me, obedience can be carried too far, Olive, and it is absurd and wrong that you should wreck your life just because your father commands you to marry the son of an old friend of his."

"But the sealed letter, Tui!"

"Oh, that's a bogey. What evil can come to you? You have your own money, good health, and the love of a most delightful man. I should defy that letter."

"But you forget I shall lose fifty thousand pounds, dear."

"What of that?" reported the romantic Tui. "I am sure Mr. Mallow is worth paying that price for. He's a darling, I think. If you don't marry him, Olive, I'll make love to him myself—there!"

"What about Lord Aldean?"

"Lord Aldean is a donkey—a dear, sweet donkey, all the same. He is too young to know his own mind."

"Indeed, he is two or three years your senior."

"Well, I never; as if you didn't know that a woman is always twice the age of a man. But you are getting away from the subject. Do you really intend marrying this horrid Mr. Carson?"

"I must," sighed Olive, ruefully; "my father——"

"Oh dear me, your father again!" interrupted Tui, pettishly, "as if he had anything to do with it. There is too much talk of obedient children, and not enough of reasonable parents. Why should people be born when they don't want to, just to be miserable slaves to those who put them in the world against their will?"

"Would you marry against your father's will?"

43

"Yes, I would, if what he wanted was to make me miserable. I would suffer for no one; and I don't see that any one—be they father or mother—has a right to expect it."

"Tui, you have been listening to that horrid Dr. Drabble."

"I know I have. Dr. Drabble is a very sensible man."

"Does he treat his wife sensibly, dear?"

"We are not talking about his wife," said Tui, evading the point, "but about him. I don't agree with everything he says, but I approve of a great deal. Every one should be a free agent. Marry Mr. Carson, and you will be miserable. Become Mrs. Mallow, and you will be happy; and, father or no father, I know which of them I would choose."

"Oh, Tui, what nonsense you talk."

"Sense, sense, sense, I talk reason, sound reason—and you know I do."

"I know nothing of the sort."

"Then you ought to," exclaimed Tui, with heat. "Now you are going to be nasty, dear, so I shall leave you till you recover your temper;" and Miss Ostergaard, holding that discretion was the better part of valour, hastily retreated.

The wretched Olive did not know whether to laugh or cry. Deserted by Tui, who had gone over to the enemy, she was more than ever bewildered. Miss Slarge, too, was all against Carson— Olive had long seen that—although neither her opinion nor help was of any great value. Olive felt desperate. The wedding-day was only a few weeks distant, and almost immediately she would have to come to a definite decision. Should she accept or reject Carson? should she forego the money and ignore the letter? The more she put the question to herself the more bewildered she became.

When they first arrived, Major Semberry and his friend had been guests at the Manor House; but as Miss Slarge (who was nothing if not conventional) did not approve of a lengthy visit, they had removed to the village inn. However, they still spent a great deal of their time at the Manor House, and it so happened that whilst Olive and Tui were pursuing their discussion, they came in for luncheon. Olive heard their voices on the lawn, but, feeling that she could meet neither of them in her present state of mind, sent a message to her chaperon, and slipped out of the house. She walked through the woods and out on to the hills, turning over and over again in her mind her ever-present dilemma.

Now, as though to settle the matter offhand, Fate had inspired

Mallow with a spirit of restlessness, and he, in his turn, feeling little inclined for Aldean's chatter or company, had strolled out alone. Thus it came about that on the breezy space of the downs the two young people met. Having met, they could scarcely pass without greeting, and they ended in sauntering side by side over the springy turf: Fate had trapped them, and Fate would have to answer for the consequences.

It was a perfect day: bland and sunny, and redolent of summer fragrance and peace. An early shower had fallen, and the raindrops sparkled on the grass, while the sheep straggled on the hillside, and the fitful breeze dispersed the sweetness of the land. A circling lark, lost in the blue, rained down its music, and the grey rabbits scuttled into their burrows at the approach of the lovers—for lovers they were, though their love was undeclared. Side by side they walked on—scarcely speaking, scarcely looking. They were alone on the lonely downs under the roof of God's sky, standing on the variegated pavement of God's temple, the strongest passion Nature knows gripping them at their heart-strings.

At first their conversation—such as it was—turned on trivial things. They skirted, as it were, the sole thought which filled the hearts of both. But their joint attempt to evade it was doomed to failure. Nature would have her own, and she seized it by force. Their idle talk dwindled into monosyllables; even these grew rare and low, and then a long silence ensued. Mallow felt his mouth dry and his heart beating furiously. He turned his eyes, eloquent with unspoken passion, on the woman by his side. With a thrill, half of joy, half of fear, she winced and shrank back.

"Don't!" she said faintly, holding up her hand, "I beg of——"

"I must," said Mallow, hoarsely, as her voice died on her lips.

"Olive, darling, what is the use of our keeping up this pretence? I—I—I love you."

"I must—I will!" He seized her hand and fixed his eyes on her flushed, downcast face. "I love you; you love me—we are for each other. You cannot deny that what I say is true. I can see the truth in your face, in your eyes. Olive, Olive,—my Olive!"

"Laurence—Mr. Mallow; you forget my position."

"I do not. You are engaged to a man for whom you do not care, whom you shall not marry. I forbid you to marry this Carson."

"You have no right——"

"I have every right—the right of love. Deny it if you can. If you go to the altar with Carson you go with a lie on your lips. You are

45

mine, mine only; and I swear to God that I will not give you up. Dearest, tell me what is in your heart. Do not deny me one little word. You love me—you love me; say that you love me."

The overwhelming force of his passion swept her away. She could no longer struggle against him—against herself. "I do love you," she faltered; then, with a sudden revulsion of feeling, she tore herself away from him, and shrank back, covering her face with her hands.

"I knew it!" he cried in triumph. "You love me, you are mine, you will not marry this man."

"I must, I must," she murmured, terrified by the way in which she felt he was breaking down the barriers of her will.

"You must not. I tell you, Olive, you shall not. I am you lover, your master, your husband—not that feeble foolish Jack-o'-dandy, with his silly smile and feeble will. Give him up, give him up; I command you, give him up."

"Laurence, you are brutal."

"Darling forgive me, pardon me, I am beside myself. I am your slave, your worshipper. Oh, my heart, my love, my dearer self, be kind to one whose life is yours."

Olive dried her eyes and became more composed as Mallow changed his tone. She turned towards him with face as white as marble.

"Laurence," she said quietly—"for I dare call you Laurence—I love, I have always loved you, and I always shall love you; but I am not my own mistress. I would to Heaven that I were; but I am helpless. I must marry this man, not for the money—ah, no; the money can go, but because my dear father left a letter for me in which he urged me to obey his dying wish and marry Angus Carson. . . . If I do not, evil will come of my refusal."

"Evil, Olive! what evil?"

"I do not know. My father's letter gave no explanation. It simply said that terrible evil would come if I did not obey his wish. I dare not refuse. I dare not ignore that solemn command. Much as I love you, I must sacrifice it—yes, and you—to the memory of my father."

"You will marry Carson?" asked Laurence, his face growing pale.

Olive bowed her head. "What else would you have me do?" she asked pitifully.

"Do?" With a burst of passion, he seized her again in his arms. "Do?—I would have you become my wife."

"My father——"

46

"Your father had no right to condemn you to lifelong misery. It shall not be. You are mine. I will not give you up."

"Cruel, cruel, when you know how I suffer," she sobbed. "If you love me, you would let me go; you would urge me to fulfil the wish of the dead."

Almost rudely he flung her from him. "Go then," he said bitterly. "I want no love so feeble that it bends to another's will. Obey your father if you think fit; marry Carson, and leave me to go-"

"How dare you to speak to me like that?" cried Olive, passing from tears to fury. "If you suffer, do not I suffer? I loathe to marry this man. I would kill myself if I dared. I——"

"You talk like a child," he said roughly.

"I feel like a woman," she retorted heartily.

"You think only of your own misery. What is it to mine? You are not forced into the arms of a woman you detest."

"If you go, you go to Carson of your own free will."

"Oh, Laurence, how can you say that I go to another man of my own free will when you know how I love you? It is unjust; cruel. If my father were alive, I might have the courage to refuse. As it is, how can I disobey? If I refuse Angus Carson some evil will surely follow, and if I marry you I involve you in it too. Would that be right?"

"Olive, I would go to hell for you and with you."

"Laurence, you do not love me—you cannot love me—or you would not make it harder for me; your feeling for me is not love, it is selfishness. I must bow to your will, I must flout my father in his grave, I must cast all to the winds that you may gain your wish."

"Olive!" His voice was husky and broken. "I would do all that and more for you. But since you hold my love so low, let us forget that I have told it; let us part here now, and for always."

"Laurence, Laurence, my heart will break."

"And for a shadow, Olive."

"No, no!" she cried, "no shadow, no folly this. It is only too real. You are right; let us—let us say good-bye."

"You tell me to go?"

"I—tell—you—to—go."

"Then listen to me. I love you, and I intend that you shall be my wife. I don't care for Carson, or the money, or the threatened evil, or anything else. I sweep all these away. I say good-bye now, and I go to London—to Athelstane Place."

Olive looked bewildered. "In God's name why?" she faltered.

"To learn if the man who was murdered there was the man you should have married."

"I—I—why, I am to marry Mr. Carson!"

"It is yet to be proved that this man is Mr. Carson."

"What do you mean?"

"I will tell you what I mean when I come back;" and without a handshake or a glance at her white face, Mallow walked abruptly away.

CHAPTER IX

"TWENTY-ONE"

On calm reflection, Mallow did not consider that he had behaved very well to Olive. His passion and impetuosity had carried him beyond himself. He had been too rough; too masterful. Instead of suing with soft words, he had sought to dominate by sheer strength of will. A cave man of the stone period could scarce have wooed in style more savage; and when Mallow had regained his self-control, he was heartily ashamed that his fiery temper had got the better of him. But his pride would not allow him to apologize to Olive. Nor did he even excuse himself by letter. He preserved an absolute silence, and kept away from the Manor House. He had not been quite sincere when he declared his intention of proceeding at once to Athelstane Place, but for very shame he could not now withdraw from a position taken up so definitely. Accordingly, on the day preceding Olive's birthday, he announced to Aldean that he was going to London.

"Oh, hang it! I do call that shabby," cried Jim, with a look of dismay. "You promised to stay here at least two months."

"I'll come down and complete the term shortly, Aldean."

"Oh, you don't wish to be here when Miss Bellairs marries Carson, I suppose?"

"Miss Bellairs shall never marry Carson if I can help it."

"Perhaps not, Mallow, but I don't exactly see how you can help

48

it. This morning I saw Carson, and he tells me the ceremony is to take place in a fortnight."

"A great deal can be done in a fortnight, Jim."

"Old man?" questioned Jim, with a stare, "have you anything up your sleeve?"

"Only my mistrust of Carson, as Carson."

"What! that old game? You are becoming a maniac on that subject, Mallow. It's all bosh, you know. Carson is Carson, right enough. Mrs. Purcell, Semberry, Mr. Brock,—they've all said as much."

"No doubt," replied Mallow, dryly. "But not one of them has explained why Carson's clothes should be impregnated with sandal-wood as were those of the man in Athelstane Place."

"You'll find nothing there to help you," said Aldean, shaking his head. "What the police couldn't do, you won't."

"Then I shall go to the police themselves."

"You'll look for a needle in a haystack, you mean. However, if you have made up your mind, I suppose you must go on your wild-goose chase. When may I expect you back from it?"

"Before Carson marries Miss Bellairs."

"Does that mean at the end of a fortnight?"

"If I make no discoveries associating Carson with the murder, it does."

"Oh, Lord! do you want to hang the man as well as rob him of his wife?"

"Jim, I'm not vindictive."

"Goodness only knows what you are, Mallow. Well, least said soonest mended; go, and good luck go with you."

After this conversation, in which, it will be noticed, Mallow gave no hint of his interview with Olive, he went to London, and was absent for the greater part of a fortnight.

Olive, too, kept her own counsel about that stormy wooing. But she felt a strange joy in recalling to herself its every detail. It was the joy of a woman who loves to be dominated and to be ruled by the man she adores. Had Mallow cut the Gordian knot of her difficulties, and, in the face of all her objection, forced her to marry him, secretly she would have been pleased and relieved. As it was, he had left her with an enigmatic utterance which she could not understand.

Yet this time of trial was in some ways beneficial to her. It strengthened the better qualities of her nature, which otherwise might have weakened in the sunshine of perpetual good fortune.

The ills of this life, like drugs, are unpleasant but necessary. They brace our mental organization as do tonics our physical.

Olive's twenty-first birthday was celebrated by a dinner to her friends and tenantry. The Manor House and its grounds were thrown open in the old-fashioned, hospitable style, and a plentiful spread was provided under a temporary tent. Here farmers and labourers toasted their young mistress in the strongest and most stinging of ales. Speeches were made and congratulations were offered, and had Mallow but been present in the character of her future husband, Olive would have been completely happy. As it was, she had to introduce Carson in his place. But she accepted the encomiums passed upon his pleasant face and amiable speeches with such show of pleasure as she could command from herself. She could not deny that the husband chosen for her by her father was both attractive and agreeable, that he was even lovable in some ways—perhaps in his very weakness. Laurence was pre-eminently a man of strength; a man imperious and self-sustaining; a man who would love a woman and master a woman, and fulfil the fundamental law of Nature that the male is the lord of creation from an oyster to a wife; in short, a man stable as the universe, fixed as the stars. Angus was pleasant, good-tempered, handsome and weak. He would have made a charming woman, Olive thought with contempt. The Indian bangle was not much out of place, after all, upon his wrist.

On this festive occasion even poor Mrs. Drabble took a holiday. She brought with her Margery, Danton, and Brutus, of whom the first-named clung to Olive's skirts most of the day. She had brought with her and presented to Olive a birthday ode, in its way a marvel of rhyme and of spelling:—

> "Oh, may no ethly cares
> Anoy Olive Bellairs,
> And may she never fear
> Her birthday every year,
> But give up teres and sighs.
> Till she most hapy dyes."

"Thank you, Margery," said Olive, kissing the little poetess, who was anxiously watching the effect of her ode.

"I hope your good wishes will come true;" and she sighed.

"I have brought Charlotte Corday," remarked Margery, holding up a battered doll with a red cap on its head. "Poor dear! she has had no pleasure since we cut her head off."

"Who cut her head off?" asked Aldean, who was close at hand.

"Brutus, because he said she must 'dree her weird.' It should have been Danton of course, but Danton was at school. I have glued her head on again, but she will never have a strong neck. But I love her all the same."

"Shall I give you another doll?" said Carson, smiling amiably.

"No, thank you," replied Margery, shaking her curls, "I must keep Charlotte Corday after she has suffered so much for the cause."

"Ah! that is my Margery," roared Drabble; "she's a true chip of the old block."

"True chip of the gallows!" growled Semberry, who hated the doctor.

"When our day comes, there will be no gallows," retorted Dr. Drabble.

"Guillotines only, I suppose," said Aldean, with a twinkle.

"There will be love and fraternity, and equality."

"Be my brother or I will kill you," quoted Tui. "I've heard that sentiment before, Dr. Drabble."

"Miss Ostergaard, I thought you were a disciple of mine."

"I stop short of murder, doctor."

Major Semberry appeared disturbed. "Nasty word 'murder,' in a young lady's mouth;" he jerked; "let's talk of something agreeable."

"Of Olive, for instance," smiled Angus. "Olives are always agreeable."

"After dinner only," said Miss Bellairs, spoiling the pun, "I don't feel complimented, Angus, by your comparison."

"My dear, you are a flower—a rose!"

"And you are a smiling cabbage," muttered Tui, turning away. "Lord Aldean, take me to the tent."

"The Major is not engaged," hinted Aldean, slyly.

"Neither am I," retorted Miss Ostergaard, "so there is still a chance for your lordship;" and she led him away wondering if he could not construe a confession of love from her last remark.

While this desultory conversation was going on, Miss Slarge had the Rector well in hand, and was bombarding him with hard Babylonic facts. "Our Good Friday hot cross-bun is an emblem of idolatry," she was saying; "we should tread it underfoot rather than eat it."

"Oh, my dear lady," remonstrated the shocked Mr. Brock, "it is stamped with the sacred symbol of our religion!"

51

"I don't care what it is stamped with; it is none other than the sacred bread of Babylon, which was offered to the pagan queen of Heaven fifteen hundred and more years before the Christian era. Even the name is the same. The sacred cake was called 'boun;' our Good Friday cake is termed 'bun.'"

"A bun!" interposed the rector.

"With or without the article, it is the same thing. 'Boun;' 'bun'— what can be plainer? The first is pure Chaldee, the last Scottish."

"I don't understand Chaldee, Miss Slarge," said Mr. Brock, in hope of changing the conversation. "What a pleasant scene this is."

"The scene is all right," snapped Miss Slarge; "but it would be better if Mr. Carson were not here. Ugh! I can't bear the sight of him."

"Why not? He seems to be a pleasant young man."

"No backbone, Mr. Brock. If you dropped him into the mud he would stay there. Mrs. Purcell said that he had a strong will and a stubborn nature; but I can see neither myself."

"It is, of course, possible your sister may have been mistaken."

"Perhaps so; but in every other respect her description of him has been particularly accurate, even to the bracelet he wears. Bangle—bracelet—" said Miss Slarge, with contempt; "the idea of a man decking himself out like a woman!"

"Still, he is agreeable enough, Miss Slarge; and you must remember that to me he is always the son of my dear old friend. In memory of his father, he intends to present my church with a new altar-cloth."

"Marked 'I.H.S.,' I suppose, Mr. Brock?"

"Well, yes; it is customary to mark them with the sacred letters."

"What do they stand for?"

"'Iesu hominum salvator.'"

"Nothing of the sort," cried Miss Slarge, delighted that the rector had fallen into her trap. "They are the initials of the Egyptian trinity: Isis, Horus, and Seb."

"Miss Slarge, how can you treat sacred things so lightly?"

"I don't treat sacred things lightly," retorted Miss Slarge. "I.H.S. is a heathen symbol; and I am not an idolater, I hope."

"Really, I do not know what to say."

"You should study more," said Miss Slarge, satisfied with her triumph, as she walked away, leaving the rector quite angry.

"I wonder where she can find all this rubbish," murmured the outraged Mr. Brock. "It is really not respectable the way she talks. Eh, what is that shouting?" he asked a bystander.

52

"The tenants are toasting Mr. Carson."

"As Miss Bellairs' future husband, I suppose?" said the rector, cheerily. "Ah, what a pity that Mark and Alfred did not live to see this happy day!"

CHAPTER X

A PRE-NUPTIAL CONTRACT

Though the passing of each hour brought her nearer to her hateful marriage, Olive felt relieved now that the celebration of her coming of age was over. She was little disposed for gaiety or for company of any kind. Her thoughts were continually with Laurence. She missed him daily, hourly. His face was constantly before her, and his words echoed everlastingly in her ears. It was not surprising that, on meeting Lord Aldean in the village, she should question him as to Mallow's return. "I sometimes wonder if he is coming back at all," she finished hastily.

"Oh, Mallow's coming back right enough," said Aldean. "He is certain to return before your marriage."

"Please don't speak of my marriage, Lord Aldean," she cried impetuously. "Have you heard from Mr. Mallow since he left?"

"Only once, Miss Bellairs. He is well and busy."

"In Athelstane Place?"

Jim was not a little taken aback by this last question. He was in total ignorance of what had taken place on the Downs. "What do you know, may I ask, about Athelstane Place?" he said, looking sharply at the girl.

"Mr. Mallow told me something about it, and about Mr. Carson."

"Oh, that is one of Mallow's crazy notions," said Aldean, vexed. "I suppose he told you that Carson was an impostor? Then, believe me, it is all nonsense, Miss Bellairs. Mallow has built up this theory on a foolish remark I happened to let drop. His idea is that the real Carson was murdered, and this fellow has stepped into his shoes."

"You don't believe that?" cried Olive, breathlessly. "Certainly not," replied Jim' vehemently; "and please don't repeat what I say. I have a horror of scandal. Carson is Carson right enough. This is only a mad idea of Mallow's."

"But why should Mr. Mallow persist in such a strange idea?"

Lord Aldean shrugged his shoulders. "The dead man's clothes were perfumed with sandal-wood, and Carson's, you know, have the same smell—it is on this ground I think that Mallow goes chiefly. He fancies there must be some connection between the two."

"And is there?" asked Olive.

"No; but Mallow is ready to grasp at straws to stop your marriage."

Miss Bellairs reddened and turned away. "That is impossible," she said in a low voice.

"Yes, if it is to be stopped only by proving Carson to be an impostor, I agree with you. Don't worry your head about such folly."

"Perhaps I ought to tell Mr. Carson," said Olive thoughtfully.

"No, for goodness' sake don't; you'll only cause unnecessary trouble by doing that. There is no doubt about Carson being the genuine article. He carries the trade mark of this Indian bangle, and Mrs. Purcell describes him exactly in her letter; besides, Mr. Brock recognised him from his resemblance to his father."

Miss Bellairs said no more on the subject. She saw that it annoyed Aldean not to be able to defend Mallow in this eccentricity of his. But on returning home she asked her aunt for Mrs. Purcell's letter, and read it through most carefully. She copied out verbatim the portions relating to Angus Carson, and committed them to memory, so that when he called in the afternoon she was able to view him through Mrs. Purcell's spectacles. A stealthy and careful examination convinced her that Mallow's fancies were moonshine. Without doubt Carson of Casterwell resembled Carson of Bombay in every particular. The graphic sketch of Mrs. Purcell was an admirable portrait of the man as he stood there unconscious of her scrutiny. Whatever way of escape from this detested marriage might open out to her, it was not here, and Olive resigned herself to her fate predestined. Her eyes followed her future husband with a look of contempt as he crossed the room with a cup of tea for Tui. His weak good nature and incessant amiability were aggressive to her. She might compel herself to marry him, but she felt that she could never feel the least respect for his character. The mere sight of his ever-smiling complacency made her resent her position more and more. Overbearing, rough, or even brutal he might have been, and

54

she might have resigned herself to him with more content. At least he would have been a man. She thought of Pope's cruel portrait of Lord Hervey:—

——"that thing of silk
Spurns that mere white curd of asses' milk."

If, as Mrs. Purcell declared, he possessed a powerful will, he concealed it only too effectually. "A stubborn nature" and "a full confidence in his own judgment" he might have—they were more in harmony with his weakness. Still, he was to be her husband—that was certain—and it only remained for her to make the best of it and of him.

"Penny for your thoughts, Miss Bellairs," said Semberry at her elbow.

"They are not worth it," retorted Olive, taking the cup of tea he held out to her. "I'll sell them as bankrupt stock. Can I give you another cup of tea?"

"If you please," and the Major took his seat beside her, much to her satisfaction, for she felt that she would rather talk to him than to his friend.

"By the way, Miss Bellairs," said Semberry, "other day you said something about a maid."

"Yes, I want a new maid; I am looking for one now."

"Friend of mine wants to find a situation for a good maid."

"Thank you very much, but I think I shall have no difficulty in finding one to suit me in Casterwell."

"But this is a London girl; very smart," urged the Major; "wants to live in country; friend recommends her no end."

"Who is your friend, may I ask?"

"Mrs. Arne; fashionable woman; clever woman. Thinks a lot of this maid. Wouldn't part with her, only girl wants to live in th' country. Spoke to me; said I'd speak to you."

"It is very kind of you to trouble about it, Major," she said, "very kind indeed; you must let me think the matter over, will you?"

"Pleasure," replied Semberry, scribbling on a page of his pocket-book, and tearing it out. "Here is Mrs. Arne's address. Write soon; might lose the girl."

"What is her name?"

"Lord! 'fraid don't know, Miss Bellairs. Never trouble 'bout these things as a rule. Mere chance I heard of this. Thought you'd

55

like to know. Hallo! who's this? By George! that Radical doctor. Can't stand the man."

Dr. Drabble bustled noisily into the drawing-room. He announced his own arrival in a stentorian voice. With his cunning grey face and close-cropped red hair and lean hungry aspect, he resembled nothing so much as a prowling winter fox sniffing round a hen-roost.

"How are you, Miss Bellairs? There's nothing much the matter with you, that's easily seen," he roared, gripping her hand. "Miss Ostergaard, you look like yourself."

"People generally do, don't they, doctor?"

"Ha, ha! very good; but I'm paying you the hugest possible compliment, if you only knew how to take it. And where is Miss Slarge?"

"She is engaged, doctor," said Olive, resigning herself too, with a sigh, to the company of this bull. "Will you take some tea?"

"Thank you, thank you; no sugar."

"Should advise sugar, Drabble," growled the Major, insolently. "Sweeten your nature."

"My nature, sir, is that of primeval man—simple, childlike——"

"And lawless!" put in Carson, smiling.

The doctor mounted his hobby at once. "If by lawless you mean the obedience of man to the dictates of his own noble nature independent of a tyrannical government, then I am lawless," he said, oratorically. "I and my fellow-workers wish to reinstate the simplicity of primeval days."

"I thought you went even further," said Olive, "and wished to revive chaos."

"Chaos reigns now," proclaimed the reformer. "Chaos means disorder; and what is the world now but a disordered mass? Look at the military burdens of Europe, at the overtaxed poor, at the insolent rich; and tell me if things are as they should be."

"No one said they were, doctor," remarked Carson; "but it is not by pitching bombs at people that you are going to mend them."

"Bombs, sir? There is no such word; there are no such articles in my scheme of reform. I would enlighten those in power by pen and speech. If they will not listen, then their blood must be upon their own heads; for the masses will rise and sweep them from out their counting-houses; hurl them from their thrones; tear them from the bench of justice on which they sit to administer evil laws. To stamp out tyranny the earth, as it now is, must be churned up,

56

deluged with the blood of the unjust; devastated, in short, from pole to pole."

"You bring, a torch for burning, but no hammer for building," quoted Olive, who had read her Carlyle and remembered him.

"The torch first, the hammer to follow. To build up we must first pull down, and on the ruins of the past build—Utopia."

"Another name for dreamland," muttered Semberry.

Olive grew rather tired of Drabble and his diatribes. Not so Tui, however. She listened to the doctor's cheap philanthropy with parted lips and eager eyes. She hung upon his every word, and, seeing that he had at least one sympathetic listener, Drabble addressed his conversation almost exclusively to her. Observing this, Olive slipped out on to the terrace, where, much to her disgust, she was speedily joined by Carson.

"I thought you liked listening to Dr. Drabble?" she said coldly.

"No; he talks commonplaces. I prefer romance."

"Romance?" echoed Olive, thinking of their relative positions, so far removed as they were from the ideal. "Romance here?"

"And where else will you find it if not in this rose-garden? Tell me, Olive," he went on, without waiting for her reply, "why do you avoid me? Have I offended you?"

"You?" she replied with contempt; "you could not offend any one. I never knew so harmless a being."

"It is better surely to be harmless than harmful?" said Carson, complacently. "I shall make you a good husband."

"You shall never be my husband," retorted Olive, flushed with anger.

Carson looked scared. "I understood we were to be married in a fortnight," he said under his breath.

"So we are! I marry you not because I love you, but because I respect the wish of my father. I can be a wife to you in name only."

"Olive, what do you mean?"

"What I say. Cannot you comprehend plain English? When we are married, you and I can be no more to one another than we are at this moment."

"And if I refuse?" he said, with a faint show of anger.

"Then I cannot marry you," answered Olive quietly. "My desire is to carry out to the letter the will of my father; and, by becoming your wife, give you the control of this fifty thousand pounds. More than this I cannot do. I pay you this money for my freedom. You are free to accept it or refuse it as you will."

Angus looked mortified and indignant. A flush was across his

57

weak but handsome face. "Do you then hate me?" he demanded angrily.

"I am indifferent to you. I do not love you; for that reason I make my bargain."

"I understand. You love that insolent Mallow?"

"I should advise you to make no assertions and to mention no names," replied Olive, keeping her temper. "What I say I intend to do. You marry me on these terms or not at all."

"I will marry you," said Carson, frowning, "if only to humble you."

Olive turned on him. "You—you humble me? You, a foolish weak——Go away, Angus, or I may say much we may both regret."

"I will not go away," he said, the latent obstinacy of his nature asserting itself. "Let us make our bargain once and for all. I will marry you——"

"And be my husband in name only?"

"Yes," he whispered, with so strange a glance that she started back, "in name only. I agree to your terms—for my own private reasons. But, should this Mallow return——"

"Leave Mr. Mallow's name out of our conversation," interrupted Olive imperiously; "there is nothing between us that you need trouble about. I do not conceal things."

"Do I?" asked Carson, with bland inquiry.

"Ask yourself, Angus." She looked at him hard. "What do you know about Athelstane Place?"

CHAPTER XI

THE NEW MAID

Any belief that Olive might still have entertained in the accuracy of Mallow's suggestion was speedily dispelled by the expression of sheer amazement upon Carson's face. He remained cool and perfectly colourless.

"What do I know of Athelstane Place?" he repeated blankly. "Why, I never heard of Athelstane Place."

"You don't read your newspaper, then?"

"No; after living all my life in India, the English newspapers contain nothing likely to interest me. But why do you ask me these strange questions?"

"I will tell you, if you will answer me a still stranger one."

"What is it?" asked Carson, apparently much mystified. "Why do your clothes smell so of sandal-wood?"

"Is that all? Why, because I keep them in a sandal-wood chest."

"Which you brought from India?"

"Yes, I bought it from a Chinaman in Bombay. I like the scent of the wood. Is the odour disagreeable to you? I hope not. Had I known I should have bought new clothes in London."

"The odour is not in itself disagreeable," replied Olive, "but in Athelstane Place a man was murdered whose clothes also smelt strongly of this sandal-wood."

"That is strange," said Carson, biting his finger-nails—"very strange. I remember now. Semberry did mention this murder to me."

"But I thought you said you had not heard of the locality?"

"For the moment I forgot. I recollect now that he mentioned the name casually. But he said nothing about any smell of sandal-wood. I should like to hear more about that. Very strange," said Carson, musingly. "But what, may I ask, can this murder have to do with me?"

If the man was acting, his powers of simulation were marvellous. Olive did not think he was acting. He had not the strength or self-control to mask his feelings so completely. The last shadow of doubt vanished from her mind. There could be no question as to the bona fides of the man.

"If you do not know, I do not," she retorted, and walked back to the drawing-room.

Carson remained where he was, deep in thought. "Murdered man——that sandal-wood odour?" he muttered, drawing his brows together; "I cannot understand it. I must ask Semberry the meaning of this." As he spoke, he removed his right arm from the sling with a sigh of relief, and let it hang for a minute or so. The bangle slipped down from under his shirt-cuff on to his wrist. Carson's eye caught its glitter, and he laughed outright.

Satisfied that Mallow's fancies had no foundation in fact, and having closed her bargain with Carson, Olive resigned herself to the inevitable, and commenced to prepare for her wedding. She retailed to Tui Semberry's proposal about the maid, and Miss Ostergaard warmly approved of it. What might suit her as Olive Bellairs, would not do in her position as Olive Carson, she observed; and it was far better at once to engage a smart young woman, thoroughly conversant with her duties, than to rely upon the primitive notions of some country girl. She advised Olive to lose no time in writing to Mrs. Arne for the girl's reference, and, if it proved satisfactory, to engage her.

Olive concurred. She wrote immediately to Mrs. Arne, and by return of post received a reply. Clara Trall was "a perfect treasure," and the writer was more than sorry to part with her; but the girl's health demanded that she should live in the country, to which argument Mrs. Arne felt she could not but yield, though it was with the greatest reluctance she did so—all this and much more, set forth on fine creamlaid note in a firm, masculine hand. The result was that Olive engaged the girl, asking that she should come to commence her duties at once.

Within a day or two of her summons Clara Trall drove up bag and baggage in a hired fly from Reading Station. She was a tall, sallow-faced girl, carrying herself with a certain hauteur. Her dress was plain though stylish, her manner respectful and self-contained, and she had a habit of drooping her lids over her black eyes demurely, as though repressing herself. On the whole she came well through her mistress's examination and cross-examination. Her knowledge of her work proved thorough; she was quick, had excellent taste and did everything she took in hand as well as it could be done. After some experience and careful observation, Olive agreed that Clara's qualifications had not been overstated by Mrs. Arne. She congratulated herself upon the discovery of a jewel, and availed herself thoroughly of the girl's usefulness. Finally she thanked Semberry for his information and advice.

"Glad it's all right, Miss Bellairs," said the Major politely; "mere chance I heard of her, you know."

"A fortunate chance for me, Major; you can't think what a comfort it is to have a maid one can thoroughly trust."

"Hard thing trust any one in this world," mumbled Semberry. "However, you'll have a husband to look after you soon."

"I can look after myself quite well, thank you," said Olive; "my marriage will make no difference to me in that respect."

"Make a heap to me, Miss Bellairs. I've been constantly with Carson last six months—got him as a kind of legacy from his father, you know. But I s'pose this marriage'll put me on one side; shall miss the boy awfully."

"You are devoted to Mr. Carson?"

"Oh, yes; weak beggar, but good sort. Been a kind of father to him, you know. Glad to see him married though, even at m'own cost."

"Oh," said Olive, "I hope you will not let me interfere with your friendship in the least."

"Must," jerked Semberry, shaking his head. "When a man marries, you know, leaves friends, clings on to his wife. 'Sides, my leave's up soon. I must pull out India way in month or so."

"You will stay for the wedding, I hope, Major."

"Oh, thanks, s'pose so; must see Carson turned off usual style."

Olive was becoming a trifle restive. She soon wearied of trying to manufacture conversation, especially for a man like Semberry, so she seized the first opportunity of slipping away and leaving him to Tui. That young lady's management of the soldier was quite masterly.

She was a born flirt, a free-lance of free-lances, all unclaimed hearts came alike to her, and she was ever ready to annex them. But however much occupied she might be in that direction, she ever kept a watchful eye on Aldean. A confession of one-half the interest she really felt in him, would have saved that young gentleman many a wakeful night and many a heartache. But, after the mystic manner of her sex, she was careful to hold her tongue on that particular subject, and poor Jim's powers of penetration were not of the highest order. Hence he was utterly wretched.

He assured himself she was a coquette, that she had no heart. He used language which sorely taxed the Recording Angel's supply of asterisks. But still she drew him back, still she tormented him, until he had a mind to turn celibate and retreat to the handiest monastery. Withal he managed to write now and again to Mallow, and to report to him, as best he was able, how Olive looked, what she said, and how she passed her time. The knowledge that Mallow was as miserable as himself was some small comfort to him.

Poor Jim took many long walks. He would then repeat to himself such poetry as he remembered, which was not much. Sauntering home in the twilight one evening, flogging his memory for rhymes, as usual, he noticed through a gap in the hedge close by two persons talking together. Closer inspection discovered a man and a woman. The man was Carson. The woman he had never before seen. Carson's arm was about the girl's waist, and she was alternately raging and sobbing, yet with a degree of caution which went to show that the meeting was a stolen one. Neither of them saw Aldean, who did not slacken his pace until he was out of both eyesight and earshot. Then he swore.

"Infernal shame!" he growled, once more increasing his stride to cool his rage; "here's this fellow going to be married next week, yet he carries on with another girl. If I were to tell Mallow how this cad is deceiving Miss Bellairs, there'd be some trouble. I wonder who the girl can be? I never saw her before, to my knowledge."

It chanced, however, that he was soon to see her again, for on calling at the Manor House a day or so after he came face to face with a tall, sallow-faced young woman, in whom he had no difficulty in recognizing Carson's inamorata. She was handsome enough in a way, he thought, but he did not like her mouth; and those dark eyes, splendid as they were, did not blaze in her head for nothing. She stood on one side as Lord Aldean passed her, and took him in—as it seemed—at a glance.

"Servant," thought Jim, as he entered the drawing-room. "Hum! doesn't look like one for all that. Carson's a—well, Carson's a blackguard, I fear."

To satisfy himself on this point, after some desultory conversation with Olive, he put a leading question:—"You have a new face about the Manor, I see," he remarked; "tall girl, dark and rather handsome. Who is she?"

"My new maid, Clara Trall," replied Olive, somewhat surprised, for it was not Aldean's habit to notice new faces.

"She seems a superior class of girl for a servant."

"Yes, she is indeed, Lord Aldean. She has been with me only a few days, but I am more than satisfied with her. I have to thank Major Semberry for finding her for me."

"Really!" Aldean was puzzled. So it was Semberry who had brought this girl, whom he had seen weeping in the gloaming on Carson's shoulder, to Casterwell. There was something queer about this. Little guessing his thoughts, Olive proceeded to relate the details of Clara's engagement. And after a few civil words, congratulating her upon the possession of such a treasure, Aldean went home more puzzled than ever.

"What the dickens can it mean," he murmured. "The woman doesn't look like a servant. It is clear Semberry got her here, and it is equally clear Carson makes love to her. There is something very queer about it all. It's too bad. Goodness knows I'm not by way of being the acme of morality myself, but—well, it's too bad altogether, making love just before his marriage to his future wife's maid."

Tui, coming round the bend of the road, scattered Lord

Aldean's contemplations to the four winds. He hurried forward and took off his cap with a blush and a bow.

"I have just been up to the Manor House," he explained, "but you were not there."

Tui laughed. "You see, Lord Aldean, strange as it may appear to you, I do take a walk occasionally for the sake of my health."

"Oh!" said Jim, "I too have been walking for my heart's sake."

"Really! I hope your heart is much benefited by the treatment," said Tui, demurely. "Does Dr. Cupid recommend solitary ambulations?"

"He recommends strongly that I should show you the neighbourhood."

"Ah, but, you see, he isn't my doctor, Lord Aldean, so I don't feel called upon to obey his orders."

"Oh, but I say, you know," blurted out her victim, "you really should let me show you round our country. You can have no idea how charming he is."

"Charm depends so much upon one's companion, doesn't it? Now Major——"

"Oh, I know he is delightful," interrupted Jim wrathfully; "at least, you think he is."

"Do I, indeed? And who told you so, may I ask?"

"Nobody; but I have good eyes."

"But not good manners, I fear, Lord Aldean, nor good temper."

Inwardly Jim groaned. "I used to be considered an amiable sort of chap," he said sadly. "But somehow I've gone wrong lately. I miss——, I miss Mallow."

The shaft went home. "Oh, I know how very fond you are of Mr. Mallow. When is he coming back that you may be amiable?"

"I cannot say. He does not tell me in his letters."

"No? Then I presume he intends letting that horrid Mr. Carson marry Olive?"

"I suppose so. I do not see how he can very well prevent it."

"Oh, he is blind, and so are you," cried Tui, indignantly. "If he loves Olive, why on earth doesn't he marry her? Mr. Carson's a smiling Cheshire cat. Mr. Mallow indeed! He ought to be called Mr. Feeble-Mind. If I were a man and loved a girl, I'd tell her so."

"Suppose the girl wouldn't let the man get that far?" said Aldean, significantly.

"What nonsense! As if any man, who was really and truly in love, ever stopped from speaking his mind."

"Well, I am in love, you——."

63

"Lord Aldean, I am not speaking about you, but about Mr. Mallow. You can tell him from me that I am ashamed of him. He's a hesitating, frightened——"

"Come, I say, Miss Ostergaard——"

"Nervous, feeble-minded rabbit; so there!" and Tui, having brought her string of epithets to a triumphant conclusion, walked off rapidly, with a glance that forbade Aldean to follow.

The young man looked after her open-mouthed. "My word! she has a power of speech," he murmured. "I wonder what she'd call Carson, if she knew of his little game with the maid?"

CHAPTER XII

"WEDDING-BELLS"

When Mallow returned to Casterwell he found the village keeping high holiday in honour of Olive's marriage. The streets and houses were gay with flowers and flags. Under the arches of green boughs, festooned with many coloured blossoms, the people moved about gazing—not without admiration, it must be confessed—at their own handiwork. The same profuse hospitality, which had distinguished the coming-of-age of the Lady of the Manor, was repeated on a still larger scale. The bells of St. Augustine's were clamorous in the old tower; the sleepy old churchyard was for the nonce alive with voices, and the sun, in sympathetic mood at so brave a sight, was shining with all his splendour. But the idol does not ever rejoice with the worshippers, and she was the most miserable girl in the whole village.

Laurence was perhaps scarcely less so. He had not advised Aldean of his return, but had come from Reading in the hired fly. Dusty and battered, it contrasted discordantly with the spruceness and gaiety of the street; and Mallow, seated far back in it, his cap drawn over his eyes, winced more than once as the full meaning of it all forced itself upon him.

"I wonder, does she feel as wretched as I do," he thought,

bitterly. "I suppose she does. My poor Iphigenia! my poor girl! Her father has much to answer for."

Lord Aldean received his friend in unbounded astonishment. He had not expected that Mallow would return on this of all days, and he fell to the conclusion that he must have been successful in his search, and have returned to stop the marriage at the eleventh hour. Yet Mallow certainly did not look as if he had succeeded. His dress was careless and his face was haggard; and he formed a striking contrast to Aldean in the smartness of conventional wedding-going garments. Indeed, as he arrived, Jim was on the point of leaving for the church. He signalled to his coachman to wait, and drew Mallow into the library.

"Well," he said, breathlessly, "what have you done?"

"Nothing; absolutely nothing," replied Mallow, throwing himself into a chair with a weary sigh.

"I was afraid your journey would turn out a wild goose-chase," said Aldean, with a shrug. "So Carson is the right man after all?"

"I have found nothing to prove that he is not."

"What about the sandal-wood perfume?"

"That is still a mystery, Jim, and, so far as I can see, is likely to remain one. I went to Athelstane Place, and I saw most of the witnesses who gave evidence at the inquest, but I could find out nothing new. I called at New Scotland Yard, but with no better result. The case remains exactly as it did when the man was buried."

"Has his name not been discovered?"

"No. Nor have his friends, if he had any, communicated with the police."

"Then you can't in any way connect Carson with the dead man?"

"In no way. Two parallel straight lines cannot meet. Carson's existence can have nothing to do with the unknown man who was murdered."

"I suppose you made no inquiries about Carson?"

"Well, yes, I did; and I found out something."

"Oh, come, that's better; I thought you said you had done absolutely nothing."

"Well, what I did learn is of so little moment, Jim, that it amounts to nothing. I called at the P. and O. office and inquired about Carson. The clerk I spoke to told me that I was the second man who had asked for him."

Aldean looked surprised. "Considering that Carson has no

65

friend in England, that's curious. How long ago was the first inquiry made?"

"Two days only before the Pharaoh arrived."

"Did you ask what kind of man he was who inquired for him?"

"Yes; a black-haired, black-bearded man, shabbily dressed. He wished to know if Carson was on the Pharaoh, and if so, when he would arrive. The clerk showed him the name of Angus Carson in the passenger list, and told him that the boat was due on July 24th."

"Did this man ever return?"

"No; he thanked the clerk and left the office. That was the last seen of him."

"He gave no name?"

"Of course not," said Mallow, peevishly. "Why should he give his name in connection with so simple an inquiry? You can see now for yourself that this information amounts to practically nothing. It neither proves nor disproves Carson's identity, and it certainly does not in any way connect him with the murder."

"Still, the mere fact of Carson's being inquired for is strange, when we know that he has not a single friend in England," said Jim, reflectively; "before his arrival, too. That is even more strange."

Mallow shook his head. "I thought of that myself," he said, "but it does not help us in any way."

"It certainly cannot assist us towards circumventing this wedding. I see you are going to it," running his eye over Jim.

"Of course. There is an invitation for you also, if you care to accept it."

"I do not are to," replied Mallow, quietly. "It is quite painful enough for me to be here on the day of the sacrifice, without attending it."

"Then why did you come, my poor old chap?"

"Because I wish you to take this letter and deliver it personally to——" Mallow paused, "to—Mrs.—Carson," he finished, slowly.

With some hesitation Lord Aldean took the envelope extended to him. He was doubtful. "I hope it does not contain reproaches," he said.

"No; it merely sets her mind at rest about—about—her husband" (Mallow could hardly get the word out), "and tells her that, if she needs me, I am always ready to do her bidding."

"Well," said Jim, placing the letter in his pocket, "I'll deliver it with the greatest of pleasure. It is not unlikely that she will need you some day."

66

"What do you mean, Jim?"

"Oh, I don't mean anything in particular," he said carelessly. "You know I neither like nor trust Carson."

"I am quite with you," said Mallow, bitterly; "but, unfortunately, neither our dislike nor our distrust can assist us to avert this ceremony."

"No, that's true. What will be will be;" and with this morsel of philosophy they parted—Aldean for the ceremony at the church; Mallow to rail at fate for having so cruelly deprived him of Olive.

It was not until after the breakfast that Aldean found any opportunity of delivering Mallow's note to Olive. As he slipped it into her hand she flushed crimson, guessing instinctively from whom it came. With a grateful glance at Aldean, she ran upstairs and hastily tore it open. It contained only a few lines, "Forget what I said in my anger about your husband. He is truly Angus Carson, and I pray heaven that you may be happy with him. But if in trouble you should need a friend, remember that I claim the right to serve you."

The lines were unsigned and ill-written. Olive sat with them crushed in her hand, the tears falling down her face. Tui discreetly held her tongue, for she had guessed that the letter was from Mallow. She roused Olive to action, whilst the maid busied herself with her mistress's clothes. A frown on her face and dark circles under her eyes, Clara seemed little less sorrowful than her mistress.

"Come, dear," said Tui, "you must dress quickly; your husband is waiting for you."

Clara looked round strangely.

"My husband," said Olive, hopelessly. "Yes, he is my husband now."

"But, dear," said Tui, "you married with your eyes open."

"Yes; and with my hands bound," retorted Mrs. Carson, rising. "Well, I suppose I must go on now to the bitter end. Help me, Clara."

On the terrace below Dimbal was conversing hurriedly with the newly-made husband. "In a few days the stocks and shares will be transferred in your name," he said, rubbing his hands; "but I suppose you won't care to be troubled with business for a while?"

"Oh, I don't know about that," said Carson, smiling. "I don't believe in neglecting business for pleasure. I will run up and see you next week. I presume I have full control of this money."

"You are aware, of course, that the capital is charged with the payment of a thousand per annum to your wife?"

"Yes; I will pay her the first year's income at once," said Carson, generously. "I suppose I can realize quickly?"

"Certainly, without difficulty; but I hope, Mr. Carson, you won't sell out. The money is admirably invested."

Before he could answer, Olive came out of the house in her travelling-dress. She looked pale, though composed. With a nod to the lawyer, Carson hurried forward and offered his arm. Having already said good-bye, Olive took it and stepped into the carriage. Then amid a shower of rice and shoes, amid smiles and congratulations, and the usual sprinkling of tears, they drove off.

Major Semberry chuckled complacently as the carriage disappeared.

"Thank God," he muttered.

From the terrace of Kingsholme Mallow watched them. He looked ill and haggard. "Heaven help her and me," he said, with a sigh.

THE SECOND SCENE

AT SANDBEACH

CHAPTER I

"THE HAPPY PAIR"

Sandbeach is a rising watering-place on the south coast. It has been rising for the last ten years, yet, in the opinion of its inhabitants, it has not yet reached that pitch of elevation to which its merits entitle it. The guide-book emphatically declares that it is healthy, pleasantly situated, within easy distance of London, and inexpensive. But for all this eulogy, Sandbeach remains unpopular. A sand and shingle beach curved between headlands of crumbling chalk, a stone-faced esplanade with wooden shelters like dolls' houses, three or four dozen Queen Anne residences fronting some public gardens—a courtesy term, surely—such is Sandbeach. In the rear huddle a score or more of untidy cottages. These represent the original village of thirty years back. There is the usual monster hotel, invariably "under entirely new management," for each season it succeeds in bankrupting its unhappy proprietor. There is also an aggressively ornate band-stand, where play local musicians who seemingly vie with their predecessors in the staleness and worthlessness of their music. Golf-links, tennis-courts, bicycle-track, all are there, but all are more or less deserted. Sandbeach possesses every attraction of the modern seaside "resort," yet people, for some inscrutable reason, decline to fill its hotel or to occupy its apartments. Even in what is facetiously termed its "season" it is but sparsely populated. 'Tis a marine Doctor Fell, and no man knoweth the reason of its unpopularity.

Olive it was who had selected this dismal spot in which to pass her honeymoon. Her one desire was to have solitude—no solitude à deux, but solitude absolute and complete. Her husband in no way interfered with her desire. He sauntered about smoking endless

69

cigarettes, and scanning such samples of modern French fiction as came to hand. Every few days he ran up to town. What he did there Olive knew not, nor did she trouble herself to inquire. But she did notice that he invariably appeared highly delighted with himself on returning from these jaunts.

Left to her own devices, Olive amused herself as best she could. But she thought more of Mallow that was consistent with her own peace of mind.

"Olive," said Angus, one day at luncheon, "I have paid your first year's income in to your account."

"Thank you, that is very kind of you," replied Olive, cheerfully; "but was it necessary to pay in the whole amount at once?"

"No; I need only pay it quarterly; but as I wished to be perfectly free to handle the money, I thought it best to get it done."

"Is it about the money that you have been so often up to London?"

"Well, yes; I have been seeing after it."

"And how is Mr. Dimbal?"

"I have not seen him. Mr. Dimbal has nothing to do with the business now, save in so far as your income is concerned. My affairs are in the hands of another firm of lawyers."

Olive was vaguely troubled.

"Of course, I have every confidence in you," she said; "but I am sorry you did not leave the business with Mr. Dimbal. He is so very trustworthy."

"There are other honest men in London," replied Carson, with his usual smile. "By-the-way, how long do you intend to stay here? We have now been exiled for three weeks."

"I was thinking of going home in another fortnight or so, if that will suit you."

"Oh, as to that, don't consider me. I am going to London myself."

"You surely do not mean to let me return alone? You really must not. Think how everybody will talk."

Carson shrugged his shoulders.

"I do not care what they say," he replied, without the least show of temper. "To tell you the truth, I am rather tired of this farce. You refuse to treat me in any way as a husband; you surely cannot complain if I betake myself elsewhere."

"I thought our relative positions were quite clear," said Mrs. Carson, coldly. "I married you simply and solely in obedience to my

70

father's dying wish; you married me—well, you married me, I suppose, for the fifty thousand pounds that went with me."

"In other words, our marriage is a bargain."

"If you please; it matters little what we call it."

"A pleasant position for me," said Carson, good-humouredly.

His wife sat silently looking at her plate, while he continued to eat his luncheon with the utmost indifference.

"Perhaps the position is a trying one for you," she said, at length; "but I dictated the terms of our union very clearly in the first instance; you were perfectly free to accept or reject them. You accepted them; your reasons were your own. No doubt they were good ones."

"Quite right; ours is purely a business marriage, or bargain. We can call it that between ourselves."

"If you were a different kind of man, if you cared for me, things might perhaps be different. But you do not care for me; you do not know what love is."

"Excuse me if I say that you are hardly in a position to judge," replied Angus, quietly. "And are you not a trifle inconsistent? If I loved you, in what position should I stand, seeing that your affections are very definitely engaged?"

"Excuse me if, in my turn, I say that you are not in a position to speak as to that."

"You may think so, but I am not blind. Oh no; it's too late in the day to talk of love."

"I wish to do my duty," retorted Olive, rather weakly, it must be confessed.

"You have done your duty," said Carson, amiably; "you have obeyed your father, and you have brought me fifty thousand pounds. You do not love me, neither do I care two straws about you."

"Then why did you marry me?"

"For the money solely," he replied, shamelessly. "I served your turn, you served mine. Were I in love with you, do you think I would rest content with the purely nominal position of your husband? By no means. For the money's sake I made you my wife. I agreed to your terms because it suited me to do so. Have I ever gone contrary to you in any way?"

"No; you fulfil your part of the bargain admirably," she said scornfully.

"Then you can ask no more of me. I shall not return to the

71

Manor House with you to hold an ignominious position. Our mutual ends are accomplished: let us part."

"Do you intend to leave me, then?" she asked, feeling herself at a disadvantage.

"I do. I shall go to London—perhaps even abroad. At all events, I intend to lead my own life."

"But think of the position I shall be placed in."

"Think of the position I am placed in," he replied emphatically.

"People will talk if you leave me so soon after our marriage."

"I must leave you to make the best excuses you can; the position is of your own making. You can say that my health is bad, or that the doctor has ordered me abroad. I'll pay you a visit every now and then to keep up appearances. More you cannot ask of me— more I am not disposed to grant."

Olive rose and struck the table with her open hand.

"I protest against your attitude," she cried indignantly.

"As I do against yours."

"You are not treating me fairly," she said, keeping back her tears with an effort.

"As fairly as you treat me, surely?"

"If I agree to be your wife, if I——"

"No," he interrupted. "I prefer matters to remain as they are. It is useless to feign what we neither of us feel."

Having so far humiliated herself, Olive was not prepared to go further. She realized that his position was every whit as strong as her own. She could resent his behaviour in no way, seeing that the original compact was of her own making. Dismayed at the predicament in which she found herself, she retired to her room to consider what she should do. Finally, she determined that, should he leave her, she would go to London for a few months. Mrs. Purcell was on her way to England, and had expressed her intention of taking a house in London. The old lady would gladly have her to stay with her; perhaps she might even invite Tui to join them. She would blind the Casterwell people, at all events; they would not know that Angus had left her so soon. It was the only possible solution she could think of.

That evening she dined in her room. She had no fancy for a renewal of the discussion. It could avail her nothing. If her husband had made up his mind to go, go he would; all she could say or do would not serve to deter him. Silence was the only dignified course open to her. So she brought to bear upon herself as much of her

72

little stock of philosophy as she could muster. But she had to confess it was poor consolation. She felt lonely and very miserable.

Later in the evening her maid came to her with a request that she might take a walk. The girl was looking far from well, and Olive did not hesitate to let her go. She had become attached to Clara. She found her a woman of refinement and capacity, and withal respectful. Never had she shown the slightest inclination to take advantage of any favour Olive might have shown her. Yet there was something strange about the girl which puzzled her mistress not a little. More than once she had surprised her weeping bitterly, and there were times when Olive had thought she was unnecessarily jubilant. Olive had questioned her about these emotional outbursts, but with no satisfactory result, so in time she ceased to notice them. The girl was always perfect in the performance of her duties.

She saw Clara go out for her walk; but no sooner had she gone than Olive felt more restless and ill at ease than ever. The atmosphere of the house stifled her. She wished she had asked the maid for her hat and things before she went. She felt she must give way to hysterics unless she did something. She could neither read nor write, nor could she sit still. She felt she must get into the fresh air. She put on her hat and cloak and went out. The night was windy and rather cold, but this suited her overstrung nerves. Rapidly up and down the esplanade she walked, drinking in the keen air, and watching the dark clouds drive across the sickly moon. Up and down, up and down, until her limbs grew weary; and with her fatigue her excitement abated. At last, slowly climbing the steps to the top of the cliffs, she returned to the hotel. Her way lay through a small shrubbery, parted from the road by a slight iron railing, beside which a gas-lamp flared in the wind. She could see a man and woman talking earnestly together. They did not hear her. As she drew near, the man stooped and kissed the woman. The next moment she swept past them wrathful and resentful. She had recognized her husband.

CHAPTER II

"THE BROOCH"

Half an hour later Carson sauntered into the sitting-room. He found Olive awaiting him. He had not seen her as she passed him in the darkness, and was, therefore, at a loss to comprehend the full significance of her present expression. He was at a loss to know why she was waiting for him. She did not usually seek him at so late an hour. However, he opened the conversation in his usual easy-going way.

"Hallo!" said he, "not in bed yet? You'll lose your beauty sleep."

"Will you be so kind as to sit down?" replied Olive coldly. "I wish to speak to you."

"And on no very pleasant subject, I should say," returned Carson, taking a chair. "Well, what's the matter?" with a yawn.

"Have you no regard for decency, Angus?"

"As much as my neighbours, I suppose. How have I been transgressing?"

"By meeting that woman to-night."

Carson started. "What woman?" he asked irritably.

"I do not know," retorted Olive, with some heat. "I did not see her face, nor would I have recognized her if I had. Your associates are not mine."

"Still, I do not understand," said Angus composedly, but seemingly relieved.

"There are none so blind as those who won't see. I was taking a walk just now, and I saw you speaking to a woman under the gas-lamp opposite this hotel. Dare you deny it?"

"I don't deny it. Why should I?"

"Angus, how can you be so shameless? I saw—I saw—that—well, that you were more than friendly with her."

"You seem to have seen a great deal," sneered Carson, coolly. "May I ask what right you have to spy upon my actions?"

"What right? The right of your wife."

"Pardon me, you are not my wife," he returned ironically. "You are my partner in a business transaction. I thought we were agreed on that point once and for all."

"When do you go to London again?" she asked. "To-morrow," he answered. "Have you anything to urge against my going?"

"No; I claim no right to control your actions. I can only say that as you agreed, for a large sum of money, to act as my nominal husband, you should fulfil your part of the bargain so far as to treat me with respect."

"And how have I failed to do so?"

"By meeting that woman to-night."

"Nonsense! No one saw me but yourself; and I must deny your right to call me to account in any way. However, that has nothing to do with my going to London. Have you any objection to that?"

"I would advise you to stop there. I never wish to see you again."

"The wish is mutual, I assure you," said Carson, rising in his turn. "I am glad that we have come to an understanding at last. I will do as you suggest."

"I think it very much better that you should. Our marriage is a very great mistake."

"Pardon me, I do not agree with you. It is surely an unqualified success, inasmuch as we have both attained our aim. But any blame there is must attach itself to you as much as to me. You might, of course, under ordinary circumstances, have had the right to object to my meeting a lady as I did; as it is, you can have no shadow of a right to do so."

"At least, you might conduct yourself as a gentleman whilst you are here," returned Olive bitterly. "But I suppose that is asking too much."

"A great deal too much; you can ask me nothing." Carson shrugged his shoulders. "This is hardly conversation," he added. "At all events, you must excuse me if I say it does not interest me. As you say, we had better part. After I leave for town in the morning, I will trouble you no more."

"Thank God," said Olive, moving towards the door of her room. "At least I shall be spared the indignity of living with you."

"Allow me," said Carson, stretching forward to open the door for her. "Good-night, and good-bye."

"You contemptible cur," said his wife, disappearing and slamming the door behind her.

He smiled as he looked after her. "A cur, am I? It is lucky for you, Miss Bellairs, that I do not use my teeth more fully to substantiate your simile; I could, you know. Ah, well!" drawing a long sigh of relief, "thank goodness, that's over. What a weary, dreary time it has been. However, at last, I can enjoy the fruits of my labours. After all, the money is well worth the trouble;" and Mr.

Carson proceeded to the bar to drink a toast to his release in a glass of lemonade. Temperance was one of his good points.

When Olive rose next morning he was gone, bag and baggage. He said no word of farewell, nor did he even leave a note behind him. She felt immensely relieved, yet she could not help feeling she had debased herself, that her self-respect was sullied. It had been a fatal mistake.

But Olive was not the woman to sit down with ashes on her head and bemoan her fate. Suppressing the fact that her husband had left her (that she intended to explain personally later), she wrote to Miss Slarge that, after a further two weeks' stay at Sandbeach, she intended leaving for London. "I don't feel like returning to Casterwell at present," she wrote, "I would rather spend the winter months in London. Please let me know when you expect Mrs. Purcell. I am most anxious to see her. When I am settled in town, you and Tui must come up that we may all be together." She sent kind messages to Mr. Brock and to Miss Ostergaard, and she inquired if Mallow was still with Lord Aldean. Miss Slarge did not omit to answer this last query. He was still there; it was the greatest comfort to her to know that.

A few days later came a letter from Mr. Dimbal, which seriously alarmed her. It drew her attention to the fact that Carson had recently sold the securities in which her money was invested, and transferred the proceeds to the Crédit Lyonnais, in Paris. Suspicious of Carson's behaviour generally, more especially when it came to taking things altogether out of his hands, Mr. Dimbal had made inquiries, and had ascertained what he now wrote to Olive. She could not understand it at all, and had she known his whereabouts, would straightway have written to him for an explanation. But he had left her without an address. He had vanished completely out of her life. Apparently it was his intention that these funds should vanish with him. Probably, the thousand pounds paid to her credit was all she would ever see of it. The position was certainly becoming serious.

She recalled Mrs. Purcell's letter, and her description of Carson. She read over the extracts she had made, with the result that she wrote again to Casterwell; this time—of all people—to Mrs. Drabble. That lady's reply roused the strongest suspicions in her regarding her husband, and she felt the time had come when she could no longer cope with things unaided. Her first impulse was to call in the assistance of Mr. Dimbal, but on second thoughts she refrained. The little jog-trot solicitor was hardly the man to deal with a clever

76

scoundrel of Carson's type, for scoundrel she now fully believed him to be. There was Mallow; he was capable beyond a doubt, and by his love for her had he not claimed the right to serve her in time of need? She would write to him without loss of time. The next day he was at Sandbeach.

Olive was in her sitting-room when the servant brought up his name. In the adjacent bedroom Clara was attending to her work.

"Ah, Mrs. Carson," he said (he had schooled himself to say the name), "I am indeed glad to see you again. But—but, you are not looking after yourself!"

"Oh, I am well enough, really," said Olive, giving him her hand, "but I am terribly worried."

"Worried?" repeated Mallow, sitting down near her, "worried? what about?"

Before Olive could reply, the door leading to the bedroom opened abruptly, and Clara came in with a hat in her hand. "I beg your pardon, ma'am," said the maid, "but do you wish this hat left out from the packing?"

"Yes, of course," replied Olive, astonished at her asking so unnecessary a question.

"Thank you, ma'am." The girl retired. Olive would have been more than astonished, had she seen her a minute later. The door was left slightly ajar, and the girl's ear was taking in every word she could catch.

"That young woman is still with you, I see," observed Laurence.

"Yes, she is a very excellent servant," replied Olive. "Why?"

"Oh, nothing. I merely remarked the fact," said Mallow, who had his reasons for keeping his own counsel. "But, to continue our conversation, why are you worried?"

"I will tell you everything shortly. Meanwhile I want you to read this." Olive placed in his hands the extracts she had copied from Mrs. Purcell's letter, and pointed out to him one paragraph in particular: "Mr. Carson has had golden wrist-buttons made to match his unique bracelet, wrought in the same style, but of vastly inferior workmanship."

"Well?"

"Now look at this." She detached her brooch and laid it on the table. It was a circular gold ornament, carved with the three faces of the Hindoo trinity encircled by a lotus wreath; a handsome, but odd, piece of workmanship.

"An Indian wrist-button," said Mallow, looking at it carefully.

77

"Imitated from Carson's bracelet, no doubt. I suppose it is one of those referred to by Mrs. Purcell."

"It is; I am sure of it."

"Carson gave it to you?"

"No, he did not. It was a wedding present from Margery Drabble; she told me it was her doll's locket. I did not notice it particularly at the time. But on reading Mrs. Purcell's letter again it suddenly dawned upon me that it was one of Carson's wrist-buttons."

"And how did Margery come by it?"

"Well, I wrote to Mrs. Drabble about that, and she replied that Margery had taken it from her father's desk on the mine-is-thine principle. Now," said Olive, "what possible connection can there be between Dr. Drabble and my husband?"

CHAPTER III

"CLARA'S LETTER!"

Mallow stared at her, astonished at the earnestness with which she spoke. "I am afraid I don't quite follow you," he said at length. "Of course Carson knows Dr. Drabble. He met him at Casterwell."

"That is just the point. Was it for the first time he met him at Casterwell?"

"I—I suppose so; but, so far as I could see, he was never very intimate with the man."

"Then why should he present him with a pair of gold wrist-buttons," said Olive—"especially the pair he wore himself; the pair he had made to match that bracelet?"

"Yes that is strange," admitted Mallow.

"It would be, if it were a fact," said Olive. "But I do not for one moment believe that he gave them to Drabble at all."

"Then how do you suppose Drabble came by them?"

"That," said Olive, "is just where I am at a loss, and where I need your help. That is what we must find out."

"But, Mrs. Carson——"

"One minute, Mr. Mallow. Am I Mrs. Carson?"

"Well, I presume so. You were married to him," said Mallow, somewhat bewildered.

"I was married to some one, yes; but is that some one Angus Carson?"

Mallow jumped up hurriedly.

"You are not thinking of that absurd story I told you?"

"I am. Not that I think it absurd now. On the contrary, I am coming to believe more in the sense of it each hour."

"No, no," said Mallow. "I made every possible inquiry in London immediately before your marriage. I visited Athelstane Place; I questioned the police. But I could find nothing, absolutely nothing, to connect your husband in ever so remote a degree with that murder. Besides, look at the facts in his favour. Mr. Brock recognized him simply from his resemblance to his father, and his appearance corresponds exactly with the description of him given by Mrs. Purcell, even to the wearing of his bangle."

"I don't remember seeing him wear the wrist-buttons," said Olive. "Women, you know, are observant of these little things. Do you remember Mrs. Slarge reading out her sister's letter in the presence of Angus?"

"Yes, perfectly. It was then Carson showed us the bangle."

"Yes. Well, I looked then for these wrist-buttons, but I noticed he wore silver sleeve-links."

"On that particular occasion, perhaps?"

"But he never wore the others," retorted Olive. "Again and again I watched for them. This is the first I have seen, and it comes from Margery, not from Angus."

"Did you speak to your husband about it?"

"No; as I say, I was busy when Margery gave it to me, and I slipped it into my pocket without thinking. It was only on looking at it again, the other day, that its resemblance to the bracelet struck me. I wear it as a stud rather than as a brooch; you see, it has no catch-pin."

"Well, I think perhaps the best way would be to ask your husband how Dr. Drabble comes to possess a wrist-button so similar to his bracelet."

Olive turned suddenly pale, and hung her head. "I cannot," she said, faintly; "he has left me."

"Left you?" repeated Mallow, scarcely able to believe his ears. "Why—when?"

"Nearly a fortnight ago. It was not possible for us to continue

79

living together. I hated him, and he did not care in the least for me. It was solely for my money that he married me; and now that he has it, he has no further use for me. We agreed it was best to separate. I was glad to do so."

"And this is the man you left me for!"

"Not of my own free will. You know I was the victim of circumstances. I told you everything about my father's letter. Here it is; read it yourself, and tell me if I could have acted otherwise."

In silence Mallow took the letter from her. He noticed that her hand trembled. In silence he read it through.

It was a strange letter, and it had apparently been written under stress of great mental excitement. The man might have been in mortal terror when he penned those lines. The warning at the close was a very cry of anguish.

"What do you say now?" asked Olive.

"I can say nothing. We seem to move in a world of mystery."

"You admit that I acted rightly?"

"I admit that you were forced to obey the letter," answered Mallow. "Whether you acted rightly is not quite the same thing."

"You are not just to me," cried Olive, passionately. "I loved my father dearly. He was always so good to me. I should have been wicked to ignore so solemn a command. Had it been only a question of money, I would readily have surrendered it all to Mr. Brock. But my father's dying wish—I could not disregard it, I could not."

"I admit that," said Laurence, reluctantly. "But what a miserable result it is!"

Olive covered her face with her hands. "I know, I know!" she cried. "The sins of the father are visited on the children. Oh, what can there have been in my father's life to make him sacrifice me so cruelly?"

"Mr. Brock was your father's oldest friend. He might, perhaps, know."

"He does not know, for I asked him the very day before this hateful marriage of mine. He could give me no answer. He could not understand the letter. Both in India and in England, he said, my father's life was above reproach."

"Yet there must be something," mused Mallow. "There are few men who have not a turned-down page somewhere in the book of their life, and as a rule it is not shown even to the dearest and closest of friends. 'We mortal millions live alone,' as Arnold puts it."

"Well, it can't be helped," said Olive, despairingly. "There is nothing to be gained by probing the past. But in the present we may be able to do something. To return to those wrist-buttons: in the first place, Carson never wore them——"

"One moment," interrupted Mallow. "You must be quite sure of that before we can accept it as evidence of any value. It is always possible he may have had them by him, yet not have worn them. Whether or no he gave them to Dr. Drabble is another matter; you had, perhaps, better write and get Mrs. Drabble to ask her husband."

"That is exactly what I did. But she replied that it was more than she dared to do. You know she is frightened to death of him. On the contrary, she implored me not to tell him lest Margery should get into trouble."

"The man can hardly blame her for following his own teaching," said Laurence, grimly. "He has been at some pains to teach her to look upon other people's belongings as her own; naturally the child thought she was doing no wrong. So Mrs. Drabble won't speak to her husband? Well, I must do so myself, then, when I get back to town."

"Have you the doctor's address there?"

"Yes. It so happens that he has been trying to enlist my sympathies towards his revolutionary projects. He gave me his town address and asked me to call." Mallow took out his pocket-book. "49, Poplar-street, Soho; that's where he lives. A veritable hotbed of foreign rascality, no doubt. Well, that disposes for the present of one more piece of evidence. What else have you?"

"Two days ago," said Olive, "I received this from Angus" (producing a letter). "He said that he was going to London, possibly even abroad. He has evidently gone abroad, for this is written from Florence."

"So I see," said Mallow, glancing over the letter. "Florence as an address is somewhat vague."

"He fears I may follow him, I suppose. Pray read the letter, Mr. Mallow."

Laurence did so. There were merely some half a dozen lines to the effect that the writer did not intend to return, that he gave his wife her full freedom, and apologizing for anything he might have done to distress her.

"He is a bad lot," said Mallow, in disgust, "Still, I cannot see how this letter is going to help you, nor, for that matter, what doubt it casts upon his identity."

"Can't you see," burst out Olive, "why he wrote that himself—

and, moreover, he wrote it with his right hand. I have seen the writing of his left. It can be read only with great difficulty. This is perfectly plain and easily legible. Yet, when he was here, he always declared his right hand was much too painful to use in any way."

"Yes, I admit there may be something in it," said Mallow; "but might not some one else have written it for him?"

"Perhaps; that is, of course, just possible. But I doubt it. I don't believe his right hand was hurt at all. He merely feigned its uselessness for his own ends."

"But Mrs. Purcell declared that it was useless."

"She alluded to Carson's hand. This man, I tell you, is not Carson. I remember one day when we were out we climbed a slight cliff. I scrambled up first. On looking back, I saw Angus climbing up with both hands. There were other times, too, when he forgot himself. I have even seen him take his arm right out of the sling and use his hand perfectly freely. When I spoke to him about it he always would have it I was mistaken. I tried to get him to remove the bandages and show me his hand, but his excuse was that the doctor had strictly forbidden him to do so. No, believe me, Mr. Mallow, I am right. That letter was written by the man himself, and with his right hand. Carson is an impostor."

"Really that is very well argued," said Mallow, puzzled. "But there are flaws. However, we can consider those later. Pray go on. What is your third reason?"

"Mr. Dimbal writes to me that Angus—let us call him that for the present—has realized all securities, and has placed the proceeds to his own credit at the Crédit Lyonnais in Paris. Now, the real Angus Carson would not do that."

"I don't quite see why he should not," said Mallow; "but I admit, of course, it is strange. Still, even so, I find it difficult to believe the man is an impostor without more direct and convincing evidence."

"He is; I tell you he is," replied Olive, resolutely. "I truly believe that man who was murdered in Athelstane Place was the real Carson. The right hand—the diseased hand, you remember—was cut off, no doubt to procure the bracelet for this impostor. This man's clothes smelt of sandal-wood—a most unusual perfume—so did those of the poor wretch who was killed. The newspaper description of the dead man corresponds exactly with the man who calls himself my husband. He never by any chance spoke to me of his father or of his life in India. He never cared for me, and was only too ready to part from me. His only action of note since we were married has

82

been to sell the stock and transfer the proceeds to a foreign bank, where he can deal with it. I am convinced, Mr. Mallow, that he was not Angus Carson. I go even further. I believe that he murdered Angus Carson in order to impersonate him. I am as sure of it as I am that—well, that I am alive; and, God help me, I am married to the wretch!"

Olive became so agitated that Mallow begged her to lie down. Do and say what he would, he could not shake her conviction. When he saw her somewhat more composed he left her and started off for a good brisk walk, that he might turn things over in his mind.

It was quite dusk when he got back to Sandbeach. Half an hour later and he would probably have failed to see a small white package lying on the path-way. He was in a narrow side street leading from the esplanade to the railway station. As it was, he not only saw it, but took the trouble to stop and pick it up. It proved to be a somewhat bulky letter addressed to Jeremiah Trall, Esq., 49, Poplar Street, Soho, London. Mallow's instinct as soon as he read this was to drop it. But the tall figure of a woman coming quickly round the corner arrested his attention. He saw that she was eagerly searching for something. She came up to him. "My letter sir," she ejaculated hurriedly. "I dropped it. Thank you." She snatched it from him, and before he had time to recover himself she was gone.

"Clara Trall!" he gasped, thunderstruck. "Shall I follow her? No, I have no right to do that. Yet the address of that letter is the address of Dr. Drabble in London. More mystery—more scheming. What on earth can it mean?"

But it was many a long day before Mallow found an answer to that question.

CHAPTER IV

"MORE MYSTERY"

For various reasons, Mallow had not taken up his abode in the same hotel as Olive. He had found a clean, unpretentious, little place near the station, which suited him well enough in his present mood. Here he ate a solitary dinner, cooked and served in thoroughly English style. Invariably fastidious over his food, Laurence was not now inclined to be any more particular about it than he was about his lodging. He ate but little. A good cigar and some strong black coffee, he felt, would do more for him just now than any food. He inquired from the waiter how the trains ran to London, for he had no doubt that on the morrow it would be necessary for him to use them. Curiously enough the waiter knew all about the trains, notwithstanding the fact that he was an aboriginal as well as a waiter.

"On'y two decent ones from 'ere to Lunnon," said this Ganymede; "you'll see 'em, sir, in the time-tables. There's one leaves ten 'o the mornin', an' another at six at night. You gits to Lunnon in about three hours; so, yer see, they ain't express like even then."

"Ten in the morning," mused Mallow. "Ah! that's a trifle too early. I may as well have another day with Olive, to cheer her up. The evening train will suit me. I can see Drabble in Soho the next morning—that is, if he is in town."

Mallow finished his coffee and cigar. Then he lit a fresh one, slipped on his coat—for the night was chilly—and strolled round to the big hotel. He was shown at once to Mrs. Carson's sitting-room. He found her almost as much agitated as she had been when he left her.

"Oh, Laurence!" she said, calling him by his Christian name in her excitement. "How glad I am that you have come. She has gone!"

"She has gone? Who has gone?" asked Laurence, pausing in the act of removing his coat.

"Clara—my maid," replied Olive. "I cannot understand it at all. She appeared perfectly content with her place, and said nothing about leaving. It was only when I sent for her to dress me for dinner that I found she had gone. What can it mean?"

"It probably seems extraordinary to you," replied Mallow, coolly; "but I confess I am not surprised. Your Clara has gone to join Carson."

Olive gasped. "To join my husband?" she said incredulously. "What has Clara to do with him?"

"That is what I should like to know. Carson has been in the habit of meeting this girl for some time past. Before you were married, Aldean saw them together; but he carefully refrained from letting me know anything about it until quite recently. I suppose he was afraid of what I should do to the scoundrel. Save, under the

84

present circumstances, I should not have told you. But, as I have little doubt she has gone to him, it is right you should know."

"Oh!" cried Olive, suddenly recollecting; "then she was the woman I saw! The night before my husband left me I saw him talking with a woman quite close to the hotel. I recognized him but her face I could not see. Yes, it must have been Clara."

"The scoundrel!" murmured Mallow, "there is clearly something between him and the girl. She was probably a spy."

"A spy—on me? For what reason?"

"Semberry could probably explain that. I understand that he was instrumental in finding the girl for you."

"That's true. A Mrs. Arne, whose address he gave me, was anxious to find a place for her; so I wrote, of course, in the usual way for her reference. It was an excellent one, and I did not hesitate to engage her. So far as that goes, she was a first-class servant.'

"She probably was no servant at all," said Mallow, bluntly. "She had neither the appearance nor the manners of one. Even Aldean noticed that. By the way, have you Mrs. Arne's letter?"

Olive nodded. "I keep all my letters for six months before I destroy them," she said, rising. "I should have hers. Wait one moment, I will go and fetch it."

Mrs. Carson returned with the letter. Mallow read it through carefully, but could gather nothing from it. He noted the address, 30, Amelia Street, Kensington, and commented on the firm, masculine character of the writing. "Mrs. Arne is evidently a woman of strong will and considerable character," he said, replacing his pocket-book. "For all we know, she may be mixed up in this plot."

"Plot?" echoed Olive, looking scared. "What plot?"

"Well," said Mallow, "I can hardly say definitely. There is certainly a plot of some kind. Sooner or later we shall know more about it. At present we must be content to know its object, which was undoubtedly to secure this fifty thousand pounds."

"For whom?"

"That is the question. Carson, Semberry, Clara Trall, or even Dr. Drabble—they all seem to have something to do with it."

"Then you think there is some connection between my husband and that horrid doctor?"

"Yes, I do. I must tell you that shortly before six o'clock this evening, as I was coming home from my walk, I picked up, in one of the small streets here, a letter, dropped evidently by this Clara of yours; for just as I was reading the address on it, she came rushing round the corner, snatched it from my hand, and flew off with it

85

before I had time to do more than notice that it was she. It is more than probable that she left by the six-o'clock train."

"For London?"

"No; I don't think she went to London."

"Oh! I see. You think she has gone off to Florence to my husband?"

"Yes, I think that; and something more, Mrs. Carson. The letter I picked up was addressed to Jeremiah Trall, 49, Poplar Street, Soho."

"Clara's father, I suppose?"

"Well, it may be her father or it may be Dr. Drabble—49, Poplar Street, happens to be the town address he gave me. It would not surprise me in the least to find that in pursuit of his Anarchistic schemes he found it useful to have—well, let us call it a nom de guerre."

"But why should he take Clara's name?"

"We don't know that Trall is Clara's real name," retorted Mallow. "Mind you, this is purely hypothetical. Jeremiah Trall may or may not be Drabble. At all events, the address is the same; and Soho is the hotbed of Anarchism in London. The possession of that wrist-button by Drabble seems to me clearly to point to some intimacy with Carson."

"The so-called Carson?" interrupted Olive.

"Well, we have not quite proved that yet. The links of the chain run something like this: Mrs. Arne, whoever she may be, gives Clara (whoever she may be) a character which is palpably false. I mean false as regards her identity, not her capability; for that you proved to be all that was said for it. From this fact we are justified in concluding that she, Mrs. Arne, is in some way implicated. I feel convinced myself that Clara was not a servant. Semberry induces you to engage her—that proves his connection; and Carson meets Clara several times, and clearly is intimate with her. The wrist-button would seem to connect Drabble with Carson, and the Soho address associates him with Clara. Save the address and the wrist-button, which, of course, are substantial facts, the rest is deduction pure and simple. But it is logical deduction, and, to my thinking, it points strongly to a secret association for some secret purpose between all these people. The purpose, I take it, was to secure this sum of fifty thousand pounds."

"But what makes you think that Clara has not gone to London?"

"That letter," replied Mallow, promptly. "It was very bulky. I believed it contained a report of our conversation here to-day. Clara

86

was in the next room. You remember how, when she heard my voice, she came in with an obviously feigned excuse? I noticed when she returned to the bedroom she left the door ajar. Overhearing us, of course, she became aware of your doubts as to Carson's identity. She probably became alarmed lest you should go further and discover her connection with him. That, I think, is the reason of her sudden departure; whilst the very existence of the letter seems to me to show that London was not her destination. Had she been going there, she need not have written it. She could have called at Poplar-Street, Soho, and said what she had to say. Do you follow? She has probably got out at some station on the way up, and is now on her way to Dover, en route for Italy."

Olive passed her hand over her forehead. "It's all very confusing," she said, in a troubled voice.

"And all very fanciful, you might add," rejoined Mallow. "Are you sure she has taken her box?"

"The chambermaid said so."

Mallow shook his head. "We had better not rest content with second-hand evidence when we can have first," said he. "Where is her room? Can we go and see?"

"Oh yes. I should have gone before, but I have been so confused with one thing and another. Let us go and search it at once."

Taking a lighted candle from a side table, Olive led the way along the corridor. The room was not far away. They could find no box there.

"She must have removed it while I was out," said Olive in dismay. "I took a stroll shortly after you left; my head was aching so. Oh, what a wicked, artful girl!"

"She is probably quite used to these fittings," said Mallow, looking round the room. "Hallo! torn-up paper in the grate! We must look at this. Hold the candle a moment, please, Mrs. Carson."

Clara had not been fool enough to leave behind anything likely to betray her. But one envelope which Mallow found proved the truth of one of his suppositions. It had an Italian stamp on the corner, and was addressed "Miss Clara Trall, Grand Hotel, Sandbeach, Inghilterra."

"My husband's writing!" cried Olive, as Mallow rose and dusted his knees.

"Yes; and from Florence—dated four days back. Look at the post-mark. This puts the matter beyond a doubt, Mrs. Carson. Your husband wrote to her to join him in Italy. She has gone to Dover, not to London."

"But, surely, what can Clara be to that man?"

"An accomplice, certainly."

They returned to the sitting-room. Mrs. Carson sat down looking hopelessly bewildered. "What are we to do now?" she asked. "Communicate with the police?"

"No," said Mallow; "we have no facts to give them. We know that Carson has possession of the money; but, you must remember, he has legal possession of it. We know that he is in Italy, and that Clara has joined him. There is nothing there for the police, is there? Beyond this we can say nothing; not even that Carson is an impostor. But it will not be long now before we are able to settle that point; Mrs. Purcell arrives from India in a couple of days' time, and a portrait of Carson——"

"I have one," interrupted Olive. "He was so vain that he actually had some done by one of these men on the beach. There were some copies in this room. I dare say I can find them. But tell me, Mr. Mallow, what do you intend to do now?"

Whilst she was hunting for the photographs, Mallow explained. "I think," he said, "I had better go to London and see this Mrs. Arne. Then I shall look up Semberry, and after that—well, then, I think I'll drop in on Dr. Drabble in Soho."

"Will you broach the matter directly?"

"No; I don't think it would be wise to do that. If things are as I suspect, we have to deal with a dangerous lot. I'll find out all I can without letting them have any suspicion—that is to say, from Mrs. Arne and Semberry. As for Drabble, I intend to join him. I shall become an Anarchist."

"Become an Anarchist?" echoed Olive, turning round, the photographs in her hand.

"Yes; it is my only chance of gaining his confidence. I must do it if I am to get at the truth."

"But you will bring trouble upon yourself."

"Oh no," laughed Mallow, "I shall stop short of throwing bombs, I promise you."

"Oh, it is dangerous," said Mrs. Carson, sighing. "How can I thank you sufficiently for all the trouble you are taking—here are the photographs."

Laurence glanced at one. It represented Carson standing straight and stiff against a stone wall for all the world as if he were going to be shot. It was not a work of art, but the likeness was excellent. Mallow nodded as if he were well satisfied.

"It will serve our purpose capitally," he said, putting it in his pocket. "Mrs. Purcell should have no difficulty in saying if this is or is not the man she saw in Bombay. Well, Mrs. Carson," he added abruptly. "I must say good night."

"Good night. What time to-morrow do you leave?"

"Not until the evening train—six o'clock. Mrs. Purcell does not arrive for two days yet, so I have plenty of time. Good night."

Thus did Mallow take his first step on the dark and tortuous way he was to follow. It led him downward into an under-world of crime and danger. But he found some good even in those sordid depths. Doubt and mystery surrounding him, holding his life in his hand, on and on he went, never flinching, never yielding, never losing sight of his clue until at last it led him to the truth.

THE THIRD SCENE

IN LONDON

CHAPTER I

"MYSTERIOUS MRS. ARNE"

For a long time past Mallow had been turning over in his mind the scheme of a new novel upon which he was most anxious to commence work. But now that Mrs. Carson had called upon him to aid her to the solution of the many mysteries by which she seemed to be surrounded, he was obliged to put all thought of it from him. With all the energy he could command he threw himself into the business on hand. Here was a romance in real life surpassing the most elaborate inventions of fiction. It was his task to round it off to a satisfactory finish. And this was not easy. Of actual fact he had but little to guide him. Neither could he hope to extract much from those chiefly concerned. He was forced to grope his way in well-nigh utter darkness. Only by the light of fresh material yet to be gathered would he be able to use to advantage that which was already at his command. And of procuring such fresh material he saw but small chance at present. Here, as in most things, it was the first step which was so important. He inclined to think that two heads were better than one. From Sandbeach he had written at some length to his friend Aldean, telling him all that had taken place there, and how he had shifted Olive's troubles (so far as he was able) on to his own more capable shoulders. The result was that Aldean came up to London almost immediately, and presented himself at Mallow's chambers in Half-Moon Street, full of curiosity and anxiety to assist in the crusade against Carson and Company. In substantiation of his belief in the old proverb, Mallow accepted his offer. Here was another head, at all events, if not an exceptionally brilliant one. And so Aldean took up his quarters at his house in Kensington, and prepared himself for an exciting time.

"It is good of you, Jim," said Mallow, at their first meeting. "I know you would much rather be at Casterwell playing with Amaryllis in the shade, according to your habit."

"Amaryllis comes to London next week," replied Jim, with something of a blush. "Mrs. Purcell has invited her."

"Oh, in that case your patience will not be put to so great a test. Has Mrs. Purcell arrived?"

"Yes, she is in town now, settled in a friend's house which she has taken over for the winter. Miss Slarge showed me a long Johnsonian missive, in which Mrs. Purcell stated she was 'elevating her shingle' in Guelph Road, Campden Hill."

"And how, may I ask, did Mrs. Purcell translate 'elevating her shingle' into English?"

"Oh, I can't remember the old lady's long-winded sentences, but she is now in Guelph Road. Miss Slarge, with Miss Ostergaard, comes up next week. Of course, Mrs. Purcell knows nothing of Mrs. Carson's matrimonial troubles, or I dare say she would have asked her too."

"She must ask her," said Mallow, hastily. "I shall call on Mrs. Purcell, and explain the circumstances. It will never do for Mrs. Carson to be left alone in her troubles."

"Take care, Mallow; your interest in Mrs. Carson may be misconstrued."

"Oh, rubbish! Mrs. Purcell is a woman of sense, I am sure. So long as I keep my own counsel, she can say nothing. I want Mrs. Carson to revert, as much as possible, to the condition of affairs before this unhappy marriage. When all this mystery is cleared up, she will be able to start fresh."

"That will depend, of course, mainly upon the identity of this man Carson," said Aldean.

"Nothing of the sort," contradicted Mallow, sharply, but wincing all the same; "whatever he is she is his wife—there's no getting past that fact."

"She may get a divorce. Carson's gone off with that girl."

"Quite so; but he has not so far treated her with cruelty, and— well, you know the idiotcy of the D.C. For Heaven's sake, Jim, drop Mrs. Carson."

"All right," assented Aldean. "I see your nerves are jumpy on that subject. Let's get to the matters in hand. About this Carson mess; what do you think of it?"

"A big business, Jim; a nasty painful business, with a strong element of criminality it it. Of course it is all very vague and confused on the surface, but beneath, I am convinced, there is a very orderly and well-constructed conspiracy progressing."

Mallow sat down and lighted his pipe. "Now, let us look at the facts," he said. "There can be no doubt that Semberry forced that girl on Mrs. Carson as a spy. Carson, too, must have known her before he came to Casterwell, or he would not have been meeting her on the quiet so soon after she came there. She overheard my conversation with her mistress in the sitting-room of the hotel (unfortunately it was not till I was about to leave that I noticed she had left the bedroom door ajar, or I would have closed it). However, she lost no time in reporting what she had heard to 49, Poplar Street, which, you understand, is the same address that Drabble gave me as his own. That, I consider, brings him into the business. Then she bolted to join Carson in Florence; that I think is proved by the envelope which I found in the grate of her bedroom. These are the main facts."

"And you really think that Drabble is in the swindle?"

"I do, from the fact of that address, and also from this wrist-button turning up; so far as we know, he could only have got it from Carson. That would seem to show that he knew Carson somewhere before he came to Casterwell. Presents argue a certain degree of intimacy."

"That is one view," said Jim, quickly, "but there is another. If Carson is a fraud, you may be sure that it was the real man who was murdered in Athelstane Place. The sandal-wood scent forms a link between the true and the false."

"Well, admitting that, even then the wrist-button must have passed through the false Carson's hands to reach Drabble. We have nothing to lead us to suppose that the doctor had anything to do with the murder."

"Humph! The papers said, you remember, that only a surgeon could have amputated the right hand so neatly."

"That is a wild theory," said Mallow. "Let us stick to the facts. Whoever Carson may be, you forget we have yet to prove him an impostor. The one thing we are sure of is that Clara Trall was a spy."

"Do you intend questioning Semberry about her?"

"No, that would put him on his guard at once. I shall go to Amelia Street, and see this Mrs. Arne."

"The same thing applies to her, surely?"

"No. I shall merely call on Mrs. Carson's behalf to inform her that Clara left her mistress's service without warning of any kind, and ask her if she can throw any light on her eccentric behaviour. It is quite natural Mrs. Carson should wish to know. I shall thus throw the onus of any explanation on her."

"She will only lie to you. She may not even do that,—probably she will express her very great regret, and confess her inability to understand it."

"Well, of course, that is probable. I must chance it. She may let fall something of value."

Aldean put on his hat and coat. "So you intend to begin with this clue?" he asked dubiously.

"Well, I think it is the most likely to bear fruit."

"And what about the murder?" asked Aldean.

Mallow pointed to a neat pile of newspaper cuttings. "I am refreshing my memory on that point. But, for the present, I think I shall leave it alone. We have not yet anything sufficiently strong to connect Carson with it. That sandal-wood is not enough. I believe in going slowly and relying on facts only."

"Well, old man, good-bye and good luck," said Lord Aldean. "See you again soon;" and he took himself off to transact some small business of his own.

The same afternoon Mallow dressed himself smartly and strolled down to Kensington through the park. Without any difficulty he found Amelia Street. It proved to be in the centre of a fashionable locality, and its inhabitants were evidently people of wealth. As he mounted the steps of No. 30 he could not help wondering at Mrs. Arne's connection with the very shady matter he had in hand. For the moment the clue did not look promising.

"Is Mrs. Arne at home?" he asked the footman who came to the door.

"Mrs. Arne, sir?" said the man with a stare; "I know no one of that name, sir."

Mallow felt a sudden shock of surprise at the unexpectedness of the answer. "But this is Mrs. Arne's house, surely?" he asked hastily.

"No, sir," replied the man, "Mr. Dacre lives here."

"Is Mr. Dacre in?" demanded Laurence, after a few moment's reflection.

"He is not, sir; Mr. Dacre is at present out of town, sir. Mrs. Dacre is at home, sir."

"In that case, please give her my card, and ask her if she will be so good as to see me for a few moments."

The footman departed, and shortly returning conducted Mallow upstairs to a magnificently furnished drawing-room, where he was received by a pretty, though vulgar-looking woman, shrill of speech and horribly over-dressed. At a glance Mallow guessed she had become possessed of unlimited cash late in life. Mr. Dacre had probably made a fortune in the rapid manner which is characteristic of our latter days, and his wife was now in the throes of acclimatization to her altered circumstances. In all directions there was copious evidence of a huge banking-account.

"Mr. Mallow," said Mrs. Dacre, assuming a dignity which suited her not at all, and looking at his card through an eye-glass.

"Yes, I have taken the liberty of calling upon you to ask you if you know anything of a Mrs. Arne who lived here."

Mrs. Dacre looked at him in surprise. "I do, and I do not know Mrs. Arne. She is hardly an acquaintance of mine; I only know her as a dressmaker."

"A dressmaker?" repeated Mallow, with a gasp.

"She is not really even that," continued the voluble lady—"pray be seated Mr. Mallow. Mrs. Arne is, in fact, a person who goes out sewing. She was recommended to me as an intelligent needlewoman by one of my friends. As I wished some costumes altered, I employed her for a few weeks."

"Is she here now, Mrs. Dacre?"

"Oh dear no. She finished her work, and I dismissed her some weeks ago."

"Do you happen to have her address?"

"No, indeed, I have not. What should I do with such a person's address. I engaged the woman; she did my bidding; I dismissed her. I am not likely ever to see her again. May I ask (this with increasing stateliness) if this person is a friend of yours?"

"No, I have not even seen her," replied Mallow, hastily; "but a lady friend of mine in the country requires a maid, and she heard that Mrs. Arne had one for whom she wished to find a situation."

Mrs. Dacre grew scarlet with anger. "Absurd—ridiculous!" she burst out. "Why, Mrs. Arne was quite a common person; clever with her needle, I admit, and quite respectful. But the idea of her recommending a maid!"

"Nevertheless she did so," said Mallow, taking a delight in touching upon the weak spot of the purse-proud little lady. "My friend wrote to Mrs. Arne at this address, and received this reply." As Mrs. Dacre's eyes, through the medium of her double glasses, fell on the letter which Mallow placed in her hand, she almost screeched.

"My own paper," she gasped, "the hussy! she must have stolen it. Clara Trall?—she recommends Clara Trall, a creature of whom I have never heard as a good maid—a maid! Oh! and she herself a sewing-woman too; a common, vulgar dressmaker. Mr. Mallow, Mr. Mallow, what are the lower orders coming to?"

"That is a very large question, Mrs. Dacre. At present, perhaps we had better confine ourselves to this one. Do you happen to know a Major Semberry?"

"No, I never heard of him."

"Did Mrs. Arne ever mention him?"

"Not that I know of. But, of course, I spoke but little to her. I will say she knew how to hold her tongue. Did Major Semberry know her?"

"I believe so. At all events, he gave my friend this address as Mrs. Arne's."

"And he a major too! Upon my word, it doesn't sound at all respectable. 'Enry (she lost her h's simultaneously with her temper)—'Enry shall know of this. Mrs. Arne recommending maids from our 'ouse on my writing-paper."

Mallow shrugged his shoulders. He had got all the information he was likely to get, so he prepared to take his leave. Mrs. Dacre was too intent upon her own grievance to attempt to stop him. At the door (whither she followed him) he asked her one more question.

"What was Mrs. Arne like, Mrs. Drace? Can you give me any description of her appearance?"

"A dark, foreign-looking person, with eyes always on the floor, and a tread like a cat. I think she was a foreigner, for all her English. Never, never shall a foreigner enter these doors again."

Mallow bowed himself out, stopping at the door for a word with the smart footman. "Mrs. Arne was in this house for some time, your mistress tells me; how is it you did not tell me so?"

"I've only been here a week, sir," replied the man. Mallow gave him a shilling and went off.

"A dark, foreign-looking woman," he repeated. "Strange again! that is very much like the description the newspapers give of the housekeeper at Athelstane Place. And Semberry knows her, and Carson of Casterwell is Semberry's bosom friend. Humph! I shouldn't be surprised if the murdered man was the real Carson after all!"

CHAPTER II

"MRS. PURCELL"

After his interview with Mrs. Dacre, Mallow's first impulse was to see Semberry and tax him with the deception he had practised upon Olive. But he was not a man who gave way to his impulses. He quickly realized that to do that at this stage would simply be to put the Major on his guard. Plainly he was connected in some way with Mrs. Arne, and it seemed more than likely, from the description of her given by Mrs. Dacre, that this so-called dressmaker was identical with the so-called housekeeper of Athelstane Place. In dealing with people so astute and so dangerous, Mallow saw that his only chance lay in gaining their confidence in some way. His next move must be to see Drabble, if necessary, in the character of a convert to his views. The doctor's vanity would be flattered, and in his enthusiasm he would not hesitate to welcome him as a member of the band. Once let him become acquainted with the schemes of these Anarchists, and he might hope for much knowledge which, by any other means, would be unattainable. The risk was considerable, that he knew well—for thus to connect himself with a set of fearless fanatics, was to play with fire with a vengeance. Once the oath taken, he was the tool of these ruffians; if he broke it—and that might be necessary for Olive's sake—he became their prey. He had no fancy to be blown to pieces or to be stabbed in the dark. But that was a risk he must perforce accept if he was to carry the thing through. He decided to take it, and affiliate himself with the brotherhood. His mind made up on that point, he found himself even looking forward with a certain thrill of excitement to the risks he was about to run. Plainly speaking, he was a spy venturing into an unknown land of snares and pitfalls. The least false step might prove fatal, not only to his hopes, but to his life. However, before actually involving himself, he called on Mrs. Purcell. He was anxious to tell her all about Olive, and to induce her to take the girl under her protection for the time being. He presented himself at Campden Hill one afternoon about five o'clock, and was graciously received by the old lady, with whom he was an especial favourite. Tui and Miss Slarge had already arrived, and were established there as Mrs. Purcell's guests, but Olive was still at Sandbeach. She shunned meeting even Tui and Miss Slarge. She knew that they would ask questions which would necessitate her explaining the invidious position in which she was placed. They were still under the impression that her husband was with her, and wondered why the happy pair did not return to the Manor House. On this point Mallow preserved a judicious silence for the present, though he had fully made up his mind to take Mrs. Purcell into his confidence. That would be necessary in order to enlist her sympathies for Olive, and to carry out his purpose. The subject was a delicate one, and would require careful handling.

A majestic female was Mrs. Purcell, with a haughty eye and a Roman nose. She was as stout as her sister was lean, and was draped with funereal pomp in silk and crape, and ornaments of glistening jet. She moved slowly and spoke slowly, and she modelled her speech on the best traditions of her hero, Dr. Johnson. Her looks were monumental, her conversations ponderous. She resembled the ideal Britannia—without, be it said, helmet or trident—in domestic life. She had flippantly been compared to Gibbon's "Decline and Fall," and, indeed, there was something of the epic about her, awe-inspiring and stately. She had never made or enjoyed a joke in her life. Pallas, Lady Macbeth, Hannah More— Mrs. Purcell was a combination of all three.

"Mr. Mallow," she said, bearing down on the visitor with full canvas, "I am glad to welcome you to my temporary hearth. With my sister, as with the vivacious Miss Ostergaard, you are already acquainted. We expect Lord Aldean, but for the time being our circle is limited, as you observe."

Mallow greeted the two ladies.

"And how is your book getting on?"

The authoress sighed.

"Only moderately well, Mr. Mallow," she said wearily. "I am at present employed in identifying the Etruscan lituus with the Pontifical crosier, and some of the accounts are so contradictory that it is not easy to reconcile them."

"How is Olive?" demanded Tui, irrelevantly. "Is she well and happy?"

"Is not that a superfluous question, under the circumstances?" replied Mallow, evasively.

Tui looked at him.

"Hardly, or I would not have asked it. On the contrary, her letters give me a different impression. I fear from them that she does not get on well with her husband."

"'Tis difficult," observed Mrs. Purcell, who had returned to the

97

tea-table, "for a newly-married pair to live in complete accord with one another. The effect of their respective trainings has to be taken into account, and only the influence of time, coupled with forbearance on either side, can adapt the idiosyncrasies of one to those of the other. Olive has been reared in our island home, Mr. Carson has not. Therefore it is not unlikely that they experience some difficulty in blending their respective dispositions into one harmonious whole."

"East is east, and west is west," said Mallow, "and two parallel straight lines cannot meet."

"Let us hope that, in this case, judicious yielding on the part of each of these young people will create an exception to the invariable truth of that axiom, Mr. Mallow. Can I give you a dish of tea?"

"Thank you, Mrs. Purcell. Ah, here comes our mutual friend."

Aldean entered. He was welcomed by Mrs. Purcell with all the pomp she considered due to a member of the nobility.

Tui was joyous. "I thought you were never coming," she said. "I see that it is out 'of sight, out of mind' with you."

"By Jove! I wish it were," sighed Jim; "I should be a happier man."

"Oh, surely I don't make you miserable?"

"Never mind; it is misery I would not be without. Tell me, how is Major Semberry?"

"Good gracious, Lord Aldean, how should I know? I have not seen him for years."

"'Tis to be hoped that you will not again come into contact with Major Semberry," said Mrs. Purcell, wagging her turban; "he is not a suitable acquaintance for a young lady."

"No, I am quite sure he is not," assented Aldean; upon which Tui at once took up arms on behalf of the absent.

"Major Semberry is the most charming of men," she declared, with a pout.

"The serpent," rebuked Mrs. Purcell, "is ever beautiful to the eye but unfortunately is possessed of noxious qualities which far exceed his beauty. Rubina, in my letter to you I think I stated my opinion of Major Semberry. From that opinion I have seen no reason to depart."

"In plain English, Mrs. Purcell, you consider Semberry a rascal?"

"Mr. Mallow, I consider him a profligate and an undesirable acquaintance. How Dr. Carson came to entrust his son to such a man I cannot understand."

"They got on very well together."

"Then the one or the other must have changed very much, Lord Aldean. In Bombay, Mr. Carson was by no means friendly with his travelling companion. His rigid sense of right and wrong did not allow him to countenance Major Semberry's laxity of principle."

"You like Mr. Carson?" asked Mallow, quickly.

"My acquaintance with him was not of sufficient duration to enable me to speak quite so definitely as that, but I consider Mr. Carson to be an admirably conducted young man, calculated to render any woman happy in the matrimonial state."

"Oh, lor!" muttered Jim; "how he must have altered!"

"Well," said Tui, outright, "I don't like Mr. Carson at all. I never did."

"You surprise me," said Mrs. Purcell, in her most majestic manner. "My judgment is seldom at fault, and I considered Mr. Carson, when I saw him in Bombay, to be the type of all that is most excellent in the male sex."

The discussion had not the remotest interest for Miss Slarge. Indeed, she had already drifted back to Babylon. Observing vaguely that the great red dragon of Revelations was the fiery serpent of Chaldean worship, she left the room to return to her beloved studies, and Mrs. Purcell was left with her three guests. Lord Aldean was carried off by Tui to a distant corner where she could torment him without fear of interruption, and Mallow at once seized the opportunity for a talk with his hostess about Olive. It took all Mrs. Purcell's philosophy to hear unmoved his tale of Carson's treachery.

"Mrs. Purcell," said Mallow, plunging at once in medias res, "you are aware that I have known Mrs. Carson for many years, and that I take a deep interest in her welfare. I am sorry to tell you that she is very unhappy in her marriage."

"Did she inform you of this fact?" said Mrs. Purcell, with some displeasure.

"She did. I received a letter from her asking me to go to Sandbeach, where she was spending her honeymoon. On arriving there I found that her husband had left her."

"Mr. Carson has left Olive!"

"Yes; he is now in Italy, and, I believe, with another woman."

"You amaze me, Mr. Mallow; I may say, you pain me. What is the meaning of this terrible state of affairs?"

"Ah! that is a difficult question for me to answer. My only way of doing so is to tell you all that I have learned concerning Mr. Carson and Major Semberry, and leave you to judge for yourself."

"That will be best, Mr. Mallow. I shall then be enabled to deliver my unbiassed judgment."

Thereupon Laurence related all that had taken place since Carson's arrival at Casterwell, and particularly detailed the steps which had led to the engagement of Clara Trall.

"So you see, Mrs. Purcell," he concluded, "she can hardly help being unhappy. Her husband has left her, and has taken her money—to spend it, I presume, on another woman. She is now alone and worried, at Sandbeach. I want you to ask her up here and take her under your wing. She needs a friend. You will be that friend?"

"You may depend upon my doing what is just and right," said Mrs. Purcell, vigorously. "I will communicate with Olive at once; yes, and I will invite her to come here. That Mr. Carson should behave so basely is a matter of the most profound astonishment to me. I had read his character otherwise. I can but ascribe this deterioration to the counsel and wiles of Major Semberry."

"That is one way of explaining it," said Mallow, taking out his pocket-book; "but there is yet another and more conclusive one. This is a portrait which Mr. Carson had taken at Sandbeach. May I ask you to look at it carefully, and to tell me what you think of it?"

Mrs. Purcell took the photograph and examined it.

"This is either an extremely bad portrait, or Mr. Carson has altered sadly for the worse," she said at length.

Mallow felt his heart beating furiously.

"In what way has Mr. Carson altered?" he asked, anxiously.

"Oh, his whole expression is quite different, Mr. Mallow. When last I saw him, Mr. Carson's face was replete with intellectual vigour; he was sad and sombre, too, not bright and smiling as he is depicted here. His moustache was very much heavier, and he certainly was not so tall as this picture represents him to be."

"It would not surprise you then, Mrs. Purcell, if I were to tell you that this was not Mr. Carson's portrait at all?"

"No, Mr. Mallow, it would not. At first glance, I did not notice many things that appear to me as I look into it. Mr. Carson's face may, of course, have changed. The circumstances of his life may have caused his expression to brighten. It is possible, too, that his moustache may be of less luxuriant growth, but I confess I do not understand how he can have become less of stature. No, Mr. Mallow, the man here represented is not Mr. Angus Carson!"

100

CHAPTER III

"A PRIVATE INQUIRY AGENT"

The same evening Laurence had a long and confidential conversation with Mrs. Purcell. He made known to her all his suspicions and theories, and the grounds upon which he based them. She listened attentively to all he had to say. Then she read through the newspaper reports, and once again scrutinized the portrait of Carson taken at Sandbeach. She prided herself upon the possession of a clear head and a logical mind, and she brought both to bear upon the case as Mallow presented it to her. She arrived at the conclusion that Carson was an actual impostor and a probable murderer—a stage further than that at which Mallow had been able to arrive.

"If you believe, as I do, that the man is an impostor," she argued, "surely he must be guilty of the murder also, else how could he have become possessed of the bangle and the wrist-buttons?"

"But, Mrs. Purcell, I cannot absolutely prove that he is an impostor, even though I firmly believe him to be one."

"Sir!" said the lady in her most impressive tone, "our human judgments are fallible, I admit, but with such evidence as is before us, there can be no possible doubt that the husband of Olive is not the man whose name he bears. She herself does not believe in him, and her reasons are in every respect sound; his dealings with her money, for instance; his silence regarding his early days in Hindoostan; his use of his right hand on several occasions when he forgot the part he was playing. The letter from Italy, too, is of great weight, seeing that the writer of it also wrote to the woman Trall. That is proved by the handwriting, which is in all respects identical. The letter to his wife, the man might possibly have dictated, but the peculiarly private nature of that which he wrote to the girl makes it highly improbable that any hand save his own was instrumental in penning it. Moreover, this is no left-handed writing, the letters are far too firmly formed. The right hand of the man must, therefore, have been uninjured, which again proves that he was an impostor. Now, although I am not actually prepared to swear in a court of law that this portrait is not the portrait of Mr. Angus Carson, yet I feel quite satisfied in my own mind that it is not, for the reasons which I have already given you."

101

"You make out an excellent case against him, Mrs. Purcell," said Mallow, "but it is only right to say that the man did know something about India."

"Naturally," she interrupted, "he would obtain whatever information was necessary for his purpose from his friend, Major Semberry."

"Then you agree with me in making Semberry an accessory?"

"Certainly. You know my opinion of Major Semberry, Mr. Mallow. He is a man utterly without conscience, without scruple, without religion. He cultivates the most extravagant tastes, while possessing means insufficient to gratify them. To place himself beyond the pinch of poverty I am convinced that he would hesitate at no crime—so long, of course, as he saw his way clear to avert the consequences."

"Well," said Laurence, "there is one method of throwing light on the matter which I would like to propose; it is that you permit me to bring Semberry here to you that you may tax him with this fraud to his face, and in my presence."

"By all means do so, Mr. Mallow. You may depend upon my acting with all discretion. In the mean time I will communicate with Olive at Sandbeach, and invite her to come to me as soon as she can. And, Mr. Mallow, permit me cordially to thank you for the infinite pains at which you have been to place me completely in possession of the facts of this very terrible matter. Together we will go into it, and see whether we cannot unravel what at present appears to be a mystery of the most complex order. Good-night, Mr. Mallow, good-night."

"Good-bye, Mrs. Purcell. I am afraid we shall find our task no light one."

"Not light, perhaps, but not impossible; and what is not impossible is always possible, is it not, Mr. Mallow?"

With this consolatory truism Mrs. Purcell dismissed her coadjutor and addressed herself to the task of writing to Olive. She did not tell her how much she knew of her story, but merely that she was aware of her husband having deserted her. She invited her to come at once to London, and urged the advantage of her being on the spot while affairs were being investigated. Mrs. Purcell rejoiced in her character of dea ex machinâ and poured forth pages of ponderous English such as would have done credit to the conduct of a political intrigue. The rôle appealed to her. She imagined herself a true Madame de Staël. Mallow could have chosen no better assistant.

He got no sleep that night. His mind was full of his projected visit to Semberry. In the morning he started off for Marquis Street, but found that, early as it was, Semberry had already gone out—on business, according to his valet, though as to the nature of the business the man maintained complete ignorance. Leaving word that he would return about one o'clock, Mallow wandered about aimlessly, until, bethinking himself that he was wasting valuable time, he determined to try his luck in Soho, and look up Drabble. He had no sooner turned into Poplar Street, than he came face to face with Semberry. Judging from his expression, the Major was in no very good tune. It was more than probable he had been calling upon Drabble, and the interview had not been to his liking.

"Good-morning, Semberry," said Mallow, blocking the way, "I'm glad to see you."

"Morning," he grunted, and made as to pass, a move which Mallow soon thwarted.

"I see you're in a hurry," he said amiably, "so I'll just walk a bit of the way with you. There is a friend of yours most anxious to renew your acquaintance."

"Very kind of him; who is he?"

"It is not a he, but a she—Mrs. Purcell of Bombay."

As was his custom when nervous, the Major's fingers sought his moustache.

"Oh, Mrs. Purcell," he said, with a desperate effort to appear at his ease, "what does she want?"

"To see you—and Carson, if you can bring him."

"Nothing to do with Carson now—better ask his wife 'bout him. As to m'self, no time to hang round old woman—leavin' town."

"Mrs. Purcell will be very sorry," said Laurence, smoothly. "Are you going abroad?"

"Don't know; depends. What makes you think so?"

"Well, I fancied perhaps you might be anxious to join Carson."

"Join Carson?" He stopped short and paled a trifle. "What do y' mean? Carson's on his honeymoon."

"Oh no, he isn't," retorted Mallow. "Carson's honeymoon is at an end; has been for two weeks or more. He is in Italy now."

"In Italy? Damme, how d'you know that?"

"Well, about a week ago he wrote to his wife from Florence. It would seem he has gone abroad to look after the money of which he has become possessed by his marriage."

"What! You don't tell me he's got the money with him?"

103

"I believe so. Mrs. Carson heard from the solicitor that he had sold the stocks and shares, to a large amount, and had transferred the funds to the Paris branch of the Crédit Lyonnais."

With effort Semberry repressed himself. A string of forcible epithets was obviously on the tip of his tongue. Although he was probably aware that Carson had left Sandbeach, it was evidently news to the Major that he and the money were together on the continent.

"Seems Carson and his wife don't pull," was all he said.

"I fear not," said Mallow, coolly. "In spite of the old adage, Carson seems to have preferred the maid to the mistress."

"What d'ye mean?" growled the Major, tugging savagely now at his moustache.

"I mean that the girl Clara Trall has joined Carson in Florence."

"It's a lie! She wouldn't dare——" Here the Major evidently thought he had said more than enough, for he stopped short.

"I am not accustomed to be told I am a liar, sir!"

"Beg pardon, Mallow; excuse, slip o' the tongue."

"And why should Clara Trall not dare?"

"Don't know," replied Semberry, uneasily; "shouldn't think a maid would dare clear out with her mistress's husband."

"I am afraid Clara is a bad lot, Major. Why did you recommend her?"

"Didn't. Mrs. Arne did."

"Who is Mrs. Arne?"

"Friend o' mine," snapped the Major, shortly. "'Scuse me, must be getting on. Kind regards to Mrs. Purcell. See her when I get back;" and the brave soldier, picking up his guilty conscience, under fire of Mallow's too-searching questions, fairly ran away.

Mallow decided to postpone his visit to Drabble. He had gained nothing of value from his brisk little interview with the Major. On the contrary, he feared he had given away a very definite piece of information, for he felt convinced that an hour ago Semberry had been ignorant of the fact that Carson and Clara were in Florence. He was fearful lest he should have aroused his suspicions in any way. He might, perchance, act upon the knowledge he had just obtained. Mallow determined he would have him watched. There and then he proceeded to a private inquiry office, of which he had informed himself in case of need. He asked for an agent to be placed at his disposal. The payment of a sum down secured this without difficulty, and in due course a personage—said by his employers to

104

be one of the cleverest detectives in Europe—was told off to serve him.

In appearance, Hiram Vraik—for that was the man's name— might well have passed for one of the worst of the class he was employed in pursuing. He was assuredly a most villainous-looking creature. He was exceedingly small, and lithe as a ferret, his face was white and pasty, his ears were enormous, and his eyes red-rimmed as those of a rat. His crop would have done justice to any prison barber. He approached Mallow with a cringing, slimy politeness, which, coupled with his appearance, made him doubly repulsive. However, argued Mallow, dirty work needs dirty tools.

"I want you to watch a man," he said, when he had got Vraik to himself in the parlour of a public-house near at hand. "Here are his name and address. Now, listen, and I'll tell you all about it."

"Yes, sir; it's best to trust me all in all, sir. If I know everything I can do as much as any man, but if I don't—well, sir, I may as well hand you back your money straight off."

As he proceeded to relate the details of the case to Vraik, the little man's eyes lit up, and he became more rat-like than ever.

"It's a big job," he said. "But I'm your man, sir; and if I get there with it I'll expect to be mighty well paid."

"Oh, you'll be paid well enough, I promise you that," replied Mallow.

"Very good, sir; I know what I've got to do, and I'd better go and do it. Whatever this Major does, and wherever he goes, you shall know. I'll lose no time as soon as I've got anything to report. Whew! The Athelstane Place business! I am in luck!" And Vraik wriggled himself off.

CHAPTER IV

"ONE OF US"

"So, at last, you come to us!" roared Drabble, rubbing his hands.

"As you see," answered Mallow, equably; "though for me it is a leap in the dark."

"Never mind, man; there'll be plenty of light soon."

"Yes, the light of infernal machines and incendiary fires, I presume," retorted the neophyte.

Drabble rubbed his hands again and winked devilishly. "You shall know all our schemes as soon as you are fit to know them," said he, significantly.

"When will that be, may I ask?"

"Of that Madame Death-in-Life must judge."

"Oh, I thought you did not know that lady?"

"Nor do I—in Casterwell. In Soho it is quite another matter."

They were in a dingy, mean room of the upper story of No. 49, Poplar Street, Soho—a neighbourhood notorious for Anarchists— and pickles. Any longings after wealth were ruthlessly repressed here. A deal table, a few chairs, a bookcase filled with revolutionary literature, and fiery pamphlets in every European tongue, and a ragged chintz-covered sofa, with a hard and suspiciously round-looking pillow, was all the room contained by way of luxury. The dirty floor boasted no carpet or covering of any kind, and the iron shutters, by which the solitary window was protected, and a brace of revolvers reposing on the mantelshelf, added in no way to the cosiness of the apartment. In all the force of blacklead and whitewash the walls displayed fierce denunciations of many things, more particularly of the various forms of law and order. Dust was over everything, and in the corners cobwebs abounded. The triumph of Anarchy was here again the apotheosis of the unwashed—the worship of the sansculottes.

Mallow contrasted strangely with these surroundings. Near him lounged the doctor, sleek and pale, and still clothed in his invariable black. But this was not the hearty, would-be-genial doctor of Casterwell, but a savage, angry, vicious, Anarchical doctor, drunk with copious inhalations of the atmosphere around him—the atmosphere of organized disorder, of crime and ruffianism and bribery. This was the real Drabble. He was at home here. No one would have known him, save perhaps his wife. Mallow, as he looked at him, found himself pitying her. The sheer abandonment of the man revolted him.

"Well, and how are the turtle-doves getting on?" he asked vulgarly.

"If you are speaking of Mr. and Mrs. Carson," replied Mallow, "they have parted, I believe, and Carson has gone off to Italy."

"H'm," growled Drabble. "As a matter of fact Semberry told me so. The maid Clara has joined him, I hear."

106

"It is highly probable. Carson is a blackguard."

"He is worse than that, Mallow; he is a thief. I understand he has gone off with his wife's money."

Now it was quite clear to Mallow, that for "wife's money" he might with safety substitute "our share of the plunder;" but for the present he must keep that to himself. It did not do to be foolhardy, especially at No. 49, Poplar Street. So he gave the doctor no hint.

"Perhaps the word 'thief' is a trifle strong, doctor," was all he said. "After all, it is more a question of conscience—or, rather, lack of it—than anything else. No man with a spark of decency would have taken advantage of a position which gave him full possession of his wife's money, by virtue of the mere fact of her being his wife. Blackguard—my word—is I think the more applicable."

"He is a fool," said Drabble, fiercely; "but let him take care. I am not to be trifled with. I wonder what Trall will say to his niece bolting with Carson?"

"Oh," said Mallow, recalling Clara's letter; "then there is such a person as Jeremiah Trall."

"Of course there is; he is one of us. But how did you know him?"

"Mrs. Carson told me," remarked Mallow, carelessly. "Clara used to talk about her uncle."

"The fool!" muttered Drabble. "I always said that girl was not to trusted."

"Not to be trusted?" echoed Mallow. "Then she, too, is one of us?"

The doctor looked at him with something approaching a scowl. "Your wisest plan," he said, "is to ask no questions in this place."

"But you forget I am quite uninitiated yet," retorted Mallow. "I don't care about committing myself to a definite course unless I am quite sure what I am about."

"Do you know what the Jesuits do with their pupils?" asked Drabble, irrelevantly.

"Yes, as a rule, they make scoundrels of them."

"Rather say they make machines of them—machines: because they are blindly obedient to those set in authority over them. That is one of their rules. It is one of ours also. Once you join us, you neither think for yourself nor act for yourself, you become a machine."

"And if I transgress?"

"Once you have taken our oaths I don't think you will care to do

107

that," rejoined the doctor, coldly. "If you do—well, I won't answer for the consequences."

"Are you a machine, Drabble?"

"No; I am one having authority. I direct—others execute."

"Really!" said Mallow. "And you fancy that a man of my capacity and experience will consent to become your tool. Understand, then, Drabble, if I join you I must know your ends, your aims, your ways, and your means. I also must be one having authority. On no other conditions will I join you. To speak plainly, I do not quite see why you want me. It is not for my money, for I possess none. It is not for my influence or my position, for what I have of either is not likely to serve you. I can only conclude, then, that it is in an intellectual capacity I am likely to be of use to you; yet you propose to place me in a position subservient to your own. No, my friend," and Mallow stood up, "if it is a fool you want, go out into the streets and choose. If you want a man, and a man with brains, I am ready; but I claim to be treated with the respect which is my due. If you cannot assure me that this will be, I must bid you good-day."

"Sit down, my dear fellow," said Drabble, hastily; "you know one cannot generalize in these sort of things, and that is what you have been doing. I quite agree with all you say, generally speaking. But whether it will apply to you individually, it is impossible to decide for the moment. Rest assured that you will have every opportunity of exercising your capacity. Ours is not a system of government under which the clever man is repressed."

"Government?" said Mallow. "I always understood that no government was the very essence of your being!"

"A common fallacy," replied the doctor, dryly, "on the part of many who misunderstand our aims. There is considerable method in our so-called madness. But Madame Death-in-Life will explain all this to you far better than I can. We shall see her very shortly."

As he spoke a distinctive rap came at the door, and on the invitation to enter being given by Drabble, a tall, bulky man, shabbily dressed, with a puffy red face, entered the room. His whole appearance was suggestive of alcohol in a severe form; but at his first words, Mallow recognized that he was a man of breeding. For the present he was quite sober, and he appeared to be in a bad temper—probably, Mallow thought, as a result of his unwonted condition.

"I beg your pardon, Drabble," he said in a refined voice, "I did not know you were——"

"Oh, I am not engaged to the extent of excluding you," said Drabble, sharply. "This is Mr. Jeremiah Trall, Mr. Mallow."

"Mr. Mallow?" echoed Trall, with a stare. (It was evident to Mallow that his thoughts straightway reverted to the report he had received from Clara.)

"A new recruit," explained Drabble, looking at him sharply. "But Mr. Mallow wishes to be quite sure of our aims before he finally consents to join us."

"Our aims are to make a heaven out of a hell," said Trall, taking the third chair. "That requires strong measures."

"Necessarily," replied Mallow; "one doesn't clean stables with rosewater."

"No, our methods are a trifle more forcible than that," chuckled Trall. "When we try this new——"

"There, there," interrupted Drabble, "that is quite enough. We will not go into details just at present."

Mallow could see even thus early that there was no love lost between these two. The alcoholic man scowled angrily at the doctor, and Mallow made a mental note of his attitude. He evidently stood in fear of his superior.

"What is it you want?" asked Drabble, after having reduced the man to silence.

"Madame wishes to see you," replied Trall, sulkily. "She did not know any one was with you."

"I am bringing this gentleman down to see her very shortly," said the doctor coolly. "You can go."

"One moment," cried Mallow, as Trall shuffled to his feet. "Have I ever seen you before?"

"Not that I know of."

"H'm. Your face seems familiar to me."

"Yes, it is the face of a sot," said Drabble, brutally—"not an uncommon sight."

"I have to thank you for making it so," stuttered Trall savagely. "I should not be what I am had I not come under your thumb. But take care, I may be one too many for you some day."

"This is not the first time you have threatened me," said Drabble; "take you care lest I make it the last. You drunken hound, clear out!"

"By the way, did you get your letter from Sandbeach?" asked Mallow of Trall, as he slouched towards the door with fierce resentment in his eyes.

109

"Eh, what?" cried Drabble, looking sharply from one to the other. "What letter?"

"Oh, merely a letter from Clara, saying she was leaving Mrs. Carson," answered Trall, hastily.

"Why didn't you tell me?"

"I didn't think it worth while."

"Everything is worth while that concerns Carson," rebuked Drabble. "Where is the letter, you fool?"

"In the fire; there were only half a dozen lines. But how do you know that Clara wrote to me?" added Trall, turning to Mallow.

"Well, she happened to drop her letter when about to post it. I picked it up, and naturally I saw the name and address."

"Oh, well, it was only a little letter—a very little letter," mumbled Jeremiah, and slipped out of the room.

"Little or big," roared Drabble after him, "you bring the next one to me. Come, Mr. Mallow, let us go and see Madame."

Mallow followed the doctor along a dark passage and into another room in the front of the house. Here at a window overlooking the street sat a pale little woman with dark hair arranged smoothly in bands. She wore a plain black dress without trimming or ornament of any kind. Her pallid face was bent intently over some wool-work she was knitting. She looked up when the two men came in, and rose to her feet.

"Mrs. Arne," said Drabble graciously, "this is our new recruit, Mr. Mallow."

Mallow turned pale and felt his heart beating wildly. In this woman, introduced as Mrs. Arne, he recognized the housekeeper of Althelstane Place.

CHAPTER V

"MADAME DEATH-IN-LIFE"

As Mallow, at Drabble's elbow, stared at the demure little figure clothed in black, he realized that this was the fate controlling all things in connection with the affair he had in hand. Instantly he

110

recognized in her the newspaper descriptions of the unknown housekeeper who had vanished so mysteriously and so completely from Athelstane Place. By name she had just been made known to him as Mrs. Arne, and he now learned that she and Madame Death-in-Life—the notorious Madame Death-in-Life who was dreaded throughout Europe—were one and the same person. He was face to face with the terrible woman with the terrible nick-name, the stormy petrel of Anarchy. At the mere rumour of her presence in their city, those in authority were wont suspiciously to look about them and doubly to safeguard their rulers. The Continental police would have given much to have had her safe in Monte Valerien, or Spandau, or Siberia. Hitherto she had always evaded them at the last moment—had thwarted their most zealous endeavours and carefully laid plans. She was Italian by birth, and had married an Englishman. She was now a widow and had made her husband's country her permanent home. As she sat before him now, so peacefully knitting, Mallow thought of Madame Defarge.

"I am delighted to see you, Mr. Mallow," she said in excellent English, with but little trace of foreign accent. "I have been expecting you for some time. You can go, doctor."

"But I want to——"

"You can go, doctor," repeated Mrs. Arne in the same unemotional voice. Without another word, Drabble, the bully, stole out of the room.

Mallow was amazed.

"It is necessary to preserve discipline here," said Madame, observing his expression. "Pray be seated, Mr. Mallow. If you do not mind, I will continue my knitting."

"I do not mind at all," replied Mallow, seating himself mechanically. He watched her firm, plump hands clicking the shining needles together as she wove her web of red wool-work.

She divined his thoughts. "You wonder at my employment," she said without a smile. "It is very feminine, is it not? Not quite in keeping perhaps, you think, with my reputation? But, you see, I am turning fiction into fact."

"Madame Defarge, I suppose you mean?"

She nodded. "A wonderful character in a wonderful book. The 'Tale of Two Cities' and your Carlyle's 'Revolution' are my favourite reading. What times, what people, what glory! I had rather work with guillotines than with bombs, but" (with a shrug) "what would you? We have improved on all that. I speak your tongue well do I not?"

111

"Excellently well, Madame; you are never at a loss for a word."

"I am never at a loss for anything, my friend," returned Madame Arne composedly. "But we must get to business. Tell me, why did you look so fixedly at me when you entered the room?"

"Madame, your celebrity——"

"Tell me the truth, please."

"Well, it was your name."

"As a celebrity?"

"No, as the lady who used Mrs. Dacre's house as the means of introducing Clara Trall to Mrs. Carson."

"Ah, so you know of that. You have been making inquiries. Why?"

"Because Clara has turned out badly, and has gone off to Italy with her mistress's husband."

"Quite so; I know it."

"From Major Semberry, I presume. Is he, too——"

"He is——what I please," answered Mrs. Arne with an odd look. "We will speak of him another time. So you are the man who is in love with Mrs. Carson! Oh, don't trouble to deny it. I know it. You made inquiries about me from Mrs. Dacre—on her behalf. A man does not take up a woman's burden—not a burden of this kind—unless he has something more than a platonic interest in her welfare."

"Excuse me, Mrs. Arne, but there are other subjects we can discuss more profitably."

"As you please. The subject has no interest for me; but I may explain that I purposely went to Mrs. Dacre's in the capacity of a dressmaker, that I might answer Mrs. Carson's inquiry from a good address. I was determined that she should engage Clara."

"As a spy?"

"Yes," admitted the woman, nonchalantly, "as a spy. It was necessary that I should have Carson watched."

"But your spy has betrayed you?"

"So much the worse for her. She shall die. How or when I have not yet determined."

Mallow shuddered. The woman repelled him. There was something uncanny in her bare statement of fact. Even a suggestion of the melodramatic would have relieved her assertion of its sheer brutality. But there was not a tinge of it. She merely stated that the girl should be killed, and went on knitting.

"You are not used to these things," she continued; "death is as nothing to us. To kill or to be killed, we are always ready."

112

"Have you no fear?" gasped Mallow.

"Of the law? No."

"Of God?"

"That is a matter between Him and myself."

"Ah, well," said Laurence, recovering his self-control, "we had better perhaps avoid anything approaching a theological discussion. But tell me one thing. Who is this Carson?"

"Why, who should he be."

"Well, he might, for instance, be impersonating the unfortunate man who was murdered in Athelstane Place."

Mrs. Arne's hands never stopped. Her colour never changed. "You have imagination, I see," she observed coldly. "That is a pity. It is apt to get people into trouble."

"Oh, as to that, I have trouble enough; and now that I have determined to join you, I shall probably have a good deal more."

"That is very possible. We are hunted like rats. Why do you wish to join us?"

"God knows," said Mallow, with a shrug.

"I also know. It is because Mrs. Carson will have nothing to say to you. It is in your despair you come to us, to throw your life away."

Mallow breathed more freely now. For the moment he had been unprepared. He had no excuse ready. He had relied upon the supreme egotism and enthusiasm of Drabble to get over any difficulty as to his intentions. But here was the most excellent of reasons already provided for him by Madame Death-in-Life herself.

Silently he acquiesced. She saw in him the foolish lover—rejected, dejected, yielding to despair. Mallow's silence convinced her she was right.

"You do not speak," she said, glancing at him. "Well, there is no need for you to do so. I am usually right in my conjectures. We have to thank Mrs. Carson for providing us with a promising brother."

Mallow protested. "I am not a brother yet," said he, emphatically. "And before I become one I must ask to know your exact aims, and the means by which you hope to accomplish them."

"Our aims!" said Mrs. Arne, laying aside her work. "We have but one aim—to establish the equality of man. The rich oppress the poor. There must be no rich, no poor, no oppressed."

"That, Madame, is absolutely impossible. Arrange it as you will to-day, you will be where you were to-morrow."

"I think not," replied Mrs. Arne. "We intend that each person shall work for the general good, and that he shall be paid by the State. If he refuse to work, then neither shall he be paid nor shall

113

food be allowed to him. In the midst of plenty, he shall starve to death."

"A somewhat drastic arrangement, surely?" said Mallow.

"By no means. It is an absolutely necessary one. At any cost the lazy and the idle must be wiped out. Under such a régime no man need starve whilst he is willing to work. His life will be in his own hands."

"And it is by the hurling of bombs and such-like missives you hope to bring about your millennium?"

"Mr. Mallow, the world and its rulers will not listen to us. So long as we are what those in power choose to call good citizens' the injustice, the great wrongs under which we suffer now, will remain unaltered. If we are to be heard, we must perforce make a hearing for ourselves. Supplication is useless, hopeless. By terror alone can we wrench the attention which is our right. That is why we resort to force; that is why you hear of bombs, Mr. Mallow. For the safety of their lives even a king, an emperor, must heed us. Persistence in that direction will in the end secure to us the attention which we claim—the attention which is our right. That will be the dawn of the new era, Mr. Mallow, for we shall conquer. Till then—but there," said Madame, resuming her knitting, "I have much to do. I must leave you. I will place you in the hands of an instructor from whom you will learn everything that is needful. Then you can come to me and say if you will join us or not. I hope you will. We want men with brains and money."

"Particularly money!" said Mallow, contemptuously. He was not to be convinced by all her rhetoric.

"I do not deny it; we cannot have too much."

"Was it not a pity, then, to lose Carson and his fifty thousand pounds?"

"We have not lost it or him yet," said Mrs. Arne, with a long breath. "Think you that Italy is in the moon that my arm cannot reach him!"

"Then you did intend to have that fifty thousand!"

"I did; it was my scheme and to a point, it has been a successful one."

"In that case," said Mallow, deliberately, "Major Semberry is with you, no doubt. Without him you would have been helpless."

"Major Semberry has not taken the oath," said Mrs. Arne coldly, "but he is one of us."

"How does he reconcile that with his allegiance to his sovereign?"

114

Mrs. Arne knitted rapidly. "You don't know our power," she said. "In every grade of society we have our adherents—yes, even in your army. I was introduced into Mrs. Dacre's house by a friend of the cause. I am not a dressmaker, but it suited me to assume that capacity for the moment. I told Semberry to give Mrs. Dacre's address to Mrs. Carson. If I could not have got into that house, I should have given another address. Mrs. Carson wrote, and her letter naturally was given to me. I replied, and secured for the girl the position I designed for her. A friend in society helped me there, and there are dozens of people who can place me in any position I choose. You don't know my power. But enough of this"—she rose and pressed an electric button. "I will introduce you to Monsieur Rouge. He will instruct you. I have other things to do."

That personage was not long in making his appearance.

A mere spectre of a man was Monsieur Rouge, with complexion, hair, and eyes of a painfully washed-out hue. A cadaverous, lantern-jawed, unholy looking person. In common with the generality of workmen of his nationality—he was French— Monsieur Rouge was addicted to dark blue. He wore trousers, blouse, and peaked cap all of that colour. He had a habit, almost equine, of blinking and glancing out of the corners of his eyes. He was evidently a nervous man, and seemed but poorly fitted for the bold and daring path he had chosen to follow. Mallow was surprised at his appearance, as he was at the fact that Mrs. Arne should have chosen him for his instructor. But that lady evidently knew what she was about. After a few curt and explicit directions, conveyed to M. Rouge in his own tongue, she introduced him formally.

"Mr. Mallow," she said, "this is M. Rouge; at least, that is the name by which he is known among us. He has been a member of the brotherhood for some three years. You will find him a most enthusiastic disciple of our cause."

"Vive l'Anarchie. A bas les tyrans," whispered M. Rouge in endorsement.

"Keep your enthusiasm for a more fitting occasion, my friend," said Mrs. Arne, as Mallow thought with somewhat unnecessary severity. "Go with this gentleman, and tell him all that is permitted to be known by one who has yet to take our oath. You," turning to Mallow, "will come to me when you have made up your mind. For the present, good-bye—or, rather, au revoir."

CHAPTER VI

"ANOTHER LINK"

On the whole Mallow was interested in his Anarchistic friends. He possessed a goodly supply of the right sort of curiosity, and this new milieu in which he found himself was unlike anything he had experienced before. He was groping in an under-world of fanaticism and crime premeditated, and it fascinated him not a little. He threw himself heart and soul into the whole question, and, in company with Monsieur Rouge, explored many queer corners, East and West. For the time he made these people's cause his own. They were a small minority, determined—ruthlessly determined—on becoming a majority, and he was curious as to the methods by which they intended to accomplish their end. Of necessity he was brought into contact with many creatures of low order; creatures often needlessly ragged and unkempt, he thought. He could only conclude that their reckless condition was of value to them as a perpetual reminder of the terrible wrongs under which they suffered. But to their fiery crusade against their better-dressed neighbours, and to their bloodthirsty plans for the removal of public buildings and public personages, Mallow lent a patient and ever-attentive ear. He was surprised to find their crusade directed against the aristocracy of intellect, as well as against that other and larger aristocracy of wealth and caste. It sufficed for a man to loom large on the horizon of public affairs—be it as warrior, orator, or inventor—for him to mark the bull's-eye for their aim. They were abominably indiscriminate. In truth, with this very aptly named Monsieur Rouge at his elbow, ever ready with some fresh diabolical inspiration of his turbulent brain, Mallow could not help likening himself to a modern Dante, bent on the exploration of a new and more terrible circle of hell, with a degraded Virgil for his guide.

But, though all very fine, this was not war, as the French say, and Mallow felt he was losing sight of his purpose. Olive was in London, safe under the wing of Mrs. Purcell, waiting patiently to see what Time and his endeavours on her behalf were to bring for her. She had taken Miss Slarge and Tui into her confidence, but for her hostess she had reserved a somewhat abridged version of her recent experiences. But, with one accord, all these ladies were consumed with feminine fire and virtuous indignation against her husband. He was a downright impostor, they declared, and no doubt he it was who had murdered the unfortunate Mr. Carson. They were strenuous in their endeavours to induce Olive to put the whole matter in the hands of the police. But to this she was not to be persuaded, although she went so far as to consult Mallow upon the advisability of such a course. He speedily convinced her that the case required a manipulation much more delicate than that which it was likely to receive at the hands of the police.

"Besides," said he, "once let the police take it up, and you will have all your details, large as life, in the columns of the morning papers, to say nothing of the evening ones, than which it is difficult to conceive a more direct method of courting failure, if not disaster."

"Still, I don't know that the straightest course is not the best course, after all," said Olive, judiciously. "Why not bring Major Semberry face to face with Mrs. Purcell, and insist upon an explanation?"

"For two reasons. First, the Major is keeping out of the way. Second, he will lie like Ananias to save himself from getting into trouble. No, Mrs. Carson, let my man continue to watch him, and when he is caught tripping—as he will be, mark me, sooner or later—then will be the time to drive him into a corner."

"Can you trust this man Vraik?"

"I think so. I have promised him a large reward if he pulls the case through to my satisfaction; and he is the kind of man to sell his miserable soul for money."

"He looks like a being of the lowest type," said Olive, who had seen Vraik.

"Then he looks what he is. It is a mere accident, of course, that he is with the law instead of against it. But I dare say he finds honesty is the best possible policy, so far as cash goes, which is all that concerns him. Have no fear, Mrs. Carson, money will keep Vraik true to us, if nothing else will."

"Unless these Anarchists find out what you are doing, and treat him still more liberally."

"Oh, I'm not afraid of their find-out," laughed Mallow. "Mrs. Arne and he gang are by no means so clever as they fancy they are. She, particularly, is blinded by her own egotism. Besides, even if they did get at Vraik, they could not bribe him. They want money badly, these people; in fact it was to your fifty thousand pounds they looked to put them in funds. Unfortunately, Carson—we may still call him Carson—has gone off with the plunder."

117

"Do you think these Anarchists will kill him, as Mrs. Arne threatened?"

"In the end, no doubt; but not till the money is safe in their hands. At present it lies in Carson's real name, whatever that may be. It is possible they may induce him to hand it over, but it will only be to save his life. While he has that money he is safe enough. It would not serve them to kill the goose with the golden eggs. These people may not be so clever as they imagine, but they are not fools enough for that."

"Mr. Mallow, I tremble when I think of the dangers to which you are exposed. Don't these wretches suspect you?"

"No!—that is, one of them does. Jeremiah Trall looks queerly at me at times, because he has read Clara's report of our first conversation. I fancy he is suspicious that it is something more than zeal for the cause that has caused me to join. But he is safe enough. He hates Drabble, and has told him that the letter is burnt. He is not likely to trouble me. Besides, he is, I think, but a very lukewarm member of the brotherhood."

"I don't trust any of them."

"Nor I! But I am safe so far, and they are not likely to give vent to any of their explosive propensities here in London, and so run the risk of being turned out of the only country in Europe which shelters them. But I must be off, Mrs. Carson. Rouge is waiting for me round the corner."

"Oh, Laurence, do take care of yourself!" implored poor Olive, anxiously.

"Be sure of that, for your sake," and Mallow left the house, sighing to think that he had now no right to say even so much to Olive. Whosoever Carson was, Olive was his wife. "And yet"—he started as the thought crossed his mind—"was she his wife? Was it not possible her marriage might be illegal? If the man were an impostor, he had not made her his wife under his real name— marriage under a false name is no marriage, surely? By Jupiter! I'll lose no time in taking Dimbal's opinion about this," muttered Mallow to himself. "There may be some way of releasing her from that scamp's clutches, after all. But the money will have to go. Well, let it go; she will gladly pay even fifty thousand pounds for her freedom."

Round the corner—that is to say, in the back of a convenient little public-house—M. Rouge, the devil's advocate, was waiting for Mallow. It was late—after seven o'clock—and Laurence needed no clock to tell him it was dinner-time. But that day he had received a note from Rouge begging for an appointment at this especial hour. He felt obliged to keep it, lest the man might wish to say something important. As colourless and shrinking as ever Rouge stood up, cap in hand, when Laurence entered. "I am glad to see Monsieur," he said in French. "Is it that Monsieur is aware that Madame desires he should come to the great meeting next week?"

"No," replied Mallow, carelessly; "what for?"

Rouge spoke again in the husky whisper he usually affected, and looked steadily at Laurence. "It is to take the oath," he said. Laurence winced.

Rouge saw his momentary hesitancy, and smiled in that uncanny fashion of his, which often caused Mallow to think he was not quite right in his head.

"It is not too late, if Monsieur is afraid," said he, with a shrug and a sneer.

"Monsieur is not afraid," retorted Mallow sharply; "but Monsieur is wise enough to consider all things before committing himself past recall. When does the meeting take place?"

"On Wednesday next, Monsieur!"

"That is a week hence. Where?"

"In the cellar of the house in Poplar Street, Monsieur."

"In the cellar?" repeated Mallow, much surprised. "Will that be large enough?"

Rouge laughed. "Oh, Monsieur does not know all the holes in which we foxes hide. Holy Blue! it must not be that he know before he swears to be true, for he might speak to the police." The wretch's expression was feline as he whispered the last word. "But this cellar! it is a great one—c'est énorme! Madame had it made, Madame preferred it. If the police came! piff-paff! whirr! Houp-là!" he pointed upwards.

"I see! we dance on a volcano," said Laurence, uneasily. Rouge nodded. "We would all die; the best and the worst."

"Sacrifice your own lives?"

"Yes, and those of others, Monsieur. When we take the oath we are already as dead. Let Monsieur reflect."

"Monsieur has reflected," said Laurence, giving the man money. "I shall be at Poplar Street next Wednesday. At what time?"

"Nine of the evening. It will be a great meeting, a grand meeting, and Monsieur will take the oath."

Mallow nodded. "Yes, Monsieur will take the oath," he repeated, and, after a second inquiring look, Rouge, with the money

119

in his pocket, glided out of the room. The cat-like movements of the man, his glistening eyes and sibilant whispers, inspired Mallow with nothing but repulsion. Still he was kind to him, and, knowing the poor wretch often went without a meal, frequently gave him the price of one. Whether Rouge was grateful Mallow knew not, but he gave no sign of gratitude, and watched the young man unceasingly. He never told him his real name, nor spoke of his past in any way. His conversation, for the most part, consisted of extracts from revolutionary pamphlets, imprecations upon those in power, and expressions of jubilation for the day when a tide of blood should roll over Europe. To Mallow he was a veritable creature of nightmare.

On leaving this red-hot destroyer of human civilization, Mallow walked quickly to his lodgings in Half-Moon Street. The walk did him good. It cooled his blood and cleared his brain. As he passed by Hyde Park he noticed he was being followed. A man was dogging him like a shadow, pausing when he paused, and following him steadily at no great distance. Brave as he was, Mallow felt a qualm. He wondered if the Anarchists, suspecting him of treachery, were having him watched. He felt that suspense was worse than danger, so he determined to right-about face and know the worst at once. He turned up a side street for half a dozen yards. Then he faced round and walked back. By this manœuvre he almost ran into the arms of his follower.

"Jeremiah Trall!" exclaimed Mallow, recognizing him in the lamplight. "What do you want? Why are you following me?"

Trall looked round swiftly, and beckoned Mallow into the comparative darkness of the side street. "I wish to speak with you privately," he said in his refined voice. "I am afraid of being watched."

"Come to my rooms, then."

"No," replied Trall, "they would follow. My life would not be safe. Better here." He led Mallow up some distance into a gloomy corner. "Mr. Mallow," he said, sinking his voice, "why are you joining us?"

"What is that to you?" asked Mallow, fencing.

"You have some scheme in your head, and I wish to know it. You are no true Anarchist; you don't care two pins about the cause."

Mallow reflected. The man might be trying to trap him into some incautious speech, duly to be reported to Mrs. Arne. Trall guessed the cause of his hesitation and laughed.

"You may as well tell me," he said; "I know so much about you, that I may as well know the rest."

"What do you mean, Trall?"

"That letter of Clara's. She reported to me all that passed between you and Mrs. Carson. You are bent on dissolving that marriage and getting back the money."

"Well, suppose I am. I can do that and still be true to the cause."

"No, you can't, Mr. Mallow. Carson was married to Miss Bellairs to get that money for the cause."

"Then the husband of Miss Bellairs is not really Carson."

"No, he is not. He is a tool in the hands of this infernal Drabble, as I am."

"What is this man's name—his real name?" asked Mallow.

"I don't know! I swear I don't know. Hush! I can't go on speaking to you here; they have spies everywhere. But I just want to tell you that no one but myself read that letter, and that it is in the fire. I know you are not in earnest for the cause, and I am glad of it."

"And why, may I ask, are you glad of it? You are one of them."

"I am not!" denied Jeremiah, fiercely. "I am a drunken fool under the thumb of Drabble. I wish to God the cause was at the bottom of the sea, and Drabble kicking his heels in gaol—or the scaffold, if I could only get him there. I had a position once Mr. Mallow, I am an outcast now, solely through Drabble, who has been the curse of my life. He treats me like a dog; but a dog can bite, and bite him I will when he least expects it. He has ruined me; he has brought my niece, Clara, into his cursed schemes. She, too, is under his thumb. Oh, my God! If only you knew my life's history, you would pity me. Some day I'll tell it to you, if only to show you how lost a man can become, body and soul. Drabble is a devil—curse him! Hush! don't speak; I'll go—I'll go. I only wanted to tell you that the secret of your real intentions is quite safe with me. If you can ruin Drabble, and with him that stony-hearted Jezebel, do it—do it, I say. Tread them under foot—make them suffer as I have suffered, as they have made me suffer."

Trall, gripping Mallow's hand, shook it violently, and disappeared round the corner of the street.

Mallow was too much astonished to follow him.

He walked on home. Almost at his doorstep a hand was laid upon his arm. He turned to see the villainous face of Vraik smirking at him.

"I've come to report, sir," whined the spy. "I've seen Major

Semberry in conversation with a light-haired, light-bearded man."

"Who is he?"

"Francis Hain, sir!—the man who was concerned in the murder. I'm sure of it."

CHAPTER VII

"AN UNEXPECTED MEETING"

"Francis Hain?" stammered Mallow, amazed. "Impossible! You must be mistaken. You have never seen Francis Hain!"

Vraik rubbed his hands and leered.

"That's as true as true," he croaked; "but if I ain't seen 'im other people 'ave. When you told me as 'ow you thought as all this business was mixed up with the murder, I went and saw the landlord, and all them tradespeople in and about Athelstane Place. From the description I got of Hain, I know 'im as well as I know my own partner. I follered that Major cove all these days till I'm fair worn out; and when I saw him talkin' to a light-'aired man with a beard as long as yer arm, it didn't take me long to recognize Hain. I tried to sneak up close and listen but they got their matter done, and parted afore I could hear a word.

"Where did you see them?"

"In Poplar Street."

"And when they parted, you followed one of them—which?"

"That Major cove, of course—didn't you tell me to keep an eye on 'im?"

Mallow was annoyed.

"I wanted you to use your own discretion," he said. "You should have tracked down Hain, and handed him over to the police."

"I didn't like to do that without orders," whimpered Vraik. "You see, I 'adn't got no orders so far as he was concerned."

"H'm. Well, of course, it is possible the man may not be Hain after all."

"Well, if 't'aint, it's 'is twin—goin' by the description," said Vraik, with emphasis. "But you just ask the Major cove about him."

"I intend to. But I'm pretty certain that the Major cove, as you call him, won't tell the truth."

"You let me tackle him, Mr. Maller, and I'll soon screw it out of 'im."

"No," said Mallow, sharply. "I'll call on him myself. You continue to watch Major Semberry until I have seen him. But if you should chance to meet Hain again, give him in charge. I'll take the responsibility."

"Oh, as long as you do that, I don't care. I'll just get back to Marquis Street, and keep an eye on the Major cove, but it's hard work, sir, and precious dry."

"Here's half-a-sovereign," said Mallow, tossing him the coin. "Don't get drunk on it."

Vraik slipped the piece into his pocket with a grin.

"Lord bless you, sir, I weren't born yesterday! I'm square, I am;" and he slunk away in the darkness, leaving Mallow more than a trifle disgusted at being obliged to come into contact with so degraded an animal.

The various side-paths along which Mallow had so carefully travelled began now to show signs of convergence.

They were pointing clearly to one principal highway, and that promised to lead directly from Soho to Athelstane Place. But in no way did he lose sight of the fact that, if at all possible, the capture of the money itself was greatly to be desired. That was an additional reason for refraining from putting matters into official hands; for, in that event, fearful of extradition, the pseudo-Carson would probably cease to affect Florence as a place of residence. On the contrary, as likely as not he would decide to place a considerable expanse of water between him and it. He decided it would be best at once to force from Semberry a complete confession, if possible; always duly heedful, of course, of that gentleman's anarchist connection and consequent powers. It would be necessary to be more than ever circumspect. Next morning, therefore, he proceeded to Marquis Street, St. James's. He found his warrior busy with the consumption of his morning meal. His reception was, he thought, unusually cordial. Had he known it, the Major's first impulse had been to refuse to see him. But second thoughts had prevailed; he determined it would be best to brazen it out. In the face of danger the weak brain is ever cunning. Thus it was that Mallow's reception was sufficiently jovial and hearty to have disarmed his suspicions entirely. But they were on too solid a foundation for that, and, though outwardly reciprocative, he was every bit as alert as the Major.

"Mornin'," said Semberry, shaking hands with his visitor, "you're out early. Had breakfast?"

"Yes, thank you. I must apologize for calling at so unusual an hour, but the fact is I want to consult you about Carson."

"Nothin' to do with that chap, now," said the Major, wagging his head. "He has gone his way, I go mine."

"And your way, I perceive, is also Italy," said Laurence, whose keen eyes had not failed to see a Cook's tourist ticket lying open on the table at "Lucerne to Chiasso."

Semberry had overlooked it. He was somewhat disconcerted; but he hastened to make the best of a bad job.

"Yes, just goin' there to see Carson," said he, sweeping the tickets into the pocket of his smoking-coat "As matter of fact, promised to take a box over for him."

"Oh. Is it a sandal-wood one?"

"How the—how do you know he has a sandal-wood box?"

"Why, easily enough. He explained as much to Mrs. Carson when she asked him why he had that everlasting smell about him. So you intend taking the box over yourself, do you? You are indeed a good friend, Major."

The Major was not appreciative of his position; but he replied bluffly enough, "Goin' for m' own sake. Carson owes me money. Not likely to see it unless I go m'self. Carson's a bit of a rogue, you know."

"Are you sure he isn't somewhat more than 'a bit,' Major? Are you quite sure he is Angus Carson?"

"Course I am; who else would he be?" said Semberry, with an admixture of indignation and ignorance in equal parts.

"Oh, don't ask me," replied Mallow, carelessly. "Only it was strange, was it not, that Mrs. Purcell should say the picture taken at Sandbeach did not represent her friend, Mr. Carson of Bombay?"

"Bad likeness, perhaps," growled Semberry. He was really uneasy now.

"On the contrary, it is a very good one—of the man who married Miss Bellairs."

"Angus Carson."

"If you like to call him so."

Semberry jumped up with a scowl.

"Do you mean to insult me; doubt m' word!" he said savagely.

124

"Carson's been with me since his father died. Didn't lose sight of him till marriage. 'S matter fact, don't 'prove the way he's treated wife; that's another reason I'm goin' Italy, to bring him back and see things square before I return t'India."

"If you can do that, Major, you will be extremely clever; but I doubt very much your being able to persuade this stray lamb to return."

"Make him, if only to prove you and Mrs. Purcell wrong."

"Oh, I!—I have nothing to do with it. Carson may be the great Cham, for all I care; but Mrs. Purcell will not be so easily satisfied. You know her."

"Rather; interferin' old cat, that she is. Says Carson isn't Carson, does she? What the deuce does the woman mean?"

"You had better ask her, Semberry, and settle the matter offhand."

"I'll ask her," said the Major, furiously. "What's more, I'll bring back Carson himself to give her the lie. Hang it! she reflects on m' honour as an officer and gentleman."

"Oh, you know what ladies are," replied Mallow, laughing but observant; "once get an idea into their heads, and there is no getting it out again. Mrs. Purcell, on the authority of that portrait, declares that the man who married Miss Bellairs is not Carson; an idle theory of hers, if you will, but one she is bent upon proving."

"She can't," contradicted Semberry, testily. "Man is Carson right enough. I ought to know, and I say so. Will bring him back, I tell you, just to prove it. Whole thing's silly nonsense."

Mallow yawned.

"Dare say. Doesn't interest me in the least. I am sorry for Mrs. Carson, and I think she has been disgracefully treated; but I should like, if possible, to see her husband return to her. However, as you are going over to fetch him, I have no doubt that will arrange itself."

"Didn't intend to fetch him!" grumbled Semberry, "but will now, just to shut up Mrs. Purcell. Can't afford to play the doose with m' reputation when I'm in the Service. Carson's box is here, if Mrs. Purcell would like to see it."

Now, a sight of this precious box and its contents would, Mallow felt, be very acceptable. But he could not say so without rousing Semberry's suspicions. In such a position many a man would have jumped at the Major's offer, and have brought Mrs. Purcell to Marquis Street; but Mallow knew better. Of all things, caution was most essential. He merely laughed.

125

"Oh, I'll tell Mrs. Purcell, if you like," said he affably. "I don't think it's the box she wants to see so much as the man. Why not call on her before you leave?"

"What's the use? She would not believe me. I'll bring back Carson, I tell you, and he can shut her up himself. I ain't going to argue with Mrs. Purcell."

"Well, perhaps she is rather a difficult subject, Major. When do you go?"

"To-morrow, night train."

"Ah, well, pleasant journey. By the way, who was that fair chap you were talking to yesterday—the man I saw you with in Poplar Street? Excuse my asking, but I can't help thinking I know him."

The Major started, and looked searchingly at Mallow, who remained unmoved.

"Oh, a friend of mine; I.C.S. man," he answered carelessly. "Why?"

"Oh, nothing. I fancied he was a doctor I had met somewhere."

"Doctor!" repeated Semberry, nervously; "no, he's not a doctor. Civil engineer. He builds bridges of sorts. You don't know him. He's been India way these last twenty years."

"Ah, strange, too—I am convinced I know him," said Mallow, rising. "Just shows how apt one is to confuse faces. I could have sworn he was a doctor. Well, I must be off. Shall I take any message from you to Mrs. Purcell?"

"No. You can tell her, if you like, that I'm going to bring back Carson," said the Major, grimly. "And if I don't prove he's the man he says he is, she can write to the War Office and say I'm a swindler. Have a peg before you go."

"No, thanks; too early for strong waters. Good-day."

"Day," replied Semberry, curtly, accompanying Mallow to the door.

When his visitor was fairly off the premises, the Major drew a long breath and returned to his breakfast. "Time I got off," he muttered. "Wonder what the chap's driving at. I was a fool to leave those tickets about; but who'd ha' thought he'd have spotted them; who'd ha' thought o' seeing him now, for the matter o' that."

In the street Mallow was looking for Vraik. He knew he was somewhere not far off: Shortly he espied a ragged pavement artist at work on a series of glaring presentments in coloured chalk within sight of the Major's door. Mallow strolled across the road to drop a copper into the man's hat. As he did so he spoke hurriedly.

"The Major's leaving town to-night or to-morrow. Watch him

126

Charing Cross or Victoria, and wire to my rooms at once when he goes."

"I'm fly," said the pavement artist, with a grin; and Mallow, satisfied that Semberry was under proper surveillance, went his way easy in his mind. Round the corner, as fate would have it, he ran almost into the arms of a stout elderly gentleman in black.

"Oh, my dear sir, my dear sir!" protested the stranger, puffing, "you knocked the wind out of me. Why, it's Mr. Mallow!"

"Mr. Brock?" said Mallow, recognizing the vicar. "Who would have thought of meeting you here."

"Surprising, indeed," said Brock, shaking hands. "But I'm on my way to see Major Semberry. Perhaps you can tell me where is Marquis Street, Mr. Mallow?"

"Just round the corner. So you are visiting the Major?"

"My dear young friend, I wish to speak with him about Angus Carson. With pain and grief I have heard of this terrible trouble between my old friend's son and Olive. I have thought it possible that Major Semberry might use his good offices to bring about a reconciliation.'

"I'm afraid that is beyond the Major's power, sir," said Mallow, shaking his head. "Was it Mrs. Purcell who told you of this separation?"

"It was. I received her letter two days back, and came up as soon as I could. I have not yet seen Olive. I decided I would see the Major first. This very painful matter must be settled."

"Mrs. Carson is not to blame, Mr. Brock. Her husband alone is at fault."

"So Mrs. Purcell said," said Brock, solemnly. "Dear! dear! Angus is not behaving in the way his upright father would have had him behave."

"His father? h'm," said Mallow, wondering if it would be wise to tell Brock that Carson was an impostor. On second thoughts he decided to hold his tongue. The open street hardly lent itself to explanations of the kind. He suggested that the vicar should call on Mrs. Purcell after he had seen Semberry.

"Certainly, it is my intention to do so, Mr. Mallow. We will put our two old heads together, and see what we can do. Good-day, good-day," and Brock trotted off.

CHAPTER VIII

"THE LIGHT-HAIRED MAN"

When Mallow returned to his rooms he found Lord Aldean seated in his most comfortable arm-chair. His expression was extremely thoughtful, and, withal, a trifle anxious. Polyphemus, as Laurence sometimes called him—in allusion to his size—was not usually given to a gentle melancholy. Mallow could only conclude there must be something wrong with the boy.

"You here, Jim?" said he, throwing hat and gloves on a near table. "What is the matter with you, man? You look as miserable as an owl."

"Mallow, you lack the delicacy of perception necessary for the correct understanding of the feelings of a man in my condition. Besides, your simile is rude."

"Oh, I see. Miss Ostergaard has been crushing you as usual."

"On the contrary, she is particularly amiable."

"That ought to encourage you."

"It does," said Aldean miserably; "so much so that I have made up my mind to propose to her this very day."

"One would think you had made up your mind to be hanged—from your expression. Why so dejected?"

"Mallow, I know what fear is now; my heart is in my boots."

"Is it? Then you had better reinstate it before you go on your knees. What are you afraid of, you jackass? Miss Ostergaard won't eat you."

"She might say 'No,'" groaned the wretched Jim. He paled at the bare idea of so terrible a catastrophe.

"She might, on the other hand, say 'Yes,'" replied Mallow consolingly. "Come, Polyphemus, you needn't go out in a coach-and-four to meet your troubles. Look at mine; they come right to my very door, confound them."

"Mallow, you don't know how fond I am of that girl."

"I must, indeed, be dull of understanding, then," said he, "for you have endeavoured to bring me to a very clear comprehension of your feelings upon several occasions. Cheer up, old man!"—he clapped Jim's broad shoulders—"you have every chance of success. The girl's in love with you."

128

"Do you really think so?" said Jim, brightening. Then, with a deeper groan, "No, no, she is always teasing me."

"Of course she is. But it is only her way. Some women are like that—especially when in love. You must interpret them contrariwise—like dreams, you know."

"In that case I may hope."

"Yes, hope and put your fortune to the test. Also, if you think you are in a fit condition to do so, answer me a question."

"What is it?" asked Aldean, accepting a cigarette. "Do you put love before friendship?"

"Well—er—no; that is not your friendship."

"You do not seem very certain on the point," said Mallow, dryly. "However, I am about to ask your aid. At present I cannot leave London. I am too heavily involved with these Anarchists, and I must remain on the spot to watch Mrs. Arne and Drabble. Now, I saw Semberry this morning, and learned, thanks to his carelessness in leaving tickets about, that he is off to Italy. I want you to follow him there and watch his little game with Carson."

"Oh, I'll go, of course," said Jim, with rather a long face; "but how do you know Semberry is going to Carson?"

"Because that blackguard is in Italy. Moreover, I told Semberry about Mrs. Purcell's assertion that the man who married Olive is not Carson. It is now the expressed intention of our good Major to bring back his friend, and—as he says—put his identity beyond doubt."

"Do you believe him?"

"No, Jim, I do not. Semberry funks Mrs. Purcell. He knows perfectly well that the man is an impostor. He is simply going over to Italy for the purpose of securing his share of the plunder. Then he will slip down to Naples or Brindisi, and board the next out-going liner for India, where he hopes to be safe. This is why I want you to hang on to his tail, and stop him clearing out."

"I'm your man, Mallow. But I don't see how I can stop the beggar without a warrant."

"Oh, a warrant is out of the question; besides, you can frighten him without that. Interview this scamp who calls himself Carson, and get the truth out of him if you can. Of course, I can't exactly forecast events for you, but you must use your common sense; you have plenty of it, you know, at a pinch. If the Major tries a bolt, tell him you will communicate with the War Office; in fact, threaten him with the most merciless exposure."

"But I can't do that."

"I can," said Mallow, with decision. "There is a man called Trall

129

who can prove that the fellow whom Semberry introduced as Carson is a fraud. And I hope, also, when I get the evidence, to prove that the real Carson was murdered in Athelstane Place with Semberry's connivance. Tell him this. I don't think you will find him refractory then."

"He is only the more likely to skidaddle, I should think."

"In that case, he'll have to chuck the army," said Mallow. "If the War Office communicates what I know to Semberry's colonel, he will not only be cashiered, but brought back to England under arrest. However, as I say, I can't foretell events; you must use your discretion."

"I'll do my best," said Jim, feeling his muscle, as though the question were best settled that way. "When does Semberry start?"

"Either to-night or to-morrow. He says to-night; but I don't trust him. I have that man Vraik watching him; and as soon as he clears a wire will be sent here. If I am in when it comes I'll advise you; but, in any case, come round and keep a look-out for it yourself. Open it—open any letter; I have no secrets from you."

"But won't you be in this evening?"

"Perhaps yes, perhaps no; I can't say. I have heard from Vraik that the man Hain, who was concerned in that murder, is hanging round Poplar Street. He was seen talking to Semberry yesterday. I must watch for him; so, if I'm not back when you receive the wire, don't wait for me. Start straight away for Italy. Lose no time; go by the same train, if you can; or follow by the next. It's a case of life or death, Jim."

"You can depend on me," said Jim, shaking Mallow's hand; "I'll hang on like grim death. If he gets away from me he'll be a smarter man than I take him to be. But I say, Mallow, don't you get into trouble with these beastly Anarchist chaps. They're a queer lot, you know."

"No fear, my boy; I know them. If I should get into any mess, however—for accidents will occur—look up Vraik at the private inquiry office I told you about. He knows Trall, and Trall is my very good friend. He hates Drabble, and will help me so far as he is able in any little difficulty."

"I understand," said Jim, with a nod.

"My poor Polyphemus, this will put an end to your courtship."

Lord Aldean looked somewhat rueful. "I am not likely to be away more than a week or so, am I? and I dare say Tui will still be free when I get back."

"Oh, you call her Tui now, do you?" laughed Mallow. "In my own mind, I do—not to her face."

"That will be a pleasure to come. Seriously, Jim, I am greatly obliged to you for your readiness to help me. Believe me, I shan't forget it."

"Oh, that's all right, Mallow. Our friendship is more than a name, I hope," said Jim, with another shake of his whilom tutor's hand. He then took his departure, in, be it said, a considerably more cheerful frame of mind.

That same afternoon Mallow walked as far as Soho, with the intention of seeing Mrs. Arne, and telling her that he had decided to take the oath. As a matter of fact, he had not; but, as there were eight days to the time appointed for his installation, he hoped that something might turn up in the interval which would render it unnecessary for him to go so far.

It was four o'clock when he arrived in the neighbourhood of Soho. The sky was growing darker every minute; but there was still light sufficient to distinguish the passers-by. At the entrance to Poplar Street he was passed by a man walking swiftly—a tall, fair-bearded man, who looked neither to right nor left, but raced on breathlessly towards No. 49. Instinctively Mallow guessed this was his enemy. "Francis Hain, to a certainty," he muttered under his breath; "light hair, light beard, tall, thin—the exact description given in the papers. Will he enter No. 49?" At No. 49, surely enough, the man pulled up, and admitting himself, evidently with a latch-key, disappeared within. Mallow's hot blood was at boiling point. Here was the wretch who had murdered the unfortunate Carson within his grasp. Heedless of the danger he was running, he knocked at the door of No. 49. It was opened almost immediately. He had given the signal knock which Rouge had taught him. The door-keeper recognized him at once, and the next minute he was standing in the dark passage of that dangerous den.

"Where is the gentleman who entered just now?" he asked the door-keeper breathlessly.

"Upstairs; he goes to see Madame," replied the man, who had no idea that anything was wrong. Mallow had given the signal, and his face was known to him. The door-keeper was quite easy in his mind.

Up the narrow stairs Mallow sprang two at a time, reckless, and full of fierce courage. He was determined to face Hain, and wring the truth from him at all costs. Caution, wisdom, fear, all went to the four winds. The hot Irish fighting blood fizzled through his veins—burned in his cheek. Rash and unthinking, he dashed forward with a courage absolutely blind—the courage which wins or loses all. On the first landing he caught a glimpse of a tall figure. He heard the click of a turning door-knob. The next moment Mallow the hero, Mallow the fool, had flung open the door and stood on the threshold of Mrs. Arne's room. She was there, and near her stood the man Hain. "At last!" cried Mallow between his teeth. "At last I have got you."

"What does he mean?" demanded Madame, in her metallic voice.

"It means that I want Francis Hain for murder."

The tall man slipped back a pace. His voice quavered. "I am not Hain," he said, keeping a wary eye on Mallow.

"You liar!" Mallow sprang forward. "You are Hain the murderer. You and that woman—one of you—killed young Carson."

"Madman! Carson is alive in Italy."

"Carson is dead—murdered! You killed him. You are Hain."

"He is not Hain," said Mrs. Arne, simply.

"I am not Hain," repeated the man. Something in the tone of his voice sounded strangely familiar to Mallow.

"No, you are not Hain," said Mallow, throwing himself at the man's throat. "I know you now—you are Drabble"—his hand twitched away the light beard, and the doctor's clean-shaven face was revealed—"Drabble the murderer!"

"Kill the spy," breathed Madame Death-in-Life; "he knows too much."

"Enough to hang you both." Mallow threw Drabble on one side, ran past Mrs. Arne, and dashed his gloved fist through the window. "Help! help! Police! police!"

"Kill him! Kill him!" shrieked Madame, fiercely.

"Spy!" roared Drabble.

The two men swung and reeled across the floor. Neither uttered a word. With clenched teeth and muscles tense they battled fiercely in the small space. Madame rushed to the door and flung it open.

"A spy! a spy! Danger! Up! up! up!" she cried down the well of the staircase. Immediately there was a noise of rushing feet—a babel of fierce voices. Mallow heard rather than saw the room filling. He had a firm grip on Drabble's throat, and the man was staggering and gurgling for want of breath. Then a hundred hands—as it seemed—plucked him back. He was hurled to the ground, and beaten and trampled into insensibility.

132

CHAPTER IX

"MAN PROPOSES"

"May I ask, Lord Aldean, if you have ever perused the biography of the celebrated Dr. Johnson of Auchinleck?"

"Yes, Mrs. Purcell, I have. Mallow made me read it when I was cramming for the 'varsity."

"Made you read it!" echoed Mrs. Purcell, majestically; "the word 'made' is misapplied, surely!"

"Well, it is a teaser, isn't it?" said Aldean, frankly; "shouldn't read it to keep myself awake. Boswell's a bit long-winded, ain't he?"

"Boswell, Lord Aldean, whatever he may be, is not frivolous."

"I don't read anything, as a rule," confessed Jim, "except the papers."

Mrs. Purcell frowned. "The general slovenliness of style of the daily journals is not such as Dr. Johnson would have approved," said she, in her deep voice. "The very letters of the illustrious lexicographer have the roll and volume of ethic poetry."

"'Paradise Lost,'" said Miss Ostergaard; "everybody talks about it and no one reads it."

"I have read it, Tui," observed Miss Slarge, rousing herself from her brown study; "it afforded me useful hints on idolatry. Moloch, who is mentioned therein, is identical with the Baal or Bel of the Babylonians. The Romish festival of St. John, at the midsummer solstice, is simply the relic of the Chaldean worship of Tammuz. One of Bel's names was Oannes: the Latinized form of John in the sacred language of the Papists, Joannes. Remove the 'J,' and you can see how the idol was converted into the prophet."

"Most interesting," said Aldean, groaning, as this deluge of hard names rattled about his head. "Do you write like Dr. Johnson, Miss Slarge?"

"Alas! Rubina does not," sighed Mrs. Purcell. "Rather does she adopt the antithetic style of Macaulay, the historian."

The conversation was taking place in Mrs. Purcell's drawing-room round a cheerful fire. In the next room Olive was writing letters. She was, in truth, somewhat depressed by the non-appearance of Mallow, whom she had expected that evening, and felt little inclined for conversation. True to his promise, Aldean had called at Mallow's rooms after dinner, but, finding there neither his

133

friend nor a telegram, had come over to enjoy himself at Campden Hill. But that the business on hand might not be neglected, he had left word that, if a telegram came, it was to be sent on to him at Mrs. Purcell's house. Mallow's absence had not surprised him. He concluded that he was in the neighbourhood of Poplar Street, Hain-hunting. As it was, Mallow was at that moment a prisoner in the Anarchist den, and, by his very warning to Aldean that his absence might be indefinite, he had done away with all chance of rescue.

Jim's true errand to Campden Hill was to propose to Miss Ostergaard. He was determined to know the worst—or the best—before leaving for Italy. But it chanced that Mrs. Purcell's Johnsonian mania was strong upon her, for she pestered the poor boy with a hundred and one details concerning her celebrated Samuel, until he fervently wished that he or Johnson had never been born—not to speak of Bean, Goldy, Reynolds, and all other illustrious old bores idolized of Mrs. Purcell. He was hopelessly dazed with it all—and looked it. Nor did it add to his comfort in any degree to find Tui heartily laughing at his plight. It became too much for the wretched Jim. He grew both desperate and rude.

"Seems to me, the most creditable thing about Johnson," said he, crossly, "was that he didn't murder Boswell."

"Murder Boswell!" gasped Mrs. Purcell. "Murder his biographer?"

"I mean the fellow who was always asking questions," explained Jim. "I can't think how Johnson put up with his silly gabble. Fancy a fellow asking another fellow what he'd do if he was shut up in a castle with a baby. Such bosh, y'know!"

"Lord Aldean," said Mrs. Purcell, solemnly rising, "you are evidently not aware that it was Boswell's object to afford the great Doctor an opportunity for the display of his unrivalled fund of argument."

"And of contradiction," hinted Tui, sweetly.

Mrs. Purcell shook her head sadly. "I perceive that you are both of you of the earth, earthly," she said pityingly. "The solemnity of the learned lexicographer's periods is lost upon you. Rubina, let us leave these unideaed young people to their own puny, foolish ways."

"Yes, Priscilla," said Miss Slarge, rising. "I must return to my desk."

"No, Rubina, not with my consent. You shall do no such thing. To tax your brain at so late an hour is the height of folly. In the next room we will play draughts; it is a cheerful amusement."

134

Miss Slarge sighed, but complied. She knew from experience the futility of attempting to argue with her ponderous sister.

As they left the room Aldean stepped forward to open the door. "Hope I haven't been rude, Mrs. Purcell!"

"Rude? Certainly not, Lord Aldean; but it must be confessed that you are sadly ignorant. Your style of conversation is neither elegant nor well considered."

Jim returned to the fire and Tui, unabashed. He was bent on proposing; and Tui, by some peculiar instinct, purely feminine, knew it. What is more, she intended to let him have his say. Lately it had dawned upon her that it was possible to play her fish too long. He might sulk away from the hook; and she had no intention of allowing that to happen. So she sat, and looked at the fire, and Jim sat and looked at her; while the hearts of both beat a lively rataplan, utterly incommensurate with so tranquil an occupation.

"I say!" began Jim, gracefully. "You don't think Mrs. Purcell's on her hind legs? Do you?"

"Oh no!" responded Tui, still confining her interest to the fire. "Women never get on their—I mean, never lose their tempers."

"Don't they?" said Aldean (this as a simple interrogation, not an assertion).

"Of course not. I am a woman; I ought to know. How silly you are."

"I'm unideaed! Mrs. Purcell says so."

"She made the same remark about me. She stole the word, you know, from Boswell, who got it from Johnson. It seems we are both of us"—Tui sighed—"'unideaed.'"

"It's a kind of bond between us, isn't it?"

"Dear me, Lord Aldean, how should I know?" (Silence for a few moments, during which, the ordinary medium for conversation proving unsuitable, recourse was had to certain more subtle means—chiefly ocular. Finally, a combination seemed to be decided upon.)

Aldean (gloomily): "I hate Dr. Johnson; don't you?"

Tui (viciously): "Not so much as I do Boswell—the nasty Poll-Pry."

Aldean: "So he is—so he was! That's another bond between us" (insinuatingly), "ain't it?"

Tui (repeating herself): "How should I know, Lord Aldean?" (Silence.)

Aldean (desperately) "Do—do you think that marriages are made in heaven?"

Tui (faintly): "I—I have heard that they are."

Aldean (speculating): "I wonder when they—whoever they are—will set about manipulating ours?"

Tui (with a maidenly perturbation): "Ours, Lord Aldean! What do you mean by ours?"

Aldean (moving his chair closer): "You know!" (No answer.) "I'm sure you know."

Tui: "Ridiculous." (Deserts the fire for the hearthrug.)

Aldean (intercepting the field of view): "Tui! Oh" (with a gasp) "Tui!" Certain physical demonstrations followed, amid which the dental emissions necessary for the iteration of the name "Tui" crackled like volleys from a machine-gun.

"Oh, Lord Aldean!" implored Tui, collecting her senses, "don't."

"Don't what, Tui?" said Jim, seizing her hand.

"Get up! If Mrs. Purcell came in, what would she say?"

"She would say I was proposing, Tui; and she wouldn't be far wrong. Say 'Yes.'"

"Why should I say 'Yes?'"

"Because I love you and you love me."

"I haven't said that I love you," said Tui, rising in feigned alarm,

"I don't need you to say it. I can see it."

Henceforth, for some time, conversation became superfluous, if not impossible.

At length Jim came to the point. "My darling!" he implored, "say that you will marry me."

"How can I? It's so sudden; you're so—so—so very demonstrative. No, no; I won't—I can't."

"Oh, very well, Miss Ostergaard," cried Aldean, suddenly releasing her. "I'm a fool, and you're a hard-hearted coquette," and he turned his back to fold his arms and sulk.

"Lord Aldean!" said Tui, faintly. There was no reply. "Lord Aldean," she repeated. Still no reply. Finally, in desperation, "Jim!"

"Oh, Tui, Tui!" His arms were round her. "Will you—will you?"

"I will," murmured Tui, with accents well-nigh liturgical.

"Dearest!"

Then there was a great silence, and what is perhaps best expressed by typographic constellations.

* * * * * *

There came a knock—a discreet knock, be it said—at the door; and, shortly following it, the footman—a concrete being indeed. His signal gave rise to a very elegant little manœuvre, whereby the width of the hearthrug was speedily, if somewhat obtrusively, placed between these two. Under his breath Jim muttered, "Hang it!"

"M'lord," said the Apollo in livery; "if you please, m'lord, there's a person below who wishes to see your lordship."

"What sort of a person?"

"A low sort of person, m'lord. His business is important, he says."

"Hope nothing's wrong with Mallow, poor chap," mumbled Aldean, driving the footman out of the room.

Then he went downstairs. In the hall he found a disreputable marionette, who, at the sight of him, at once commenced profusely to scrape and bow. This creature confessed to the name of Vraik, and addressed Lord Aldean in a husky whisper—presumably that the lordly footman should not hear.

"Mr. Mallow told me to send a wire to his rooms, m'lord," said the man—"that is, when I saw the Major cove off. But bein' a bit late for a telegram, I thought I might as well trot round myself. Mr. Mallow wasn't in, and they told me you'd left a message for this place, m'lord."

"Yes, I did. Well, what about the Major?"

"He's off to the Continong, m'lord; cleared off by the nine hexpress from Victorier—took three boxes with 'im."

"Went off to-night, did he?" mused Jim. "That is just what Mallow expected. He's a bit of a liar, that Major. Very well," he said to Vraik, "I will convey your message to Mr. Mallow."

"What am I to do now, m'lord?"

"Call and see Mr. Mallow to-morrow. He will give you your orders. You can go now, Vraik."

"Foggy night, m'lord—fog will get into the throat som'ow."

Aldean construed the remark correctly, and produced half-a-crown. The creature slipped it into his pocket, and sneaked out with the abasement he judged befitting to the occasion.

"Well," said Aldean, re-ascending the stairs, "I can't say Mallow's particular as to whom he employs. But one can't work in mud, I suppose, without getting a bit dirty. H'm! so the Major's off. That means I'll have to go to-morrow. There's a nine o'clock, I think, as well as the midday mail from Victoria. I had better take it, I suppose. Hang it!" grumbled Jim—"just when she's said 'Yes.' This comes of sticking closer than a brother."

On re-entering the drawing-room, Aldean found Tui the centre of manifest congratulations. Olive and Mrs. Purcell, assisted by Miss Slarge—who had returned from Babylon for the purpose—were showering upon her many expressions of delight, osculatory and otherwise. Tui, of course, was weeping. How things had progressed thus far, in so incredibly short a space of time, Jim was at a loss to comprehend. He felt a little out of his depth, and wondered if all was as it should be. He supposed it was all natural enough. Still, he was obviously disconcerted when the trio bore down upon him, brimful of compliments and general expressions of goodwill. He blushed, and sought a corner with as much speed as he felt to be compatible with politeness. But even so he was only protected in the rear. Olive shook one hand and said, "Oh, Lord Aldean, I am so glad." Mrs. Purcell took the other, and continued, "Lord Aldean, I congratulate myself that beneath my roof you have met the future partner of your joys and sorrows."

"I knew it would be all right," said Miss Slarge, beaming. "One marriage invariably brings another. That superstition we can trace back to the land of Uz."

"Thanks, awf'ly," muttered Jim, nervously.

Then once again Tui became the centre of attraction.

"Dearest Tui," said Olive.

"My sweet girl," said Miss Slarge.

"It will be a pleasing spectacle for me to witness the progress of Love's young dream," rolled Mrs. Purcell, still majestic.

"Oh dear! you are all very kind," wept Tui. "How—how—how very happy I am!"

"I fear you are not to see the progress of Love's young dream just yet, Mrs. Purcell," blurted out Aldean. "I am going away, you know."

"Going away?" echoed the combined trio.

"Oh, Jim!" wailed Tui. "Oh, Jim!"

Aldean steeled his heart. "Major Semberry has bolted to Italy," he said. "I must follow him—promised Mallow.'

"And why has Major Semberry departed so suddenly?"

"Guilty conscience, Mrs. Purcell. He's gone off to see Carson."

"To see my husband?" cried Olive, turning white. "Are you following him?"

"Yes; by the nine train to-morrow. Don't want to go, but promised Mallow. I can't break my promise, you know."

Tui jumped up and kissed him before them all. "Jim," she cried, "you are a darling!"

138

CHAPTER X

"WOMAN DISPOSES"

For a young gentleman to face with equanimity four ladies, each one more or less gifted in her particular way, especially when the said young gentleman has just proposed to one of them and been accepted, requires a considerable amount of moral courage. Aldean confessed he felt the want of it when Tui kissed him, and the three onlookers smiled sympathetically. It was only when they quitted romance for reality, and became interested in Olive's troubles in place of his engagement, that Jim recovered his equanimity. Mrs. Purcell adjusted the situation to the lower and less romantic topic with her usual majesty.

"Be seated, Lord Aldean," she said, enthroning herself on the nearest and most comfortable chair; "let me hear your opinion on this unexpected and suspicious departure of Major Semberry."

"My opinion is the same as Mallow's," replied Jim, bluntly. "Semberry has gone off to get his share of this money. It is my business to stop him getting it."

"That will be difficult," said Olive, despondently.

"It would be, Mrs. Carson, if the Major were irresponsible as well as a scamp, and if he did not happen to be in the Service. As it is, I have the pull over him, and so has Mallow. We are in a position to prove Carson's imposture through a third party, and—as Semberry must have been accessory to the swindle—I can get him cashiered if he doesn't leave the money alone and make a clean breast of his conspiracy."

"How can you prove that Olive's husband is an impostor?" asked Tui.

"By bringing forward a man called Jeremiah Trall as a witness."

"Clara's uncle!" said Olive, nodding. "I know. Mr. Mallow told me all about him. Oh! and I am married to this man."

"No, you are not, Mrs. Carson—or, rather, I should say, Miss Bellairs."

"Lord Aldean!" cried Mrs. Purcell, while Olive remained silent, too amazed for words, "I trust that you are not about to inform me that this profligate has contracted a previous matrimonial alliance."

"No, but he is not Angus Carson, and he therefore married Miss Bellairs under a false name. To do this wittingly nullifies a marriage."

"Are you certain of that?" asked Olive, pale and anxious.

"Certain. Mallow saw Dimbal about it, and, to make doubly sure, they took counsel's opinion on the subject. You are not married."

Tui threw her arms round her friend's neck.

"Oh, Olive," she said aloud, and then whispered slily, "I know why Mr. Mallow consulted the lawyer."

"The iniquity of the fellow is preposterous," said Mrs. Purcell, in her most stately tone; "nevertheless, if our dear Olive can be freed from her matrimonial bonds, I shall rejoice sincerely and without reserve."

"I should like to punish the wretch," cried Tui, vehemently.

"I'll punish him for you," murmured Jim in her ear. "Shall I kick him, or wring his neck, or throw him into the Arno?"

"Well, I think the last would be best; it might wash the sin out of him."

"Water was used for lustration by the Chaldeans," said Miss Slarge, her ruling passion strong within her. Then the genuine woman asserted herself. "Olive, my poor love, I trust indeed that this may be so, and that you will escape from the power of this bad man."

"I was never in his power," cried Olive, proudly; "he was never my husband. I hated him. I will throw the ring—no"—she stopped suddenly, and replaced the wedding-ring on her finger—"I must not cease to wear this until I am certain of my freedom. Lord Aldean," she asked suddenly, "you go over to Italy to-morrow?"

"Yes, by the nine o'clock express from Victoria."

"And you will see this—this man who calls himself Carson?"

"It is probable. I must put a stop to his game and Semberry's. I promised Mallow to do so."

"Then I will go to Florence with you."

Mrs. Purcell stared. Her face assumed an expression of horror.

"My dear," she said, aghast, "are you in your right mind?"

"Of course I am. I must and will know the truth about this man, and, what is more, I intend to hear it from his own lips."

"But—but that woman!" gasped Miss Slarge.

"If I am not married to the man, she is nothing to me. Lord Aldean, will you take me to Florence?"

"Certainly," said Jim, promptly; "and I think that you are brave and right to face your troubles so boldly."

"She is a heroine," cried Tui; then whispered softly, "and you are a dear."

140

"Pray consider the feelings of society," boomed Mrs. Purcell.

"I prefer to consider my own, thank you. It is no use talking, my mind is made up, and Lord Aldean has consented to take me. I must know how I stand towards this man. I must hear from himself that he is not Carson, and I must recover the money stolen from me."

"Oh dear me!" wailed Miss Slarge. "Can't you wait until Mr. Brock calls? He is in town. He writes to say that he will visit us to-morrow afternoon."

"Can't wait," struck in Aldean, judiciously; "promised Mallow to follow Semberry next train. Must be off nine sharp."

"I shall be at the station at half-past eight," cried Olive. "You get the tickets and engage a carriage, Lord Aldean."

"Consider the feelings of Mr. Mallow.'

"Oh, he will be glad I am going. Mr. Mallow is not a prude. I'll write him a note to-night. Perhaps he will be at the station in the morning."

"No need to write," said Aldean, rising; "I am going round to his rooms now. I'll tell him, if I see him, though it's just possible I may not see him. He's so mixed up with these Anarchists that he never keeps regular hours now."

"I cannot but condemn this insane determination."

"Oh, but, Mrs. Purcell, you can trust Olive with Lord Aldean," coaxed Tui. "I am sure you ought to, when I trust him with her."

"I have a great mind to undertake the journey myself," cried Mrs. Purcell, with energy, "but I fear that the excessive travelling would prove highly injurious to me."

"Two days and two nights," hinted Aldean; "it's a corker of a trail."

"You must not think of going, Mrs. Purcell," said Olive, resolutely. "I will go alone with Lord Aldean, so that is all about it. Good-night, Lord Aldean; there is none too much time. I must go and pack."

When Olive had left the room, both Aldean and Tui brought their persuasive powers to bear upon Mrs. Purcell. After no small amount of trouble, they succeeded in reducing her to a more pliable state of mind. She confessed that Olive's position was so extraordinary, that perhaps extraordinary measures were justifiable for the adjustment of it. In the end, she went further, and expressed her opinion that it was right the girl should go.

"But for her own sake," said Mrs. Purcell, severely, "the more so, seeing that she has been so wantonly deceived by that unprincipled profligate, you must take the greatest care of her, Lord Aldean."

"I will treat her as I would a sister of my own," said Jim.

This seemed to suffice Mrs. Purcell. She fussed out of the room to help Olive with her packing, followed in a few minutes by Miss Slarge, tearful and doubtful: The room was empty, and the two young people grasped their opportunity for saying good-bye, after their own fashion, and in their own time. Jim—in this instance, at least—was nothing if not thorough, and fully twenty minutes elapsed before he descended the staircase. As he lay in bed that night, he confessed to himself that the love-scenes of fiction were not so highly coloured after all. The course of his true love had at last begun to run very smooth indeed.

But before going home to dream of his good fortune, Lord Aldean had not forgotten to call at Mallow's rooms, only to learn from the night porter that their occupant was still absent. Little thinking how Laurence's impulsive Irish spirit had led him into difficulties, Jim scribbled a few lines on his card, to say that Major Semberry had left that evening for Florence, and that, with Mrs. Carson, he intended to follow by the nine o'clock morning mail from Victoria. This card he gave to the porter, with strict injunctions that it was to be handed to Mr. Mallow immediately on his return. That done, Aldean abandoned himself with a clear conscience to the full enjoyment of his dreams.

Shortly before eight o'clock next morning he drove to the station, arriving there on the stroke of the half-hour. He quite expected to find Mallow waiting for him; but there was no sign of him. Jim could only conclude he had not received the card.

"Been out all night, I suppose," grumbled Aldean, in no very good temper. "In the thick of it with the brutes in Soho, I expect. I only hope he won't get into trouble with them. Must have spotted and followed Hain; he's probably hanging on to him till the police run him in."

It was a cold, raw morning, and Jim, in a fur-lined coat, rolled about the platform like a giant bear. He took two through tickets to Florence, bought a couple of morning papers and some illustrated weeklies, and, with the assistance of the guard, engaged a carriage supplied with foot-warmers. Hardly had he completed his preparations when Olive made her appearance, accompanied, to his great delight, by Miss Ostergaard. Both ladies were in the best of spirits.

142

"But I don't see Mr. Mallow," said Olive, her face falling somewhat. "Does he not know that I am going?"

"Told him so last night—that is, I left an explanatory card for him; but he can't have got it."

"Oh, Lord Aldean, I trust nothing is wrong with him."

"No fear of that," replied Jim, confidently. "You can trust Mallow to look after himself; besides, he told me he might very likely be away for some time over this Hain business."

"Is that the man connected with the murder?"

"Yes; Vraik reported that he had seen him talking to Semberry in Poplar Street, so Mallow determined to catch him himself."

"Talking to Major Semberry?" said Tui, thoughtfully. "That looks as though the Major had something to do with poor Mr. Carson's death."

"I have not the slightest doubt about it. Semberry knows a good deal more than he is inclined to tell. But you needn't worry about Mallow, Mrs. Carson—or, shall I say, Miss Bellairs?"

"No, no," said Olive, hurriedly. "Don't please do that for the present. Have you the tickets?"

"Yes; tickets, and carriages, and papers. Everything is square."

"Are you well wrapped up?" asked Tui, with an air of proprietorship.

"Warm as toast," said Jim, laughing, and they walked down the platform.

"You have left nothing behind, Jim?"

"Nothing, except my heart."

"And that is in good keeping," said Olive, smiling. "Lord Aldean, wait in the carriage with Tui while I buy a paper."

"Plenty of papers here," said the stupid Aldean, not seeing her kindly intention.

Tui, more quick-witted, turned over the journals.

"Telegraph, Morning Post, Daily Mail, Sketch, and Graphic," she counted, "and not a single fashion-paper amongst them; so like a man."

Jim looked depressed, and Olive went off, laughing, in search of publications of a more particularly feminine nature. Tui and her lover were left alone in the carriage.

"Oh, what a donkey!" she said, shaking her head.

For the moment Aldean failed utterly to understand. Then a comprehension of her meaning dawned upon him, and doubtless he did his best to make amends.

Tui's farewell left him in a state of ecstasy, which endured long

143

after the train rolled out of the station. He stared solemnly out of the window, and Olive, who knew well where his thoughts were, had not the heart to break so sacred a silence. She let him dream on, and secluded herself behind her morning paper. He had been indulging himself for the best part of half an hour, when a startled exclamation from Olive aroused him.

"Oh, how dreadful!" she said.

"'What's the matter?" said Jim, shortly. "Anything wrong?"

"I should think so. Poor Mr. Brock has been run over."

"By Jove! you don't say so? When? Where?"

"Yesterday evening, in Marquis Street," said Olive, referring to the paper. "He was crossing the road, when a hansom, coming too quickly round the corner, knocked him down. His leg was broken, and they took him to Charing Cross Hospital."

"Poor old chap!" said Aldean, sympathetically. "Deuced hard lines on a man of his age. Marquis Street, did you say? Why, that's where Semberry lives."

"He intended calling on Major Semberry, I know," said Olive. "In his letter to Miss Slarge he said so. Dear me, I am sorry for him."

"So am I. He's a good old chap, is Brock. May I see the account?"

Olive passed him the paper. He read the account, but beyond being sincerely sorry for his friend the vicar, he attached no especial importance to it. Little did he think how significant it really was. This particular ill wind, in common with others of its kind, blew great good to somebody. That somebody was Major Semberry. How good a wind it was for him they neither of them knew till it was too late.

144

THE FOURTH SCENE

IN FLORENCE

CHAPTER I

"ON THE LONG TRAIL"

The efforts of some people to convert what is purely a business errand into one of pleasure are rarely crowned with success, though there are times when the process can be inversed with some degree of profit. "An extreme busyness is an invariable sign of a deficient vitality." There never was a greater truth than that. Complete enjoyment of the picturesque argues the possession of a large capacity for dreaming and dawdling. One must, so to speak, supply one's own atmosphere, steep one's self in romance, acquaint one's self with the mystery of the past for the toning down of an all-too-obvious present. The successful pursuit of pleasure is every whit as arduous as the compilation of pounds, shillings, and pence. Nay, more so, because for every man who achieves the one, there are a thousand who achieve the other. True enjoyment is, of all prey, the most elusive—the most horribly tantalizing. You think you have it, and "heigh, presto!" the wily thing is "right about face," and grinning at you half a mile away! Call art a jealous mistress if you will. Pleasure is twin sister to her. She demands and will have, the absolute abandonment of you—all or nothing.

And so it was that neither Aldean nor Olive succeeded in extracting any pleasure out of their well-nigh meteoric flight to Florence. They could not give themselves up to the thing. Their object was ever before them, and they were conscious only of it and the hundred-and-one petty annoyances of a continental railway transit. They ate, they slept, they talked, they read—not for the sake of eating, talking, or reading, but merely to pass the time. They were acutely aware of an all-pervading mustiness, of the rumble of

145

wheels, and of the fussy interference of various individuals terming themselves officers—customs and otherwise.

Each station seemed more draughty than the last, and with each mile it seemed to grow more cold. At last—in the early morning of the second day—they found themselves at the Florence Centrale, in a temperature and fog which would have done credit to the estuary of the Thames.

From Milan Aldean, ever practical, had telegraphed for rooms to the Hotel Magenta; and thither they proceeded in course of time, in what is known as an omnibus. A good breakfast, and both of them felt more at peace with themselves, though Olive had to give in and lie down for an hour or so. Aldean, whom nothing seemed to tire, shaved and bathed. He dressed himself in fresh clothes and felt as fresh as paint. (The simile was his own). Then, lighting a strong cigar—former experience had proved to him the luxury of tobacco in these parts—he took a brisk walk for the consideration of campaign details.

In a city of the size of Florence you have the disadvantage of being able to run up against your next-door neighbour half-a-dozen times a day. From the Via Tornabouni—haunted by forestieri—to the end of the Lung 'Arno or Cascine Gardens is no very great stretch, and here, in the Hyde Park of Florence, Aldean had a notion that his stroll might prove most profitable. Failing that—the gentleman of whom he was in search having no very pronounced artistic cravings—he argued that Giacoso's rather than the Duomo, the Gambrinus Bier Halle rather than the Uffizi should prove remunerative as a hunting ground. But nowhere had he any luck. Perchance it was that Messieurs Semberry and friend were resting for the moment. At all events, they showed no signs of life, and Aldean, having drawn blank, returned to the hotel.

Olive was up and waiting for him—sufficiently refreshed, she said, to get to business straight away. That their conversation might be unfettered—it was certain to revolve round the one topic—they lunched in a private room.

Aldean deplored his bad luck. "It's worse than looking for a needle in a haystack," he declared.

"Have you examined the visitors' list?" asked Olive.

"No—no use. Semberry only arrived yesterday. They require somewhat longer notice for these things in this part of the world. As to Carson—well, of course, he will not be known as Carson here, and for his other name we can hardly look, seeing we don't know it."

"What do you think is best to be done, then?"

146

"Well, Mrs. Carson," said Aldean, reflectively, "I think perhaps you had better stay in this afternoon. It might frighten these young birds did they happen to see you. They won't take so much notice of me; at all events, they would not be likely to connect me with the business. I'll walk round the town and keep my eyes open! Somewhere about five I'll drive in the Cascine. If they show anywhere it will probably be in the gardens."

"And if you do see them?"

"Oh, I'll keep them in sight, be sure. My next step then will depend upon what they say or do. Semberry I can manage by threatening to report his conduct at the War Office; but it will not be so easy to deal with Carson."

"I think it will," said Olive, scornfully. "The man is a poor, cowardly creature. You can terrorize him into obedience."

"In that case, I'll bring him here and let you deal with him. When we get the truth out of him I shall—let me see," mused Aldean, "did I promise Tui to kick him or drown him? One of the two, I'm sure."

"I almost despair of ever getting the money back," said Olive.

"Depends upon what he has done with it. I expect we shall have to get him arrested, after all, and prove that he has annexed that fifty thousand pounds under false pretences. The British Consul will help me in all that. In the mean time I'll bring him here if I can."

Olive agreed that this seemed about the most feasible line of action. She remained at home—glad indeed of the opportunity for rest—while her coadjutor cast around for the trail. But in all his peregrinations Jim caught no glimpse of those he was in search of. In no very good temper he hailed a carriage and drove to the Cascine Gardens. His last hope lay in that direction.

"If I don't see them here," he grumbled, "there's no chance of coming across them to-night. I dare say I shall have to persuade the Consul to take up the matter, after all."

As the wretched vettura bumped over the pavement of the Lung 'Arno, Aldean scanned the faces of the chattering and gesticulating crowd. The sun was dying in splendour over Bello Sguardo Hill. The river—yet to be swollen by its winter rains—caught up the golden light, and spread it over its vast gravel bed. To the green avenue of the Cascine a variety of carriages, from the springless conveyance of the streets to the imposing equipage emblazoned with armorial bearings commensurate in size only with the age of the families they represented, were hurrying there to parade between the mounted gendarmes at either end. These latter were quite admirable in their capacity of ornate signposts. Aldean found plenty to amuse him, but still there was no sign of either fugitive. His patience was beginning to show signs of wear, though there was no one to observe them but the cocchiere, and he was impervious to everything of that nature. Just then he became conscious of a man and a woman talking and laughing together in a smart green victoria. They were travelling in the same direction as himself, and, as they passed him, he noticed the coachman was in livery. With something like a sigh of relief Aldean leaned forward to instruct his man to follow—a somewhat difficult task to him, for his Italian was none of the best in his calmest of moments.

"Cocchiere! Carozza! la carozza verdi, subito, presto." The Italian jehu nodded and cracked his whip. At the same moment the green victoria was stopped in the crowd. In another moment he would have been alongside. "No, no!" shouted Aldean, laying his hand on the man's arm. The bewildered cocchiere pulled up. Then Carson's carriage began to move out of the throng. "Si! Si!" cried Aldean, in answer to the interrogative aspect of his coachman. "Adagio! piano! slow, you fool!"

Jim's driver became suddenly inspired. He caught sight of a lady in the green carriage. He was evidently driving a jealous husband bent upon the spoliation of an intrigue. This appealed to him in every way. With the greatest skill he kept in the rear of Carson's vehicle, and turned only to hold up his five fingers twice. "Dieci lire!" he said, as his inspirations—now aspirations—took definite shape.

"Si! si! venti lire si vi piace! adagio! comprenez? Parlezvous Francais? non! ah quelle dommage. Allez! piano! Go slow, you ass!" Thus did Aldean frantically endeavour to make himself clear. But those two words, "venti lire," had done their work, and Jim congratulated himself on his linguistic attainments. "Easier job than I thought," he said to himself. "I'll stick to Carson till I catch him. The brute! he doesn't know I am at his tail. Gigglin' and laughin' with that girl—hang him! hang her! hang 'em both!"

By this time it was getting dark, and people were beginning to leave the Cascine for dinner. Quite ignorant that he was being followed, Carson, in the highest spirits, drove along the Lung 'Arno, and in a short time his carriage turned into the Piazza Santa Trinita, where it stopped before the door of the Hotel du Sud, opposite to the column. Clara and her friend alighted and disappeared into the hotel. Aldean jumped down, and, bidding the coachman to wait, ran up the steps in mortal terror lest he should miss them. The concierge—a vision of gold lace and moustache—advanced with a smile, and in French begged to know what Monsieur might require.

"I want to see the lady and gentleman who have just come in," replied Aldean, in the same language.

"Signor and Signora Boldini," said the man. "Assuredly, Monsieur; they are on the first floor. Shall I present the card of Monsieur?"

"There is no necessity. Take me upstairs and show me the room; Signor Boldini expects me," said Aldean, making the best excuse he could think of at the moment.

"In that case, I shall conduct Monsieur with pleasure," replied the gold-laced personage, in his magnificent way. "Will Monsieur give himself the trouble to ascend?"

Monsieur did, and was speedily ushered into a gilded and ornate salon. In Italian the man announced that a gentleman desired to see Signor Boldini. He closed the door, leaving Aldean face to face with Carson.

Clara paled somewhat as she recognized the visitor, but she kept her head. She evidently meant to see things through. Carson shrank back at the sight of Aldean as though expectant of a blow, and collapsed into a chair nerveless and terrified. Jim looked on grimly.

"Well, Mr. Carson," he said, in no very amiable tone, "you have given me a considerable amount of trouble. What have you to say for yourself?"

"What need he say?" cried Clara, seeing that her accomplice was incapable of speech. "How dare you come in here uninvited, Lord Aldean?"

"Dare is not a word, young woman, that I am accustomed to hear from domestic servants."

"I am no servant," replied Clara, with a flash of anger.

"Thought not," said Jim, coolly. "I never believed you were, but I hardly expected to find that your real profession was that of spy."

"A spy, a spy! What do you mean?"

"Oh, I think you know pretty well. The report you made to your uncle Jeremiah was the work of a spy."

"My uncle!" gasped Clara, steadying herself by the table. "Yes; your uncle. I know all about him, so does Mr. Mallow, so does Miss Bellairs."

"My wife?" murmured Carson, speaking for the first time.

"Oh, you have found your tongue at last, have you?" cried Jim,

149

striding over to the trembling coward. "I wonder why I don't throw you out of the window."

"This violence—this insult——" panted the man.

"Oh, don't be afraid; I'm not going to make a mess of you just yet. How dare you call Miss Bellairs your wife?"

"I—I was married to her."

"You were—under a false name, to rob her of her money. Perhaps you are not aware that such a marriage is void. Miss Bellairs is not your wife; her money is not yours. I am going to give you the chance of handing it over. Take it, or go to gaol like the swindler you are."

"How dare you call him a swindler?" said Clara, savagely.

"Because I like to call things by their right names. It's a case of speaking by the book. I know all about your Anarchist schemes, and Madame Death-in-Life, Drabble, Rouge, and all the rest of the gang. However, I didn't come here to waste breath on either of you. You come along with me, Carson, or Boldini, or whatever else you choose to call yourself."

"Where do you want me to go?" whimpered the wretched creature, looking up at the towering figure of Aldean.

"To my hotel. Come along, up with you!"

Clara dashed to the bell. "I'll call the landlord and have you turned out!" she said viciously. "You can't bully us!"

"Don't want to. Sorry if I'm not conducting the business according to etiquette. You know more about this sort of thing than I do. Ring the bell by all means, and I'll have up the police. Ring; go on."

"No, no, Clara, don't!" shrieked Boldini, leaping out of his chair at the mention of the police. "He knows too much."

"Hold your tongue," said the woman, between her teeth. "He can prove nothing, you fool."

"The police can judge of that," replied Aldean, quietly. "Ring."

But Miss Trall did not ring. She knew better. She recognized that whatever he might know, Lord Aldean knew quite enough to make the intervention of the police unpleasant. The game was up, she saw plainly. So reluctantly she yielded.

"We can do all that is to be done here," said she, sullenly, fighting every inch.

"I'm afraid not," answered Jim, suavely. "My hotel is the best place. There's a cab waiting." Then, seeing that Clara was still irresolute, he took out his watch. "I'll give you just two minutes."

150

Clara moved slowly across the room to where Boldini sat in sheer terror. "What shall we do?" she asked, in a low voice.

"Go, go," moaned the man. "We must go; perhaps we can make terms."

Aldean overheard the remark. "It is my right to make terms," he said, "and I make these. Give back the money; confess the whole conspiracy, and you can go where you will."

For a moment or two the pair looked at one another. Clara bent forward and whispered something in Boldini's ear. He nodded, and a gleam of hope passed across his face as he rose, holding a handkerchief to his mouth.

"We are ready to go with you," said Clara, turning towards Aldean.

"Very good. Come on."

CHAPTER II

"ONE PORTION OF THE CONSPIRACY"

Certain features of the present position appealed to Lord Aldean. It was his first experience of the kind, and perhaps what gratified him most was the consciousness of the power which so suddenly had become vested in him. The knowledge that in this human rubber he held all the trumps in no wise lessened his enjoyment of the situation. There still remained to play them, and he felt pretty confident that in the end he and his partner would not have many tricks to deplore. For the moment his antagonists were absolutely in his hands—the man frightened to death of his skin; the woman believing that for the time being, at least, discretion was surely the better part of valour.

He hurried them off to the Hotel Magenta, there to be dealt with by the woman they had deceived and plundered.

As he fully expected, Olive was greatly agitated. He supposed it was womanlike for her to show most anger at the sight of her whilom maid. Her husband, after all, had at no time been anything

151

to her—for him she had nothing more than the contempt she had always felt. She ignored him completely.

"How dare you come into my presence?" she said to the woman. "How can you have the face to look at me, after the shameful way in which you have behaved?"

"Blame your friend for that," answered Clara, doggedly. "I would not have come at all had I known you were here."

"Exactly. That is why I did not think it necessary you should know of Mrs. Carson's presence here," exclaimed Aldean, smoothly.

"Mrs. Carson!" sneered Clara, with a contemptuous laugh. "Oh yes; Mrs. Carson, of course."

Olive looked at the woman with a flush of anger. "No insolence, if you please," she said. "And you!" turning on her shrinking husband—"who and what are you, pray?"

"Carlo Boldini," he replied almost inaudibly.

"Are you an Italian?"

"My father was. He married an Englishwoman."

"So I am Signora Boldini?" said Olive, bitterly.

Clara laughed again. "Oh yes! Signora Boldini," she repeated, seating herself complacently beside her companion.

The two sat there like prisoners in the dock. Aldean began to feel positively judicial. The woman was horribly insolent.

"I would suggest, for your own sake, that you endeavour to restrain yourself," he said, moving to the end of the room in search of pen and ink. "You are in quite enough trouble as it is."

"Oh, I don't mind her insolence, Lord Aldean," said Olive, quietly; "she can do me no harm."

"Don't be too sure of that!" flashed out Miss Trall, vindictively.

"Clara, Clara!" implored Boldini, "it's best to say nothing—least said, soonest mended."

Aldean, arranging his writing materials on a table at Olive's elbow, looked up. "I fear you will find that proverb doesn't apply to what is to come," said he cheerfully. "Mrs. Carson, as this lady may be called for the present, will question you sufficiently closely as to the various details of the conspiracy. You will answer her questions categorically while I write them down. The little précis will then be signed by you both and witnessed by myself."

"And if we refuse this confession, as you call it," questioned Clara, who withal was obviously uneasy.

"Oh, in that case, as I have told you before, I hand you over to the police. Now, then, come along; we have no time to waste on you. Begin."

152

Jim dipped his pen into the ink and waited; while Olive, after a sharp glance at the two before her, launched into the examination. Reversing her previous attitude, she addressed herself exclusively to Boldini. She judged a studied indifference to be more effectual from woman to woman.

"Who are you?" she asked.

"I have told you that my father was an Italian named Boldini. My mother was an Englishwoman. I was brought up and educated in London."

"Are you an Anarchist?"

"Yes. I was affianced to the cause by my aunt, Mrs. Arne."

"Oh, so Mrs. Arne is your aunt?"

"My father's sister," explained Boldini, who was recovering his self-possession somewhat. "He was an Anarchist, but he is dead. My mother also is dead."

"Is Major Semberry in Florence?"

"No!" said Clara, loudly, before her accomplice could speak.

"Useless to lie," said Aldean, looking up; "we followed him here from Victoria Station. Suppose you put your question in another form, Mrs. Carson?"

"Where is Major Semberry staying?" amended Olive.

"At the Albergo della Pace, on the Lung 'Arno," replied Boldini, seeing it was hopeless.

"Have you seen him?"

"Yes, once—this morning."

"Have you known Major Semberry long?"

"Since he came to England in the Pharaoh. I never met him before. But I had heard of him."

"From whom?"

"From Dr. Drabble and my aunt."

"Is he an Anarchist?"

"No; his connection with us has to do merely with this money."

"You have the fifty thousand pounds in your possession?"

"Yes; part of it is in Paris."

"And where is the remainder?"

Boldini wriggled uneasily and looked at Clara. She gave him no assistance, but kept her eyes fixedly on the floor. "I have the other part of it at my hotel in circular notes on the Crédit Lyonnais."

"How many have you, and what is the value of each?"

"I have twenty of one thousand pounds."

"Twenty thousand," reckoned Olive. "Major Semberry's share, I presume?" she added, with unconcealed scorn.

"Y-e-s," said Boldini, reluctantly, with another wriggle. "And the remaining thirty thousand is at the Crédit Lyonnais in Paris, you say?"

"Yes. That is my share."

"We will talk of the money later," she said. "By the way," with a glance at Boldini's hands, "I observe you have recovered the use of your hand."

"It was never in need of recovery," snapped Clara.

"I guessed as much—one of the smaller embellishments of your very ornate conspiracy. Boldini, since you confess that you are not Mr. Carson, please to hand over that bangle."

Boldini shook it down on to his wrist. "You can have it with pleasure," said he, sullenly, "but I can't get it off."

"How was it got on?" asked Aldean.

"It was filed through and joined on my wrist."

"Ah, well! I am afraid that process will have to be reversed to-morrow. It can't be done here to-night. Who gave you that bangle?"

"Dr. Drabble.'

"Was it he who killed Angus Carson?" asked Olive, with embarrassing suddenness.

"I don't know."

"Come, come!" cried Jim, sharply, "the truth, please."

"I am telling you the truth," retorted Boldini "I do not know who killed Carson. I did not even know that he was killed until Miss Bellairs there asked me about the smell of sandal-wood. Then, as I read the account of the murder in the Morning Planet, it occurred to me that the dead man might be the person I was representing. I asked Semberry about it, and he admitted I was right; but he refused me all details."

"Then Angus Carson was really murdered in Athelstane Place?"

"According to Semberry, yes."

"Did Semberry say that he had killed him?" asked Aldean.

"No. He swore he did not kill him; and that he did not know who did. Drabble also declares himself innocent."

"You are all innocent, according to your own showing," said Olive, ironically; "but I can hardly believe, Signor Boldini, that you were so simple as to assume the impersonation of an original of whom you know nothing."

Clara looked up with a strange smile on her sallow face. "You evidently know nothing of the Anarchists," she said coldly. "Implicit obedience is the first law with them. Carlo was told to represent a man called Angus Carson. He did so without asking questions. How

154

much longer is this to go on?" she cried furiously; "it is now seven o'clock. I am tired of it."

"I don't care for the Socratian method myself," observed Aldean, blandly. "On the whole, I think it would be best, perhaps, for Boldini here to acquaint us with the particulars of his share in the conspiracy straight away."

"Tell them, Carlo!" commanded Miss Trall.

"Shall I tell them everything?" whimpered Boldini.

"Everything," she repeated emphatically. "We have cut ourselves off from the brotherhood—so it really does not matter. Lord Aldean has promised to let us go if we tell the truth. You had better tell him."

"Tell the truth and restore the money," murmured Jim, politely.

Boldini winced at the last remark, but nevertheless applied himself to his most unpalatable task. He evidently intended cutting it as short as possible. He started off at top speed. Aldean wrote down the gist of what he said.

"As I told you, I am an Anarchist," he explained shortly, "and by the oath I took to the cause I was bound to render obedience. In June last Drabble came to me and stated that the brotherhood could obtain a sum of fifty thousand pounds; and that I was to help. He introduced me to Major Semberry, and told me that I was to assume the character of a man called Angus Carson, from India. Semberry had a portrait of this man, and I altered my appearance in some degree so as to more clearly resemble it. This was not difficult, as I was very like the portrait. I cut my hair short and parted it at the side instead of in the centre; I let the ends of my moustache droop instead of twisting them up. Then Drabble told me that I must pretend that my right hand was injured, and wear it in a sling, which I did. The bracelet was produced by Drabble and placed on my wrist. Major Semberry then told me all about Carson's life in India, and took some trouble in seeing that I acquired a sufficient knowledge of the country. He took me to his rooms in Marquis Street, St. James's, and made me dress in Carson's clothes, which he showed me in a sandal-wood chest. Afterwards I think that he and Drabble must have seen the leader in the Morning Planet about the sandal-wood scent, for they took Carson's Indian clothes from me and supplied me with new ones in place of them."

"But how was it that Mr. Mallow smelt sandal-wood on your clothes, if this was so?"

Boldini explained. "There was a smart coloured waistcoat," he said, "which belonged to Carson, which I admired very much. When

155

Drabble took the clothes from me I kept that back without his knowledge. When I met Mr. Mallow I was wearing it, and, of course, it was scented by the box. That was how he noticed the perfume."

"Did you never suspect that this smell was in some way connected with the murder?"

"No; how should I? I did not know that the real Carson had been killed; and, although I myself read the leader in the Morning Planet—which was the only report of the case I did read—I never thought for a moment that the dead man was the one I was representing. When you, Miss Bellairs, spoke to me of this sandal-wood odour and Athelstane Place, I was really and truly ignorant of the murder. It was only on reflection I put two and two together. I remembered the severed hand and the sandal-wood perfume referred to in the paper; I knew also that the Carson I represented came from India. Then it was that I made Semberry tell me the truth. He admitted the murder, but swore he was ignorant as to who committed it. Then I married you, Miss Bellairs, and got the money."

"For the Anarchists or for yourself?"

"For myself and Clara," admitted Boldini, shamelessly. "I hated the Anarchists, and grasped the opportunity to be free from them. I sold out the stocks and shares, and transferred the proceeds to my real name at the Crédit Lyonnais. I have the twenty thousand pounds here in circular notes, because I have to give them to Semberry to-morrow."

"Why did you not give them to-day?"

"Because I would only give them to him in return for the sandal-wood box and the clothes of Carson—which it contains."

"Why do you want that chest?"

Boldini showed himself in his true colours. "I like Carson's clothes," said he, with the simplicity of a child. "He had nice clothes. I am to have them to-morrow, and then I will pay him the twenty thousand pounds."

"I am afraid you will have to forego both those pleasures," said Aldean, grimly. "Your vanity must, in this instance, be sacrificed to your safety. I will trouble you to hand over those circular notes."

"They are at my hotel," said Boldini, rising with alacrity. "Shall I go for them?"

"Oh, pray don't trouble. Miss Trall can go for the notes."

Clara looked at Boldini, and Boldini looked at Clara.

Aldean made a shrewd guess that the man was attempting a trick to gain time, for every now and then his hand wandered mechanically to his breast pocket. It was probable that the notes were there. Jim expected a fight for the spoil; but Clara laid down her arms without a murmur, and instructed Boldini to do the same.

"Give him the notes," said she, curtly.

One by one they were counted and laid on the table before Aldean. Boldini winced as if he were having a tooth drawn. Olive counted them and found them correct. There were twenty notes of the value of one thousand pounds each—printed in francs on the Crédit Lyonnais paper.

"Good," said Aldean, with a nod. "Now for your cheque-book."

"I won't! I won't!" cried Boldini, childishly. "The rest of the money is mine."

"We need not argue that question over again," said Olive, coldly. "Write a cheque in my name for thirty thousand pounds—that is, seven hundred and fifty thousand francs. If not, Lord Aldean shall call up the police."

"Oh, Clara! what shall I——"

"Give it to them," she interrupted fiercely. "What is the use of fighting?"

With tears of rage in his eyes Boldini wrote the cheque and gave it to Olive. She looked at it with a nod, and passed it on to Aldean.

"So far so good," said the latter, cheerfully. "Now, Signor Boldini, sign this confession."

Without a word the man took pen and signed it, Jim attesting it with a flourish. "I think that is all," he remarked, rising. "You can go now."

"Am I not to sign it?" asked Clara, scowling.

"There is no necessity. Beyond that you are a spy, you are of small account."

"I am of this account," said Clara, furiously, "that Carlo is my husband."

"Your husband!" exclaimed Olive.

"Yes; we were married a year ago in St. Chad's Church, Marylebone. Carlo Boldini to Clara Trall. I am his wife—not you."

"Thank God!" said Olive. "Oh, thank God!"

"You are an infernal scoundrel," cried Jim, advancing on Boldini. "I have a good mind to wring your neck."

Clara threw her arm round the man. "Let us go, Lord Aldean. No words can alter things now. I am Clara Boldini, and she"—pointing to Olive—"is nothing."

"I am a free woman, at least. Heaven be praised, I never was that man's wife. I know now why you agreed so readily to our

157

bargain," she said, turning on Boldini. "Go, you miserable creature, and lead a better life if you can."

"I have no money," said Boldini. "Will you give me some?"

"We will arrange that to-morrow," struck in Aldean, sharply. "You don't deserve any help; but as the Anarchists are after you, Miss Bellairs and I will give you some help."

"The Anarchists!" repeated Clara and Boldini. Both paled to the lips.

Without another word, they left the room. At last Aldean saw how it was. Throughout he had been a trifle uneasy at the extreme and unexpected smoothness with which things were progressing. He had not looked for the process of disgorgement to be accomplished with so little difficulty. Boldini's attitude had been subservient; Clara's altogether too unreal to convince him. In the most abject coward there is at least a modicum of obstinacy when at bay; and he could not understand how a plunder thus arduously come by should be disgorged with so little resistance. The mention of the word Anarchist explained everything to him. The effect of it upon both miscreants left nothing to the imagination. They were thoroughly scared. This, then, was what they had dreaded; for this it was they had been ready to throw everything by the board—for silence. Exposure to the police would have revealed their immediate whereabouts to their fellows. That meant pursuit speedy and relentless; and that, in its turn, meant death to them both.

For some minutes after they had left neither Jim nor Olive spoke—he, occupied with his ruminations; she, with her own innermost thoughts. Jim broke the silence.

"Poor devils," he said, closing the door, "they have worse before them than what they have just been through. And I think they know it. At the hands of their brethren they are likely to meet with treatment a good deal less clement. But what, may I ask, are you thinking of, Mrs.—I mean, Miss Bellairs? You look most supremely happy."

"I am thinking of your friend and mine," said Olive.

CHAPTER III

THE SANDAL-WOOD CHEST

"Well, Lord Aldean," asked Olive, when she met her companion, hatted and gloved, in the saloon next morning, "what next?"

"The next item on our programme is an official visit to Semberry," answered the young man, promptly. "A bit early for a call, perhaps; but I'm the bird, you know, after the worm—the Major's the worm. Won't do, you know, to let him and the Boldinis come together and arrange their little plans. Union's always strength, isn't it, Miss Bellairs?"

"Miss Bellairs!" repeated Olive, after him, with a long breath of satisfaction; "how good that sounds! But about Major Semberry. For all we know he may have seen the Boldinis last night."

Aldean wagged his head judiciously. "Not likely; they'd not seek him, believe me. Now that we have Semberry's share of the loot, both Boldini and his wife would rather be excused that interview. They are too anxious about their little selves to bother him."

"Perhaps; at all events, let us hope so. Shall I come with you?"

"I'd rather you didn't, if you don't mind. Better let me tackle Semberry in my own way. He won't climb down like Boldini, you know; in fact, I don't anticipate he will be an easy customer to deal with at all. He'll fight," said Aldean; "so shall I."

"I can't understand now why the Boldinis gave in so utterly."

"Had to—no choice for them," replied Jim promptly. "Case of devil and the deep sea, you know. Let's assume we are the deep sea, and the Anarchists and police and all of that ilk are the—well, the other thing. You see, police would have meant publicity, and publicity would have meant extinction for them, so far as this world is concerned; and that, though probably a relief to them in the future state, was not exactly what they sought at present."

"Could we have them arrested even now?" asked Olive.

"Well, perhaps, with an infinite amount of trouble and red-tapeism, we might get the British Consul to help us so far; but that sort of thing takes time, and they might bolt at any moment. I'm glad they had the sense to climb down. It's all right now. We have the money and the confession. They are no use to us any longer."

"Yes, we have the circular notes; and they, I suppose, are safe," said Miss Bellairs, reflecting. "But that cheque, Lord Aldean—Boldini might stop it by telegram."

"He'll only tumble back into the pit if he does," said Aldean, decisively; "but I won't trust him any more than you do. Before I see Semberry, I'll drop in at a bank I know here, and ask them to cash the cheque."

"They won't cash so large a cheque without inquiry, surely?"

"That's just the point; if not, the banker'll have to wire to the Crédit Lyonnais in Paris, and we'll soon know if Boldini's been up to hanky-panky. That's the worst of playing a game like this with a rascal," added Aldean, musingly; "he's always got an ace somewhere."

"We must watch his sleeve," laughed Olive. "Well, Lord Aldean, off you go to Major Semberry, and I'll wait here till you return."

"Bringing my sheaves with me," said Jim, with a grin, and forthwith departed.

Left alone, Olive sat down and wrote a long letter to Tui, in which she praised Lord Aldean's common sense and willing help in the most glowing terms. With joy she told Tui of her freedom; how Clara was Boldini's, alias Carson's, true wife; and how everything had gone off so much more quietly than either of them had dared to hope.

Her letter ended with a casual inquiry after Mallow, and expressed a hope that Tui had seen him. As the strength of a chain lies in its weakest link, so the strength of Olive's letter lay in the pointedly trifling allusion to Mallow. Small wonder if Tui smiled to herself at the studied indifference of those few lines. Women understand those things.

As Olive directed and stamped the envelope a knock came to the door, and a smiling waiter entered with a letter addressed in lead pencil to Miss Bellairs. She did not know the writing, but, when the man had gone, she soon discovered that the letter was from Clara. There were two hurriedly pencilled pages commencing abruptly, without date or address, as follows:—

"I don't want you to think worse of me than you do, for the trouble I brought on you was not of my making. I am—or, rather, I was—a tool in the hands of the Anarchists, and against my will I was forced to play what I know was a mean part. My father, Michael Trall, was a gentleman, and at one time very rich. But he gambled away all his money, and left my mother and myself to starve in London. I am now thirty years of age, but never since an infant have I seen my father. Neither have I heard of him; nor do I even know what he is like in appearance. But I do know that he was a bad father and a bad husband, who broke his wife's heart. My poor mother died when I was only two years of age; and I might have been an outcast in the streets but that my good uncle Jeremiah took charge of me. He had a little money, and until I was twenty we lived on that. He was kind to me; but, alas! he was the slave of drink—and, by indulgence in it, so weakened his will and self-respect that he was the prey of any scoundrel who cared to meddle with him. Dr. Drabble met him ten years ago or more, and, seeing in him a useful tool, inveigled him into the toils of the Anarchists. I tried to rescue my uncle as he had rescued me, but in vain; so, to protect him, I also took the oath to the brotherhood. I was forced to implicit obedience—I was ordered to Casterwell as your servant, in order to spy upon you. I confess that, in one sense, I went willingly—for I am Carlo's wife; and, as Dr. Drabble had arranged that he was to marry you for the sake of the money, I was jealous. I consented to keep quiet, only because I wanted the fifty thousand pounds. I had made up my mind that Carlo and I should use it, and once and for ever free ourselves from the brotherhood. You have taken that hope from us; but I don't blame you even now. The money was yours, and we swindled you. Carlo and I are going away, and you will never see us or hear from us again. He is a poor, weak creature in your eyes; but in mine he is the man I love, and I hope to be happy with him in the future—if only we can escape the relentless hand of the brotherhood. If I knew who killed Carson, I would tell you; but I do not. I suspect Drabble, since he brought the bangle to Carlo; but this is mere suspicion. Did you know the miserable life I have had, you would pity me. I am sorry if I was rude last night. I do not wish to be rude; but I am surrounded on all sides by terror and death, and care not sometimes what I say or do. You have been very good to me; and I thank you. Marry Mr. Mallow—I know he loves you—and forget Carlo and the miserable woman, Clara Boldini.

"P.S.—When Carlo and I are safe and settled we intend to send for my uncle to live with us. We will rescue him from the brotherhood. Carlo is not a bad man—indeed, he is not. Weakness is his only fault. With me he begs your pardon for his wickedness; but remember his character, his oath, his helplessness, and forgive him.—C.B."

It was a sad letter, written by a woman who, surrounded by better people and under good influence, might have remained true

161

to the better part of her nature. By the tides of life she had been swept to the lee shore of disaster. Olive felt that in no small degree fate had been against her, and in her generosity she was unwilling to be the one to cast a stone at the unfortunate woman. On the contrary, her impulse prompted her to help Clara with money and advice—to rescue her and her weak husband from their danger, and to help them to their first step on the way to a new life.

With such philanthropic intentions she started off to the Hotel du Sud.

An hour later Aldean returned, followed by a man with a hand-barrow. It was laden with a curious-looking chest of yellowish wood, bound with brass. Dismissing his porter, Aldean had the box taken upstairs and placed in a corner of the salon. He was disappointed that Olive should be absent when he returned with this trophy of his victory over Semberry, but, to pass the time, he set to work to examine the chest's contents. A thin brass key unlocked it, and Aldean was soon so deeply interested in his search that he almost forgot the absence of his fellow-worker. By the time he had reached the bottom of the trunk, the floor of the room was strewn with wearing apparel of all kinds. The chest was literally packed with garments of every colour and pattern imaginable. Shooting-suits of rough home-spun; tropical garbs of white boots, riding-breeches, high brown boots, shirts, scarves, collars, under-wear—all more or less impregnated with the scent of the wood. But amongst all these now useless articles not a scrap of writing. Aldean was disappointed. He had fancied that a stray letter or a journal, or even a card, might have been forthcoming to throw some light on the owner's past. Yet he might have guessed that all evidence likely to inculpate Semberry, or Drabble, or Mrs. Arne would have been removed by one of them before the chest left London. Two out of the three, at least, were old hands at obliterating tracks.

With an observant eye and a careful ear Aldean overhauled the box outside and in. He rapped at the sides, pushing here and tugging there; but, so far as he could see, there was no hollow space either at the sides or below. The chest was plainly made of five thick slabs, which sounded dead and dull when he tapped them. Then Aldean turned his attention to the lid, which was clasped with two broad brass bands dividing it into three equal spaces. These were carved in the laborious Chinese way with impossible flowers and stiffly flying birds.

"Rum thing," muttered Jim, shaking the lid. "Looks like an overgrown glove-box." Round the lid ran a deep rim, fitting down

162

on to the lower portion of the box when locked; and, on examination of the inner side of this, Aldean found a row of brass nails—ostensibly mere ornaments. With infinite patience he pressed every one of the decorations hard. He found that one behind the hasp yielded with difficulty to pressure. Two other nails, one near each end of the lid, proved equally loose. Jim pressed and pressed all three, until suddenly with a click the whole inner skin of the lid fell down, and between this and the top there proved to be a narrow space extending to all four sides. With the lid fell a long blue envelope, sealed with a coat-of-arms in red wax. "Clever dodge," said Jim, picking up the envelope and admiring the workmanship which so skilfully concealed the space in the lid. "But a chap could hide only thin things in it; there's no room for anything else." He looked at the envelope. "The Rev. Manners Brock, Casterwell," he read. "Jupiter! that's queer. Wonder what's inside? feels like dozens of pages. 'Spose this is a letter from Carson, senior, to his old friend. Wonder why Carson, junior, hid it so carefully?"

While he was turning it over, his fingers itching to break the seal, and see if the contents could in any way explain the mystery of Carson's death, Olive came hurriedly into the room. Without stopping to comment on the disordered floor, or the extraordinary figure of Lord Aldean grovelling before the chest with the blue envelope in his hand, she burst out into excited speech the moment she saw him.

"Lord Aldean, they have gone away—Clara and Boldini. They left the hotel last night about nine o'clock!"

"I'm not astonished," replied Jim, getting on to his legs. "Where have they gone to?"

"The people at the hotel couldn't tell me," said Olive, exasperated somewhat at his calm reception of the news. "They paid their bill, packed their things, and went off in a cab to the Central Station. A porter wanted to go with them and look after their luggage, but Clara would not allow him. They have gone!'

"Best thing they could do, Miss Bellairs. Dare say they are afraid of the Anarchists tracking them here. Wonder where they have cleared to?"

"I went to the station to try and find out," said Olive, disconsolately; "but, although I saw the stationmaster and described the appearance, he could give no information. I believe they disguised themselves."

"Well, it doesn't matter much," said Aldean, soothingly; "we have the money and their confession. Let 'em go, if they want to."

"How did they get away without money? They said they had none."

"Another lie, I suppose," said Aldean, sagaciously; "must have had some coin somewhere. Don't you bother, Miss Bellairs; we're done with them—yes! and with Semberry too. Look here," and Aldean produced a packet of papers from his inside pocket. "Here's the Major's confession."

"Did he confess?" gasped Olive, taking the papers.

"Rather. What's more, he wrote out his confession, and I stood over him until he did. There it is, signed by him, witnessed by me, and giving a full account of the conspiracy from first to last."

"Wonderful! However did you manage it?"

"I threatened him with the War Office," replied Aldean, complacently; "told him that Boldini had owned up; and let him see that I knew quite enough to have him cashiered, if nothing else."

"Then he didn't show fight, as you expected?"

"Oh yes, he did. He blustered about his name and position. But I told him I'd take 'em both from him if he didn't own up. In the end he did. You have the gist of it in your hand. He'd have wrung my neck if I hadn't told him I'd wring his if he tried that game. First-class fighting man the Major."

"And what is all this?" asked Olive, with a glance at the sartorial chaos.

"Oh, this is Carson's chest, which Semberry was bringing over to Boldini. I made him give it to me; and for the last half hour I have been hunting for papers and things to see if I could find out anything of importance."

"And you have found nothing?"

"Yes; a secret hiding-place. Look at it, Miss Bellairs. Clever thing, isn't it? Found it by chance. Only a letter in it addressed to Mr. Brock."

Olive took the letter and read the inscription. "It's from Dr. Carson, I suppose," she said, turning it over. "I wonder what's in it?"

"Don't know! Can't be anything about the murder if Carson, senior, wrote it. If we are to believe Boldini and Semberry, the whole scheme was invented by Drabble and this Madame Death-in-Life."

"And which of them killed poor Carson?"

"Ah!" Jim shook his head gravely. "That is just the one thing Semberry could not tell me. He doesn't know."

164

CHAPTER IV

"ANOTHER PORTION OF THE CONSPIRACY"

Olive and Aldean could not but confess themselves well satisfied with the results of their journey. Their achievement had been very tangible. Not only had they extracted from these prime movers of the conspiracy a full and clearly-set-forth confession, but they were in a position comfortably to contemplate repossession of the money itself. In the space of two days they had done this, and, as they now sat at luncheon, they could not refrain from mutual congratulation. The only thing about which there was any doubt in their minds was the wisdom of accepting from Boldini the cheque for thirty thousand pounds. In truth, Aldean, now that the pair had flitted, blamed himself heartily for having done so. He was a trifle young and inexperienced—more particularly in the shady financial tactics, to be expected from people such as he was dealing with—and, at the moment, it did not occur to him that the risk he ran in taking Boldini's cheque was considerable, seeing that there was really nothing to prevent the man bolting right away. Certainly he had confessed that he had no money; but Aldean realized now that either this obstacle had not proved insurmountable or that it had not existed. Long habit had made him so accustomed to look upon cheques as equivalent in value to the sum they represented, he decided to dismiss the uncomfortable sensation that was creeping over him, and to hope for the best. He said nothing more about it to Olive.

"And now, Lord Aldean," said that young lady, joyfully, "we can return home. You, no doubt, will be as glad as I to do that?"

"You can measure my pleasure by your own, Miss Bellairs; we are both in the same galley, I think."

Olive blushed at this allusion to her feeling for Mallow, and thereby, of course, only accentuated its truth.

"When shall we start?" she asked.

"To-night, by the 9.30 express," said Jim, promptly, "unless you want to have another look round the city before you go."

"I would rather get back to Casterwell, Lord Aldean. Let us get away to-night. There is nothing to detain us—except that cheque. What about that?"

"Oh, that's all right, Miss Bellairs. I sent a wire through the

165

bank this morning to Paris. They'll have a reply this afternoon. But are you sure you can bear the fatigue of another long journey so soon?"

"Oh yes; I'm quite recovered now."

"In that case, I'll drop in at Cook's and get the tickets. We'll return in glory, bringing our sheaves with us. Mrs. Purcell shall deliver an address in her best Johnsonese, and Tui shall oblige on the piano with 'See the Conquering Heroine Comes.'"

"Oh no," protested Olive; "you have done the work. Tui shall hold to the original text. But, seriously," she added, stretching out her hand, which Jim grasped warmly, "I give you my best and most sincere thanks, Lord Aldean, for the great kindness you have shown me. I shall never, never forget your good humour and attention, and all your hard work on my behalf."

"Oh, please, please don't, Miss Bellairs," protested Jim, flushing. "Only too jolly glad things have turned out so well. Can't help being sorry I didn't kick Boldini, though; I promised Tui I would, you know."

"I am very glad you didn't. So abject a creature doesn't merit even a kick from you. By the way, is Major Semberry returning to England?"

"What, to fall into the clutches of his Anarchistic friends? I think not. He knows better than to do that. India's his goal. That's where he's making for. Even Mrs. Arne can't reach him there. But what's the use of bothering about any of them now? Let 'em all go to Jericho, or any human rubbish-heap they fancy, for that matter. Will you come out with me, Miss Bellairs, and see about the telegram and tickets?"

"No; I think I'll stay in and devote myself to Major Semberry's confession."

"Oh, you'll enjoy that, I'm sure. It's like the concluding chapters of a sensational novel. I'll leave you to read it, then, while I see about these things."

After he had gone, Olive settled herself in a comfortable chair—that is to say, as comfortable a chair as is to be had in that country—by the window, and plunged eagerly into Semberry's confession. Jim having promised that the statement should be kept strictly private, the Major had not been at all half-hearted about it, but had set forth his iniquities in extenso. Indeed, his vanity would seem to have led him to make the most of his misdoings. As a human document, the confession of Major Horace Semberry was well worth perusal. It ran somewhat after this fashion:—

166

"I am one of those unfortunate devils who have extravagant tastes and no money with which to gratify them. I was brought up extravagantly by an extravagant father; went from an extravagant school into an extravagant regiment; and have had my tastes so fostered by luxury that it is absolute pain for me not to satisfy their cravings in every way. I am always in debt, and never out of difficulties, and I would willingly dispense with the necessaries of life if only I could procure its luxuries. By nature I am not a bad man. It is the want of money that has induced me to do many things I would not otherwise have done. It led me from borrowing to swindling; but I have stopped short at that. If I am accused of murder, I am wrongly accused. Angus Carson was not killed by me. By whom he was killed I know no more than the man in the moon. Four or five years ago, while on leave in London, I met with Dr. Drabble. He is about as big a scoundrel as ever deserved the gallows. He is, moreover, an Anarchist, and by means of his dupes in society—of whom there are many—he contrives to mix with very good people. To do him justice, he hates and despises them all, but 'for the good of the cause'—words which are never off his lips—he feigns an interest in those with money or position, solely that he may recruit his infernal army of destroyers. Somebody once called Drabble 'a wrecker of humanity,' and the title fits him well enough, though it by no means does justice to his devilish ingenuity and wickedness. Why he should approach me with friendly advances I could not understand at the time, but when I came to know him I learned the truth. When he likes, Drabble is a fascinating man, and by finding out the weak spot in people's characters he usually contrives to net them somehow or other. He soon found out my weak spot—want of money—and insisted on being my banker. Like a fool, I borrowed at first a little, then more and more, until I was so deep in his debt that he had it in his power to force me to leave the army. He was not wealthy himself, and I was always puzzled to know how he came by his money. When I was completely in his power he told me. He was an Anarchist, he said, and the money he lent me was taken from the funds of the Brotherhood. To repay that money and something more, he suggested that I should help him in a scheme of his for obtaining a sum of fifty thousand pounds. This was the story he told me:—It appeared that at Casterwell, where Drabble was the parish doctor, there lived a young lady named Miss Bellairs, who, by a family arrangement, was to marry one Angus Carson by name. This man she had never seen. Miss Bellairs—as the doctor had discovered in some way—was possessed of fifty thousand pounds. On her marriage this money was to be paid over to Carson (her husband). Drabble's scheme was this: He knew that I came from India, and was returning there, hence the reason of his friendship. He proposed that I should make the acquaintance of Dr. Carson and his son Angus, and, when the latter came to England to marry Miss Bellairs, that I should contrive to accompany him. I was to introduce Carson to Drabble, and let him persuade the young man to join the Brotherhood, so that he (when married) should hand over the money for their benefit. 'Become intimate with Carson,' said Drabble, 'make yourself indispensable to him, and when you bring him to England introduce him to me. I'll do the rest.' Seeing that Drabble could easily have introduced himself when the young man arrived at Casterwell, I naturally asked why he wished to employ me as a go-between. To this he answered that it was his desire Carson should join the Anarchists before seeing Miss Bellairs; that is, before he went to Casterwell at all, as, were he to fall in love with the girl, which, considering she was both pretty and attractive, was more than probable, he might point-blank refuse to join Drabble in his scheme for the regeneration of mankind. To make a long story short, I agreed to take part in the conspiracy provided I received twenty thousand pounds out of the fifty, but I swear solemnly that neither at the first interview nor at any subsequent one with Drabble, was there any mention of murder. I was to bring Carson home; I was to introduce him to Drabble, and when his enthusiasm had been roused sufficiently to induce him to hand over the fortune which he would acquire by marriage, I was to receive twenty thousand pounds. Is there any roguery in such a scheme?—I think not.

"Shortly after making this arrangement I returned to India, and for some months I had to pay with hard work for my holiday. I was compelled so to attend to my duties that I had no chance of seeing the Carsons. However, I made inquiries, and learned that the doctor was a recluse somewhere up in the Hills, and that he kept his son constantly under his own eye—to educate him for Miss Bellairs, I presume. After several disappointments, extending over twelve months, I obtained leave of absence, and started out on a shooting expedition in the neighbourhood of this modern hermit. As I made it my business to become acquainted with him, it was not long before I attained my object; how, there is no need for me to explain. I became very friendly with Dr. Carson, also with his son, and in time the friendship ripened to intimacy. I got on better with the doctor than with Angus. The latter was a solemn prig, I thought, with the most Puritanical ideas. Still I adapted myself to his humour, and I think he liked me fairly well; but it was no easy task to break down his stiff reserve. For two or three years I visited regularly the elder Carson, until I became so old and so good a friend in his eyes that one day he told me—what I already knew, of course—about Miss Bellairs and her fortune. I suggested that, as Angus was still young, the possession of so large a sum of money might lead him into dissipation, and I further suggested the advisability of some one accompanying him to England, so that there might be at least some check upon him there. Dr. Carson approved of my idea, and when he died, about a year afterwards, he made Angus promise that I should accompany him to Europe. At once I wrote to Drabble and assured him of my success, after which I left India for London with my charge. So far all had gone well. Lord Aldean informs me that Mrs. Purcell wrote to her sister a full description of Carson, of his looks and dress and priggish conversation, and of the sacred bangle he wore on his right wrist. I hated that bangle. It seemed to me effeminate and foolish. But it would not come off, owing to Carson's swollen and diseased hand, and he refused to have it removed. I had written to Drabble about this hand being diseased, and, when the Pharaoh arrived at Brindisi, I found a letter from him containing the programme of the plot. That letter I kept, and now attach to this confession, at Lord Aldean's request. Drabble, from my description of the state of Carson's hand, declared that an operation would be necessary, and suggested that I should state to the young man that he (Drabble) was a skilful surgeon, who would perform it. If Carson consented, I was to take him to a house in Athelstane Place, and there introduce him to Drabble as the surgeon. Drabble, on the excuse of the hand, engaged to keep Carson there for some weeks, and hoped, by his own persuasions and those of Mrs. Arne (another Anarchist), to inspire Carson with a desire to benefit humanity. He and Mrs. Arne hoped to talk Carson into a state of red-hot enthusiasm, so that he might take the oath to the Brotherhood. Once he did so, and bound himself to this band of wild fanatics, he would have to part either with his money or his life. Drabble and I and Mrs. Arne were in great need of this money, but there was no suggestion that the goose with the golden eggs should be killed. I followed closely the directions in Drabble's letter. I talked to Carson about the necessity of getting his hand cured, and said that I knew a skilful surgeon called Mr. Francis Hain (the name supplied to me by Drabble), who could cure it. Carson, whose hand gave him pain, readily agreed to

169

try the effect of an operation, and it was arranged between us that I should take him to Mr. Hain's house on our arrival. From Plymouth I wrote to Drabble advising him of this, and when the Pharaoh docked, I first took Carson and his luggage to the rooms in Marquis Street, which I had already engaged, and afterwards to Athelstane Place. The luggage, including the sandal-wood chest, was left at my rooms, and with only a small portmanteau Carson arrived—at night—at the so-called Hain's house. Mrs. Arne was the housekeeper, Drabble the surgeon under the name of Hain, and all was highly respectable. Carson had no suspicions; and when Drabble said that he would have to remain in Athelstane Place for at least three weeks, while his cure was being effected, he readily agreed to do so. He gave me a letter to post to Miss Bellairs, telling her how through this operation he was detained; but, of course; I destroyed this. I left Carson in Athelstane Place, and I returned to my rooms in Marquis Street. That was the last time that I saw the poor fellow alive.

"A day or so afterwards I was hurriedly summoned to the house in Soho by Drabble and Mrs. Arne. With much agitation they declared that Carson was dead—had been murdered. I asked with horror if they were guilty. Both denied it in the strongest manner. Carson, they said, had been left alone on the previous night, as they were both obliged to attend to some Anarchistic business. When they returned they found him dead. On examination, Drabble discovered that death had been caused by a knitting-needle thrust into the man's heart. It had evidently been taken from some wool-work of Mrs. Arne's, which had been left in the drawing-room, where the body had been found. Mrs. Arne searched the house, but could find no one; the doors were all closed, the windows also. However, in Carson's bedroom she discovered his portmanteau open and the contents tossed about, as though the murderer had been searching for something. Both declared again that they did not know who had killed Carson, and in the end—seeing that they had no reason for murdering the man—I believed them.

"I thought the whole conspiracy was at an end. Not so Mrs. Arne or Drabble. The doctor produced the bangle, which he had obtained by cutting off Carson's hand at the wrist, and declared that Mrs. Arne's nephew, Carlo Boldini, who greatly resembled Carson, could impersonate the dead man, and wear the bangle. At first I refused; then, as I was in desperate straits for money, I agreed. Carlo was called in, and told that he was to represent a man called Angus Carson, wear the bangle, and marry Olive Bellairs. That done he was to hand over the money to Drabble and myself. Being already married to Clara Trall, he declined at first to act the part; but his aunt forced him to do so in the end. It was not till long after this that Carlo knew of the murder of Carson at all.

"We dressed him in Carson's clothes, taken from the sandal-wood chest, but afterwards, on reading the leader in the Morning Planet, we changed these clothes for new ones, lest the scent should arouse suspicion. The bracelet was placed upon his wrist, and I instructed him in Carson's history, manner of speech, and action. It took me some time to train him in; but at last he was turned out with so close a resemblance in appearance and personality to Carson, that he might well have been taken for the dead man's double.

"I then accompanied him to Caster——"

Just as Olive reached this part of the confession, Lord Aldean, very red in the face, entered the room hurriedly.

"Here's a pretty kettle o' fish!" he cried, "Carson's cheque's no good. I'm very much afraid we've lost that thirty thousand."

"Lost it!" cried Olive, starting up. "Is the money not then in Paris?"

"No; not to Boldini's credit, at all events. Bank have received a reply to their wire, saying that the money was withdrawn a fortnight ago, and the account closed. Not a cent has the beggar got at the Crédit Lyonnais. The cheque is mere waste-paper. They either have the money, with them, or have transferred it to the place they are bound for. What a—what a fool I was! I might have known there was something dicky up the brute's sleeve when he gave in so meekly. They didn't mind dropping Semberry's share, but they were determined to stick to their own. What an ass the devil must have thought me! I fear we shall have a bit of a job to trace them now."

Here the presence of Olive must be held responsible for the string of peculiar sounds proceeding from Aldean. They were comparable to nothing, and cannot be expressed in type.

"Never mind," said Olive, soothingly. "At any rate, we return with twenty thousand and the confessions. Half a loaf is better than none. We have lost much, but, on the other hand, we have gained more than I——"

A knock at the door interrupted her, and a waiter entered with a telegram for Lord Aldean. It proved to be from Tui.

"Come back at once. Mallow in danger," read Aldean, blankly.

Olive turned grey, and literally dropped into her seat. "The

171

Anarchists!" she cried with a gasp. "Oh, Lord Aldean, we must go back at once."

"But the thirty thousand pounds, Miss Bellairs?"

"What do thirty, forty, a hundred thousand pounds matter if Laurence is in danger?" cried Olive, excitedly. "We must not lose an hour. God grant we may not be too late."

"Amen to that," said Aldean, gloomily.

By ten o'clock that night they were on their way to London.

THE FIFTH SCENE

IN LONDON

CHAPTER I

"THE MISSING MAN"

Clothed, and in his right mind, Hiram Vraik sat in the bare room, which he and his brother-tenant grandiloquently termed "The Office."

He was absolutely at a loss to account for his employer's disappearance. For several days he had called regularly at Half-Moon Street, only to be told as regularly that Mr. Mallow was still absent. The porter of the chambers was not alarmed by Mr. Mallow's continued failure to put in an appearance, as that young gentleman was most irregular in his comings and goings. But Vraik's reasoning differed from the porter's, perhaps because he knew more than the porter. Mallow was involved with a dangerous gang of Anarchists; and it was always possible, indeed probable, that some incautious speech or misguided confidence might get him into trouble. The more Vraik reflected on this possibility the stronger became his belief that Mr. Mallow was now in difficulties—up to his neck in them.

"He'd hev tole that young lord chap if he'd bin goin' to stop away," said Vraik, stroking his newly-shaven chin; "but the lor' chap he tole me to git Mr. Mallow's orders nex' day, so he don' know nothin', an' he's gone arter the Major cove, as I foun' out by follerin' him to the stashun. But Mr. Maller! here's a rum go."

Later on Vraik put things in this way before his partner, a heavy-jowled, coarse-faced, military ramrod, who answered publicly to the name of Serjeant Jorran, privately to the endearing appellation on the part of Vraik of "m'pal."

"It's a rum go this, m'pal," said the little man, gravely; "an' I'm blest if I knows what's come t'him."

173

"He may have gone abroad with Lord Aldean," suggested the sergeant.

"He ain't. I sawr the lor' chap orf at Victorier, an' he went with a gal. No, m'pal, I'll lay any odds as them revolutionary busters hev laid Mr. Maller by the heels."

"Why don't you find him, then?" said Jorran, tartly; "the job's in your hands, and it's a paying one. If Mr. Maller doesn't turn up we'll lose the money."

"I knows that, m'pal—none better; an' I'm looking for him proper. Mr. Maller's bein' makin' free of that crib in Popl'r Street, an' I dessay he's got onto trouble there."

"Can't you find out his whereabouts from some of these Anarchists?"

"I'm goin' this very minit to pump one of 'em," said Vraik, looking at his watch; "a swipy ole cove called Trall. Mr. Maller, he interdooced me to him, an' tole me t'look arter him. Th' cove's loose in the shingle, so I may get somethin' out of him."

"Has this man Trall anything to do with the Poplar Street den?"

"He's shoe-black and bottle-washer there, I thinks," replied Vraik, jumping up. "I'd like to fin' all about that crib, I would, an' put a stop to their blowin's up. There'd be noospaper pars and lots of coin in a job like that."

"It isn't a bad idea," said Jorran, reflectively; "keep your weather-eye open, Vraik, and let me know when I can sail in to help."

Vraik winked and whistled through his teeth, after which pantomime he swaggered into the street, conscious of an exceptionally smart appearance. But he never promenaded the main thoroughfares. Publicity was contrary to his principles of business. Like the rat he was, he slunk through alleys and by-streets, down passages, and into disreputable quarters, until he found himself in Poplar Street. Here he strolled casually past No. 49, and took a stealthy survey of its battered front. Then he dived into the squalid depths of Soho, to cut the trail between himself and Poplar Street, and came to the surface in the greasy little parlour of a public-house in Bloomsbury. Here Jeremiah Trall, dissipated, but still gentlemanly of aspect, was seated at an oilcloth-covered table with a glass of whisky before him.

He had arrived at his "cross-drop," and was in no very good humour when his visitor sneaked into the dingy room.

"I have finished three glasses while waiting for you," said he, in a complaining voice, "so you will have to pay. I have no money."

174

"Y'never have anything except a thirst," replied Vraik, sitting carefully down on a horsehair sofa. "Lanlor', 'nother Scotch cole, for this gentleman, and gin for me—smart as y'know how."

Provided with such refreshment, the two men came to business; that is, Vraik did, for Trall's energies were in the main devoted to a dreamy contemplation of the liquor before him.

"I'm glad you've turned up, Mr. Trall," said Vraik, raising his glass; "here's m'respec's t'you. Now you an' me's got to tork. D'want t'make money?"

"I should not mind," replied Trall, on whom the fourth glass was now exerting its soothing influence. "How can I earn it?"

Vraik came to the point at once. "By tellin' me 'bout Mr. Maller," said he, bluntly.

The question had a paralyzing effect on Trall. He dropped his glass and his jaw at the same time, turned a dingy yellow colour, and cast a terrified glance round the four corners of the room.

"I—I—I do not know anything about Mr. Mallow," he gasped.

Vraik's eyes glittered, and he lifted a lean admonitory forefinger. "Mr. Maller he interdooced us pals, an' he tol' you I was helpin' him with this case as you knows of; so I arsks you agin, ole cove. Where's Mr. Maller?"

"I—I don't know!"

Vraik still shook the warning finger. "Lyin' agin, an' at yr'age, I'm ashamed of y'. I noo y' was an Anarchist, but not——"

"Hush!" entreated Trall, with another glance round. "Some one may hear!"

"Not they, ole cove! there ain't none of 'em about here."

"You don't know—you never know," moaned Trall, shaking and white. "They hide everywhere—they see everything. They listen and punish."

"Lor'! t' 'ear y' tork one 'ud think this was Africay."

"It is worse much worse. There men fight openly; here the Brotherhood stabs in the dark. Hush! Oh, hush!"

"Have they stabbed Mr. Maller in th' dark?"

"No; he is safe, quite safe!"

"Oh!" said Vraik, briskly; "y' know that much, do you? Now where is he?"

"I don't know? don't ask me."

"Oh, won't I? but I will." Vraik bent across the table and spoke rapidly in Trall's ear. "Mr. Maller is in that Poplar Street crib."

"No, no, he is not!" Trall shrank back.

"Ole cove, why d'y' lie? He is there. Y' knows it. If y' don't tell me 'bout him, blest if I don't have the perlice into that den."

"You—you would not dare——"

"I mightn't, but the peelers would. Lor'"—Vraik wriggled himself—"jes' to think of the coppers raidin' that crib, an' you bein' blown kite-high for splitting on yer pals. Wot a Sun'y School picter!"

"I have told you nothing," moaned Trall, thoroughly terrified.

"Don't I know that?" snapped Vraik. "Ole cove, I knows enough 'bout you an' them t'make y' tell m'all. If y' don't, I'll go strite to the perlice an' 'ave a raid on yer den. Then I'll say 't was you rounded on the lot."

Trall moaned again and wrung his hands. Drink and terrorism had destroyed the man's brain and nerve. The mere suggestion that Vraik would tell the police about the Soho house was enough for him. If a raid were made there, and he were denounced as an informer his life would be at the mercy of those who were truly merciless.

"Ave some more comfort," said Vraik, who was watching the beads of perspiration roll off his victim's forehead, "then y' can tell me 'bout Maller."

More whisky was brought. Trall dispensed with all water now. He saw that he was in a cleft stick, and since Vraik knew so much, the only way to save himself was to tell him more. Moreover, Trall hated Drabble, and—if he could do so with safety to himself—would with pleasure ruin him. He stretched a trembling hand across the table.

"Swear you will keep my name out of the business," he said, looking round again.

"I swear," said Vraik, promptly. "Bless y', I don't want t'arm y'. I on'y wish t'save Mr. Maller, cos I won't git m' money paid if I don't. Now where is he? Tell me strite."

"In that house—in Soho."

"Is he a prisoner, ole cove?"

"Yes; he said too much, so Drabble and Mrs. Arne had him locked up."

"Drabble and Mrs. Arne!" repeated Vraik. "Who's they?"

Trall shut up promptly. "Oh, you don't know so much if you don't know who they are."

"Ho! that's it, is it?" squeaked the rascal, with a puckered forehead; "now I jes' tell y', ole cove. I knows enough to mess up you and them bomb-pitchin' cusses, so you speak strite. Who's Mrs. Arne an' t'other chap?"

176

"Anarchists," faltered Trall. "But it's not necessary to talk about them," he went on rapidly, "but about Mr. Mallow. He is a prisoner in the Soho house."

"'Ow can I git im out?"

"You can't get him out except at the risk of your life," said Trall, coldly.

Vraik twisted his lean body and winced. "I've on'y one life, not bein' a cat," said he; "and I ain't goin' to chuck that away for Mr. Maller's. But I'm agoin' to 'ave 'im out if I rip that blessed shanty of yours from top to bottom."

"There is only one man who can help you, and that is Monsieur Rouge."

"Who's he? another of 'em? Wot's he like?"

"Tall and lean, pale, light——"

"Dressed in rummy blue bags? A furrin' cove! Ho, I've seed him goin' t'yer rabbit 'ole. And 'ow can 'e 'elp me?"

Trall rose heavily. "Ask him, if you dare to. I'll tell him you want to see him."

"Right y'are! He won't bring bustin' things with him?"

"No." Trall reflected. "Where's Lord Aldean?" he asked. "Mr. Mallow talked of Lord Aldean."

"He's gone to the Continong. He'll be back soon."

"Then take Rouge to Lord Aldean. I don't think he'll deal with you."

"My h'eye, won't he?" spluttered the little man; "e've horty pride, ain't it! oh, no! Well, jes' you fetch this cove along 'ere to-morrow at this time. I knows where Lord Aldean lives, an' I'll take 'im there."

"I'll tell Rouge. He shall meet you here to-morrow."

"No larks, min'!" said Vraik, sharply. "If 'e ain't 'ere, the perlice 'ull be at Soho, y'bet."

"Rouge shall come. But keep my name quiet."

"I'm dumb. Y'treat me strite, an' I'm yer pal. If y'don't—well, y'know my game."

On this understanding the conference came to an end, and Trall rolled off half terrified, half assured. If the Anarchists could be captured, if his tormentor, Drabble, could be imprisoned, he would be free. "I can join Clara and Carlo then," thought the poor sot, "and be happy for the rest of my life. Ah! Michael had the head of the Tralls. If only I had been like Michael." He heaved a sigh, and, finding sorrow thirsty work, lurched into the nearest bar for another drink.

In the meantime Vraik took a dive into the depths, and wriggling westward in his own slimy way, rose once more to the surface in the respectable neighbourhood of Campden Hill. He knew that Lord Aldean visited at the house there, and he had made up his mind that he would see the occupants and get them to communicate to Lord Aldean Mallow's peril. Confident in his new clothes, he stepped jauntily up to the door, and rang the bell. It was answered by the footman, who remembered his face from his previous visit.

By means of a very free use of Lord Aldean's name, in addition to some capital lying, Vraik succeeded in introducing himself into the presence of Mrs. Purcell and Tui. To them he told his story—that is to say, as much of it as he deemed necessary to fetch back Lord Aldean to London.

"Mr. Mallow in the power of those wretches!" cried Tui, tearfully. "Oh, what will Olive say? What is to be done?"

"The officers of the law——" began Mrs. Purcell, when Vraik cut short her stately periods.

"'Scuse me, lady," he said, "but if the peelers come in there'll be a mess, there will; and Mr. Maller 'ull git the worst of it. Y'jes wire the lor' chap to come back, an' I'll striten out the rest."

"Yes, yes," cried Tui, "let us wire to Lord Aldean at once."

"The matter shall receive my immediate attention," said Mrs. Purcell. "And if this individual——"

"I'm orf, lady; but I'll come back an' see when the lor' chap 'ull be here. It's dry work, this, tho', ain't it?"

After which speech Vraik retired with five shillings clinking in the pockets of his new clothes. Ten minutes later, Mrs. Purcell sent off a telegram of recall to Lord Aldean in Florence.

CHAPTER II

"MONSIEUR ROUGE IS CONFIDENTIAL"

At breakfast, under his own roof-tree, Aldean reviewed the events and incidents of the last six days. Without doubt, they had been fast and furious. But, even qualified as it was by the news of Boldini's trickery, his work had been largely successful—the more so, considering that four days out of the six had been spent in travelling. The telegram bringing such serious news of poor Mallow had made it absolutely impossible to take any steps towards following the Boldini pair. First and foremost, Mallow's position— whatever it might prove to be—demanded his entire energies. On arrival the previous evening, he had listened earnestly and anxiously to Mrs. Purcell's majestic account of Vraik's visit. But all that her ponderous periods succeeded in conveying to Aldean was the mere fact that Mallow was a prisoner. He felt he must know more at once, and he there and then despatched a wire to Vraik, which brought the little man to Campden Hill in an incredibly short space of time. From him Aldean learned all details, among them that Rouge had refused to move in the matter until brought into personal communication with himself. He arranged with Vraik to see Rouge the next morning between ten and eleven. He felt he could do no more that night save comfort Olive with the assurance that Mallow should be rescued at all costs. Moreover, for once in his life, Aldean felt physically exhausted. He hoped much from the mysterious Monsieur Rouge, though at first thought it was difficult to see how so red a sans-culotte was going to help him. As a devoted Anarchist, it was the duty, and no doubt the wish, of Rouge to keep Mallow in prison, and prevent all attempt at rescue rather than assist towards it. Yet Trall, who was plainly against the Brotherhood, had hinted that Monsieur Rouge could, and would, play the part of a beneficent Deus ex machinâ. The more he thought of it, the more puzzled Aldean became at this dodge of Vraik's. He finished two pipes trying to solve the problem, and concluded by hoping, as usual, for the best.

"Monsieur Rouge," announced Lord Aldean's valet, just as he was filling a third pipe.

"All right; show him in." And Jim, standing with his back to the fire, was face to face with his enigmatic visitor from the depths.

179

Monsieur Rouge, thin, sad-faced, and more colourless than ever, glided into the room like an unquiet spectre. He saluted his host with grave dignity. Aldean nodded, and when the door was closed pointed to a chair.

"I am glad to see you," he said in French. "Sit down, please. Would you like to eat, or drink, or smoke?"

"If Monsieur permits, no; I come to talk."

"About Mr. Mallow?"

"But certainly, Monsieur, about myself also. I discharge myself of a mission in thus presenting myself."

Lord Aldean, who had not once taken his eyes off the white, haggard face, nodded again, and sat down. With easy grace his visitor slipped into a chair, and placed his peaked cap on the floor beside him. Then he looked fixedly at the young Englishman, and waited to be questioned. Evidently M. Rouge was a discreet personage, and not inclined to venture in further than he could withdraw. Nothing of the rash revolutionist about him.

"Did Vraik bring you here?" asked Aldean, settling himself.

"Assuredly, yes. He gave himself the trouble to lead me to the door. But," Monsieur Rouge waved his hand, "he is gone. I dismissed him. It is not for him to hear what I would say."

"What do you wish to say?"

"Monsieur, I would make you a confession; I would deliver myself of a story. But that later. Let us concern ourselves with Mr. Mallow."

"By all means. Is Mr. Mallow safe?"

"Safe and well. But what would you?" Rouge spread out his hands and shrugged. "He is in the power of Madame. She knows not mercy."

"Does she intend violence?" asked Aldean, hurriedly.

"But what can I say? As the votes go, so will Mr. Mallow be dealt with by the Brotherhood. Attention, Monsieur. Your friend is brave, but rash—oh, most terribly rash! He comes to Soho, and he tells Monsieur the doctor and Madame that he knows of their wickedness about this money, about this murder. Eh! they are afraid that he may tell too much, these brave ones, and they call out 'Spy! spy!' Mr. Mallow fights well, but he is conquered. Behold, Monsieur, your friend most dear is a prisoner in a little room on the top of the house in Soho."

"Have they ill-treated him?"

"But no; it is not necessary. Monsieur, your friend eats and drinks like one of the aristocrats. To-morrow night there is a great

180

meeting of us in the cellar—oh, a very great meeting! Mr. Mallow will be taken down to be judged. All will be told; and if they say 'Kill!' Monsieur will disappear."

"You don't mean they will murder him!" cried Aldean, aghast.

"First, they will murder him," replied Rouge, significantly; "afterwards his body will disappear. We have chemists who do these things. Mr. Mallow will be no more."

"But the police?"

"Eh! what is it that can be done by them? No body, no murder, no trial. Madame and Monsieur the doctor they know well what to do. There is no one else who has seen Mr. Mallow enter—no one. Trall can speak, I can speak; but," with a shrug, "will he speak?"

"I hope so," said Jim, anxiously. "You came here to speak."

"Behold, Monsieur, I do so; and why? Figure to yourself the reason." Rouge rose slowly from his chair. "I—I am no Anarchist."

"You—are—no—Anarchist?" repeated Aldean, stupefied.

"No, I am become one to destroy them. It is my vengeance."

"Vengeance, Monsieur Rouge?"

"That is not my name. I am Emile Durand, citizen of Paris, who devotes himself to destroying those who would destroy the world. Ha! ha! Superb, magnificent. Monsieur," with a sudden solemnity of tone, "I avenge my wife and my child."

"Why, did the Anarchists kill——"

"Yes." Rouge covered his face, and dropped back into the chair, sobbing. "Ah, yes, alas! My dear Sophie, my little child! the good God was silent, and they died—died, and I—I still live."

Lord Aldean looked with pity on the frame of the man, shaken with the violence of his grief. He succumbed to a veritable nerve-storm which swept over him. He wept, he cried aloud, he rolled in his chair, until, beaten and prostrate, he fell back limply.

"My poor fellow, I am sorry for you. Some wine——"

"No, no; Monsieur need not give himself the trouble. No wine." After a time a faint colour came back to him. With an effort his muscles reasserted themselves, and he pulled himself together. But he kept his eyes fixedly on the floor, and spoke rapidly, though almost inaudibly. "Monsieur, five years ago I was a chemist in Paris—Rue Flaubert—and, my faith, what a charming shop! Sophie, my dear wife, was there, and the little one, an adorable little one of four years. Ah, how I loved them—how happy we were! Monsieur, that she-devil of a Madame commanded that Paris should be terrorized by bombs. She wished for a revolution. Close by my little shop a bomb was thrown one night. It burst. Oh, most terrible name

181

of names! Shall I ever forget the bursting of that hell-bomb? It killed my Sophie and my dear little Therese." His voice broke with a dry sob. "They were buried in the ruins of our happy home. I lived; conceive to yourself, Monsieur, I lived. Yes," his voice rose, "to destroy those who destroyed them."

Rouge flung up his arms with a theatrical gesture of despair, and paced hurriedly to and fro. Aldean did not speak. He did not know what to say in the face of such grief.

"Yes, Monsieur, I lived to plot vengeance. I was ill long, long. When I was again myself; I was not myself—not Emile Durand, but Monsieur Rouge, the Anarchist, as you see me now. I joined the Brotherhood, I took the oath. I used my knowledge of chemistry to invent explosives. I wormed myself into their confidence, their counsels, their secrets. Now I am the friend of that she-devil. Figure to yourself, Monsieur, the dear friend of Madame. I make the bombs; I place them. I work, work, work—not for them, but for myself. They shall all die to-morrow."

"Good Lord!" cried Aldean, in horror. "Do you intend, then, to blow them up?"

With an insane light in his eyes Rouge turned on him.

"Monsieur seeks to know what I care not to tell. Holy blue! I know when to be silent. To you I speak of Monsieur Mallow; to him I have related the story of Emile Durand, and he knows that Emile Durand will rescue him. But Rouge—ha ha!"—he broke into a peal of laughter not good to hear, "he will not rescue Madame, or Monsieur the doctor. No, no, not death in life for the innocent, but death in life for her. Ah! ha! it will be a pretty sight."

Frankly speaking, after the first natural feeling of horror, Jim did not care two straws if the Anarchists were blown to atoms or not. On the whole, he considered that some such wholesale destruction might be beneficial. It would assuredly rid the world of a lot of these pestilential wretches, and frighten the others. Moreover, there was something ironically just in their being hoist on their own petard.

"But about Monsieur Mallow?" he observed.

"I shall save him," replied Rouge. "He is in a little room on the top, with a skylight window on the slope of the roof. In the next house I have a room, with a little window, too, through which I can climb. Behold, Monsieur, I take a rope, well strong, and to its end I fasten a stone. I climb on the roof opposite to my window, and throw the stone at the skylight on the slanting roof. Crash! It falls in, and Monsieur Mallow will knot it to his bed. Then he will climb up, like the little cat, along the slanting roof and round its corner, until he slips into my window. Then I will lead him down the stairs to the door, to the street. There you will be, Monsieur, and receive this unfortunate."

The plan of escape appealed to Aldean as simple and skilful and safe enough. Forgetting their relative positions, he sprang to his feet, and shook Rouge heartily by both hands.

"Thank you! thank you!" he cried. "Neither Mr. Mallow nor myself will ever forget your kindness."

"Bah!" Rouge shrugged his shoulders. "It is nothing. What would you have? Monsieur Mallow has been good to me. He has given me money and kind words. No, Monsieur, I am no ingrate to permit one so beneficent to perish. Death is for the evil, not for the good."

"Suppose his escape is discovered?"

"Only when it is too late for them," said Rouge, with a cruel smile. "They will not care for Monsieur Mallow's escape. No, my faith!"

"But what of yourself?"

"That shall be as the good God designs. Ask me no more, Monsieur, but be you in that street at eight o'clock to-morrow night. I will bring your friend to your arms. I swear it! I, Emile Durand, by the head of my Sophie, by my little Therese But when you have your friend, go far—there will be danger."

"If we can ever repay you——"

"Repay me?" Rouge seized Aldean by the hand, and looked into his face with earnest eyes. "Monsieur, have masses said for the repose of the dear ones. It is all I ask, If the good Lord give me death in my vengeance, buy a mass for the poor Emile Durand."

He sighed, dropped Aldean's hand, but still looked at him.

"I promise," said Jim, earnestly. "Masses shall be said for Sophie and the little one; but I hope you will escape."

"It is as the good God wills," sighed Rouge, and walked to the door. As he put on his peaked cap he looked back. "Not a word of this to a soul," said he, hoarsely, "or your friend is lost."

"I understand."

"Good. At eight o'clock to-morrow night in the street of Poplaire. There you shall see your friend, and my vengeance."

When the man glided out, Jim turned to the mantelpiece, and rested his forehead on his clasped hands.

"Thank God!" he muttered. "Mallow will be saved. I must tell Olive."

CHAPTER III

"A TERRIBLE ADVENTURE"

In the old-fashioned drama of mediæval complexion, the prisoner—usually the hero of the play—was "haled to the deepest dungeon beneath the castle moat." The Anarchists of Soho having no castle and no moat, and having moreover other uses for their cellar, so far improved upon this bygone fashion as to sky their prisoners—when they had any. In the present instance Mallow was perched in an attic on the top of the house. The window was overhead, set in the slant of the roof, and the door was kept double-locked. A safer or more isolated cell could not well have been devised. It was impossible to reach the skylight even by standing on the bed; and it would have been a difficult task to break down that four-inch door. Had the prisoner even succeeded in boring through the walls, he could scarcely hope to escape by dropping fifty feet on to the pavement; and let him shout and kick as he would, no one— other than his gaoler—was likely to hear him.

He was absolutely powerless; and his sole comfort lay in the thought that Aldean was carrying on the campaign. When Jim returned he would find that Mallow was missing, and would undoubtedly guess that he was in the power of the Anarchists. If these latter did not kill him in the meantime—as they might, in self-preservation—Aldean would surely apply to the police and have the Soho house searched. Then freedom, and Nemesis upon his enemies.

This was one hope, but there was yet another. Monsieur Rouge, who had brought Mallow's food to him several times, had on one occasion thrown off his revolutionary mask so far as to promise to aid the prisoner's escape. And, although Mallow did not well see how he was to do this—seeing that Rouge had not divulged his scheme,—there was comfort in the thought that, if Aldean should fail, he might succeed. So he resigned himself to the inevitable, and waited.

Since his imprisonment Drabble had not appeared, nor indeed had Mrs. Arne; but on the sixth day, when Mallow was wondering what they were thinking of doing with him, the lady herself came into his attic. She re-locked the door, sat down on the one chair— which she placed so that she faced Mallow sitting on the bed—and, with the most amiable composure, signified that she wished to converse. The mere sight of her infuriated Mallow, but the memory of his previous folly taught him to control himself. He was as self-possessed as Madame herself.

"You are no doubt surprised to see me, Mr. Mallow," began Mrs. Arne, in her unemotional tones; "but you will be less so when you hear what I have to say."

"Nothing you could do would surprise me, Madame, after your daring to shut me up in this illegal manner."

"Oh"—Madame shrugged—"everything we do in this house is illegal. The Brotherhood is outside the so-called law, and against it. If there is any one to blame, it is yourself. As a spy, you can hardly expect mercy."

"I am not a spy."

"Then your interpretation of the word differs from mine. You came here under the pretence of joining us, from conscientious motives; but your real errand is to criminate myself and the doctor in the murder of this man Carson. Your intentions were dangerous to our personal safety; ergo, we lock you up! Can you blame us?"

"If the tiger has the tiger's nature who can blame him?" retorted Mallow. "You killed Carson; I dare say you will not hesitate to murder me."

"As to yourself," said Madame, smoothly, "we will speak of that later. But you are wrong about Mr. Carson; I did not kill him, neither did Drabble."

"I find it difficult to believe that. You and Drabble—he under the name of Hain—rented the house in which the man met his death. He was stabbed with a knitting-needle. I have observed that you knit a great deal, Madame."

"True; but I confine my needles to their proper use. The doctor and I left Mr. Carson alone in the house; when we returned he was dead. Who murdered him I know no more than you—or the police," finished Madame, with a sneer.

"Your explanation is too diaphanous to be convincing."

"I did not come here to convince you," said Mrs. Arne, dryly, "but to inform you that we intend to give you a chance to save your life."

"Save my life?" echoed Mallow (he could not repress a slight tremor). "Your meaning has been murder, then?"

"We never use that word; but call it so if you will. In three nights from now there is called a meeting of the Brotherhood in the cellar of this house. You will be brought down to take the oath."

"And if I refuse?"

"Then we—remove you," said Madame, in silky tones. "Take the oath and you go free, for you can break it only at the imminent risk of your life. A hundred eyes will be always on you, a hundred feet will dog your steps. One rash word, one hint to the police about our affairs, and you die."

"You dare not kill me."

Madame laughed.

"Put that to the test if you will by refusing the oath," said she, indifferently. "For myself, I think you better dead. It is the doctor's wish that you have this chance."

"I suppose you know the risk you run? My friends will search diligently for me."

"No doubt. But they will not come here. No one saw you enter this house. If your friends are clever enough to trace you to this place they will find nothing. We have chemists who can convert your dead body into nothing more tangible than gas. You will vanish into thin air. We have arranged all that."

"You are a fiend."

"I am Madame Death-in-Life. You know why I am called so? No? Because those in authority live on my sufferance. I have but to lift a finger and they die. Monsieur Rouge, whom you have seen, is something more than a chemist. He invents explosives. He designs bombs."

Mallow thought of the explosion in Paris, when the wife and child of Emile Durand were killed by the lifting of Madame's finger, and he drew comfort from the recollection. A man with such wrongs would surely rescue him, even at the eleventh hour.

The thought gave him courage to listen to the woman.

"Well, whether you kill me or not the fifty thousand pounds are gone," said he, rather spitefully. "All your schemes have come to nothing."

"All our schemes are not ended," said Mrs. Arne, rising. "I see your friend Lord Aldean has not yet got back the money."

"How do you know that?"

"I know that he is in Florence trying to force my nephew into giving back the money which is ours."

"Your nephew! The false Carson!"

"Yes. Carlo Boldini is his real name. He is a fool if he thinks to escape with that money from me. But that reptile, his wife, is to blame for all that."

186

"How dare you use such language towards Mrs. Carson?" cried Mallow, indignantly.

"I am speaking of Clara Trall, my nephew's real wife. Miss Bellairs is not that."

"What—what do you——"

"I should advise you to take the oath, Mr. Mallow, and you may yet live to marry Miss Bellairs. Otherwise——" She shrugged, and opened the door.

Mallow tried to detain her, but she drew her dress gently from his grasp, and with a sudden dart was outside. Before he could fling himself after her the door was slammed to and locked.

The last communication of Madame was skilfully made. It left Mallow in a storm of mingled joy and grief.

For the next two days he thought and thought over his terrible position, and contrived a hundred ways to escape without having the resolution to attempt one. On the third day, at five o'clock, Rouge brought up his food. Mallow—who had almost given up hope of seeing him again—sprang forward with an exclamation of delight. Rouge laid a lean finger on his lips.

"Hush!" he whispered, glancing at the door, "we may be overheard. To-night you will be brought to the meeting at ten o'clock. Is it not so?"

"Yes, yes!" said Mallow. "Madame told me. But you will help—"

"Hush! No word, Monsieur. To-night at eight I will throw a stone at the window above. It will fall inside here, and a cord will be tied to it. Fasten the cord to your bed, and climb up it. Get through the window, and climb on the cord, round the corner of the roof; then slide down the slope. The cord will lead you to my window. I shall be there."

"Thank you! Thank you! But the noise—the falling stone—is it not dangerous?"

"No! no! We shall all be down in the cellar. The meeting begins at eight o'clock. They expect me to bring you at nine. But then, Monsieur, you will be free. Milord will await you in the street."

"Lord Aldean! Does he know, then?" +++233/247 "He knows all. Hush, Monsieur, be careful to fasten the rope well. If it slips, and you roll off the roof into the street, you are dead."

"I will be careful. How can I thank you——"

"Hush! no word!" Monsieur Rouge again laid his finger on his lips, and slipped silently out of the room.

Mallow was in darkness, for, lest he should fire the house, he was not permitted a light. But he cared little for that. His heart beat high at the prospect of escape, even in so perilous a way. He shook his bed, and found that the feet were clamped to the floor. All the better; it would hold the rope fast. Overhead the skylight was black in the night, and Mallow heard the raindrops rattle like small shot on the pane. Up through that black square was his sole way of escape, with the risk of death if he made a false step. But his courage was high, and his nerve did not fail him.

Never had the hours seemed so long. The chimes of a near church marked them at century distances, as it seemed, to the strained ears of the prisoner. He ate heartily of the food Rouge had brought, but the wine he left untouched. He would need a cool head and a clear brain. Down below the wild beasts were, no doubt, creeping into their jungle. He pictured them slinking through alley and by-street in the rainy, stormy night: unclean prowlers menacing humanity. In the depths of the earth they would scheme the destruction of the dwellers thereon—innocent men and women, little children, even the kindly beasts of the earth. All! all would be gloated over by those now stealing to their wicked hole. Mallow was as brave as a lion, and he burned with rage as he thought of those demons below.

At last eight o'clock clanged loudly in the night air. Then a dead silence. Mallow could hear his heart thump furiously. Still no stone fell, and he clasped his hands in nervous dread lest, after all, Rouge might have deceived him. What if the man were in truth an Anarchist? what if his promised deliverance were not fulfilled? suppose—crash! smash! and a heavy body shot like a meteor through the window amid a rain of splintered glass.

"The rope! Thank God!"

With feverish hands he felt in the darkness for the stone, and found it. As he gripped, the rope shook away more glass. He listened for a moment to hear if the noise had attracted attention. All was quiet. Joyfully and hopefully he groped for the bed and drew in the rope until it was taut. At this end of it was prison, at the other liberty and Olive. Mallow bound it in tight knots to the iron framework of the bed. He felt these over and over again to make sure they would not slip. His life depended upon his care; and he anxiously tugged and strained until he poured with perspiration.

At last the task was complete. He ran his hand along the rope. It was taut as a bobstay—but at best it was but a frail bridge to safety. Yet it was his only one. Going to the door, he listened. Again silence. Taking off his shoes and socks, so that his bare feet might cling to the slates, Mallow sprang on the rope and swung himself upward.

The rain, spurting in through the window, splattered on his upturned face; a piece of glass, loosened by the swing of the rope, fell and cut him; but the man set his teeth and climbed hand over hand to freedom. At last his head emerged through the skylight. He saw the dark and stormy sky spitting rain, and the light of the city glimmering through the mist. Luckily the skylight was large enough. Clinging tightly to the rope, Mallow thrust his shoulders against the glass. It smashed, splintered, broke in a hundred fragments. He was through in the fresh air, on the roof of a house fifty and more feet from the pavement. With desperate courage he clung to the frail rope, and lay flat on the wet slates, his toes digging into them to relieve the strain on the cord. The blood surged and gushed in his head, and he feared he would roll off insensible. Below was the abyss of the street, above the sloping wet slates at an acute angle, and, over all, the tearing, sweeping drench of the rain driven before the gusts of wind.

Then a new terror gripped his heart. The edge of the rope lay amongst the sharp angles of the glass. It might fray through, and he would be dashed over the parapet of the house to swing like a spider at the end of a thread. For a moment or so he lay flat in his soaked clothes, prone on the slant. Then, with a violent effort, he drew up his knees, and clawed his way along the rope. His trousers were cut to ribbons; his nails torn, hand and foot; and a piece of glass had cut one of his feet severely. But he was too excited to feel any pain. Slowly, but surely, he drew himself along the slates, ever ascending to the summit of the roof. There was no moon to help him; only a flurry of flying clouds and the steady thresh of the rain. It seemed a century, until he put out one hand and felt the ledge. With renewed courage he lifted himself over this, cutting his knees with the rough slates as he did so. The next moment he was safe from the abyss, and sliding carefully down the slant to a leaden gutter between two houses.

"Hush!" whispered a voice. "Hold to the rope, Monsieur; give me your hand."

Mallow gave a gasp of joy and relief as Rouge hauled him, wet and exhausted, through the window. He would have fallen, but that the man kept him upright by main force, and carried him through the candle-lighted room out on to the landing. How he got down the stairs he never knew. In the grip of Rouge he seemed to be falling, falling, falling into eternal darkness. Then he must have fainted for the moment. When he came to he was in a hansom, his head lying on Aldean's shoulder, and Aldean holding him with a grip of iron.

189

"Thank God! Oh, thank God!" he heard Aldean say as in a dream. "And you, Rouge—how can I thank you?"

"Adieu, Monsieur!" said a far-away voice. "Forget not the prayer for Sophie and the little Thérèse."

CHAPTER IV

"THE ISHMAELS OF HUMANITY"

At the head of a bare deal table, set on a dais at one end of the cellar, stood Madame Death-in-Life. This subterranean place of congress comprised the whole area of the building. Excavations had been made, indeed, extending some way below the street. These were bricked in with stones, rough whitewashed. The low roof was actually the concrete floor of the basement. It was supported by pillars and arches. Entrance and exit were effected through a trapdoor with a movable ladder. There were neither chairs nor benches. The Brothers stood huddled together like sheep in a pen before the daïs—the tribune of their infernal parliament. The lanterns slung at intervals along the wall shed their faint gleam only to make obscurity more obscure. It was curious to note on the faces of these men—faces shaven and unshaven, fierce and dreamy, bearded and haggard—one common expression of determination. The flash of fanaticism was in the eye of every one of them. Some of well-nigh each European nation were present here; and their spokeswoman addressed them, first in one language, and then in another. She was no longer the icicle. She was the zealot. She made herself felt solely by means of the sense of conviction which consumed her by the right of imaginary wrong. She communicated her feelings to those about her. She dominated them by sheer force of her own enthusiasm. She renounced, she denounced, she exhorted. "Our ruler is our enemy," she declared. "We Anarchists are without rulers. We fight against all the usurpers of power— against those who wish to usurp it. Our enemy is the landowner who keeps the land for himself, who makes the peasant work for his advantage. Our enemy is the manufacturer who fills his factory with

190

slaves. Our enemy is the State, be it Anarchical, Oligarchical, or Democratic. Its official and staff of officers, magistrates, police-spies—all these are our enemies. Our enemy is every thought of authority, call it God or the devil, in whose name the priests have so long ruled the people. Our enemy is the law which oppresses the weak by the strong to the justification and apotheosis of crime. But if the landowners, the manufacturers, the heads of the State, the priests, and the law are our enemies, we are theirs, and we boldly oppose them. We will reconquer the land and the factories, we will annihilate the State, under whatever name it may be concealed, we will regain our freedom in spite of priest and law. We despise all legal means. They are the negations of our rights. We want no so-called universal suffrage, since we cannot get away from our own personal sovereignty. We cannot and will not make ourselves accomplices in the crimes committed by our so-called representatives. We will remain our own masters, and he amongst us who strives to become a chief or leader is a traitor to our cause. Our work it is to conquer and defend common property, and to overthrow governments by whatever name they may be called. To do this we must work, we must invent, we must sacrifice. Brains, money, labour, lives—let all go for the attainment of our end. And I have a thought—a great and glorious thought, a master-thought, which, if put to execution, will give us victory." For the first time she threw out her hands, and shouted, "Air-ships! that is my thought. Conceive to yourselves, brothers, the value of this. It is superb—magnificent. There are men of genius amongst you. Get you to work, then, with all your powers. Think, strive, experiment; dedicate yourselves to the fulfilment of this great project. Succeed. You shall have money, time, help—what you will, but succeed. This is no idle dream, I say. It is the vision of my faith. I see it now before me. It rises from the ground, it soars over the earth, it poises like a vulture o'er the cities. Death—death—death it deals around. Unassailable, unapproachable, ever victorious, our engine or right. Let this be your task, comrades, and France with her armies, and England with her navies, are puny and powerless against us. The dreams of to-day are the truths of to-morrow. Have we not proof of it? The steam-engine, the telegraph, the phonograph, the telephone—all these were but dreams, once. To-day they are with us. Again I say, work, toil, beat your brains, make the great secret ours; solve the mighty problem of the air, and make us victors over the kingdoms of the oppressors!"

Madame sat down. One after another the men leaped up on to

191

the daïs, each in his own tongue striving to give vent to the frenzy she had raised within him. They discussed the subject hotly. The problem of aërial navigation had plainly caught their fancy. Then up spake Dr. Drabble.

"Dreams," he said; "yes, brothers, at present these are but dreams. But they are dreams which it is for us to make realities. Brothers, I bring no inventive powers to this task. But I bring you the sinews of war. I bring money—money amply sufficient for our present needs—fifty thousand pounds. A million and more of francs, a million of marks, a million of lire, two hundred and fifty thousand dollars. I give it to you—all to you—all to the Brotherhood."

A roar of applause from the crowd, then a dead silence, at the words that followed. They were as a douche of cold water on red-hot iron.

"But there are difficulties," he said calmly, "not wholly unsurmountable. A brother has this money, gained through a scheme of mine—of Madame here. To-night that money should have been with us. Alas, it is not." Drabble then paused to give due effect to his next words. They came with a hiss. "The brother who has that money is a traitor."

No outcry this time, no openly expressed disapprobation, only a low deadly murmur of hatred and contempt. Every face expressed loathing for the traitor. Every hand itched to be at his throat. The wild beasts seemed to crouch for the spring.

"The traitor's name is Carlo Boldini," said the doctor. "Remember that name, that you may engrave it on his tomb."

"My nephew this man," cried Madame, with a cruel smile. "My nephew whom I devote to death. I spit on the traitor. I stamp him under my foot. To betray the great and glorious cause of humanity— robber, beast, one lower than the brutes. Here, you always-to-be- trusted comrades of Germany, the cause has been by my nephew— most vile of creatures—betrayed. When you beside him stand, kill. Brothers of France, the fraternity call upon you to execute the vengeance. Understand you the horror of betrayal? Children of Robespierre, I delegate to you the task of giving him the death. Down with the traitor. Death to him—death."

"Death," "death," "death"—the word echoed in all languages through the cellar. Every one present, man or woman, doomed Carlo Boldini to death from that moment. His aunt smiled approval. She would have slain him herself for the cause.

"Brothers"—the doctor was on his feet again—"the traitor, with a woman, has fled to Italy—to Florence. He has been followed. Our brother who has watched him there reports that he and his wife have escaped in disguise to Genoa. Our brother still follows. The traitor has taken ship for South America, with the money so hardly won. On that ship our brother watches him. Wherever he goes the eye of the Brotherhood marks him. Fear not! Vengeance shall blot him out from amidst the humanity he has so basely betrayed. My comrades, you volunteer to punish this traitor and the woman Clara Trall."

Before any one could speak, Jeremiah, haggard-faced, with terror in his eyes, broke through the throng and flung himself on his knees.

"No, no!" he implored, with shaking voice; "not Clara, not my little girl. Spare——"

"Remove him," cried a dozen voices; and a dozen hands clutched the wretched creature and forced him to his feet. Weeping and imploring, he was dragged mercilessly to the further end of the cellar. The Juggernaut of Anarchy had rolled over his heart, and crushed it without extorting a sigh or a glance from its fierce worshippers. With terrible composure two men were then selected to hunt down Boldini and recover the money and punish the traitor. Money and instructions were given to these trackers, and they were bidden to return with their task completed. Without a word the pair slipped through the crowd, through the trapdoor, and went out into the world to pick up the trail of the victims. From that moment Boldini, flying over the seas though he was, stood doomed. There was something devilish in the menacing silence in which the hunters departed to run down their prey.

"My brothers," said Madame slowly, "I have a secret to disclose. When this money comes back to us, we go to Switzerland—to Geneva—there to work out our great invention. Here the police have heard of the Brotherhood. There is danger. Some day the tyrants will send their dogs here to drive us from this refuge. We are ready for their coming. Our brother Rouge has prepared this cellar for their reception. Here, under this floor," she pointed downwards, "there is a mine formed of a new explosive, the invention of brother Rouge. We stand now on a volcano. Behind me," she turned to the wall at her back, "behold this button. It communicates with the mine by electricity. One touch, and all who are here would be destroyed, the house would be destroyed, and the street would be torn up. This is the work of brother Rouge."

A murmur of approval followed. Some of the weaker creatures looked down to the concrete floor, as though their gaze could pierce

193

to the deadly mine beneath, and shuddered. But the rest smiled grimly. No one made comment of any kind.

Madame continued, "Rouge, my brothers, declares that he will sacrifice himself for the glorious cause. When these dogs come here they will not find us. We shall be in Switzerland, with wealth, and brave hearts working out our scheme for the benefit of the slaves of humanity. The police will explore the house, they will descend to this cellar. Here, where I stand, they will find our brother smiling at his prey. He will speak. He will proclaim our glorious mission. He will doom them to die for it. One touch, and our enemies are as dust. Rouge dies indeed, but his glorious memory will live in our hearts. Brothers! salute the name of Rouge!"

The Anarchists shouted exultantly, and the name of Rouge, with words of approval, flew from lip to lip. They did not pity him, they did not lament his coming fate, but they lifted up their voices and saluted the mention of his name all-glorious. There was not one man or woman present who would not do the same if bidden. "To save humanity, my brothers, we must die. Sacrifice a hundred lives, so that one despot may fall from his throne. Over our graves the happy world of the future will live, and those who have won freedom by our death will strew those graves with flowers everlasting. To the glory of the cause, shout, my brothers, shout— and, if needs be, die."

Drabble glanced at his watch, turned a significant look on Madame, and spoke. "To-night, brothers, a neophyte will take the oath to aid us. He is a gentleman, clever but rash. He entered our house to spy. He learned our secrets, and, should he go abroad, much harm may be done. Madame says kill him. I say not so. If he refuse the oath, then let him die. If he take it, I say let him live. It is for us to win all we can to our Brotherhood, so that we may be strong. This man can aid us. Therefore, let us keep him if we can. Rouge brings him here in a few minutes, and according to his wisdom shall he be dealt with."

There was an interval for rest. The meeting broke up into chattering groups. Madame passed swiftly to the end of the cellar, where the unfortunate Trall still moaned over his niece. With a look of contempt, the woman stirred him with her foot.

"Rise," she said sternly. Slowly he got on his feet, a dishevelled, tumbled object, and muttered something about Clara. "You fool!" said Madame. "Is that all you have learned with us? To value your own miserable life or that of any other man or woman? When we take the oath we surrender our lives, to be saved or lost for the good

194

of the cause. Clara has proved false. She must die. Nothing can save her."

The wretched man sobbed. "Have mercy," he said. "Oh, have mercy."

"It is no question of mercy, but of necessity. You are not fit to be here. This is no place for tears. Leave the house, I say. When you are wanted you shall be sent for."

"Madame——"

"Go," said Mrs. Arne, sharply. "Have I to speak twice?"

Trall's head dropped on his breast in utter despair, and, without a word, he slouched through the throng and up the trapdoor. As he went out, he passed Rouge about to descend. Rouge was alone, grave, colourless, composed. As he dropped down, the Brotherhood saluted him with a volley of applause.

"Where is the prisoner?" called out Madame from the daïs.

"He will be brought down by me shortly, Madame," said Rouge; "but I have come to make a communication to the society. First, I must make all safe."

So saying, he removed the ladder, and laid it flat on the ground. Then he took up his position in the corner directly under the trapdoor, and leaned lightly against the wall. To right and left the crowd parted, so that Madame and Drabble saw him as down a long lane. A lantern overhead shed a heavy yellow light on his pallid face, and he looked as a ghost in the shadows. The Brotherhood was uneasy, not at his action, for he was a much trusted member, but on account of his reference to making all safe. Even Mrs. Arne seemed anxious.

"Rouge," she cried, "what is the matter?"

"I propose to tell you, Madame," he replied in a loud, clear voice. "Listen, all of you, to what I say. You know me as Rouge, the trusted brother of the society. Five years ago in Paris I was known as Emile Durand."

They looked at one another. Madame, with a premonition that something was wrong, half rose from her chair, and Drabble leaned forward anxiously. In dead silence every one hung upon the speech of Rouge. He spoke in French, the tongue best understood of the greatest number.

"Emile Durand," continued Rouge in a calm, even voice, "was a chemist in Paris, with a wife and child whom he dearly loved. He was a good citizen, a good father, a fond husband. The good God bestowed on him happiness, but his happiness was destroyed by death."

195

"What does this foolishness mean?"

"You will soon know, Madame," said Rouge. "It means that you and your cursed assassins threw a bomb into my shop. You killed my wife and child wickedly and cruelly. I lived but to avenge them. To-night I do so."

"Seize him! drag him forward!" shouted Drabble.

"Stand back, murderer!" shrieked Rouge, his face scarlet with rage, his eyes sparkling. "You see, I have my hand on the wall. I press it, and the mine below is fired. You will be——"

A wail of terror rose from the crowd. They shrank back from the man. Madame flung herself across the table, less afraid than furious.

"Seize him!" she cried madly. "Traitor! kill him; he lies! The button which explodes the mine is at my back."

Drabble whipped out a revolver, and the crowd reeled forward, mad with terror and anger.

"Who laid the mine?" cried Rouge, undaunted. "I did. The wire yonder is a false one. The real communication is here, under my hand."

"Betrayed, betrayed!" yelled Madame, throwing herself down. "Shoot him! kill him!"

Up swung Drabble's revolver to a level with Rouge's heart. The man never flinched. "Shoot, and I fire the mine!" he roared. "Your lives are in my hands, and I doom them. Make your peace with the God you have offended, for you are to meet Him now."

With an oath, Drabble flung himself forward and fired, but a terror-struck woman seized his arm, and the shot struck the roof. The scene which ensued was indescribable. The wild beasts groaned and howled, some, returning to the religion they had forgotten, fell on their knees to pray. Drabble was overset and trodden underfoot. All shrank back from their judge and executioner. Madame, on the daïs, colourless and silent, stared at Rouge. She alone knew how lost all was.

"O God," Rouge's voice rose clear and steady, "I am an instrument in Thy hands to rid this earth of devils. I sacrifice myself to avenge my wife and little one. To help humanity, I slay these demons. Judge them in their wickedness."

His voice became inaudible in the turmoil. With uplifted hands, they implored pity, besought mercy. And Rouge smiled.

"In the name of God," he shouted.

Madame rushed forward, stumbling over the terror-stricken men and women. She dashed straight to the mark. Silent, deadly pale, her eyes flaming, her hands extended to tear this man to pieces.

"Sophie, Therèse," cried Rouge, and, as Madame flung herself like a tigress upon him, he pressed the button hard. The next moment he was borne down by the woman.

The turmoil ceased. There was a dead silence—a terrible silence. And the earth rocked and heaved, and opened her mouth to vomit fire, and the jungle with its wild beasts of humanity hurtled through the air. With a roar of thunder, belching flame and smoke, the house split from cellar to attic. The end of the world had come for them all. And the smoke of their torment went up to heaven.

Sophie and Therèse were avenged.

THE SIXTH SCENE

AT CASTERWELL

CHAPTER I

"AN UNEXPECTED ARRIVAL"

A week after the catastrophe at Soho, Olive and Laurence were seated before a blazing fire in the Manor House drawing-room. Winter was upon them in earnest, and the rose-garden of July lay covered thick with snow, and the naked woods surrounding fought with the whistling blast.

Mallow had recovered from his cuts and scrapings, but his nerves were still suffering from his recent experience. There was no doubt that his system had received a severe shock, although he pluckily made light of it. Even Mrs. Purcell, suddenly entering the room, made him jump in his chair, and Olive laid her hand on his arm to soothe him. The two had come together only within the last three days, and at their first meeting Mallow had kissed her. That kiss was the outward and visible sign of their engagement.

"My dears!" Mrs. Purcell, with voluminous skirts, sank into a chair a wide-spreading billow. "My dears," she spoke ex cathedrâ, "I have been considering your position. Olive, my dear, outside this house you are still known as Mrs. Carson. Have you formed any plausible scheme for the amelioration of this unpleasant state of affairs?"

"None, Mrs. Purcell. I suppose I must tell the truth."

"That seems to me an extreme view to take. The truth is so very strange."

"Stranger than fiction," chimed in Mallow. "But if fact will poach on the domain of fancy, our friends will have to enlarge their swallowing capacity. I think it is best to be straightforward, Mrs. Purcell, and make a clean breast of it, from the arrival of Carson, the impostor, to the Soho explosion."

198

"I regret to say, Mr. Mallow, that I do not concur," said Mrs. Purcell, shaking her turban. "Exclusive honesty is not the best policy; and in this case it would only provide the daily journals with sensational matter. I am averse, and I feel sure that you are also, to our dear Olive's name being in the mouth of the multitude. There is no need to be too explicit."

"Then how am I to account for my marriage being a false one?" asked Olive.

"By telling the truth, my dear, within limitations. Say that the marriage was a nominal one, contracted with Mr. Angus Carson in obedience to the expressed wish of your father. Add, that during the honeymoon you unfortunately—or, rather, fortunately—discovered that Mr. Carson was the husband of another woman, and at once left him to resume your own name. Finally, let it be known that Mr. Carson and his true wife have left England together, and will return no more. Mr. Carson, you understand, my love, not Signor Boldini."

"You would make no explanation?" demanded Mallow.

"Assuredly not. You are not bound to satisfy the curiosity of the public. Though, indeed!" added Mrs. Purcell, "so much as I would have you reveal, should be sufficient to answer all questions. Moreover, I most earnestly advise Olive to accompany me abroad for a few months, and at the end of that time to marry you, Mr. Mallow, before returning to England. Then both of you can take up your position in this house without giving cause for scandal or public animadversions. It is true people may talk about our dear Olive's first marriage; but, for want of details, which I advise you strongly to withhold, such idle chatter will die of inanition."

There was good sound sense in what Mrs. Purcell said. A bare statement of the facts which enabled Olive to reappear in society as Mrs. Mallow was all that was necessary. And none was better calculated to enunciate the facts than Mrs. Purcell, for one reason because she knew every one in the county worth knowing; for another, because her very prolixity made impressive what otherwise might have been looked upon as a bald and feeble narrative. She would take care that the sympathies of one and all were with her beloved Olive, and, when, after a sufficiently judicious absence, she returned to the Manor House the wife of Laurence Mallow, her reception would be something more than cordial.

"What a relief!" sighed Olive, when the old lady had departed in triumph. "The whole thing has been quite a nightmare to me lately. I am so thankful that Mrs. Purcell has found a way out of it."

"Mrs. Purcell is a sensible woman," said Mallow, warmly, "and her opinion carries weight. What she says is perfectly true. You were so unfortunate at first as to be placed in the position of marrying a man who was not your choice, and, further, having married him, of discovering the fact that he was already married. The sequel is, I think, sufficiently obvious to the dullest of our neighbours. At all events, there is the whole business in a nutshell, and it shall be for Mrs. Purcell to present it to the county to crack. No word need be said of any connection with these Anarchist people. Thank goodness, they and their diabolical schemes have been very effectually disposed of."

"Don't, Laurence!" Olive shivered and covered her face. "It is terrible to think of how narrowly you escaped death."

"Dearest, a miss is as good as a mile. Thanks to that poor fellow Rouge, I came through all right. My only regret is that the death of Mrs. Arne, of Trall, and Drabble does away with any hope of our learning the truth. The reason for poor Carson's murder will remain a mystery."

"It is no mystery to me," cried Olive, petulantly. "Mrs. Arne killed him."

"She denied it most solemnly."

"I dare say. Such a woman would deny anything."

"To gain her ends, she would," replied Mallow judiciously; "but, in this case, she gained nothing by denial. I am inclined to think she told me the truth. Until Carson proved recalcitrant it would have been foolish for her to kill the goose with the golden eggs. Olive, whoever killed Carson, the Anarchists didn't."

"Well, innocent or guilty, then the wickedness has put an end to them. That man Rouge is a hero."

"I agree with you, but the world does not know of his heroism, and never will. The police, the papers, are absolutely at a loss to explain the explosion, and it is my intention that neither Jim nor I should enlighten them. The Morning Planet declares that the Anarchists were experimenting with a new explosive. Such an explanation is quite sufficient for the masses, the classes, and the quidnunc asses."

"Will not Vraik say something?"

"What can he say, save that Rouge was one of the Brotherhood? It was only to Jim and me that he revealed himself and his plans. No, Vraik is safe enough. I shall pay him, and dismiss him."

"You won't go on with the case, then, Laurence?" Mallow shook his head. "There are no clues," he said.

"Surely you forget; there are still two clues," cried Olive, vivaciously. "What about the man who inquired at the P. and O. Office?"

"Oh, no doubt he was an Anarchist sent by Drabble to learn when the Pharaoh would arrive—perhaps Drabble himself, in disguise. I dare say, whoever he was, he was blown up with the rest of the gang. No clue there, Olive."

"Then there is the packet Lord Aldean found in the sandal-wood chest."

"H'm," Mallow reflected, "there may be something in that. Of course, it depends upon what the packet contains. Have you given it to Mr. Brock?"

"No; I thought of doing so to-morrow. He has been too ill to see any one lately."

"What! Is his accident so bad as that?"

"It is as bad as it can be," said Olive, emphatically. "He is old, and not very strong. Besides, he would insist upon being brought back to Casterwell; and the journey has shaken him. The nervous shock has affected his heart, so the doctor says."

"That's bad. Poor old chap! Don't suppose he'll pull through."

"Come and see him with me to-morrow, Laurence."

"Yes, dear, with pleasure. We'll ask him about the packet. I dare say he'll show us what is in it." Mallow rose and began to pace the room, musing as he walked. "It might turn out valuable," he said, at length, "from the care Carson took to conceal it it is evidently a document of importance."

"I wonder why Mr. Carson did conceal it?"

"Because he mistrusted Semberry," replied Mallow, promptly. "Depend upon it, Olive, Carson soon realized that the Major was a shifty scamp, and hid his papers where there was no likelihood of their being read. I see no other explanation for their concealment."

"I shall make a point of seeing Brock to-morrow," he said, looking out of the window and whistling softly.

"Laurence," said Olive, who was still staring into the fire, "do you think Dr. Drabble was blown up?"

"I'm certain of it. As Madame Death-in-Life's right-hand man, and general adviser to these rascals, he would certainly not be absent from so important a meeting. Yes, I think Drabble has received the wage of his sins."

"Poor Mrs. Drabble!"

"Happy Mrs. Drabble, you mean. She has been rescued from the torment of an unscrupulous bully. Besides, Drabble would have poisoned his children's minds. He was in a fair way to ruining

201

Margery." Olive rose and came laughing across the room. "Margery has improved," she said, with some amusement; "her Anarchistic mood has passed. She now concerns herself chiefly with religion."

"At her age? Nonsense! There must be a limit even to her precocity."

"A child's religion, of course. Margery is older than her years, and very, very clever, as you know. She now reads her Bible, goes to church, and writes hymns on the model of Keble. I found her with Keble's poems the other day."

"Poor child! her father has quite unsettled her mind. It's a lucky thing for Margery, and for the rest of the family, that he's gone. I suppose the news of his death will, have to be broken to his wife. But if Mrs. Drabble is wise she will rejoice, not sorrow."

"Oh, Laurence! After all he was her husband, the father of her children."

"And a nice blackguard in either capacity. Hullo, who's this tramp?"

Across the lawn stumbled a ragged Guy Fawkes, grotesque and unsteady. He laboured in the snow like a liner rolling in a cross sea. At his nearer approach he raised his head. Those at the window started, and stared eagerly.

"Laurence! look! a black beard, a long beard; can it be——"

"Wait, wait," interrupted Mallow; and throwing open the French window, he ran across the terrace down the steps. With a yelp the man scrambled back, but stumbled full length on the slippery crust of snow. Mallow gripped his shoulder as he dropped. "Who the devil are you?" he said roughly.

"Mr. Mallow?" The ragged creature gave a howl of joy. "I'm— I'm Trall!"

CHAPTER II

"THE PENANCE OF MARGERY"

"I'm Trall," repeated the man, staggering to his feet.

He plucked off a false beard, thereby throwing into prominence the haggardness of his face.

"Trall?" echoed Mallow, as though taking in the man's identity for the first time. "Good God, I thought you were dead!" The man whimpered, and fawned on Mallow as a whipped dog fawns on its master. "I'm alive; I'm Trall," he reiterated. "I'm so glad it's you, Mr. Mallow. I thought they were after me. But I'm Trall; you know me, don't you? You'll save me, won't you? I'm afraid of them.'

"Whatever is the matter, Laurence?" called out Olive, at the window. "Who is it?"

"It's all right, Olive; it's only Trall. I'll explain later; go inside now.—Good God!" said Mallow, again looking at the wreck of humanity before him. "Alive after all."

Jeremiah Trall nodded, and laughed vacantly. His life of terror and strong drink, added now to want of food and sleep, had scattered the poor creature's wits. He clung to Mallow like a child, reiterating his prayer for protection, and ultimately sliding into an incoherent gabble, disconnected though continuous. Seeing that nothing was to be got out of him, in his present state, Mallow soothed him with repeated assurances of his safety. He then led him round to the back of the house, and had him supplied with food. In another half-hour the wretched man was safely tucked in bed, with one of the men-servants to watch over him. The food and warmth and sense of security relaxed his nerves, and shortly he fell into a deep sleep. His relief had come just in time.

Meanwhile Mallow returned to the drawing-room and explained the situation. How Trall had escaped death he did not know, but he understood the man's instinct had led him to seek the protection of the only person who had treated him with kindness.

"We shall hear his story to-morrow," concluded Mallow; "and a queer one it will be, unless I'm very much mistaken."

"Laurence, do you think this can be the man who inquired at the P. and O. Office? He has a black beard."

"False, my dear; assumed no doubt to escape the Brotherhood, although, seeing they are all dead, I can't understand what it is he fears. It is quite possible he may be the man who inquired at the shipping office; we shall know all about that in the morning. And Olive," added Mallow, in lower tones, as the servant entered with the tea, "say nothing about this for the present to Miss Ostergaard or the old ladies. I'll tell Aldean myself later on."

Olive readily assented. She had no wish any of them should be alarmed. When they, with Lord Aldean, came in to tea, no word was said about Trall's strange arrival. Later on Mallow found an opportunity for enlightening Jim.

203

"Jove!" said the startled Aldean. "How the dickens did he escape?"

"I can't say. Perhaps he wasn't at the meeting. Don't alarm the ladies, Jim. We'll get it all out of him in the morning. He's worn-out now, poor devil."

"Do you think he knows the truth about this Carson business?"

"It's possible, and probable. At all events, whatever he knows he'll tell me."

But, in spite of all precautions, it was not long before Mrs. Purcell knew all about it. Her maids were of more than ordinary loquacity. She immediately declared her belief that they would all be murdered in their beds, and communicated her fears to Miss Slarge. The two ancients reappeared in the drawing-room in a nervous flutter, and, in the end, if only to quieten them, Mallow thought it best to explain matters fully. Contrary to his expectations, they were only the more alarmed.

"An Anarchist," cried Miss Slarge, tremulously, "with a bomb!"

"I don't think he has a bomb," replied Mallow, gravely. "He is quite harmless, Miss Slarge. He hasn't strength just now to kill a fly."

"Has he rebelled against established authority?" demanded Mrs. Purcell. "Has he crime upon his soul?"

"His worst crime is hard drinking. I'll look after him, Mrs. Purcell. Please give the servants no particulars."

Mrs. Purcell expressed a pious hope that the Manor House would be still whole in the morning; but finally agreed that Mr. Mallow had acted with his usual judgment, and was quite right to succour the oppressed.

When, after every one had gone to bed, Mallow and Aldean visited Trall, he was still sleeping, so they left him. But early next morning Mallow was in his room. He was awake, and professed himself much easier in his mind. Amid a profusion of thanks for all his kindness, he told Mallow how he had escaped the common fate through Madame having ordered him out of the house.

"I don't know how it all happened," he said. "There was a mine laid under the cellar, I know, but I feel sure Madame didn't fire it. I hope they won't think I did it. It was for fear of that I came down here."

"You are safe enough here, Trall. Besides, that section, at least, of the Brotherhood is done for."

"Oh, but they were not all there. There are others. Two of them have gone after Carlo and Clara. I protested, but Madame would send them, and she turned me out of the place."

"Where are Boldini and your niece now?"

"They have left Genoa for South America. One of the Brothers followed them. He wired to Madame they had taken ship, but he did not say for what port. But they're as good as dead," moaned Trall; "the Brothers who were sent after them had instructions to kill them."

"Oh, let us hope they will escape," said Mallow, soothingly. "By the way, that disguise of yours, Trall. Did you wear it to visit the P. and O. Office before Carson arrived?"

"No, Mr. Mallow; I was never in the P. and O. Office in my life."

Mallow looked searchingly at the man, but saw by his simple denial, and from his manner, that he was telling the truth. "Do you know any one else who went there?" he asked, shifting his ground.

"No, I never heard of any one."

"Did Dr. Drabble?"

"I am sure I don't know," said Trall, plucking at the clothes. "He never told me, if he did. But Drabble wore all kinds of disguises; sometimes he wore a light wig, at others a black one. He was never twice the same."

"I dare say it was he," said Mallow, thoughtfully; "he was the person most interested in Carson's arrival. He is dead, I suppose?"

"Blown to pieces, Mr. Mallow. He was in the cellar when I left. Not one of those present escaped alive. They are dead in their sins, Mr. Mallow, and black—black indeed are those sins. If I had not spoken for Clara, if Madame had not—well, I have sins of my own to repent of. God saved me for repentance. I'm sure of that."

"Rouge was in the cellar, of course?"

"He came down the trapdoor as I went up. I liked Rouge; he hated the Brotherhood, as I did. It might have been Rouge who caused the explosion. He laid the mine; he knew how to fire it. Yes, I believe Rouge killed them all."

"I am sure he did," said Mallow decisively. "Mrs. Arne had Nemesis at her elbow, although she thought, no doubt, it was the devil. But how did you know that I was alive, and here?"

"Rouge told me. He said that he intended to aid your escape, because you had been kind to him. As he passed down the trapdoor, I heard him say, 'Monsieur is safe.' I didn't know what he meant at the time, but afterwards I recollected he was speaking of you. When I heard of the explosion, I was nearly out of my mind. I thought the surviving Brotherhood would surely suspect me. I went to your rooms to ask for your protection. They told me there that you were at Casterwell, so I came down. I walked the whole way. I begged, and slept out-of-doors. Oh, the cold was bitter. I knew you would protect me, for you were always kind, Mr. Mallow. Always, always," and Trall stretched out his hand timidly.

"Well, now you are here, you shall stay," said Mallow, kindly. "They won't look for you here. I dare say they think you perished with the rest; and later on we'll see what had better be done."

Trall sat up eagerly.

"I know what to do; I have my plans," he whispered, with a glance round, as was his habit. "Give me money, and I'll go out to South America. Clara will look after me. Carlo has a lot of money; Drabble said so. I'll warn them of their danger, and we'll hide in the mountains. They'll never find us there. Clara is so clever; Clara knows."

"Is she your only relative?"

"So far as I know. I have a brother—her father—my brother Michael; but he may be dead. He left his wife and Clara many, many years ago. His wife died. I looked after Clara. I had money then. But when I met Drabble"—Trall burst into childish anger—"I hate Drabble; he made me what I am. He was my curse. I'm glad he's dead; glad, oh, so glad. If he'd only died before he ruined me. I was once—I am now—oh!" and the man, weeping senile tears, dropped back exhausted on his pillow.

"Hush, hush!" said Mallow, smoothing the bed-clothes; "you are with friends now; I will take care of you. But don't say a word as to who you are or what you have been doing. That might be dangerous even here."

"No, no—not a word; you won't let them get to me if they come?"

"They won't come, Trall. Believe me, they think you dead."

"Dead?" echoed Trall, his wits wandering. "Dead, dead, yes, these many years. Drabble killed my soul. Dead—yes, the man is dead; the beast lives on."

With tactful words and many promises, Mallow managed to calm him and dispel his morbid mood. The man was not really so ill as worn with fatigue, and stupefied with terror. Rest, and a belief in his safety, were the medicines he needed, and these were now forthcoming. His narrow escape seemed to have turned his thoughts towards religion, for he requested the use of a Bible with childish eagerness. Mallow left him grappling desperately with the Psalms, striving to extract hope from the more comforting.

206

"I am glad the poor man is better," said Olive, when she heard Mallow's report; "he seems a harmless creature."

"There is good in him, but circumstances and Drabble have done their best to destroy it."

"Well, let him stay here and rest, Laurence. See, I have the letter for Mr. Brock. We must call on him now. Talking about Dr. Drabble," added Olive, as they stepped out into the crisp air; "I think I ought to call and see his wife, and tell her."

"Do you think that is wise?" asked Mallow, dubiously.

"Of course it is wise; suspense is worse than the truth. Besides, she is without money and food. I had to send provisions to her yesterday. The sooner she understands her position, and makes the best of it, the better."

"How can she make the best of it?"

"I shall help her; and Lord Aldean has promised his assistance."

"Good fellow; you must let me do something too."

"My help is yours, Laurence," said Olive, softly.

A brisk walk soon brought them to Drabble's untidy home. In a room more slatternly than ever, they found the unsuspecting widow. She was, if possible, more worn and downcast than before.

"I'm sure I don't know what I should have done but for your kindness," she said to Olive. "But I expect the doctor will be back soon. It is too bad his leaving me destitute like this. The tradesmen won't send in food without money."

"Dear Mrs. Drabble," said Olive, touching her arm gently, "will you take me to your room? I have something to tell you."

The significance of Olive's tone was not lost upon her. "I hope—hope nothing is the matter with the doctor?" she said tremulously.

"I'll tell you in your own room," insisted Olive, leading her to the door.

"Excuse us, won't you, Mr. Mallow?" called back the widow; "and if the children should come in send them away. Danton is in bed with the mumps, and Margery has been converted. Please talk her back to some sense, Mr. Mallow, if you can. Dear, dear! my children are so dreadful."

Mallow sat quietly amid all the litter, in no wise inclined to laugh at these last words, albeit there was some humour in them. On all sides there was the noise of children creeping, scuffling, and whispering. At times a head would pop round the corner; its owner, meeting Mallow's eye, would shriek and scuttle away, and then would be swift scampering and a continuous patter as of hard little hoofs on a frosty soil. Shortly the door swung open to its widest, and

Margery appeared, so astonishing a spectacle that Mallow could not but stare at the child. She was draped in a sheet; her feet were bare, and she carried a lighted candle.

"I'm doing penance!" announced Margery in solemn tones. "I should stand at the church-door and proclaim my sins, but mother won't let me."

"Your sins?" said Mallow, suppressing a strong desire to laugh; "have you any?"

"Dozens! I have sinned deeply," sighed this guilty little person. "I have been cross, I have stolen, I have perverted the truth. Would you like to hear about any particular sin, Mr. Mallow?"

"I should be delighted, Margery. Only don't shock me too much."

Margery waved her taper. "This sin was done to Olive!" she chanted. "Listen, oh people, to the sin done to Olive! I gave her a golden ornament of fine gold with wrought-work. She asked where I obtained it. I declared that I had taken it from the desk of my father. That was a lie. That was a sin. I did steal it. Wicked woman that I am—but I stole it from the study of Mr. Brock."

"Margery!" Mallow jumped with sudden interest. "Did you find that wrist-button in Mr. Brock's study?"

Margery dropped her candle and became the child she was, even to the length of bursting into tears.

"Yes," she sobbed, "I was wicked. I went to see Mr. Brock; he left me to play in his study, and I found the button in the drawer of his writing-table. I—I—I took it."

CHAPTER III

"MR. BROCK AND THE LETTER"

Margery's conscience had now the upper hand of her. All her acting was cast to the winds. "It was wrong to take it," she wept. "I can see that now, Mr. Mallow, but I did not think. Father said that all property should be shared in common, so I thought I would share with Mr. Brock; he has very nice property," she added, naïvely.

208

"Was this wrist-button put away carefully?"

"No-o-o. It was lying loose in a drawer; I didn't think it was of much value. I am very, very wicked."

Mallow drew the child towards him and consoled her. "Don't cry, Margery," he said, wiping her eyes with his handkerchief. "A fault confessed is half-redressed. Did you tell Mr. Brock that you were sorry?"

"Yes; I told him that I was converted, and that I repented of my wickedness. He said it did not matter; that I was not to trouble about what I had done."

"Then don't trouble, dear. There, there, it's all right. So you have given up the Anarchism?"

"I am a Christian now. I believe in——"

Before Margery could state her religious beliefs, Olive, looking rather anxious, came into the room. "Laurence, would you mind calling on Mr. Brock alone? Mrs. Drabble is not well enough to be left at present."

"Oh, is mother ill?" cried Margery, scared.

"She is not very well, dear. Put on your stockings and shoes, child; you will take cold. Laurence!"

"I'll go to Mr. Brock. Is that the letter, Olive? Thank you. How long will you stop here?"

"Until Mrs. Drabble is better. When you return home, Laurence, please ask Miss Slarge to come here. Margery!"

The child was shaking and white. "Please, please, what is the matter?" she asked, catching Olive by the hand.

Olive looked at her in silence and with pity. If it had been a painful task to inform Mrs. Drabble of the truth, it was a much more terrible one to inform Margery. With a nod to Mallow, she led the child from the room; and Laurence, feeling somewhat de trop in this scene of domestic grief, slipped away, not ill-pleased to have the opportunity. It was vexing, in one way, that Olive could not come with him; but on reflection he could not regret her absence.

At the corner of the Vicarage he was confronted by a she-Cerberus, in the person of Mr. Brock's deaf housekeeper. This grim and lean spinster might once have been a human flower, but the sap was now gone out of her, and she had withered on the stalk in a state of single-blessedness. Even Mallow's good looks and polite inquiries failed to impress her. She was the sworn enemy of all male-kind. At the outset she declined to admit Mallow; "indeed, he's much too ill," she said. But in the end she was so far prevailed upon as to consent to convey a message. This resulted in prompt permission for the visitor to enter the sick-room, whither the sour spinster led him with obvious reluctance. She closed the door on him with a bang, and returned to vent her ill-temper in the kitchen.

The vicar had transferred himself from his bedroom to the study. He was lying on a sofa drawn close up to the window. His eyes were unnaturally bright and sunken, and his skin was the colour of wax. The few weeks of confinement to the house had aged him inconceivably. But he appeared to be in good spirits, and received Mallow most cordially.

"You find me much afflicted, Mr. Mallow," said he, cheerfully, "but I am not without hope of recovery. I contrive to keep up my spirits, which is, I suppose, a greater preventive of inanition than the most stringent of medicines."

"I am indeed glad to know you are better, Mr. Brock. Will conversation tire you?"

"Not at all. It is a pleasure to converse intelligently. How is Mrs. Carson?"

"Miss Bellairs is quite well," said Laurence, prepared for this question. Brock turned an astonished look on his visitor. "But why do you call Olive by her maiden name?"

"Because that is her name for the present. She is not Carson's wife."

"Not Carson's wife, man? I married them myself" said the vicar, with a searching glance, not unmixed with uneasiness.

"True enough, Mr. Brock. But I am sorry to tell you that Carson has proved a scamp and a bigamist. At the time he married Olive he was already the husband of Clara Trall, the maid. They have left for England, and Olive has returned here as Miss Bellairs. She is shortly to be married to me."

"Angus already married?" gasped Brock, when he took in the full import of it. "Angus, the son of an upright man, act so basely? Surely, surely there must be some mistake."

"I—am—afraid—not. Lord Aldean followed the runaways to Florence, and saw them together. They confessed their marriage."

"But why did Angus so deceive Olive?"

Mallow shrugged. "To get her money, no doubt," he said carelessly. "It will come to you now, Mr. Brock, since the marriage has not taken place."

"Alas! I fear I have done with all use for worldly goods, Mr. Mallow. I am not so strong as I thought I was. My heart has been weakened by my accident, and any sudden shock would probably be fatal to me. If this money does come to me now, it will not remain with me long, for my days are numbered."

"Nil desperandum," said Mallow, not very originally. "You have years of clean living behind you, sir, and may mend sooner than you think. After all, you are better off than Drabble; he has met with a violent death in common with many others of his kidney."

"Drabble dead? Well, I am not surprised. I have been wondering if he was in that Soho explosion of which we have read lately. As that was his town address, it struck me that he might possibly have been. Ah!" sighed Mr. Brock, "a terrible end to a mistaken life. But I thought that Drabble was more of a Socialist than an Anarchist?"

"He was everything that's bad," said Laurence, shortly. "Olive is now comforting Mrs. Drabble, poor soul! By the way, Mr. Brock, Margery told me about that wrist-button."

"Dear, dear; the poor child must not worry about that. I forgave her taking it; children will finger things, and Margery's mind was quite perverted by her father's peculiar views.—Still," he added, with a smile, "Margery really had more right to it than I. It originally belonged to Drabble."

"What! did you get it from him, then?"

"As a gift—yes. I saw it lying on his desk one day, and took it up to examine it. As it was of Indian workmanship, I asked him to give it to me as a curiosity. I was a missionary in India once, you know."

"Yes, I know. Did Drabble give it to you willingly?"

"Certainly. I should not have taken it otherwise. It is a pretty thing; Margery tells me that she gave it to Olive."

"Olive wears it as a brooch," replied Mallow, gloomily. He was distinctly puzzled.

He noticed, too, that the vicar was half dozing, and felt that perhaps he was overtaxing his strength.

"Well, I must be going now. Mr. Brock," said he, producing Dr. Carson's letter, "my principal reason for coming was to hand you this."

"What is it?" asked Brock, taking the blue envelope drowsily.

"A letter from your old friend, Dr. Carson."

Brock woke up with a start. He was clearly agitated. "From a dead man? What does it mean?"

"A message of some import, no doubt," said Mallow. "Young Carson brought it home with him, but forgot to deliver it."

"A voice from the grave!" muttered Brock, unheeding. His hands were busy with two papers—a closely written letter, and a

211

dozen long pages of foolscap of aggressively official appearance. Mallow's fingers itched to take them up, but he judiciously restrained himself; and watched the vicar skim his eye over the letter. Its perusal seemed to move him greatly.

"Wrong, wrong," he said, folding it up. "Better to let the dead past bury its dead," and shuffling the papers into their envelope, he slipped it under his pillow.

Mallow was struck by his remark. It tended to confirm his long-entertained suspicions.

"Mr. Brock," he asked, after a moment, "was there a secret in the life of the late Mr. Bellairs?"

"Why should you think so?" said the vicar, nervously.

"I have not forgotten about the sealed letter which forced Olive into marrying Carson. She asked you what its hint of evil meant. You told her to take no notice of it."

"That was her best course," said Mr. Brock, still agitated. "So long as she married Angus, there was no need for her to trouble about the letter."

"Then there is a secret?" insisted Mallow.

Mr. Brock shifted uneasily. "Whose life is free from sin?" he said, in low tones. "Yes, there—is—a secret."

"Had it to do with Olive's marriage?"

"Yes; if she had refused Angus, there might have been trouble."

"What kind of trouble?"

"Don't ask me," said the vicar, with a shiver.

"I must ask you. Olive guesses that there is a secret, and she wishes to know it."

"She shall never know it from me," said the vicar, his face more pallid than ever. "I say let the dead past bury its dead."

"You said that before when you read that letter. The secret is told in that enclosed document?"

"Yes," said Brock, reluctantly.

"Then Olive must read it—I must read it. We must know the truth."

The vicar remained silent, and his brow wrinkled. "Who gains knowledge gains sorrow," he said, aphoristically. "It will do neither you nor Olive any good to learn the follies of a young man. However, I will read the document, and—if I can legitimately do so—I will send it to Olive."

"Is the secret so very terrible, then?"

"It is very terrible."

"Is her father——"

212

"Mr. Mallow," protested the vicar, wiping his wet forehead, "I have said all I intend to say, until I read this letter. If I can send it to Olive, it shall be sent. Please leave me. I—I have overtaxed my strength. Touch the bell, please, as you go out."

Although Mallow would fain have stayed, there was nothing left for him to do but to obey this peremptory request. He could not but acknowledge that Mr. Brock was acting in an eminently reasonable way. A secret of such moment as this appeared to be could not be communicated hastily and without due consideration.

When next he saw Olive, Mallow told her what she might expect. With characteristic firmness, she chose to abide by her decision.

"I must know the truth," she declared, "at whatever cost. So long as you and I are together, Laurence, nothing can hurt us."

"You tempt the gods, my dearest," replied Laurence, and sighed.

The events of the last few months had shaken his nerve, and he was apt at times to give way to despondency.

Mr. Brock did not seem in a hurry to come to his decision. One, two, three days passed before word came to the Manor House. Having implicit faith in the vicar's judgment, Mallow did not urge him at all. He did not even go near the Vicarage, but curbed his impatience and that of Olive as best he could. Virtue was rewarded—if reward it was—for on the fourth day the document was delivered to Miss Bellairs, with a letter from the vicar.

"I send you the history of your father in India," wrote Mr. Brock, "though it is somewhat against my better judgment. I do so, however, as I can guess that your curiosity will allow you no rest. I give you the opportunity of appeasing it. Still, even at this eleventh hour, I would most earnestly advise you to put the enclosed paper in the fire unread. Its perusal can only give you pain, and remove from its pedestal the idol of your youth."

All this, and much more, Mr. Brock wrote, and Mallow read. He was alone with Olive in the library. He looked questioningly at her. She was silent, and for answer placed the document in his hands.

"Am I to read it?" he asked. Olive bent her head. "As you think wise, dear; or shall we burn it, as Mr. Brock advises, unread?"

Olive clasped her hands tightly together. The question was a weighty one. She hesitated. Then she crossed the Rubicon.

"Read," she said, in low tones; "at whatever cost, read."

Mallow silently spread out the paper and began.

CHAPTER IV

"THE TREASURES AT KIKAT"

"I, Alfred Carson, M.D., who relate to you this story, do most solemnly swear to you by all a Christian gentleman holds most sacred, that though stranger far than any fiction, it existed in fact, and that the relation of it here set forth—to which my signature is duly appended—is in each and every particular true. At the time these events occurred, I occupied the post of physician to the Rao of Kikat, which was an unconsidered kingdom in the Northern part of India. I say 'was' advisedly, for since the year of the Mutiny it has been absorbed in our Asiatic Empire. But in 1859—the date of the facts herein related—it was still an independent state, reigned over by Rao Singhapetty, it is true, but free and wealthy nevertheless. Still the Rao, in a small measure, was tributary to the H.E.I.C., and it was to release himself from a nominal payment that he engaged to take part in the great rising. To his folly in this respect this story is due.

"In those days, I was young, poor, rash, and ambitious, yet not without, I think, good parts, mental and moral. If I failed to control the one by the other, the blame for such must lie with Michael Trall. He was one of those rascally adventurers who then infested India, in the hope of becoming Nabobs; fertile in resource, of great courage, and one of the most unscrupulous scoundrels who ever played the part of Mephistopheles for the seduction of weaker spirits to ruin and crime. Whence he came I know not. I conclude his past life was too disreputable to be disclosed, but my knowledge of him dates from the year 1857, when he appeared at the Rao's court, and used his impudent arts to secure an ascendency over the mind of that weak potentate. There he came into contact with me, and with Bellairs.

"Mark Bellairs, my dearest and oldest friend, had come out to India with me. He was then in the army, but having quarrelled with his father, his allowance was cut off, and he was forced to sell out. I suggested that he should travel Eastward in my company, and turn his military knowledge to some account at the court of some petty Rajah. As there was nothing for him to do in England, he agreed to try his luck in the East, and together we arrived in Bombay, with no money, and great ambitions. Of our adventures I need not speak, as

214

they have nothing to do with this story; but we wandered here, there, and everywhere, until Fortune brought us to Kikat. Here, as the Rao was in need of a resident physician, he engaged me, and afterwards, finding that Bellairs had been in the English Service, he placed him in command of his small army. I swear that before the meeting Bellairs and I were quite content with our positions. We had power, the salaries were large, and the Rao was our very good friend. In a few years we hoped to make our fortunes, and return wealthy, and honoured to the Mother country. But for Trall, we might have continued in the straight path, but, like the Belial he was, he drew us from it to earn money and lasting shame.

"I must admit that Trall was a most fascinating man. Handsome, strong, clever, full of conversation and tact, he had acquired complete power over Singha. Then, finding that we had no little say in matters of state, he set his clever wits to work for our conquest—not without success. No doubt, it was weak of us to yield, but the man had a tremendous strength of will, and a power of fascination which could control—and did control—all who personally came in contact with him. Remember, both Bellairs and myself believed him to be an honourable gentleman; and it was not until we were well entangled in his nets that he threw off the mask. Then it was too late.

"There is ever an exception to a rule, and an exception to the well-nigh universal popularity of Trall was to be found in the person of the Rev. Manners Brock, a missionary, who had engaged himself in the hopeless task of converting the Kikat heathen. The pleasant manners and simplicity of Brock made him a great favourite with us all; even the Rao liked him, in spite of his Christianizing propensities, and placed no barrier in his way with the people. Brock was candid almost to the verge of folly. He told us how he stood alone in the world, without parents or relatives; made us acquainted with all the details of his early life as a sizar at Oxford, as a poor London curate, and made a frank declaration of his 'call' to enlighten the idolaters of India. I knew Brock's life as well as I did my own, and felt great respect for his principles and zeal. Trall was studiously affable to him, and tried his hardest to fascinate him into obedience, but somehow Brock managed to avoid his snares. He kept out of Trall's company, undermined his influence with the Rao—which was exercised for no good, you may be sure—and altogether showed our Belial plainly that he considered him a rascal. Naturally, Trall grew to hate him, and would willingly have done him an injury, but as Singha protected the missionary, open warfare

215

was out of the question. However, Trall watched his opportunity, and it came at last—the Mutiny with it.

"When all India blazed with fanaticism from north to south, Rao kept himself and his kingdom out of trouble, although he did not go so far as to side with the English. He adopted a neutral attitude, and no doubt would have maintained it to the end, but that Trall, ever at his elbow, persuaded him to revolt. Singha did not declare open war against the foreigners—he could scarcely have done so while an Englishman headed his army—but he tampered with the mutinous princes, corresponded with them, and declared that he wished to be rid of his tributary necessity. With devilish ingenuity, Trall conducted the whole intrigue, and kept urging Singha openly to declare himself. Bellairs and I protested at first, but in some way, I can hardly say how, Trall involved us in his schemes. What would have been the end of it, had the Rao taken the field, I hardly know, but he hesitated, and hung back until it was too late. The Mutiny was suppressed, and puppets at Delhi were driven into exile, and with them, Trall's hopes of becoming the Vizier of an Eastern king. For a while he raged furiously over his disappointment; then, making the best of a bad job, he began to look about him how best to turn the tide of affairs to his own advantage. It is at this juncture that Bellairs and I come into the story.

"The troubles at an end, Singha naturally wished to make his peace with the victors. It is true that he had not declared himself an enemy, but he had intrigued deeply; he had written compromising letters; and what with the knowledge of myself, Bellairs, and Trall, there was evidence ample to have him dethroned and exiled. He grew afraid of what might happen to him, and implored us all to help him. At this critical moment Trall showed himself in his true colours.

"I have mentioned the compromising letters, and treaties with mutinous Rajahs. Well, Trall had kept copies of these, and also possessed some of the originals. If these documents had been shown to the H.E.I.C. or to Sir Henry Lawrence, there is no doubt that they would have ruined the Rao beyond all hope of keeping his kingdom.

"Singha knew this, and so did Trall, so did Bellairs and I, for the letters were shown to us. Trall proposed to blackmail the Rao; we refused, and then it was he unmasked his batteries. The man—as we then discovered—was a skilful forger, and had signed our names to many of these letters, besides the actual signature of Singha. If he was guilty, we were also, and in a worse degree, seeing that,

216

according to the forgeries, we were ready to massacre our own countrymen. It is impossible to explain how deeply we were involved; but Trall showed us clearly, that if we did not work with him, he could, and would, ruin us. The choice lay between ruin and crime, for in no way could we have proved our innocence. Trall had the letters and treaties, with the Rao's real signature, and the false ones of myself and Bellairs; he had provided himself with more than a dozen witnesses to swear that we were renegades to the British cause; he had entangled us in the political criminality of the Rao, and we saw very plainly that our lives were ruined should the documents ever reach the Governor-General. Bellairs and I took a night to choose between our ruin and crime. Next morning—I blush to set down the fact—we chose shame.

"Consider, I pray you, our position. Trall, as I have shown, had us completely in his power. Guiltless, we should have appeared guilty, and would have been punished and despised—perhaps shot by our own countrymen. No declaration of innocence would have done away with the forgeries. The evidence of our guilt as conspirators with the Rao against the H.E.I.C. was down in black and white, and only our word on oath contradicted it. We were—as the saying goes—in a cleft stick—mere pawns shifted on Life's chessboard by an unscrupulous intriguer. There was nothing for it but to obey Trall, if we wished to save our names from the world's knowledge as those of traitors and renegades. The devil and the deep-sea proverb applies to our position.

"Well, as I have said, we gave in, and Trall proceeded to round off his plot. Money was what he wanted, and money he intended to have, even though he were to share it with Bellairs and myself. He saw Singha, and fixed his price for the inculpating documents. The price was three diamonds—famous not only in Kikat, but throughout India. Three stones of the purest water they were, a large gem and two small ones, valued together at some forty thousand pounds, more or less. Trall intended to keep the most valuable gem for himself, and to give us the other two, 'and I should advise you both to clear out then,' said he, 'for there may be trouble.'

"He was as cool in the midst of all this rascality as though he were engaged, like Brock, in missionary enterprise. When he went to have it out with Singha, we expected he would be killed there and then; but Trall, knowing his risk, knew also how to circumvent it. Of course the Rao was furious and amazed when Trall made his statement and demanded his price; and, of course, being an Indian, his first instinct was to kill the man who had deceived him. But Trall was ready with a counter move. He told Singha that the incriminating papers were in the hands of a third person, and that if he killed him these would be sent on to the Government at Calcutta. As this meant ruin, Singha was not fool enough to resort to violence, and seeing no way out of the snare, he gave up the diamonds. They were called the treasures of Kikat, and were guarded by the priests. Then the blackmailer promised that the papers should be sent back to Singha. Two hours later he presented us with our share, and slipped his own jewel into a chamois leather bag. 'Now,' said he, 'you had better skip. I'm off myself.'

"But before he could get away, the Rao made trouble. Afraid lest Trall should not return the papers, he made a clean breast of the whole thing to Brock. The missionary was fearfully angry, and without trusting himself to Trall's mercies, started straight away for Calcutta, there to lay the whole matter before the Government. He promised to get Singha out of his trouble, and have Trall arrested for his wickedness. There was no mention of Bellairs or myself, as the Rao did not know how Trall had been plotting with us. Brock got away, though Trall heard of his mission through his spies, and followed him, determined to stop his visit to Calcutta at any cost should he prove unreasonable. Bellairs and I remained with the Rao, and made up our minds to get away at the first opportunity with our diamonds. We did not know what might happen, and thought it best to be on the safe side and save our skins, at all events. In time, Singha received the papers, and, of course, saw our signatures. He applied to Bellairs for an explanation. I was absent at the time, so Bellairs saw the Rao alone. What took place at the interview I hardly knew, for Bellairs was never very explicit. But it seemed that Singha accused Bellairs of betraying him, and tried to stab him on the spot. The end of the struggle was that Bellairs passed his sword through the Rao's heart, and then came to tell me what he had done. As I saw that everything might come out, I advised immediate flight. That same night we both left Kikat.

"Shortly afterwards we learned how Singha's heir had found his father's dead body and the treasonable papers. Fearing that these, if exposed, might cost him his newly acquired throne, he wisely determined to let sleeping dogs lie. Whether he knew that Bellairs killed Singha or not I cannot say, but he probably guessed that we were implicated, from our disappearance. His measures were prompt and judicious. He burnt the papers, gave out that his father had died of apoplexy, and took possession of the State. As there was nothing to compromise, he made matters right with the

218

Government, and when Singha's corpse was burnt on a pile, in accordance with the Hindoo custom, there was nobody to show the violence of the death. The new Rao did not pursue in case we might get him into trouble. He simply let the matter die out, and commenced his reign with the support of the Government.

"I believe, if the truth were known, he was glad his father was dead. What became of Trall I never heard; but Mr. Brock was not afterwards molested by him. He was probably satisfied with his spoil. Mr. Brock returned to England, and was presented by Bellairs with the living of Casterwell; but before leaving he put the whole facts of the case before those in power. But they, taking into consideration that Singha was dead, and that Trall had decamped, and, moreover, having regard to the then distracted state of the country, decided to let well alone. Thus it was all made very easy for Singha's son. The priests, I believe, made some fuss about the removal of the treasures of Kikat, but the new Rao soon put an end to them. He judged it better to lose the jewels than his throne. And so the trouble ended without in any way inculpating either Bellairs or myself.

"I made up my mind that I must part from my friend—my friend no longer, for I could not forgive the murder of Singha. Nor would I touch the money which had been gained by the price of dishonour and of blood. I gave my diamond to Bellairs, and, turning my back on him, went to live like a hermit in a corner of the Himalayas. That my nerves were shaken by my late troubles I do not deny. And I must also state that Trall's treachery, Singha's death, and Bellairs' wickedness disgusted me with the world. I felt the only life I could endure was one of solitude. Bellairs returned to England, made his peace with his father, and shortly after became the Squire of Casterwell, with Brock as his rector. Trall had dropped out of sight with his ill-gotten gains. He may be dead or alive, rich or poor, I know not; what is more, I do not care. The man ruined my life, soiled my honour, and I hate him.

"Years afterwards I grew weary of my solitude, and married a young Eurasian lady. She died when my son Angus was born, and, alone once more, I devoted myself to the education of the boy. As he grew up he displayed such talents that I reflected seriously how best to advance him in life. He was poor; I was old, and when I died Angus would be penniless. Then it occurred to me how wrong I had been in giving up the diamond. For my boy's sake I resolved to make peace with Bellairs, the more so when I heard that he also was married and was the father of an only daughter. With sudden resolution I wrote to Casterwell, and proposed that my son should marry his daughter, and that the value of the two diamonds should be given to them when they became man and wife.

"To this Bellairs replied that the gems were not so valuable as we had thought. He had sold both for thirty-eight thousand pounds, and this money he had deposited in the bank to accumulate. His father had left him well off, so he had himself made no use of the money. With the interest that had accrued, he said that it amounted to some fifty thousand pounds. He intended to invest this, and would share the income arising therefrom with me; but he refused to let his daughter marry my son. I replied that he was at liberty to retain the income to himself. I told him that I would not touch the money; but that if he did not consent to the marriage, and on the marriage-day give to my son Angus the capital sum of fifty thousand pounds, I would write to the Home Government, and divulge the murder by him of the Rao Singha. On this Bellairs gave in, and consented to the marriage. I drew out the clause relating to the money, which was to be incorporated in his will, and sent it to him. Out of the fifty thousand pounds which Angus would receive on his marriage with Olive Bellairs, he was to allow her a yearly income of a thousand pounds. This I considered was fair, and Bellairs thought so too, for he made his will as I directed.

"The present document I now send to Manners Brock by the hand of my son Angus. I wish him to deal with it in this fashion: If the marriage takes place it is to be destroyed. If Olive refuses, he is to show her this statement, and threaten to publish it unless she consents to the match. Bellairs is now dead, and it is possible he may have tricked me in some way. But I am not to be tricked. Unless my wish is carried out this story is to be laid before the authorities. They will then confiscate the Rao's money, and publish to the world the wickedness of Bellairs. It lies with Olive to save the money and protect the memory of her father by marrying Angus. If she declines—well, she knows what will happen. Brock, whom I admire and respect, will never let my son lose the money that I wish him to have, and, by our old friendship, I conjure him to obey me. Angus knows the story as it is here set forth, and will respect, and aid towards the consummation of my wish. For the rest, I maintain I am more than liberal in allowing my son to marry the daughter of a murderer.

"(Signed), Alfred Carson, M.D."

CHAPTER V

"LET THE DEAD PAST BURY ITS DEAD"

The insulting peroration of Dr. Carson's effusion was suppressed by Mallow; for Olive was already suffering severely under the knowledge of her father's misdeeds. He was a murderer, a blackmailer, a thief—he, her dearly-loved father, whom from a child she had set up as her idol. Who could cherish, nay, even respect, the memory of a man guilty of what she now learned he had been guilty? Small wonder, indeed, that he had implored her to conceal that guilt, even though it cost her a life's happiness in the doing. She had a rigid sense of right and wrong, and, despite herself, her idol crashed from off the pedestal whereon she had so lovingly set it up just as Mr. Brock had prophesied it would. And with it went all her dearest memories—all the recollections which she had cherished for so long—which in the cherishing had become a part of her self—perhaps, even the better part. She wept bitterly at the ruin of her world. And Mallow let her weep. He felt it was better so. And when she grew more composed he left her, holding over the fire, as he rose from his seat, the leaves that had brought such sorrow with them. She divined what he would do, and sanctioned it with a slow bend of her head. And then the flames destroyed for ever the tangible evidence of Mark Bellairs' sins.

When Mallow returned she was more herself. She had dried her eyes. "Would you like to talk about this, Olive?"

"No, dear, no. Of what use! Nothing we can say can alter such truths as these."

"Perhaps not; but we can at least hide them. No one save you and I knows this story. No one must know it, Olive—for your father's sake."

"Mr. Brock knows it?"

"Mr. Brock, yes. But we can trust Mr. Brock. Indeed, he has done all a man could do to spare you. I feel I am in no small degree myself to blame for the knowledge of this having reached you at all. I urged him to it."

"Oh, it is better I should know it, Laurence. At least, we know the worst now. Nothing—oh, surely nothing could be worse than this. Poor father is gone. But, Laurence dear, I have you, Laurence—I always have you. Thank God for you, Laurence."

"But remember, Olive, if your father sinned, he repented—bitterly repented."

"Yes, Laurence, I know. But he was willing I should be sacrificed to hide his sin—I, who loved him so—that hurts me terribly, Laurence; that is not easy to forgive."

"Is it not possible that he agreed to this man Carson's proposal to save you from the truth—that you might never know?"

"Even so, it was for his own sake—for his memory's sake."

"May be, yes. But that was only natural, Olive. Would it not be his great desire that you should think the best of him? And, after all, dear, this act of your father's was the act of days long bygone—thirty years or more ago—and from then to the time of his death he led an upright, honest life. Think of him, not as Trall's accomplice, dear, but as the father you knew. Try and do that, Olive—will you?"

"If you wish it, Laurence—yes, I will try."

And so the fateful missive was destroyed, and they made up their minds that they would put their knowledge behind them, and slip back again into the old life as though it had never been. Their Hegira was before them—from their marriage they would date it. And that was to be very soon now. Yet there were details which must be settled before they finally dismissed the past. And with these Olive prepared to busy herself. Great as was her sorrow, she did not allow it to sadden her. She determined it should permeate her every-day existence. She was quietly cheerful, and ever amiable to her guests. She was kindly sympathetic to Aldean and Tui, and listened with all patience to the disquisitions of Miss Slarge, even unto the doings of Ala Mahozim, the god of fortifications. Of Mrs. Purcell she saw little in these days. That good lady was indefatigably scouring the county, renewing early friendships, and conducting an orderly canvass in favour of Olive, and to the denunciation of her bigamist husband. Maids and matrons lifted up their hands in horror at Mrs. Purcell's revelations; men, old and young, expressed violent desires to have Carson within boot-reach. So vigorously did the clever old lady raise the countryside in Olive's favour, that the tide of sympathy soon set strongly towards the Manor House, and Miss Bellairs—Mrs. Carson no longer on friendly tongues—was pitied, petted, called upon, and duly wept over.

As a Dea ex machinâ, Mrs. Purcell had been successful far beyond the thanks of those whom she sought to serve.

Meanwhile Trall had picked up his health in no small degree, and with it a courage long foreign to his timid nature. But, lest he should revert to his old habits, Mallow feared to let him out of sight.

222

He kept him always within the grounds of the Manor. There he pottered about, from day to day, and the servants understood that he was a decayed gentleman pensioner of their mistress. Jeremiah, collecting his rags of gentility, supported the character well enough. He never alluded in any way to his stormy life of the past. His mind taking a religious turn, he dismissed his former state as one of sin, and not to be referred to; and he spent hours reading the Bible in preparation for his summons to another existence. And, seemingly, that call was not very far away. The man's once bulky frame had shrunk and dwindled greatly, so that his clothes hung loosely upon him now.

After the burning of the document, Laurence called at the Vicarage to tell Mr. Brock of what he had done. But this time the deaf spinster was successful, and he obtained no admission to the Vicarage. Mr. Brock sent out a message that he was much engaged, and could see no one for a week at least. Surprised somewhat, Mallow took himself off, and on the road up to the Manor met little Mr. Timson, the doctor, pounding along on his broken-kneed mare. At Mallow's halloo, he reined up—no easy task with his hard-mouthed veteran.

"The Vicar?" asked Mallow, gazing into Timson's red face—red with pulling; "how is he getting along?"

Timson was a pessimist, with a high average of deaths amongst his patients. He shook his flaxen locks dolefully. "Very bad, Mr. Mallow; I don't suppose he'll see the winter through. His heart is weak—very weak. Nasty murmur there—mitral valve wrong; any sudden shock—in fact, emotion of any kind—and he's done for," said Timson, solemnly.

"But under normal conditions, doctor, he'll pull through, won't he?"

"Oh, may last for a time; but he's bound to go—bound to go. The leg is obstinate, too. If he'd only rest, there might be a chance; but he goes on writing, writing."

Laurence pricked up his ears.

"Writing! What is he writing?"

"Some sort of diary, I should think—pages and pages of it. To make matters worse, he uses a cipher. Very bad for him that, you know—very bad. By the way," added the little man, "I hear poor old Drabble is taken."

"He is blown to bits, if that is what you mean by 'taken,'" said Mallow, grimly; "he played with fire once too often."

Timson sighed. "I know that he held pernicious doctrines, Mr.

Mallow, and his medical methods were not such as I could endorse. I've taken over a good many of his patients. They are in a sad state— a sad, sad state!" and he shook his little head again. "Poor Drabble! Ah! well, we must all come to it."

"But not necessarily in the same way, I trust. Well, good day, Mr. Timson."

As the doctor's animal stumbled down the hill, Mallow, climbing upward, felt somewhat uneasy at the news of Mr. Brock's industry. It might be that there was yet more to tell of Bellairs' wickedness, and Mallow fancied that the vicar might be setting it down in black and white.

"Precious queer amusement for a clergyman on the point of death, anyhow," he muttered to himself. "He has no relative that his scribbling is likely to interest, that I know of."

That same evening, leaving Aldean and Tui at whist with the old ladies, he led Olive into the library.

"I want to talk to you, Olive about this money. You were saying something the other day about getting rid of it."

"Yes; I wouldn't use it for the world. Thirty thousand of it has gone with Clara and Boldini to South America. I want to give the remaining twenty back to the Indian Government."

"H'm; the Government will ask questions. We don't want that."

"Can't it be returned as conscience-money?"

"Even so, I fancy, some explanation would be necessary. It is a large sum, you see. Besides, there is another point which you have overlooked. The money—or, rather, what is left of it—is not yours."

"Not mine? Then whose is it?"

"You forget the will, Olive. In the event of your not marrying Carson, the money was to go to Mr. Brock. Well, as a matter of fact, the provisions of the will not being complied with, that is where it ought to go."

"He can have it, with pleasure; but I feel sure he won't touch it now."

"Perhaps not; but he said if he got it—that was before he read the story—he would give it back to you."

"I don't want it. If he does, I shall only forward it to the proper quarter. Strictly speaking, it should be given to the Rao of Kikat."

"There is no Rao now. Don't you remember how Dr. Carson said that the kingdom was absorbed in the Empire? I think it will be best to ask Mr. Brock's advice—and, not only ask it, but take it."

"Mr. Brock is an honourable man; he will agree with me that the money should be restored. I am half sorry we recovered it now."

"I'm not," said Mallow, grimly. "At least, we have done Semberry out of his haul. But I'll see Brock."

"Laurence, do you think Mr. Brock knew of my father's wickedness?"

"No; Carson explicitly says that Trall did not tell the Rao about either him or your father. When Singha got the papers, Brock was already on the road to Calcutta, and they were burnt before he returned. No; Brock did not know until he read Carson's story."

"He would never have published it, as Dr. Carson wished."

"No; that I'm sure he would not," said Mallow, warmly. "Carson was quite mistaken in his estimate of Brock's character. But, if Angus had lived, and you had refused to marry him, he might have held it over you as a threat."

"But the envelope was sealed?"

"Of course. Still, Angus knew the story as related there. Dr. Carson said that he told it to him. But things are square now. Carson is dead, with his story untold; the paper is burnt, and Mr. Brock will keep his own counsel for our sakes."

"After we see Mr. Brock, dear, we will never talk of these things again," said Olive. "But there are one or two questions I feel I must ask him."

With a sudden recollection of the cipher diary and its possible further revelations, Mallow withheld his approval. "Better let sleeping dogs lie, dear."

"But I want to know more of my father's life at Kikat."

"Don't, Olive, don't. What you do know has brought you nothing but unhappiness."

"That's just it, Laurence. Nothing can make me more unhappy. I may as well know everything there is to know."

"Well, as you please. But you must let me see Mr. Brock first."

"Why; to warn him, I suppose?"

"No, n-o-o. I think I ought to tell him of Angus Carson's death."

"What good will that do?"

"None, most likely. Still, I think he ought to know. I've always thought the motive for Carson's death was to be found in India."

"There was nothing in the story to lead one to think so."

"Nothing. But Mr. Brock may know something. At present he is under the impression that Boldini is the genuine Carson; but, when I tell him of the murder, and the whole conspiracy, it is possible he may recall some incident likely to throw light on what is now absolutely Cimmerian."

225

"I doubt it, Laurence. Are you still so bent on getting to the bottom of this murder?"

"Why not? An undiscovered mystery is like an unfinished tune. You feel a tantalizing desire for the closing cadence. All my life I shall worry about that poor fellow's death, until I really know how he was killed, and who killed him. Only one more try, Olive, I promise you. If Mr. Brock fails to help me, I suppose I must give up the chase."

"Well, see Mr. Brock, and then tell him the story. But I fear you will be disappointed."

"Who knows, dear. His knowledge of your father and Carson's life in Kikat should be precise. For all we know, Michael Trall may have done it."

"I can't think that, Laurence. Michael Trall has not been seen or heard of for thirty years."

"True, true. His own brother doesn't know of his whereabouts. I dare say the scamp is dead."

"And even if he were alive, I can't see where his motive could have been."

"True, again. But I think I'll ask Mr. Brock, nevertheless."

CHAPTER VI

"MR. BROCK'S ADDENDA"

In spite of herself Olive fretted. Her trouble had taken firm hold of her mind, and bade fair now to make havoc of her body. She lost flesh rapidly. In vain Mallow tried to combat this brooding over her father's wrong-doing. He pointed out the futility of it; he urged her—implored her—to make the effort to rouse herself. But without result. Her father's sin became with her an ever-present enormity. She was continually dwelling upon it. They tried to get her to work— to use her hands, employ herself actively, anyhow—at anything—so long as, for the time being, it was capable of absorbing her, and thus releasing the terrible tension under which she laboured. At last

226

Mallow saw there was nothing for it but an entire change of scene and surroundings.

"You must go, Olive dear—away from here, away from all that reminds you of yourself. You shall go abroad at once, Mrs. Purcell shall go with you, and later I will join you, and in six months' time you will return, dear, a totally different woman—no longer Olive Bellairs, even in name, for we will be married, and you will laugh at yourself and these wretched phantoms of your own raising."

"You speak as though I were a child!" she cried petulantly. "Phantoms indeed!—facts, you mean. My father was a—oh, don't speak of it, the very thought drives me beside myself. And I have to keep it all to myself—all, all!"

"Oh, Olive," said Mallow, reproachfully, "am I not some help to you?"

"A man never understands—he does not feel these things."

"Really, Olive, I think the sooner you get away from Casterwell the better."

"I shall never be better—never, never!"

Mallow did not argue with her. He saw that it was quite useless. Actions, not words, were necessary if Olive was to be restored to a proper sense of what was due to herself and to others. Laurence recognized this, and took an early opportunity of calling at the Vicarage. Again Mr. Brock refused to see him; but next day Mallow received a note requesting him to call. He obeyed promptly.

On his way through the village he met Jeremiah looking distressed and lonely. "I want to see a clergyman," he whined peevishly; "I have so many sins to confess. I can find no one to help me."

Mallow looked at him. It appeared that Trall, under stress of religious emotion, might confess to a priest, much more than he would be likely to confide to a layman. In such circumstances it was not at all improbable that he might let drop much that would be useful.

"I will take you to see a clergyman, Trall—the best in this parish. I am now on my way there. If you will call at the Vicarage shortly—left-hand side of the church from the roadway—I will leave you with him. Then you will be able to unbosom your mind quite freely."

"Oh, thank you; thank you, Mr. Mallow. I have many sins to confess—many, many. When shall I come?"

Mallow glanced at his watch. "In three-quarters of an hour. Say

227

about four o'clock. I would take you with me now, only I want first to see Mr. Brock myself on private business."

Trall was more than satisfied with this arrangement, and hobbled off, profuse in his expressions of gratitude. Mallow continued his way to the Vicarage.

"Good-day, Mr. Brock," said he, as the deaf housekeeper showed him into the study (now the sick-room); "I am glad to see you at last."

"Indeed, I must apologize for not receiving you before," replied the vicar, wearily, "but I have been busy arranging my papers against my death."

"Oh, come now, you are not going to die."

"I shall never leave this house alive, Mr. Mallow. My days are numbered. You can guess now that the reading of Carson's statement gave me a severe shock. All these years, I never suspected that it was Bellairs who murdered Singha. Indeed, I did not even know that he was murdered, for Rao Chunder, the heir, gave out that his father had died of apoplexy."

"Did you never return to Kikat?"

"No; I failed altogether to induce the Governor-General to move in the matter of the blackmailing, and, as the Rao's son was not very friendly to me I judged it wiser to keep away. Besides, I heard that Bellairs and Carson had left Kikat, and believed that their departure was due to the enmity of the new Rao. God forgive me, I never guessed the truth."

"Rao Singha never told you that Bellairs and Carson were inculpated in the blackmailing?"

"No. Trall made it out to be his own conspiracy, entirely, and kept their names out of his confession. Moreover, Singha had not received the incriminating letters with the forged names. They were afterwards burnt by the new Rao. He kept his own counsel. I never saw them; I never suspected that Bellairs and Carson had fallen so low."

"Do you think the names were forged, or do you believe that your friends were willing accomplices in the conspiracy?"

"I believe the names were forged," declared Brock decisively. "So far as I knew, both Bellairs and Carson were thoroughly honourable men. Trall entangled them by means of the forgeries, and, for their own sakes, they were compelled to act as accomplices."

"Did Bellairs ever hint at the truth?"

"Mr. Mallow,"—the vicar sat up and flushed indignantly—"had I

228

been told the truth by Bellairs, do you think that I would have remained Vicar of Casterwell? No! For Olive's sake, perhaps I might have held my tongue but my first act would have been to vacate the living. Bellairs was as silent as the grave about Kikat. He hardly ever alluded to his life there, and then only casually."

"Guilty conscience, no doubt," suggested Mallow. "As a rule, a man doesn't particularly care to reperuse the smudged pages of his life-book. I suppose Bellairs never told you his reason for the betrothal of Olive to Angus?"

"Never! never! I thought it was simply and solely the outcome of his strong friendship for Carson. As to the will leaving me the money in the event of the marriage not taking place, I did not know its contents until Bellairs was dead."

"Well, the money is yours, now, Mr. Brock. Will you take it, knowing how it was earned?"

"My dear friend, believe me, it is superfluous to discuss what I will do with it. I am a dying man. By my will, I have restored the money to Olive; she can deal with it as she pleases."

"In that case it is her intention to restore it to the Indian Government."

"What good will that do?" said the vicar, with a sigh; "there is no Rao of Kikat now—the name, the family, the very kingdom has died out. Let Olive make restitution, if such be her wish, but the money will go into the wrong pockets if she sends it there."

"I don't care whose pockets it enters, neither does she," said Mallow; "the main point is to get rid of it—and there is twenty thousand pounds."

Mr. Brock started. "Only that. I understood——"

"That there was fifty. True enough; but thirty has gone across the seas with Boldini and his wife."

"Boldini! Who is he?"

"I forgot, you don't know the story. It is a long one, Mr. Brock, and not a pretty one for a clergyman to hear."

"As a rule, we hear the worst stories. But you talk strangely, Mr. Mallow. I do not understand. This Boldini! Who is he?

"Well, he is the man who masqueraded here as Angus Carson."

"As Angus Carson! Do you mean to tell me that it was not really Angus Carson who——"

"I will tell you all about it, if," said Mallow, with some hesitation, "you think you are quite strong enough to hear."

"Quite strong enough, and most anxious to hear" said Mr. Brock, feverishly. "Come, Mr. Mallow, explain this mystery."

"You may well call it a mystery, Mr. Brock, and it seems likely to remain one. I can begin the story and continue it to a certain point; but you must finish it for yourself."

Then Mallow related to the astonished vicar all the intrigues of the last few months. He was most minute in his recital, giving even the reasons which had induced him to take various steps. Mrs. Arne, Drabble, Boldini, Clara, he introduced all these people to Mr. Brock, placing them before him in their different capacities as vividly as he was able. But he refrained from expressing to the vicar his hope that Jeremiah would shortly aid towards the solution of the mystery. He could see that the old man was becoming exhausted as well as bewildered by what he had heard.

"Terrible, terrible!" he murmured. "Poor Olive! poor Angus! Oh, why, why did you not tell me all this before?"

"There was not much use in telling you," said Mallow, gloomily; "you could not have helped us. We are no nearer finding out the truth than we were before. Why was young Carson killed? that is what I want to know. What was the motive?"

"I can't think," replied Mr. Brock, staring before him; "it is all so dreadful. You don't think Drabble murdered the poor lad?"

"No; Drabble's interest was to keep him alive, unless he proved stubborn. Then——whew!" Mallow drew a long breath. From his experiences in the Soho house, he had little difficulty in guessing what Mrs. Arne would have done had young Carson proved obdurate. "But I don't think they killed him," he added; "no, I am sure they didn't."

"But who else could have a motive?" asked the vicar, wrinkling his brows. "They left him well, you say, and returned to find him dead. Some one, according to your theory, must have been in the house meanwhile."

"Undoubtedly. And that some one is the murderer. But who is he?"

"It is impossible to say. Angus lived all his days in India; he knew no one in England. Perhaps Major Semberry——"

"No." Mallow shook his head. "He denied it strenuously, and, so far as I can see, he had as much interest as the Anarchists in keeping Carson alive. Come, Mr. Brock, are you sure there was nothing that happened at Kikat likely to lead to this?"

"After thirty years—nothing. Besides, Carson was not married then; the boy was not born."

"I wonder," said Mallow, musingly, "if that bangle had anything to do with it?"

"How could it?" asked Mr. Brock, amazed.

"Well, I understand it was taken from an idol."

"No." Brock shook his head. "That is not correct. Singha gave the bangle to Carson—my friend—with the full permission of the priests. He cured the Rao of a severe illness, and the priests approved of the reward."

"Then Michael Trall must be the murderer."

"How do you make that out? Trall disappeared from Kikat thirty and more years ago. He has never been heard of since. Probably he is dead."

"Probably. But possibly he may be alive; and he may have killed young Carson."

"On what grounds—for what reason," said Mr. Brock. "Killing Angus would not give him the money, if that is what you are thinking of. No, I am sure Trall is dead. He was too restless and ambitious a man to remain quiet; and when he had exhausted his own share of the blackmail, he would, in all probability, come here for the purpose of blackmailing Bellairs."

"Perhaps he knew you were here, Mr. Brock."

"Perhaps. And, so far, I may have been a safeguard to Bellairs. But knowing Trall well as I do, I think he would have run even the risk of my denouncing him, had there been money to be gained."

"When did you see Trall last?"

"At Kikat. He followed me with the intention of frustrating my plans; and he would have done so at the cost of murder, I make no doubt. But I changed the route I had intended to take, and, I am thankful to say, he missed me."

At that moment the voice of the housekeeper could be heard raised in anger—evidently, from the deeper tones which followed, against some man. Mr. Brock grew deadly pale, and his heart beat wildly with sheer nervousness.

"See—see what it is, Mr. Mallow!" he gasped, "Oh, this will kill me!"

The young man ran to the door and threw it open. As though he had been waiting outside, Jeremiah shambled into the room amid the shrill expostulations of the sour spinster.

"I came as you told me," whimpered Trall, clutching Mallow. "Where is the clergyman? I must see the clergyman."

"Trall, this is disgraceful. Mr. Brock——"

"Aha!" breathed the vicar, and both men turned at the strangled sound to see him sitting up looking at the newcomer with vacantly staring eyes. On his side, Jeremiah released his hold of Mallow, and,

231

as though drawn by a magnet, approached the sofa. The sick man and his visitor gazed blankly at one another.

"Why," whispered Trall, still gazing, "it's you—it's—it's—it's—why, it's Michael!"

"Michael?" repeated Mallow. "What Michael?"

"Michael Trall—my brother. Oh, Michael, I'm so glad to see you. I'm Jerry."

The man on the bed stared and stared, but spoke not a word. His face was blanched with fear, and he repeatedly put out his hands as though to keep the other back. Then quietly, silently, without a sign of recognition, he fell back dead.

CHAPTER VII

"THE CIPHER DIARY"

Even in the first shock of this untimely death, though timely discovery, Mallow kept his wits about him. That Brock was truly Michael Trall he made no doubt. For, in truth, Jeremiah had neither the capacity nor the reason to simulate relationship of the kind. Moreover, nothing surely could be more conclusive than the fatal effect which this unexpected meeting had had for Brock, beside whom now the wretched man dropped into prayer and supplication. He called upon him to recover, implored him for a sign—a look. He wept bitterly. Mallow did not molest him. He was totally unfit for rational conversation. Poor Brock—he may still be called so for the avoidance of confusion—was quite dead. Mallow slipped his hand under his clothes on to the heart to make quite sure. The sight of his brother, and the knowledge of what would follow, had done their work and snuffed him out of this life.

"Come now, Trall," said Mallow. "You must try and pull yourself together, and, what's more, you must not say a word about this. No one must know—understand, Trall, no one. As Mr. Brock he lived—as Mr. Brock he died."

"But he is my own brother Michael."

"I believe you, Trall; but reticence, absolute silence on that

232

point, is necessary, if only for your own safety. Remember the Brotherhood!"

That was quite enough for Trall. He promised implicit obedience. "And I'll sit in this corner as quiet as a mouse, Mr. Mallow," he concluded, "if only you'll let me. Don't! oh, don't take me away."

"Well, you may remain there for the present. But, remember, not a word to any one about this."

Mallow deemed it advisable to alarm the household. He rang the bell, and the acidulated housekeeper duly appeared. She immediately lost all control of herself. She cried out aloud, and gesticulated wildly. Her fellow-servants followed suit, and in a very few moments the usually tranquil Vicarage was a very pandemonium of weeping and wailing Promptly Mallow sent a messenger for Mr. Timson, and another for Lord Aldean, with strict injunctions not in any way to alarm the ladies at the Manor House. He determined not to leave the place himself until he had possession of the cipher-diary. Seeing now that without doubt this was Michael Trall, he expected much in the way of revelation from the diary. It is a passion with some of perverted instincts to set down their deeds and misdeeds in black and white, and such documents are invariably to be relied upon. They are usually perfectly unfettered in their utterance—the tangible communion of such people with themselves. Mallow anticipated difficulty only so far as the unravelling of the cipher was concerned. This might prove obstinately difficult, or it might not. But, he argued, there was no cipher invented by man that man could not unravel—and unravel it he would, even though he took years in the doing of it. It remained now to secure the document itself. Within an hour Mr. Timson arrived, and seemed in nowise astonished at the suddenness of Mr. Brock's death.

"Just what I expected," he chirped in his pessimistic way. "Cardiac failure—pure and simple. He was excited in some way, I presume, Mr. Mallow?

"Yes; he became very excited while I was talking with him," said Laurence, evasively.

"Quite so—quite so. I warned him. I told him how it would be. Dear, dear! Most regrettable, but natural all the same—quite natural." Mr. Timson was moved not a hair's-breadth from his habitual complacency.

"Don't you think the body should be removed to the bedroom?"

233

said Mallow. He hardly liked to begin his search for the diary with the dead man's body lying there.

"Certainly, certainly! More decent. Quite right."

So, superintended by the little man, Mr. Brock's remains were carried out of the study. The progress to the bedroom drew forth further lamentations from the female servants. Timson took himself off then. As he went out of the hall Lord Aldean entered. He was full of sympathy, and amazed.

"Poor old chap!" he said, as Mallow conducted him to the study. "Died of heart failure, I suppose? I'm awfully sorry for the poor old fellow. He was a good sort—Brock."

"Yes, I'm sorry, too," said Mallow, grimly, "but not quite for your reasons. The dead man is Michael Trall—not Brock."

"Trall! What do you mean?" Aldean cast a glance at Jeremiah. "Is not this Trall, then?"

"It is Michael—my poor brother," sighed the creature in the corner.

"Mr. Brock your brother! Well, I——"

"Wait a moment, Aldean, I'll tell you all about it directly." Then, turning to Jeremiah, Mallow asked, "Was your brother a good man?"

"No—o—o," replied Trall. "He was clever, but he was not a good man. He deserted his wife and poor little Clara. But I was fond of him; a brother is always a brother."

"Oh!" Mallow paused. He did not wish to reflect in any way upon the dead man, and he was afraid to trust Jeremiah out of his sight, lest in his weakness he should reveal his connection with the late vicar. "I wish to speak privately with Lord Aldean," he said at length. "Go you, Trall, into the next room for half an hour. Stay there, and, mind, not a word to any one about what has happened."

"Very well, Mr. Mallow," replied Jeremiah, submissively, creeping towards the door.

Laurence followed him and made him comfortable in the dining-room. The sour spinster—now a very Niobe—all tears—was informed that Mr. Trall was suffering from shock at the unexpected death of the vicar, and was not on any account to be disturbed. Having arranged thus for Jeremiah's seclusion, Mallow returned to the study, where he found Aldean in a state of intense expectancy. The situation and hints of mystery puzzled him.

"What's all this business about?" he asked, when he saw his friend lock the door.

"It's about Michael Trall, alias Brock, who, I truly believe, Jim, is the murderer for whom we have searched so long."

"Mr. Brock the murderer of Carson! Impossible! You must be mistaken, surely!"

"Well, perhaps; but I don't think so. I will give you my grounds for saying so, and I think you will agree, Jim, that they are pretty strong."

Rapidly, but tersely, Mallow related the story as set forth by Dr. Carson. He concealed nothing, not even Bellairs' guilt. Finally he expressed his conviction that in Mr. Brock's diary would be found the key to the whole mystery. Jim was amazed; still, he could not agree with his friend.

"Murderers don't write accounts of their crimes," he pronounced, decisively; "not such fools as to make up their own brief for the prosecution."

"That's just where you're wrong, Jim. There are not a few cases on record," said Mallow. "I can recollect one, in particular, where a clerk wrote in his diary: 'To-day, fine and hot; killed a little girl in Croft's spinney.' That line hanged him."

"Glad it did," growled Jim, in disgust, "for being such a fool. I confess I have no sympathy for a man who gives himself away like that."

"Perhaps not, Jim; but there seems to be a peculiar fascination about confession which some of these men can't resist. It may be that there is great relief for them in unburdening their minds, even on paper. If we can judge Michael Trall's character from Carson's story, he has heaped up a goodly pile of wickedness these thirty and more years. Moreover, if his diary were guileless reading, he would not resort to cipher. No, Jim, I believe the man has sought to ease his conscience by setting down his sins."

"May have, Mallow; but the cipher's a teaser."

"No doubt. I don't anticipate it will be child's play, by any means. Still, it is a fact that there is no cipher invented by the ingenuity of man which—given time and application—cannot be unravelled. This diary may take days, even months, to straighten into Queen's English; but, sooner or later, I shall master its contents, if only to learn why Brock killed Carson."

"You speak confidently, Mallow. But Brock may be innocent, even yet."

"Possible; but, to my mind, improbable. If Brock be not guilty, I don't know who is. However, it's no use theorizing when we have facts before us. Brock's keys are under the pillow."

"Sure we have the right to search, Mallow?"

"I'll take the risk of that," said Laurence, with composure, and forthwith went to work, assisted by Aldean.

Manifestly, the most promising hunting-ground was the escritoire near the window, at which Michael Trall in clerical capacity had been accustomed to compile his sermons. Mallow first explored the pigeon-holes and their papers, scrutinizing the writing of each in turn; but, so far, failed to find anything at all incriminating. He unlocked the drawers, and went through them systematically from top to bottom. In the right-hand corner of the lowest drawer they found the diary carelessly thrown in without attempt at concealment. It was contained in a stout volume, bound in red cloth, and on the back was written, in ink, "No. 21."

"Oh!" said Mallow, examining the neat cipher writing. "The rogue evidently posted his criminal ledgers with the utmost regularity. Where are the other twenty?"

They were not in his desk, for by this time they had searched every inch of it. Jim examined the bookcases filled to overflowing, and occupying three walls of the room. Near the top of one of them he found, shamelessly exposed, the remaining twenty volumes. The astute Mr. Brock had evidently acted upon the conviction that in attempting no concealment he aroused no curiosity. His readings had no doubt included the stories of Edgar Allan Poe.

"Cheek of the beggar," grumbled Aldean, tumbling down these ledgers promptly; "he had every faith in his cipher."

"And in his reputation as the Rev. Manners Brock," said Mallow, receiving the books below, and arranging them on the table. "I expect there is material enough for a dozen detective novels in this lot. Eh! What's up now, Jim? Don't swear!"

Aldean, suppressing further imprecation, scrambled down the ladder.

"Look here, Mallow! Just look!"

"Watch, chain, studs, and the missing wrist-button," counted Laurence, coolly; "it is no more than I expected. There can be no doubt after this, Jim. Here is the dead man's jewellery. The lying brute—he said that Drabble gave him the other wrist-button as a curiosity."

They surveyed the tarnished gold and the double pile of red books in silence. Then said Aldean slowly—

"God! to think of that murderous scoundrel saying he was a parson. Makes me sick to think of it. Might have lived to marry Tui and me. By Gum!" Jim started as the discovery slowly evolved itself in his brain. "Say, Mallow, all the marriages in this parish must be wrong 'uns. What's to be done about them?"

"We must wait until we read the diary before considering matters of such minor importance as that," said Mallow, tapping the books. "I expect it won't be easy to straighten out Brock's crooked ways."

"Don't call him Brock. Makes me feel bad."

"Brock he must be called, Jim, for the present. None of the ladies must know the truth until we get through these books. Manners Brock is dead, not Michael Trall."

"I understand. But Jeremiah——"

"I'll manage him. Ha! there he is, I expect. Open the door, Jim."

Aldean did so, and Trall, looking white and agitated, crept into the room. "I'm afraid to be alone," he whimpered. "Can't I stop here?"

"We must go home now, Trall," said Mallow, soothingly. "Can you read this cipher?" and he opened out a book to Jeremiah in the faint hope of receiving an affirmative answer.

To his surprise and delight it came.

"I can read it, Mr. Mallow. It's Michael's cipher. I taught it to him when we were boys."

"Hurrah!" sang Aldean, slapping Trall's back. "You shall translate it, then."

"Michael's diary!" said Jeremiah, quicker in understanding than might have been expected. "I see. Ah, Michael was always clever with his pen."

"Been a sight too clever this time," muttered Jim, assisting his friend to tie up the books in neat bundles.

Here operations ceased for the moment, and Mallow and Aldean, with Jeremiah in charge, returned home after a few directions to the deaf housekeeper. Then came the difficult task of explaining certain rumours which had already reached the Manor House. Jim discreetly held his tongue and left things to his friend, who vouchsafed as little information as was consistent with allaying the general alarm. Mr. Brock had died suddenly from heart failure, he declared, refraining carefully from all mention of the dead man's identity with the Michael Trall of Carson's story, and from any reference to the cipher diary. In the lamentations which ensued, further questions were spared him.

"The man must be buried as Mr. Brock," said Mallow to Aldean, a day or two later. "There is no other course open, if the story is to be kept quiet."

"Yes, I suppose so. It will save all trouble over those marriages. Better let him have a decent name over his tombstone, though he doesn't deserve it."

As the pseudo Brock had no relatives—for Mallow insisted that Jeremiah should suppress the fact of his relationship—Olive, as the Lady of the Manor, charged herself with the funeral. So the scoundrel was buried in fine style, although it is only fair to state that he had kept his false name clean enough, so far as concerned the parish. They could not but feel his loss, and there was much weeping and eulogy by the graveside as Michael Trall, of Kikat, was laid under the turf of the churchyard in the odour of sanctity. Mallow thought this was one of life's greater ironies.

"Good Lord!" was his aside to Jim, "how the rogue must chuckle at this mummery if his spirit has eyes to see. He might be a canonized saint for the fuss they make."

"Must have had some good in him," replied Aldean, meditatively; "as Mr. Brock he was straight enough. That I know."

"A serpent in a bamboo cannot be otherwise than straight," said Mallow. "Casterwell Vicarage was our friend's bamboo. But a triple murderer! Faugh!"

"Triple! How triple?"

"He murdered Carson, I'm certain. Brock was despatched by him so that he could assume the missionary's lambskin, and I shouldn't be surprised to learn that he, and not Bellairs, made away with Rao Singha. He was capable of it."

"But as Mr. Brock——"

"As Mr. Brock, Jim, there should be inscribed upon his tomb the couplet of some Byronic imitator—

He settled with a little pious leaven
To give the fag-end of his life to Heaven."

Jeremiah did not attend the funeral. Mallow induced him to remain at home, lest in his grief his tongue might get the better of him. So he sat in his room and painfully translated the rascalities of Michael into plain English—and he taught Laurence the cipher, and Laurence toiled likewise. It was an affair of many weeks—indeed, it lasted until Mrs. Purcell announced her determination to take Olive abroad. At the same time Tui received a cablegram announcing that her delighted parents were on their way to England.

Much of the diary has no bearing on this story, but in the last volume or so there were notes which shed a flood of light upon

238

much that was before hopelessly obscure. One discovery in particular was of the greatest satisfaction to Mallow. Indeed, it led him to communicate the latter portion of the diary to Olive, Miss Slarge, and Mrs. Purcell. Tui the matter did not concern.

It must not be supposed that Laurence gave this information in the precise words of the diary, for this proved to be a hastily compiled composition, thrown together at odd moments—Heaven knows what for, unless for the sheer egotistical gratification of its author. He shifted all extraneous matter, translated the notes of the earlier to the later years, and in one way and another drew together the story of the Carsons and the events at Kikat into a concise narrative. This he wrote out carefully, and one evening, when Tui and Aldean were love-making over the billiard-table, he read it out to an audience of three. So it is that the following narrative must be regarded strictly as Mallow's version—compiled by him from the materials supplied by the twenty-one volumes of the diary, and told by him, in the first person, from its author's point of view.

CHAPTER VIII

"A ROGUE'S MEMOIRS"

"Bad luck, bad luck, bad luck—there's my life's history in one word. The day I launched myself on the world misfortune established herself at my elbow, and my most persistent endeavours have failed to oust her from that position. Only so far as to allow me perfect health from first to last has she relented. Yet even that has had its disadvantages. It has whetted an appetite, already omnivorous, for the luxuries of life—luxuries for the acquirement of which the means have ever been withheld. How I have pursued them—how they have eluded me! It is this quest for luxury, this craving to satisfy an appetite abnormal and insatiable, that has brought upon me so much of trouble. I have had the worst of luck. Ten thousand a year might have made an honest man of me. But I defy St. Paul himself to have stood in my place with my mind, my body, my soul, and not have done the things that I have done. He

239

would have been another Michael Trall. I do not say I could ever have been like St. Paul. That is another matter. My passion has been the cakes and ale of life—I have never had enough of them; I could not have enough of them. But I was not gifted even with the means for their procuration in a moderate degree. So I don't blame myself. I cannot blame myself. No one can justly blame me. It is nature that is responsible for what I am—for what I have done. Blame her, or whosoever, or whatsoever inspires her to bestow upon a luckless man passions strong and undeniable—passions overwhelming and senses insatiable, while denying him the wherewithal to gratify them. That is the most refined torture. I can conceive nothing more ubiquitous, nothing more merciless.

"Well, that is what has ruined me.

"I was unlucky at the start. I was the second son of a Pharisee, provincial but respectable. So I suffered from the amiable custom of primogeniture. My brother Jerry, two years only my senior, received a home and lands and a thousand pounds a year. He did not receive over much in the way of brains. I, in this latter respect, received, perhaps, more than my share, with senses to match. With such gifts, and some five hundred pounds all told, I was pushed off to sink or swim. I just kept afloat. First of all I lost all my money in a most determined—and, I think, thoroughly well conceived—attempt to double it on the card-table. It was pure misfortune that it proved inferior in practice. I was obliged then to borrow from Jerry. He was a stay-at-home ass. I did not approve of his way of life at all; but I had no option but to borrow from him. Again misfortune dogged me, for somehow or other—it passes my recollection now—I got into trouble about somebody else's name on a cheque. I remember those concerned made a great fuss about it, altogether out of proportion to the circumstances; and I remember distinctly how disgusted I was at the puritanical island upon which it was my lot to be cast, so I decided to leave it. For some time after that I lived on the Continent—upon my wits, which were duly sharpened in the process. It was hard that this should prove to my disadvantage, but it did, for at Baden-Baden my misfortune culminated in a row at the tables. I was utterly disgusted, but it was wiser that I should leave so I dropped South over the Equator and turned up at the Cape in a new character, and with a brand new name. Those were prehistoric days, and the South African millionaire had not yet invented himself. The Boers disapproved of my more civilized ways with the ace, and, as I could not repress my repugnance for their psalm-singing barbarisms, I could not make myself at home there. It

240

seemed as if a resting-place was ever to be denied me. But I plucked up courage, and in a rackety ocean tramp, carrying a cargo of rats and cockroaches, I sailed for Bombay. I had a very few pounds, but no little experience. Arrived there, I was obliged to make my living somehow. It was a hand-to-mouth existence, and I saw no prospect before me. I had a certain amount of luck with my dice, though on one or two occasions aspersions were cast upon their equilibrium. 'Give a dog a bad name, and hang him!' seemed to hold good even here. I was driven North. Then, Heaven knows why, Fortune gave me her hand for once and led me to Kikat, the kingdom of one Rao Singha.

"This petty prince was an up-to-date Hindoo, with an English army leader and a European physician. Bellairs—he was the leader—proved to be a fool, with no brains and some scruples. Dr. Carson, on the contrary, possessed some brains, but was quite unfettered by scruples. I saw that I should have to adapt myself to the idiosyncrasies of each. I did so, and a sort of triune partnership for the making of our several and joint fortunes was the result. Singha was sufficiently acute, but I beat him on his own ground. He loved me like a brother—indeed, I did all I could to civilize him. I taught him cards, introduced him to billiards, and instructed him in the orderly and methodical compilation of a betting-book. I don't say that, one way and another, I did not profit by him; for I did. But the profits were inconsiderable, and in no way sufficient to satisfy me. Besides, I was conscious of certain ambitions then. I felt that this great state treasure, not to speak of the command of some two million heathen, would be much more rationally dealt with were they in my hands. In a word, I coveted the viziership of Kikat But the priests were one and all against me. Moreover, there was an English missionary there, named Manners Brock, who seemed to be mistrustful of me. I could make nothing of him. In his moral and religious convictions he was absolutely rigid—a most unsympathetic soul, I thought him. It soon became plain to me that nothing short of re-adjustment of the existing political system would clear these obstacles from my path. My chance came with the Mutiny. By carefully playing upon Singha's ambition and feudal pride, I managed to get him mixed up in it. At my instigation he made certain treaties with the Delhi princes, and wrote certain letters professing hostility to the H.E.I.C. Then he watched for a favourable opportunity of declaring himself. This opportunity never came, for the Rao, over-persuaded by Brock, delayed action until it was too late. The Mutiny smouldered out when Delhi was captured, and I—

unlucky once more—reverted to the post of idle companion and powerless buffoon, with the priests and Brock ever on the alert to ruin my credit with Singha. It became a choice between my downfall and the Rao's; so, of course, I chose the Rao's.

"To strengthen my scheme I appended Carson's and Bellairs' names to some of the letters, and thereby so implicated them in the Rao's conspiracy that, for their own safety, they were compelled to join me. Carson was willing enough to throw in his lot with me, but Bellairs made some absurd objections, until I was obliged to show him how completely his life and honour were at my discretion. When matters were thus arranged I saw Singha. I told him plainly that I should have no option but to send the letters to the Governor-General, unless he gave me the three diamonds which were known as the treasures of Kikat. He blustered a good deal, but in the end I gained my point. Singha gave me the diamonds. The largest I kept to myself, the other two I handed to Bellairs and Carson. All went smoothly until the Rao made trouble by confessing his position to Brock. The missionary, with the usual meddlesomeness of his class, made tracks for Calcutta, declaring his intention to inform the Government of my plot and protect Singha. He was afraid of me, I fancy, for he slipped off without my knowledge. I saw that his denunciation meant unpleasantness, so I followed close on his heels, met him, and argued the question with him. I did my best to persuade him to my way of thinking, to show him how utterly foolish and misguided he was, but all to no purpose. He was hopelessly unreasonable, so I killed him. There was nothing else for it.

"I returned to Kikat, but with the utmost caution. This was necessary because the Rao, being now in possession of the papers which I had directed were to be sent to him, might be plotting vengeance. I then discovered he was dead. On noticing the names of Bellairs and Carson appended to the papers, he had become unruly, so Carson had poisoned him, and with Bellairs had fled. I managed to come across the fugitives, and together we waited events.

"As it happened, the new king was afraid lest his father's conspiracy should cost him his throne, so he hushed up the matter, and gave out that Singha had died of apoplexy. As the danger from this quarter was over, we three could now enjoy the fruits of our success. I told Bellairs and Carson that I had killed Brock, so there was nothing to be feared from the Government through him. Bellairs returned to England, taking with him both his own diamond and Carson's. The latter had found a rag of a conscience

242

somewhere, since he had murdered the Rao, and talked of the diamond as the 'price of blood.' He refused to take it, and let Bellairs carry it off, although I should have liked it for myself. However, I was quite satisfied with my share, for I sold the diamond for thirty thousand pounds. With this money I went back to Europe, where I married, became the father of a daughter, and altogether had a glorious time. Carson, in a fit of repentance, retired to some Himalayan hermitage, haunted, I suppose, by what is called a guilty conscience. Fool! My shooting of Brock troubled me not in the least.

"But what did trouble me was another run of bad luck. I lost everything. I returned to London, and placed my wife and child in the care of Jerry, who was a bachelor, and could better afford to keep them than I. Then I determined to look up Bellairs, who was now Squire of Casterwell, and horribly prosperous. On making inquiries, I learned that the vicar of the parish was dead, and that the living was in Bellairs' gift. I was terribly weary of wandering, and it occurred to me that such a position would suit me very well; at all events, for a while. It was quite a simple matter for me to impersonate Manners Brock. I had all his papers, and I was well up in the details of his early life, as well as his life in India. The creature had been a confirmed babbler, and had told me everything about himself. I had some trouble with Bellairs at first, but he soon saw it was no good. He was desperately jealous of what he called his good name. He had everything to lose; I nothing. So he did the wisest thing he could do, and gave in. I became the Reverend Manners Brock. I had no difficulty in deceiving the old Bishop of the diocese. I had all the papers, and was well up in all the necessary details. The living of itself was a poor one, but of course Bellairs had to alter that. He told me, when I approached this part of the subject, that he had sold the two diamonds for some thirty-eight thousand pounds. Then he, too, indulged in some silly nonsense about the 'price of blood' and so on, which he said had prevented his touching the money. For the last ten years it had been lying in the bank at compound interest, and had now reached something like fifty thousand pounds. I soon settled that. I made him invest the money securely, yet profitably, and pay me the interest. I felt now that I could settle down in comfort to my hardly-earned repose. I had an assured position, a good name, and a most comfortable income. There were times, of course, when I grew weary of so much respectability; but then, all I had to do was to assume some disguise and run up to London for a few days and enjoy myself. But I never went near Jerry. My wife was dead, and he looked after my daughter. So, as the Reverend Manners Brock, my life, if quiet, was pleasant enough. For years all went well, until one day there came a letter from Carson regretting that he had surrendered his diamond, and suggesting that his son—he had married in the mean time—should marry Olive Bellairs, and that the proceeds of the diamond should be given to the young people on their wedding-day. At first Bellairs refused; but Carson replied threatening exposure—more than that, he plainly gave Bellairs to understand that he would accuse him of Rao Singha's murder. For the sake of his jealously-guarded name, Bellairs was forced to yield. But he wrote to Carson telling him how, in the person of the Rev. Manners Brock, I had become vicar of Casterwell, and how he had been obliged to pay me the interest on the money. I did not wish to be selfish, but naturally I refused to give up my income, so in the end I compromised the matter. It was arranged that I should have the interest until the marriage took place, when I was to surrender it. As this could not be for twenty years I agreed to the arrangement, provided that if it did not take place the money should revert to me. Bellairs made a will to this effect. Carson insisted that the fifty thousand should be settled on his son, with a discretionary clause that he should pay one thousand a year to his wife. I did not know at the time—though I learned it later—that Bellairs had left a letter for his daughter imploring her to marry Angus, as he feared, did she not, that Dr. Carson would make known the truth, and thus tarnish his memory. So-the matter was arranged.

"The years slipped by, and Bellairs died. Then Carson wrote to me that he had told his son the story, keeping back, however, his own guilt of Singha's murder. He had also put the story on paper, though in doing so he had carefully refrained from connecting me, as Brock, with Michael Trall. This account, he intimated, he was sending by his son to me, so that I might, if necessary, use it to force Olive into the marriage. I refused so to further his desires. Angus, his son, was to denounce me, and to accuse me of the murder of Brock. Needless to say, I was greatly alarmed at the existence of this document, and by the knowledge that young Carson had it in his power to ruin me. Even when Dr. Carson died I was not reassured, as I still knew that Angus was in possession of the document and the story. The first could not ruin me, since my identity with the Brock of Casterwell was not shown; but if Angus proved difficult to deal with, it might be very awkward for me. To make myself more comfortable I resolved to see Angus before he arrived at Casterwell. I should then know, at all events, how he was disposed towards me.

Mrs. Purcell's letter, which had been shown to me by Miss Slarge, plainly hinted that Angus was a religious prig, and I foresaw that he might not prove so easy to manage as his father had been. From the letter I also learned the name of the steamer in which Angus was coming to England. Shortly before the Pharaoh arrived I repaired to London in disguise, and inquired at the office when the liner was expected at the docks. On obtaining this information I went down to wait for her. I wore shabby clothes and a false black beard.

"Of course, I was not aware that Major Semberry was in any way connected with Drabble, although, from Mrs. Purcell's letter, I knew that he acted as bear-leader to Angus. When the steamer arrived I mixed with the crowd on deck, and managed to have Carson pointed out to me. I recognized him easily from his resemblance to his father. When he left the boat with Semberry I followed them, still disguised, to Athelstane Place. I determined to take the first opportunity of speaking to Angus. I waited for some time, but they did not come out. I realized that it might be some considerable time—perhaps days—before I found the opportunity I wished for. See him I would, and that alone. While hanging round the house I saw a man—it must have been Drabble disguised as Hain—but at the moment I failed to recognize him. I saw also the housekeeper. She was a stranger to me. These two were always about the place, although Semberry had left, and I was beginning to despair of ever seeing Angus alone. At last one evening they both left the house together, and I, having seen them well out of the way, walked up to the door and rang the bell. Angus answered it himself, and when I said I was Mr. Brock of Casterwell (for I had put my false beard in my pocket) he at once asked me to walk upstairs. In the drawing-room I had an interview with him, and a stormy one it proved. He was a stern, religious young man, and he declared that he intended to tell Olive the truth, to pay back the money to the Indian Government, and to denounce me as Brock's murderer. He also informed me that he had the document securely concealed, as his father, having repented of writing it, had tried to regain possession of it. To prevent his doing so, Angus had placed it in the secret drawer of his chest. I implored him not to ruin me—indeed, I offered to give up all claim to the money. I even went on my knees to him, but all in vain. He was adamant, and insisted that I should be exposed as an impostor and a murderer. Then, in my turn, I threatened him. I told him that if he denounced me I would reveal his father's sin. He did not know the truth, and asked me what I meant. When he heard that his father had murdered Singha he fainted, as he generally did when violently excited, by reason of his weak heart. This I knew from Mrs. Purcell's letter. I was quite determined that, as I had him at my mercy, he should not live to ruin me. I looked about for a weapon to kill him, and saw the wool-work left by Mrs. Arne with the knitting-needles in it. I opened his shirt as he lay insensible on the sofa, and pierced him to the heart with one of the needles. He died very quietly and, I think, without pain. Then I took his studs, wrist-buttons, watch, chain, and money, so that the murder might look like the work of a robber. In the next room I hunted for the portmanteau, and turned it out to see if I could find the document. It was not to be found, nor the sandal-wood chest, so I stole away from the house, leaving Carson dead, and, later on, returned to Casterwell.

"I read in the newspapers how futile had been the search for the assassin. But I could not quite comprehend what they said about the severed hand. I guessed that it had been cut off in order to remove the bangle, because I myself had been unable to remove it owing to the swollen condition of the hand. But I could not understand their motive for taking away the bangle. It was not until I met Boldini, as Carson, in the churchyard that this became quite clear to me. Then, of course, I guessed at once that it was necessary for his impersonation. I almost fainted at the sight of him. He was so like the young man whom I had been obliged to kill. I explained my emotion to Mallow by saying that the son had reminded me so forcibly of his father—my dear old friend. Moreover, I made no doubt that a conspiracy was in progress for obtaining the money. Of course, I could have denounced the imposture there and then, but that might have led to my own undoing; so I decided to let sleeping dogs lie. The money would be lost to me by the marriage, as, on reading her father's letter, which she showed to me, Miss Bellairs was bent on carrying out his wish. Still, now that Angus was dead, no one could identify me with Michael Trall. I was safe, if poor.

"The marriage ceremony I myself performed. So I lost the money by my own act. I was surprised to learn that my daughter Clara had engaged herself as maid to Olive; but, as Mr. Brock, I dared not interfere. I regret now that I did not, for through her I might have found out all about Boldini's scheme. When Mr. and Mrs. Carson (so-called) departed, I discovered that one of the dead man's wrist-buttons had been taken out of my desk. This alarmed me greatly, and I forthwith hid the rest of the jewellery in my bookcase. Afterwards, Margery Drabble confessed to me that she was the culprit; so when her father was killed I told Mallow that he had given it to me. There was no one else to contradict the statement. I was most anxious to find the document in the sandal-wood chest, and thought it might be with Major Semberry. Having gone up to see him I unfortunately met Mallow, but I explained my visit on the plea that I wished the Major to bring about a reconciliation between the young couple. I did not see Semberry, nor did I enter his lodgings. As I was coming away, a cab knocked me down and broke my leg. Then one day, a few weeks later, to my great surprise, Mr. Mallow himself brought me the document. It had been discovered by Lord Aldean in the secret hiding-place of the sandal-wood chest, where Carson had concealed it from his father. Olive, as Mallow informed me, wished to read it. She thought, perhaps, it might throw some light on the sealed letter left by her father. On consideration I promised to show it to her, if, after reading it, I judged it fit for her to read. I found I could do so with safety. Carson had made no mention of Brock's death, and had accused Bellairs of the murder of the Rao Singha, which he himself had committed. True, he spoke in no measured terms of Michael Trall—in fact, he abused him roundly; but since that adventurer was dead, and Brock was alive in his person, such blame of him and praise of me served only to strengthen my position. I resolved, therefore, that Olive should read of her father's guilt, hoping that thereupon she would refuse to touch the money—granting it was recovered from Boldini—in which case it might come to me.

"So the matter stands. All who may know of my identity with Trall are dead. The existing document strengthens my position, and in no way can the death of Carson be traced to me. I shall die in the odour of sanctity, after all; and, indeed, if what the doctor says is true, this cursed accident is going to bring about that event very shortly. Well, if I die, I die; my life has been a hard one, and if I have sinned, I repeat, Nature is to blame, not myself. I have directed by my will that the twenty-one volumes of my cipher diary are to be burnt, since it is only for my own gratification that I have written them. I have no wish to be maligned after my death. Even if the diary is not destroyed I feel safe, seeing that no one can read it save Jerry, and I dare say that he is dead by this time; he must be dead, or Clara would not have gone out to service. I wish, now, I had asked her about him.

"Mr. Mallow is about to marry Olive Bellairs. I wish them joy. I have no ill-feeling against either of them. If I live, I may, of course, get back this money. I don't suppose for one moment that Olive will touch it. If I die—well, there is an end of Michael Trall and his bad luck. But no one will ever know that the revered and beloved Vicar of Casterwell killed Angus Carson. I die a respected member of society, and on my tombstone shall be written words of praise. Many a stone has lied about him who sleeps beneath it, so why not mine? I murdered Brock, I murdered Carson, but their ghosts have never haunted me. I have baffled the world, and I have kept my secret in the face of every danger. Mallow is coming to see me again. Well, let him come, I say. I do not fear him now. The bad days are over for me. Michael Trall has gone into limbo, and Manners Brock, the worthy vicar, has beaten Fortune after all."

EPILOGUE

Letter from Miss Slarge, of Casterwell, to Mrs. Purcell, at San Remo:—

"The first of January, 189—.

"My Dear Sister,

"I hasten to thank you for your kind invitation to join you at San Remo. I regret to say that it is not possible for me to accept it. Although my book is now rapidly approaching completion, there still remains much to be done in the way of verifying sundry minor details. For example, I am desirous of expanding the statement of Diodorous Siculous, in which he identifies Osiris with the god Bacchus; and that means that I have still many works to read. The impossibility of taking my library with me, alone precludes me from leaving here until my manuscript is finished. I have decided to call my work 'The New Babylon; or, the Migration of Chaldean Idolatry to the Seven-hilled City of the Revelations, according to St. John the Divine,' a title which, I think, sufficiently well explains its meaning. May its publication tend to keep our island free from the superstitions of Semiramis and Peter.

"You will be glad to hear that Olive and Mr. Mallow are now comfortably established at the Manor House. Their serene happiness is pleasant to contemplate. A year has elapsed since the death of Mr. Brock—as I may still call him—and with him is buried the sad story of the past. His brother, Jeremiah, as you know, died six months ago. He lies beside him in the same churchyard. In life they were divided: in death they lie side by side. What a moral your favourite Dr. Johnson would have deduced from this. Mr. Mallow, I think now, was right when he decided not to reveal the truth about our late Vicar. The confusion which would have arisen in our village had he done so, would have been terrible to contemplate. 'What the eye does not see the heart does not grieve at'—that is a wise proverb, my dear Priscilla, and peculiarly applicable in the present instance.

"Lord and Lady Aldean have returned to Kingsholme from their honeymoon—if possible, more in love with one another than ever. I am bound to say that Tui conducts herself with great dignity in her new position; and that, seemingly, Lord Aldean is not without a due sense of his social and marital responsibilities. At the next drawing-

249

room both brides are to be presented to their Sovereign; and I am glad to know that you will be with us for that ceremony. Olive and her husband express themselves very gratefully to you for the judicious manner in which you anticipated any scandal which might have arisen through the chain of incidents connected with the impostor Boldini. As it is, they have been received with open arms by the county, and, of course, no reference is ever made to poor Olive's untoward entanglement. Socially she occupies her proper position, and, as Mrs. Mallow, she is, if anything, more popular than before.

"Mr. Mallow is engaged upon a new novel, which bids fair to secure for him a high position in the world of letters. Olive, I know, would like him to enter the Commons; but, so far, he has shown no inclination in that direction. Lord Aldean has taken his seat in the House of Lords, and, urged by Tui—who has more ambition than I gave her credit for—intends taking an active part in the politics of his country. Mr. and Mrs. Ostergaard have returned to New Zealand well satisfied with the elevation of their daughter to the rank of a peeress. They were delighted with Lord Aldean, and parted from him with great regret. He hopes soon to return their visit, and talks of buying a yacht for the purpose; but this scheme is as yet quite in embryo.

"Of course, you know that Mr. Mallow, with his wife's approval, paid over the twenty thousand pounds to the Indian Government. I believe he told the whole story to the Secretary of the India Office. Indeed, there was no reason why he should not, seeing that every one who was implicated in the death of the Rao Singha has now passed away. The story of Kikat must now be relegated to the domain of legend. For my own part, I never wish to hear of it again. Poor Olive! she was so much relieved to know that her dear father was not guilty of bloodshed. She has put everything else behind her, and feels able to cherish his memory as she loves to do. That is as it should be. I always thought highly of Olive's moral principles.

"Between them, Lord Aldean and Mr. Mallow have arranged Mrs. Drabble's affairs. That is to say, that, as the doctor died absolutely penniless, they allow her a small income. The children have been put to school, and I am glad to say that the discipline is already exercising a most salutary effect upon Margery—pruning, as I may say, the exuberance of her temperament. She is much less flighty, and altogether improved; and I feel confident she will at length emerge into a clever and notable woman. Her tastes lie chiefly in the direction of poetry, and, when she comes here for her holidays, I endeavour myself to assist her as much as I can. As a widow, Mrs. Drabble is infinitely happier than she was as a wife. This is reflected in her home, which now presents something like an orderly appearance. She is full of praises of her benefactors, which, indeed, is just and right.

"I received a short time back some news from India, which, I think, will interest you. It appears that Major Semberry, through financial difficulties, has been obliged to resign his commission. Reports say he has gone to Chili, with the intention of there entering the service of the Republic. It is to be hoped, whether he does this or no that he will take his lesson to heart, and endeavour to mend his ways even at this somewhat tardy stage in his career. You, Priscilla, with your usual acuteness, were perfectly correct in your reading of his character. He is a thoroughly bad man; and he never did a worse thing than when he conspired to ruin the life of our poor, dear Olive. It just shows how far beneath the standard of honour and moral rectitude it is possible for a gentleman to fall.

"There is still one other, and a most extraordinary circumstance, in connection with the conspiracy, that I must tell you. A week ago, Mr. Mallow received a visit from Clara Boldini. She told him that her husband had gambled away every penny of the money with which they decamped. Is it not terrible to think of such depravity? Imagine a young man like that squandering thirty thousand pounds in twelve months in gambling. And not only did the wretched fellow lose his money, but his life. It appears that, directed by the terrible creature whom they call Madame Death-in-Life, two of her followers tracked Boldini to Lima, in Peru, and shot him one night in a gambling den. Their efforts to obtain the tangible fruits of his wickedness were frustrated, of course, through his having squandered them. In their fury at thus being baulked of their spoil, they determined to kill this unhappy Clara. She, however, managed to receive timely warning, and escaped to England. She looks old, and worn, and poor; and seems possessed with the idea that she must ultimately be killed by these ruffians. Mr. Mallow and Olive tried all they could to induce her to remain safe at Casterwell; but she would not, because she said she could not bring more trouble upon them. That was good of the girl, I think. She visited her uncle's grave, and wept bitterly over it. Mr. Mallow did not tell her that her father, too, was buried close by, and I think he was right. It is best that this sad story should pass into oblivion. Clara remained only one night here. She then returned to London. But, before she left, she gave to Olive the famous Indian bangle, which

251

she had removed from the dead body of her husband when he met his death in Lima. Olive keeps it as a curiosity; though she does not need anything to remind her of the troublous times with which it is connected. Where Clara is now we none of us know. We can only hope she will be spared any such violent death as she fears, and that, indeed, some amount of peace may be vouchsafed to her after the stormy life which she has led. How truly thankful should we be, my dear Priscilla, that Providence has cast our lot in pastures so peaceful and so far removed from the strife and turmoil of the world!

"There is really no more news to give you, save that I am well and happy. Neither Olive nor her husband would hear of my leaving the Manor House; so I am still here in my old position. I have great comfort in the thought that Olive is now so well protected by an honourable and upright husband; besides which, the presence of a literary man in the house is a source of unmixed pleasure to me. The friendship between Mr. Mallow and Lord Aldean still stands as firm as ever, cemented only by the fact that their wives are as sisters to one another. We are, indeed, a happy family down here; and it needs only your presence, my dear sister, to compete our joy. We all of us look forward to seeing you in London this season. Perhaps then we may persuade you to take a house in Casterwell, so that you may spend at least some part of the years that are to come amongst us who love and esteem you. We are blessed, indeed, for we have health, wealth, and happiness; and, so far as our finite intelligence can perceive, our troubles all are at an end, and the future before us is tranquil. This letter leaves me, I may confidently say, the happiest woman in the three kingdoms.

"Write to me, my dear Priscilla, and tell me when you propose to arrive in London, as my book will be published this year, and it will be a great joy to me to feel that I am to have your valuable aid in correcting the proofs.

"Now let me conclude with a verse from the Book of Books, to show how thankful I am for the great mercies of the Almighty: 'I cried unto God with my voice, even unto God with my voice, and He gave ear unto me.'

"How truly that has been fulfilled, my dear Priscilla, you know.

"Believe me, my dear sister, ever your loving
"Rubina

"P.S.—Will you enter some Roman Catholic place of worship, and see if any image of the Virgin Mary is decked with a turreted crown? The Diana of Ephesus wore such a one and I connect her with the Virgin. The crown itself is probably a reminiscence of the Tower of Babel.—R."

THE END

Milton Keynes UK
Ingram Content Group UK Ltd.
UKHW040912011224
451619UK00015BA/124/J

9 798889 424895